Needing Gil
Bad Boys Book Eleven

Christine Young

Published by Rogue Phoenix Press, LLP
Copyright © 2022

ISBN: 978-1-62420-678-8

Editor: Sherry Derr-Wille
Cover Art: Designs by Ms G

Chapter One

Bordeaux countryside 1826

What little was left of Jenna Bonnet's luck ran out at the bottom of *Colline du Cimaron,* the hill leading to a past she'd rather forget. Nonetheless, the *Cimaron* vineyard along with the chateau sitting at the top was a place of demons she had to confront for the sake of her son, the heir to the vast land. The holdings, now that Jacques was gone from this world, should be in the will with Brice's name at the very top. When she shielded her eyes from the hot rays of the sun, she clearly saw the chateau she lived in two years ago with her husband, the Count of *Cimaron.*

Once a very long time ago, she'd been a countess. Supposed she still was since they never divorced.

For herself she didn't mind the walk up the mile long road to the front entrance. Both her son Brice as well as the aged horse that stopped pulling the small cart containing all her belongings exactly in front of the gatehouse would not be able to make the distance to the place she once called home. The ancient mare balked at taking one more step. Now the old lady was contentedly munching grass.

Jenna wasn't at all positive why she returned. All along, she understood her reappearance could be foolhardy with nothing to gain added to the fact she had so very much to lose. There were valid reasons though. None of which made sense at the moment when she wanted nothing more than to turn tail and run in the other direction. She let out a long slow breath of air deciphering the facts in front of her as she tried to put reality in the front of her befuddled mind.

One could call this attempt to regain what had been lost a disaster. It wasn't, not truly. She had such convoluted emotions. Somehow, she would find a way to get her belongings to the chateau. It was, after all, hers now that her husband passed away. Well, legally, as the only heir to the Bonnet fortune it was Brice who inherited. In any case, she had rights simply because she was his mother.

Fortune, she mused, if there was anything of monetary value except the jewels she left behind when she fled. The money was in the grapes then the wine. She didn't have the means to take care of the vineyard, to hire the hands needed for harvest along with making the wine. After more than a year of neglect, much would have to be done to make a profit.

"Maman?"

Her son's tiny voice shook her from her reverie. Brice was the reason she was reminiscing. "What my *petit rayon de soleil?*"

She had used up the last of her spare francs in a shabby hotel in the town of Bordeaux. At the moment she possessed enough for a couple days of food but naught else.

"Do we have to walk up that road? It looks so far. I'm tired."

Brice was always so well-behaved. He never complained even when she knew he was hungry or tired. To get here she pushed them too hard. Even the horse protested.

"Not today, *mon petit chere.* We'll stay in the gate house tonight or in the cart as we have before if the door is locked."

She did pray the old cottage would be open to them, as she wasn't looking forward to spending another night sleeping in the wagon. A soft bed would certainly be nice.

"I don't like sleeping in the cart," Brice said with his little boy voice that always managed to make Jenna feel guilty about the life she forced on him.

If she hadn't run from his father, if said father wasn't abusive to both of them. While he never hit her, he made them both feel as if they were useless as well as inadequate. He treated her as if she possessed no brain. After she gave him his heir, he ignored her. She was thankful for that small fact. She could not believe how a woman would ever want to be with that man in his bed.

Staying with her husband along with his family who moved unannounced into the chateau a year after Brice was born had not been a choice she could live with. Every moment she spent in their midst she feared for Brice as well as herself. Her aged husband was unable to defend them even if he'd wanted to. Jenna had never been certain the man cared. His brother was after the land, resented the fact he was the second son and would never inherit.

Jacque Bonnet was a selfish man, a greedy man who had feelings for no one other than himself. The night she fled, she took her son along with a few meager possessions, vowing to never return. She sewed coin into her cloak. The money was gone now. To feed them she worked wherever she could find a job. In the threadbare pocket of her frock, she had twenty-five silver francs. Before she left the village below the chateau, she bought bread and cheese. They had food tonight. If she rationed the meager fare, Brice would be able to eat in the morning. She didn't know what awaited them. Her luck had to change sometime. Now would be nice.

"We should go on up the hill to the house up there." Brice stared up the long drive pointing a tiny finger in that direction. He was saying the words she wanted to hear. "Did I used to live there?"

"Yes, you did. Maybe tomorrow we will have enough energy to walk the distance."

She patted her son on the head, wishing she could give him everything his little heart desired. She was afraid for the boy. He'd been terribly sick a few months ago. Even now, he still showed signs of the ailment. He was weak and thin. He coughed too much. Of course, he'd never been a large boy, never actually strong as many others his age.

"Are we going to die?"

At the question Jenna's heart lurched. Too many times to count she asked herself that same question. Day-in and day-out, life for them had been precarious. *"Non mon petit chou." Not today.*

"Maman! Don't call me a little cabbage. I'm a boy." He stared at her with his deep blue eyes, a tiny, little boy frown creasing his forehead. "I don't like it when you do."

No, now that they were back at the chateau, their lives would be different, better. At least she prayed their lives would improve. She smiled, supposing he'd outgrown the endearment.

"We just have to find a way to change our luck, that's all. Why don't you get down from the cart, perhaps run around a bit, stretch your legs? Don't go very far. Make sure you can see me and I can see you." With a half-hearted sigh, she watched him leave.

While he struck off in the direction of the gatehouse, she rummaged through their limited belongings. After that, she saw to the horse hoping the old girl would be up to the trek to the chateau in the morning. One more night in the cart would be survivable.

She cringed.

A carriage whipped by her on the road behind them much too fast in her estimation. The horses would be winded; exhausted by the time the people reached their destination. Jenna looked down at her dress, smoothed the worn skirt. It seemed to hang shapeless from her bony shoulders. Her hair was lank. Once she had clothes that fit, a body that was not all skin and bones. Her hair had been shiny and thick. While she'd never been considered a beauty, she was passable fair.

Jenna fought back the tear that wanted to slide down her cheek. She sniffed a few times pushing all thoughts of self-pity behind her where they should be. She didn't have time to wade around in the depth of despair. At least she'd not been forced to sell her body to put food in Brice's stomach along with clothes on his back. Drawing in a long drink of air, she held it inside until her lungs burned. She let it go with a startled gasp when she heard the deep rumble of a man's voice from behind her.

As she turned, thinking she needed to check on her son, she saw Brice held fast by the collar of his shirt. A large man, hair as dark as midnight, eyes cold as the inside of a tomb, carried him along, his toes barely touching as he tried to walk. Anger flared inside her. At her sides her fists tightened. The urge to swing her knuckles at this man simmered deep in her gut. How dare that man misuse her boy? Only prudence stopped her from her foolishness.

"Get him out of here." The voice emanating toward her was gravely and harsh with bitterness. "Don't want to see either of you again. You're trespassing."

"Why? What has he done that could possibly merit this anger toward a little boy?" Her back stiffened as all motherly instincts to protect her child rallied inside her. "I'm sure he's done nothing wrong."

"He peed on my vines," the man seemed to grit out as he let go of Brice.

He peed on his vines? They were her vines.

Brice scampered away. Jenna wasn't sure she'd ever seen her boy move so quickly.

When he stumbled toward her, she met him half way pulling him protectively into the shelter of her arms then positioning him behind her as if the feeble gesture would protect him. "Relieving one's self on vines can't possibly be a crime that would cause a grown man to treat a little boy so scathingly. Haven't you ever peed on a plant?" she shot out without thinking, her body shaking with the anger simmering deep inside.

She wanted to lash out. Give that boorish man something to think about besides harming children. She blushed slightly, realizing she never before talked so boldly.

He didn't blink. Kept coming. With a slash of his large hand, he spoke again, "Get out of here! Both of you! Don't want you on my land. Don't want anyone especially not little boys anywhere near me."

His eyes glistened with the anger that seemed to be boiling over as he strode closer. His brows were drawn tight together, frown lines marring what could have been a handsome face with eyes nearly as dark as his hair. His forearms were thickly corded with muscle, his legs long as his loose-limbed strides seemed to eat up the ground.

Well, she would leave if she could, however, she couldn't. This wasn't his land. The little boy he terrorized owned this little piece of Bordeaux. "It's my land. You get off! You leave!" She was sure he meant to dispute her claim.

His grin turned feral, "My land. Bought this piece of paradise at auction two weeks ago. What makes you think the vineyard is yours? If it was before I purchased it, you've a sizeable number of francs in your pocket from the sale. You can go anywhere."

The shiver erupting within swept cold waves into her belly. No, oh god, no... no. What was she to do now? He was wrong. She didn't have anywhere. "Whoever sold the land to you had no right. It wasn't theirs to sell. You will have to give it back. In this, the law will be on my side."

Foolishly a small measure of courage erupted. This was Brice's inheritance, his legacy left to him by his father. For her, she didn't care about the chateau, the grapes or the wine. All the memories she had of this place left a sour taste in her mouth, curdled in her belly. She needed the income though. Wished to find the jewels that were hers by right. To find the gems, she had to get inside the chateau. Wasn't going to give it up for this arrogant man. She tilted her chin.

"All the papers were in order." His broad shoulders stiffened as he spoke while his voice deepened. "Nothing you can do about this person who sold it. Wasn't truly a sale though. Man lost it because of back taxes due. So, suppose you wouldn't have francs in your pocket, now would you?"

"That can't be." At the moment, she was all bluster and no thoughts. It wasn't a winning combination. "My husband would never let his land..."

"Rumor has it the old Count Bonnet was bankrupt. Owed back taxes from several years. When I paid them, the land was mine. No one actually knew how the family was able to maintain this little piece of paradise after the revolution. The count should have lost his head to *Madam Guillotine*. Somehow, he managed to elude the *madam*. Kept the land for a while. Now it's mine."

His relatives, the same ones who succeeded in chasing her away caused this. Nevertheless, she meant to stand firm, fight for what was rightfully her son's. "I'll pay you back." She found she was holding her breath, waiting, nerves stretched taut.

Haughtily, he sauntered around the tiny cart, ran a hand over the weary ancient horse. He pulled out the small basket holding all their possession. He looked inside then to her, as he seemed to peruse everything. The odious man even allowed his gaze to travel the length of her then back up to settle on her bosom. Instinctively, she placed a hand where he was staring.

His grin didn't reach his eyes, eyes that were cold, frigid.

"Stop that! You've no right to go through my things. To look at me as you just did." She grabbed at his thick forearms understanding she would not be able to deter him from his quest. He would choose what he was about.

"You're trespassing, Madam. Seems I don't need permission to toss you off my property on your scrawny arse. Don't need consent to go through this bundle of nothing."

If his eyes were indeed frigid, they didn't come close to the coldness seeping from his dark, despairing words.

She choked back the not-so-subtle contemptuous retort she had for this man. Jenna didn't mean to let him get the better of her patience. Tried to think of some way to soothe the icy fury that was so evident in his eyes. Eyes that seemed to turn from dark brown to black the farther the conversation proceeded. She did nothing to be the recipient of this hatred.

"Maman?" Brice tugged on her gown, fabric slipping. With more insistence, *"Maman!"*

She pulled the gown back onto her shoulder. His steely-eyed glare followed her movements. He found her lacking. She didn't care. She found him equally as lacking.

"Oui, mon chere?" She pulled Brice's hand into hers hoping the gesture would give some measure of reassurance to her boy. He was so small, so young.

"Is the bad man going to make us leave? He's not nice. You tell me to always be nice to people."

His little boy voice melted her heart. He had such a tiny hand. His limbs were so thin and frail. He would not survive another sickness. She wanted to bundle him in her arms, keep him safe from the world as well as men such as this one. She realized long ago, despite her best efforts, she could not do so.

The man did want her to leave. Was certain there was no way she would give up ground, at least not tonight. No matter what he told her, tonight she was going to sleep on a bed within the cottage. They had nowhere to go. Even if they did, they had no way to get there. She was going to do everything in her power to remain on this land that was Brice's birthright.

"Could we stay in the gatekeeper's cottage for the night. I would pay you in work tomorrow if you'd allow it. I'm a hard worker."

"What would you do with the boy? Don't want him around," he asked leaning back on the cart, his huge arms crossed in front of him while he glared from the boy back to her. Fear for her child crawled up her spine.

If he didn't have a perpetual scowl on his face, he might have arresting features. His dark brows tightly drawn together did nothing for his appearance except make him look threatening. She would give him that. He was intimidating.

"Brice would have to stay with me. There is...he's too young to leave him here by himself. He would never get in the way. You won't even know he's in the house." She was pleading, begging him. They both understood the fact. It seemed her words weren't swaying him.

The man pinched the bridge of his nose. "It won't work then. Don't want the boy anywhere near my home or me. Don't want the boy on my property. Don't want to see him or hear his voice."

That was more than obvious. She wasn't stupid. She got the picture he painted. "I know the chateau. Know what needs to be done. You won't find anyone more competent than me to help clean. Please." God, she didn't want to beg this man. She would.

"No." He turned her back on her stomping up the trail to the house. He looked over his shoulder. "There is nothing for a woman to do. Don't plan on hiring women for any reason."

Especially not you, she heard the words he didn't say.

Frantic with need, she ran after him, tugging on his arm to stop him. "I will do anything." It was true. She would do anything to put food and clothes on Brice. "Anything at all." She wanted him to live, to have things normal children had.

One of his eyebrows slanted upward in question. A crooked demonic smile lit his face. "Anything? I'll keep that in mind."

She understood she just offered herself to this man. Knew what she told him was true. Desperation had been a solid part of her life for so long now. "Yes, I've no other choice. I'll work twice as hard as anyone, as any man. Do the chores no one else will want. The place must be a mess. How long since anyone lived there? You said you purchased it two weeks ago. The grapes will have to be harvested. I'll fix up your home."

Several seconds passed while he stared at her. For a moment, she noticed a partial smile then it vanished replaced by the frown she was getting used to seeing. "I want you and the boy gone tomorrow morning. Stay in the cottage if you wish overnight. Vacate the place by six. If you aren't gone in the morning, I just might take you up on your offer. If I see you again, be prepared to let me see more of you, perhaps all of you." His gaze roamed the length of her until it settled on her breasts.

The breath she'd been holding rushed out in a loud whoosh. Thank God, for one night. Instead of leaving, she intended to be at work at six. Perhaps her luck changed a tiny bit. She would work so hard he wouldn't be able to turn her out. She would make him need her. Tonight, they had shelter as well as food. With the francs he would pay her when he discovered she was working for him, she could walk into town. She was certain Brice could ride the mare. She would buy more food. Living was day to day. This time she thought perhaps she found some place she could stay.

His long-legged stride took him quickly up the hill. He didn't look back. Jenna found she was once more holding her breath while she watched. It seemed to her she was waiting for the next explosion of his wrath. *Demain*, tomorrow it would come. For now, there would be peace.

"*Tete de butt*," she mumbled under her breath before realizing she didn't want Brice to hear the words.

She made sure he knew swearing was wrong. However, this was apropos. He was exactly as she said. Her muttered words were not a lie.

"I thought I wasn't supposed to say bad things." Brice tugged on her skirt.

She whirled. Embarrassed, she let the man blind her to the fact her son heard her frustration. "You aren't."

This time she didn't know how to get out of the conversation that was certain to follow. How was she ever going to explain herself? She knelt so she could be eyelevel searching for the right words. She didn't believe she could think of any.

"How come you can?" He sounded a little indignant as well as curious.

Tenderly, she pushed an unruly lock of hair from his eyes. He was so precious, his question so innocent and pure. She wished she could simply tell him it was because she was an adult. Being older didn't make it right. "I'm not supposed to either. It's just that he was acting like a butthead. I'm sure he is not that way most of the time. I couldn't help myself."

"*Tete de butt*," Brice murmured seeming to agree with her. "He's a bad man. I don't like him. You shouldn't want to work for a man like that. We need to find somewhere else to go."

Jenna was sure he was right. Knew she shouldn't have offered herself to the loathsome man. In any case, the coldness in his eyes when he looked her over told her he wouldn't want her. By his expression, he found her lacking. She didn't have to worry about him taking her up on the offer of her body. "Don't say the words in front of him. Can't lose this opportunity. Shall we see what the gatekeeper's house looks like?"

"He told you we had to leave. Told you he didn't want to see us. How are you going to work for him?"

"I'm hoping that if I'm already in the house working, he won't send me away."

Well, he most likely would. She would have to stand her ground, as she was desperate for the money. Stubborn was her second name. He would discover just how stubborn she could be.

"We really don't have to sleep in the cart tonight? Will I have a real bed?" For the first time in weeks, Brice sounded eager to see what would happen next. His little boy smile so warmed her heart.

"Yes, and probably not. I would want to make sure all the linens are clean before you sleep on them. Maybe things inside are just dusty. What do you think? Shall we go see?" Her hand settled on his shoulder as they walked.

"If they are not too bad? Wouldn't be any worse than the bottom of the cart and our old blankets," Brice said looking up as if to see into her eyes.

"No, it probably would not. Let's find out if I remember this place."

The heavy wood door creaked on its hinges when she opened it. Before she did anything else, she pulled all the draperies wide to let the sunshine inside the dreary room. Dust flew as the fabric was swept aside. Muted light from a setting sun filled the drawing room. Particles of grime left by years of neglect swirled in the warming rays of the sun.

Hope filled her. The cottage wasn't much, nevertheless it would be their home. She would find a way to stay.

"Shall we look at the bedrooms? If I remember correctly, there are two. Do you want to sleep with me tonight or in your own room?"

She understood he would start in one before he came to her later in the night. He did like to snuggle. They were a team. Had been so, for a very long time.

"My own." He looked at her sheepishly through lowered lashes while he clung to his wooden pony. One time in his life he had an entire army of ponies and soldiers. Now he had the one. Their lives had been reduced to nearly nothing.

She did have her love for her son. One could not sneeze at something so valuable as love.

If the ill-humored man allowed her to stay and work, would he pay her? How much was the next question. She knew she was getting ahead of herself. Feeding and sheltering Brice was now her sole concern. In his present mood if he allowed her to work, he would most likely pay her next to nothing. She needed to save so she could pay the back taxes.

That thought did not put a smile on her face. The taxes were paid. It didn't seem the man would sell the land to her even if she possessed the desired coin. He probably didn't even need this place. He had the markings of wealth about him.

He could possibly make her work for the food and shelter without paying her. As a man in another village did, he could ask her for other services. She fled that place. The man was ghastly. He stunk of garlic, his teeth rotten. Even for food she couldn't let him touch her. Couldn't sleep with him. During the month to reach the chateau, there were times she thought she should have closed her eyes and spread her legs for him. In doing so she could have kept Brice healthy. Could have fed him. He might not have taken sick. She pushed those morbid thoughts to the back of her mind. The past was just that, the past. For Brice's sake she wouldn't make that mistake again.

Jenna thought of this man, the man in her future. Would it be so bad if she shut out all sounds and thought of other things? If he didn't scowl, he would be handsome. She knew women who did just that in order to survive. For a brief time, she worked as a maid for Angelique in her bordello in the city of Bordeaux. She saved every franc. Eventually, she had enough francs to move on.

Now, she was here. She offered herself to the man. The mean man, she amended. Jenna realized she didn't even know his name.

Brice disappeared into the smaller bedroom. When he returned, he was grinning. "It's dusty like everything else."

"We'll take the bedding outside. Give it a good beating. You can sleep there. First, however, we are going to have dinner. Are you hungry?"

After Brice ate, they took the bedding outside. The beating didn't take long. Before she knew it, she was tucking Brice into bed, his wooden horse under his arm. She hugged him then kissed his forehead. "Sleep tight."

"When are you going to eat? You never eat anything, *Maman*. Your clothes are going to…"

"I'm not hungry," she whispered then gave him another tender kiss on his forehead. "I'll have something as soon as my tummy tells me it's time."

No, she wasn't hungry. She'd gone so long without eating she barely recognized hunger pains. Keeping Brice healthy was all that mattered to her. Once every couple of days, if there was extra bread, she would have a piece.

With everything done for the evening, she didn't want to sit inside the stuffiness of the house. Needed to feel the fresh air on her face. The old swing still sat on the porch. She remembered sitting on the porch steps while Oliver told her stories. He was ancient. Seemed as old as the hills. He must have been forced to move on when the chateau was sold. Often, he spoke of the revolution along with the reign of terror.

The scent of ripe grapes hung on the air. Harvest season was upon them. If the vineyard was in working order, there would be people from the village tomorrow milling around waiting for orders as to what they should do.

Lost in thought, Jenna didn't hear the soft tread of booted feet on the grass as she hummed a French lullaby she used to sing to Brice. Those days were a very long time ago, the memories nostalgic. In any case, she didn't wish for them back. All she wanted now was to move forward.

She jumped when the man cleared his throat. "Thought you and the *enfant* might be hungry. Didn't see a lot of food in the basket. Also brought the two of you clean linens. My cook suggested I bring this to you."

At the bristling of her back, the man's eyes narrowed. "Are you asking for favors in return?" While only a few minutes ago she thought she could give herself to this man, she now understood it wasn't what she wanted. Even though when he let his guard down for a second, he was handsome as sin.

When her question registered, it seemed the words also burrowed under his skin. "Didn't come down here looking for sex. Just making sure you understand you can't stay longer than tonight. Want you to be comfortable."

His gaze once again roamed over her, heating her from the inside out with what appeared to be raw hunger. She didn't understand.

"Thought a bit of ham might go with the cheese and bread coupled with a bottle of *Cimaron's* finer Boudreaux. A vintage from two years ago."

That was when she fled the *Cimaron*. "You don't want anything from me?"

Her pulse pounded as her breath caught deep in the back recesses of her throat. If she offered herself more blatantly...

Turning her head, she watched him walk into the cottage to return with two glasses and an open bottle. He set the sack of meat on a tray, emptied it. "Eat. Don't want sex at this moment if that's what you're asking. Maybe another time, though there won't be another opportunity. Just want to make sure you have enough stamina to get your skinny butt off my land tomorrow morning. No offense intended. You don't appear to be very strong. Look as if you could just faint dead away any second."

"Stronger than I look," she muttered as she set aside most of the meat for later, for Brice.

She didn't remember the last time they had meat. He still wanted her to leave. Well, she wasn't about to do something so stupid.

"It's not all for the boy. Want to see you eat and drink then I'll leave. Not a second before." He poured two glasses of the wine.

She accepted when he handed her one. She sipped, closing her eyes as the liquid warmth slid down her throat. The wine was delicious, a reminder of another, better time.

"So, you used to live up there on the hill? Jacques Bonnet is your boy's papa? You know, the people around here, in the village, the ones who worked for him, didn't like him. Suppose that's mild, they hated him. Don't like you either. That's all I hear when I go to the village."

He wasn't telling her anything she didn't already know. "Jacques wasn't a nice man." Seemed to run with the territory. He certainly wasn't a very nice man either.

"I didn't know him. Been away for a long time."

"Who are you besides the man who stole my son's inheritance," she asked as she watched him close his eyes almost as if he tried to ward off immense pain.

When he opened them, he was staring at the rows of vines as if they didn't exist.

"Look...if I didn't pay the government what was owed on the land and chateau someone else would have. You still wouldn't own this place. *Cimaron* will never be yours again."

"That doesn't answer my question."

"Gill Allemand."

"What do you need these vineyards for? I recognize the name. Your family owns several a little north of here."

Silence stretched across the small distance separating the two people. "Haven't seen you eat anything. If you don't, I'm taking this with me so the kid won't get any of it. Is that what you want? No, I don't suppose it is. Eat. I'll leave you alone after that."

His one word sounded as a command. She didn't want to eat anything she could save for Brice. He'd been so wrong about not seeing her eat. To appease Gil, she did have a piece of ham along with a slice of cheese. If she didn't eat anything more, there was enough left for breakfast as well as lunch for Brice. She wasn't going to allow her son to go without food. Brice needed to regain his strength.

After eating two pieces of ham and cheese she looked at him. "I'm Jenna," she told him as she watched his strained features smooth slowly.

For a fraction of a second, his eyes warmed, golden flecks dancing in them.

It didn't seem he meant to stay that long. "Jenna, finish the wine. Save the rest of the food for the boy, breakfast for both of you. Make sure you eat something before you leave in the morning."

"I'm not leaving tomorrow. We're too tired. You're going to have to give me another couple of days to recover."

She rose. Must have been too quickly. She swayed slightly her head dizzy. Trying to hide what just happened she sat down.

"See that you eat."

His command didn't go unnoticed.

As Jenna watched Gil walk up the hill, she understood she hid nothing from him. He had this way of looking at her, one that seemed to burrow into her soul. She wondered what he was thinking.

~ * ~

Gil sat in the darkness of his room. His body trembled as a seething darkness encompassed him. Seeing the boy, who would have been the same age as his son when his child died along with the boy's mother, sent ice pouring into his veins. He didn't even know about the two of them until his son was four. They shared one year together. That wasn't enough time. After Etienne Dubois wed the woman, he thought to be in love with, Elisa Moreau, he aimlessly wandered France visiting old haunts. He didn't go back to his work for the French government. Didn't function with the same lethal nonchalance as he had previously. He discovered he yearned for a family along with peace and quiet of a rural life.

That was when he discovered his child. Unlike Jenna's boy, his son was robust, big for his age. The boy could run and climb. He laughed easily. For that one year, he slept with Chantel, played at having a family. Unlike his son, he didn't truly love the woman. When she died though...

When she died, he found himself haunted by thoughts of her. Found there was a hole left in his heart that needed filling. It seemed he would look into a room and he would sense their presence. At times in bed, he felt sure Chantel slept beside him. He might have made a life with her, just to be close to his son. Had been thinking of marriage even while he knew wedding a woman he didn't love would be a mistake.

Thoughts of his first love, Elisa, disturbed his nights. Still, he missed Chantel simply because she came with his son who he adored. Now, alone with his memories, the emptiness in his life bled into his soul. Too many times to count, he didn't see a reason to live. Without his son, thinking of his son, he could not breathe. Air refused to enter into his lungs. He wanted to die.

The room he slept in was black, pitch black. He reached for the pistol beside his bed. His hand shook. He turned it over in his hands, thinking to end his misery. If he did, too many people would be hurt; his family, his friend Etienne along with Etienne's wife, Elisa. Every step he took each day was filled with pain, not the physical variety but the mental. No one dared mention the boy or his wife. They were terrified he would collapse. Perhaps they were correct in their assumptions. Without them he felt broken.

Jenna...

Her son Brice...

Gil couldn't manage to swallow the lump in his throat. Couldn't condemn himself more when he wished it was Brice and not his son, Lance, who perished in that fire. He should have been there, perhaps made a difference. If he'd been able to get him out, Lance would still be alive. That was a long time in the past.

Head in his hands, he sobbed. Copious tears rolled down his cheeks in an unbroken flow. His head pounded painfully with each new breath of salted tears slipping between his lips.

He didn't want to see Jenna or her son in the morning. Prayed they would be gone when he checked on them. Didn't know what got into him when he allowed her to offer herself to him. Lord help her, the woman was all skin and bones. The soles of her shoes were coming lose from the tops. Her threadbare dress might be ripped to strands if threatened with a stiff wind. When he looked into her basket of possessions, she owned one more dress, which was in just as bad shape as the one she wore. While the little boy didn't have much, he possessed a great deal more than his mother. Clothing that was new, a shirt plus another one, two pairs of shoes that were not falling apart. He owned a warm coat tucked away at the bottom of the basket. She possessed a threadbare shawl.

It wasn't his place to improve her life. The reasons for her leaving the winery years ago were unknown to him. Though the motives must have been very real and valid. What little he knew of Jacques Bonnet, he didn't blame her for running. Now, with the passing of her husband she returned thinking to take up where she left off, believing her son would inherit the vineyard.

He wouldn't.

It was almost dawn. He told her to be gone at six. Not knowing why, he expected her to stiffen her shoulders; after that beg him for another night. She'd already done just that. Perhaps his expectation had something to do with the boy. She would have to get him ready, feed him before she could leave. He hoped she didn't give all the food he brought her last night to her son. He wanted her to be able to put that old mare to the cart and leave. If she couldn't, he wasn't positive how he could get her to leave. A sick woman to care for was not high on his list of priorities. He had enough trouble getting himself out of bed each morning. If she continued in this vein, she would be sick sooner than later. If she meant to take care of her son, she needed to take care of herself first.

The next morning when he made his way to the first floor, it was five thirty. He needed to make certain the cleaning supplies were out and available to the workers he meant to retrieve from the nearby village. Striding through the kitchen, he grabbed a slice of bread hot from the oven. He would eat later or perhaps while he worked.

"She's out there working her skinny backside off." The woman, Gaby, who cooked for him all his adult life, pointed toward the main hall. "Seemed to know where everything was located. Got herself a rag and some soapy water, says she's going to use the lemon oil when she finishes to make the wood shine. Been working since I started baking bread this morning around five o'clock. You tell her she could work for you?" Gaby asked sounding skeptical while appearing even more surprised.

"The devil you say. No, told her to leave by six. Apparently, she didn't listen."

That didn't surprise him. Where Jenna Bonnet was concerned, it seemed she had a mind of her own. She didn't obey direct orders either.

He stabbed his hands in his hair as he strode the distance into the entrance. She was humming softly, working on the staircase with what smelled like lemon oil. She must have found the cleaning supplies. When she heard him, she looked up. Smiled softly.

"Where's the boy?"

The soft smile vanished at the penetrating sound of his gruff voice. Despite his feelings about this woman and her child, he found he wanted to see the soft curve of her lips again. Cursed himself for the weakness. He didn't like feeling vulnerable. When he asked about her son, her entire demeanor changed. Well, hell, of course she would be protective of her son.

Her shoulders squared while her back stiffened. "He's not in the way," she told him, her voice curt, her blue eyes icy. "He's playing with his toy horse."

"Eating, I see." He turned his attention back to her. "Did you eat?" He couldn't help asking even though he knew the answer.

"What do you think? Not that it's your business," she spoke softly as she continued stroking the wood, making it gleam more with each swipe of the soft rag. The transformation was vividly apparent.

"You were supposed to be gone by six. Instead, I find you working. Told you I wouldn't hire you. Haven't changed my mind. You're doing this for naught. There is no pay for work when you haven't been employed."

His voice was harsh, gruffer than he intended, but her visible grimace was the effect he wanted. He knew she didn't eat. Saw her hang on to the railing as she pushed hair from her face. Didn't expect her to so blatantly defy him.

"I never thought it was a bad thing to be early to work," she spoke as she watched Brice completely ignoring the fact she wasn't authorized to do anything she was doing.

He'd just been blatantly honest. She ignored every word. "Hope it was alright that your cook, Gaby, gave Brice a glass of milk."

"You need the nourishment more than your boy. You're all skin and bones. When are you going to leave?"

When she followed his orders, he wanted to send a year's supply of food with her.

At his words she flinched, red suffusing her cheeks. He supposed that wasn't candid of him. Candid was not something he sought. If his disposition was nasty enough, he prayed she would decide on her own to depart the premises. No job could possibly be worth the belittling he'd already directed her way. As her lips moved, he was positive she was calling him a *tete du butt*. Well, she had him pegged right, a butthead. That's exactly the way he intended to carry out this relationship of theirs that was going to be extremely short-lived. He figured the meaner he was, the sooner she would takeoff.

"Do you need some help departing?"

He strode toward her ready to do whatever was necessary. Pick her up then carry her if she continued the defiance. He could put her in that cart as well as hitch the old mare to it.

She stiffened then, her shoulders squaring as it seemed to him she prepared to talk. "Not going anywhere. Can take care of myself. Besides..." she paused sipping air just to keep herself standing as she once again wavered.

He was certain she was about to tumble down the steps to land at his feet. The question in his mind was whether he could snag her before she tumbled down the steps.

"Besides?" he queried as he started up the stairs. If she was going to fall someone needed to be there to keep her from hurting herself. While he wanted her and the boy to vanish, he didn't wish anyone harmed.

"What I do is none of your business," she finished on a soft whisper.

"It is when it seems I'm paying your wages. Wages I didn't intend to pay you since you were never hired. You will be gone first thing tomorrow." He didn't understand why he backed off.

"Please, let us stay. I'll do anything." She paused looking as if she just heard his words. "You're actually going to pay me?" Now she sounded wistful, a bit of apprehension thrown into the mix.

"I'm not that big an ogre that I expect you to work for nothing. Today at least, nevertheless if you turn up tomorrow unexpected, I'll send you on your way with no wages to speak of."

"Oh."

"Oh?" He lifted an eyebrow as he studied the expression on her face. "What did you think?"

"I hoped." She ran her tongue across her bottom lip, leaving it dewy with moisture.

He stared. A feminine ploy to entice him, he just might take her up on the blatant offer before sending her on her way. It had been a long time since he had a woman beneath him. "Well, your fondest wish just came true. Not paying you if you faint making me rush to Gaby for the smelling salts."

"Wouldn't expect you to do anything like that. We can stay then?" She sounded so hopeful and sincere.

"*Madam*, look here." His voice was stern but it didn't seem she listened.

"We can stay."

"I'm not hiring you."

"Of course you are. You need this chateau cleaned up from top to bottom. You need to harvest your grapes so you can do what this place does best, make wine. Don't see anyone lining up to get rid of the dirt and grime in the house. If you want to live here...well, there is much to do."

All this talk of food was making him hungry. Her arguments were having the same effect on his stomach while managing to make his head throb. *Tete du butt.* "Carry on."

He strode back to the kitchen ignoring her question as well as her statements about his needs. He didn't want her to stay or to ever see her again. Gaby set a plate of food on the table that she took from the warming oven. "You going to bring the little lady here to eat. It's the least you can do. She needs some more meat on her bones. If she filled out a mite, she'd be quite attractive."

"You're meddling in what doesn't concern you, Gaby. Save the matchmaking for your mama. She's not staying."

Gaby huffed as if she was indignant. "I'm the better matchmaker, besides just looking at her one would know she's not eating enough."

"Says she's eaten."

"Well, I'm sure she is lying."

Couldn't help the following heavy sigh. "So am I. Jenna gives all her food to her son. Doesn't eat a thing. I sat at the cottage last night until she ate two small slices of ham and cheese. She did sip a glass of wine."

"Doesn't need wine. The girl needs food, good French cooking would put some well-needed meat on her bones. Then you'd want her stay to around for more than just the cleaning."

"Give her anything at all and Brice will have the food. I'm telling you; she won't eat."

"If you give her more than the little tyke can eat, she'll have to eat some of the leftovers before they spoil. Won't she?"

"One would think." He did sit down to eat. As always whatever Gaby cooked was delicious. Before she left for her home, she set about making sandwiches leaving them wrapped and on the table. Gaby would be back in time to cook dinner.

In the meantime, he had to oversee the collecting of the grapes. Harvesting was one of the most important parts of the vineyard. He wanted wine this year. While the grapes had been neglected, it was only for a year and a half. They would do fine. The harvest might not be as bountiful this year as in the past, but his manager assured him this year's crop would produce a wonderful red Bordeaux.

Gil spent the remainder of the morning and well into the afternoon talking with the manager about his vines as the man gave him a tour of the property. He brought help with him from his family's vineyard closer to St. Emilion. The men and women had over a hundred years of experience in wine making. All would go well. Yes, it would go well if Jenna Bonnet would leave as he instructed. He didn't want a woman in his life nor did he want anything to do with the child. Just seeing the boy tore his heart into shreds.

By the time he finished, he was dusty and dirty which suited his mood. When he walked into the entrance, Jenna was finished with the stair railings. She was no longer on the steps. The wood was smooth and polished. The lemon scent of the oil she used filled the air. He breathed in deeply.

When he found her, she was sitting on the floor, scrubbing the stones with skim milk. Where she cleaned, everything reflected the sunlight. He looked around for Brice. Finally catching sight of him, he was sitting beneath the piano, playing with his toy horse as if he didn't have a care in the world. The boy didn't. His mother certainly did. His heart lurched. Gil didn't appreciate the protective feeling toward Jenna that surfaced blindsiding him. He doused that feeling with a cold dose of realism. The pain in his gut was too raw and deep. All he wanted was to be left alone.

He pushed the sensation away with an angry nod toward the boy. "Has he done nothing today but play and eat?"

She stopped mid-scrub, lines on her forehead deepening as her eyes seemed to draw together with a pointed scowl. They flashed blue ice shards at him. He didn't care. He wanted an answer.

"He's just a little boy. What is it you want him to do? Get down on his hands and knees? Scrub the stones?" Sarcastic venom filtered through the air severing his mind with the ridiculousness of his words.

Her question was valid even though it reeked of disrespect. She should quell her unruly thoughts if she wanted to get paid. Gil didn't have an answer for her. Children were supposed to play. Why would he want him to work? *To ease her burden.*

Jenna shouldn't have Jacques Bonnet's child to look after. She should have had better than a man who was despised by almost everyone who knew him or worked for him. All he heard was rumors. He had not been around to know the man first-hand. Gil had been in Paris most of the years since he turned twenty. Even before that, he'd spent a great deal of time there. Most of what he knew he'd heard since his arrival. At the time he didn't care what was said. He bought the winery. It was his now. Eventually, the land his family owned adjoining this one would be merged.

22

He couldn't bear to be such a burden on his family. That was why he moved out. Thought he could work so hard it would take his mind off his losses. Since the death of his boy, he didn't want to be around people who cared about him. Saying he was morose would be understated. The people he cared most for him sidestepped the issue that overcame his mind. He never spoke of Chantel or Lance. He liked it that way. Needed his thoughts to be bleak and dark, desolate was best.

He didn't want to think about these two either. Just looking at the woman and her child brought painful memories to the surface. Seeing her love shine so clearly for the little boy brought him to his knees. It was the way he loved Lance.

"Hell, if I know. Just don't want to see him when I'm in my house. If you expect to work for me, keep him somewhere I don't have to look at him."

He didn't miss the tiny look of relief that crossed her face to be changed when she spoke. "Can't leave him by himself in the cottage. What do you propose I do with my son?"

"Maybe you should quit. Move on. Find some other means of employment." *Some other man to torment.* "A place that will welcome you with open arms."

Angrily, he fisted his hands while his gut coiled then soured. He didn't know what else he could say to her.

"There is no place like that. It doesn't exist," she gritted out through teeth that were clenched hard together.

"It isn't here either, *Madam.*"

Blinking a few times, she then ran her tongue across her bottom lip. At the sight he hardened, his arousal blatantly evident to anyone who looked. He knew he was looking at her with raw hunger in his eyes. He didn't like his reaction, despised what the sight of her automatically did to his body. She told him she would do anything.

Jenna Bonnet wasn't a virgin. She was a widow. So, what did he care? He should take what was offered and enjoy her sensuality. Hell, it wouldn't be given willingly. He would always know she gave herself to him to feed her son. That knowledge didn't settle very well in his gut.

If he took what she blatantly proposed, he'd be no better than dirt, lower than dirt. He understood her desperation to some extent. They were both dying inside but for different reasons. She wanted to keep her son alive while he mourned the death of his.

If he'd only had the chance to try to keep Lance alive, to rescue him from the fire that consumed his tiny body. Lance would be seven now. The boy had been strong and vital, so different from Brice. Gil hated the comparison.

What he did know was that he'd never again put himself in the position to love so thoroughly that the loss of that love would devastate him. He couldn't go through anything like that another time.

Not ever.

"You should understand. I'm not going anywhere," she spoke softly as she slowly pushed herself off the floor. "I'm staying."

Her foot caught on the threadbare dress she wore. He heard the fabric tear. Quickly, she moved her foot before rearranging her skirt.

"What time do you put your boy to bed?" he asked as he studied her swaying form.

Her body was small. She was skinny except what curves she possessed were womanly, tempting even to a hard-edged, jaded man who'd been through hell and back. Her blue eyes were warm when she looked at her boy, turned to ice when she directed her gaze to him. If she eased some of his pain, he didn't care if ice flowed in her veins as it did his. Perhaps together they could thaw each other. One time with her would never melt the ice that was so much a part of him now.

"Why?"

Her question didn't surprise him even when he saw the immediate change from blue to frozen silver. Her lips trembled as if she guessed the answer to his question.

She might propose giving her body to him. He had no doubt giving herself to him to use was not something she wanted. What she didn't know was that he would never take something from her she wasn't willing to offer. All he wanted at the moment was to scare her out of his life. So far, she didn't seem to catch onto any of the clues.

"Come, eat. Gaby left sandwiches. Enough so you don't have to give yours to your son."

A whisper of air left her lips as she wiped her hands down the front of her dress. As if he could see into her mind, he knew she was trying to figure out how to save one for Brice's dinner.

"Don't get me wrong, although I'm a bit skeptical you're asking us to eat with you."

Her voice held a wealth of censure while the summer-sky blue eyes sparkled with bits of sharp, silver-ice.

"We all need to eat. If you're going to insist you have a job, I don't want to be picking you up off the floor when you faint dead away."

"Truth be told I'm not hungry. I'll give Brice his. He can keep playing while he eats. I need to start on the wall paper."

"No, you don't. Since you defied my order of leaving this morning, this employer wants to get a full day of work out of you. The only way that can happen is for you to finish off that ham sandwich. Won't take no for an answer."

"If you insist."

Her quick answer surprised him. He expected some half-witted argument. It seemed she capitulated too easily. "I do."

"Gil." The male voice coming from behind him caught his attention.

"What is it?" Gil asked as he turned to see Stephan, the manager of his vineyard, striding toward them, a grim look on his face. "Something wrong?"

"No, not at all. Need for you to check out the vats in the cellar. There are years of wine kept in a second cellar. You should take a look there. Figure out what you want to do with everything."

He turned to Jenna. "You can relax now. Looks like I'll be gone for a couple of hours."

Gil didn't leave though. He waited for Jenna to head to the kitchen with her little boy in tow.

When she didn't move, he nodded in the direction of the waiting food. "Take the boy with you. I won't be there."

She nodded, grimacing as she tried to stand. He knew she was feeling the pain of working all day, part of it on her hands and knees. Wondered too if she ate any of the meat and cheese for breakfast he left the night before. He doubted it. Now that he wasn't going to watch her down the sandwich, he was sure she would wrap the food up and save it for Brice tonight.

More food could be brought to her tonight. Food she would hand over to the boy. It wasn't as if Brice didn't also need meat on his bones. Jenna, however, appeared to be starving herself to death.

Why did he seem to harbor a soft spot for this woman? The faster she moved on the better. *Enfer!* He smashed a fist into his palm. All he wanted was to see her leave the chateau behind. Would do just about anything including intimidating her to succeed. He couldn't keep up the pretense of intimidation despite how hard he tried.

Gil grabbed his lunch on the way out the back with Stephan. "What is it you wanted me to see?"

"Viens."

Once inside the building housing the cellars, they made their way down a flight of steps to the area where the vats were located. The cellars smelled of darkness and wine. Hoses ran the length of the floors leading to each huge vat.

"They all seem to be in working order. If we go on through this hall, we'll see the real interesting part of the estate."

The cellar was cool, dark as well. He remembered playing inside the family cellars with Etienne. Wondered if his son would have enjoyed some of the same pastimes.

"What is it?"

"Wines going back to the early seventeen hundreds. They are all labeled and dated. Just thought you should see this. If you want, we can sell some of the bottles for hefty prices. Buy more vines to plant on some of the unused land."

He thought of bringing one of the vintage bottles with him tonight when he visited Jenna.

He should bring food too.

Make sure she ate.

~ * ~

"Tomorrow I should visit Gil. Don't want to leave him by himself too long. He might do something we'd all regret."

"Not sure what he'll do," Elisa spoke softly as she watched Etienne sip his wine.

They were all afraid for Gil. The desolate and sometimes desperate look in his eyes was so different from the jovial man she first met. The man who helped her get over the loss of Etienne those first years as well as played with her son, Masson, when she had no one except the boy's grandfather to help her. "He shouldn't be left alone this long."

Masson played with their little girl, Margo. A blanket was spread out on the floor, toys scattered haphazardly around her. Margo turned one a month ago. She was a precocious little thing. She had her big brother wrapped around her tiny little finger. Masson would do anything for the child. When it came to Gil, Elisa felt fear for his life. His eyes were haunted dark pool of depression.

"Gil doesn't like to visit. Don't think he enjoys watching Masson. Brings back memories he'd rather forget. Lance and Masson were the same age. Don't want to push the man to do something too soon."

"Seeing Masson makes him remember all he lost," Elisa agreed with her husband as she watched their children. "At least to some degree, he shouldn't hide from the memories. Sometime soon, he needs to embrace what he once had as well as except the fact it is gone. It would be nice if he could learn to live again." In her heart she understood Gil didn't want to live.

Etienne missed the first four years of Masson's life simply because she kept the truth about his son from him. It wasn't well done of her. Now, she regretted keeping the facts of Masson's birth to herself, regretted it with all her heart. None of that time could be made up to the man she loved since she was a little girl.

Her husband would feel some of the pain Gil felt, however the trauma wasn't the same. He didn't lose his child forever. They'd both been so happy for Gil when he discovered he had a boy. Elisa knew Gil thought for a time to be in love with her. She never could return the sentiment. Now, Gil loved that boy with all his heart. Gave everything he was to him. Wound up devastated when Lance died. At the moment, everyone tiptoed around the man whose mean temperament was so different than the light-hearted, loving man she once knew. They all wanted to hear him laugh again. Needed to see the permanent scowl wiped off his handsome face.

Elisa didn't acknowledge there was anything Gil loved more than playing with Masson until he was reunited with Lance. The joy carried over to his son. She was certain Gil was meaning to ask for Chantel's hand in marriage. She didn't think Gil loved Chantel though.

Now they were both gone, the mother as well as the child, leaving Gil a shattered man who seemed to barely live in the shell of his body. In Elisa's mind, the man she once knew so well needed a swift kick to his backside. Etienne continued to tell her he just needed to be handled with care. If everyone left him alone, he would eventually come out of his melancholy. When they were around him, she was warned not to speak of her children and especially not of Lance.

"He shouldn't be coddled," she told her husband who glowered at her in disapproval. "You know he has to find a way to adjust to this, to learn to live again. He needs to find a woman to love, one who can give him more children. There are so many things he can do beside hideaway in that big old chateau of his."

"Gil doesn't need those thoughts of yours brought to the forefront. Whenever you speak them, he withdraws farther away. If you continue thinking you know best, he will end up a shell of himself."

"Every time we see him, he is worse. You know it's true. Coddling does not work. He needs to be confronted with this disease of the mind that possesses him. You are the one who is wrong in this matter."

Etienne wrapped her in his arms. "What we need is to start another child so you can stay out of Gil's business," he told her nuzzling her neck.

In response, she shivered.

Trying to ignore him, she spoke again, "Remember the children."

"Always do. Isn't that what I just intimated?"

"We should go see him."

Elisa had reasons her husband would not agree with nonetheless she intended to visit soon. It would be fun. The weather was nice. Fresh air linked with new scenery would do her good. Masson as well as Margo would love to spend time with their grandfather while they would be gone. She did agree that Gil seeing her son brought more despair to his eyes. A sleepover would be wonderful for Masson and Margo.

"We're not traveling that great distance. Not with the children or without them. I know what you're trying to do, Elisa. This time your meddling won't work. Mind your business. Stay out of Gil's."

Etienne picked up Margo, cuddling her for a few seconds. "I'm putting her to bed then Masson. After that I'm going to put you to bed. No arguments."

"Why would I argue?"

She smiled softly, lowering her lashes. Elisa let her fingers hover over the fastenings to her dress. "I'll get a bottle of wine and something to eat. We can sit on the balcony."

She loved the breezes on the balcony whether it was cold or hot. If cold, she could wrap herself in a heavy blanket. Etienne would always find ways to get his ever-questing hands beneath the covering to heat her more thoroughly.

"Watch the stars?" he queried, his voice husky, his eyes warm with the desire she hoped would never waver.

"The moon as well." The laces to her gown were unfastened far enough she knew he could see the swell of her breasts.

"I'll hurry," he told her.

"Make sure that you do."

Chapter Two

From her spot on the stone floor Jenna watched Gil saunter through the kitchen, his strides long and quick. He would want to distance himself from her. There might be hell to pay when he discovered she was here and not in her cart leaving the chateaux behind. The tiny breath of air she drew into her lungs wavered as a small measure of air slowly found its way in then out. She looked to her son, who was also staring at his back.

"I don't like him, *Maman*." Brice spoke in a small voice that seemed to break when he finished. "He's not nice. He's always frowning at me. He's mean to you too."

"While I hate to admit to the fact, we need him." *Need his money.* "We have to make sure we keep him happy. His displeasure will not put food in your belly."

She would do anything to keep the man contented. At least his breath didn't reek of garlic and his teeth weren't yellow. His stomach didn't overflow his belt. If she had to give herself to him, she would endure it much more easily than the other man who gave her no choice except to flee.

Deserting the chateau was not going to happen, not an option for them. There were things she needed to do. Her jewelry for one thing. Before she left, she hid the gems. Somehow, she needed to find an excuse to clean in the attic. She would do whatever she had to do to stay on this land. The vineyard was her son's legacy. Perhaps the sale wasn't done legally. She could look into that.

"Is it lunch yet?"

"Come, he must be nicer than we think. He's feeding us. Haven't heard your little belly grumbled since we arrived. Your stomach has been filled with food thanks to *monsieur*."

True to his word two sandwiches were wrapped and sitting on a plate on the kitchen table. Brice raced to a chair. Chuckling, she was certain she heard his stomach rumble, nothing like suggestion to cause something to happen. A pot of tea was there also along with milk and honey. She poured herself a cup. Gave Brice a glass of milk.

She unwrapped Brice's sandwich handing it to him. Hungrily, he bit into it. Devoured half before he looked up.

"Aren't you going to eat yours?" he asked sounding a bit worried. "I never see you eat."

"Not hungry."

Jenna ruffled his hair. She had every intention of saving the food for Brice's evening meal. Between last night and this morning most of their meager fare was gone. She would have to find the time to walk to the village. For now though, she didn't dare leave the chateau during working hours. He might find a way to lock her out. The place was so big, she didn't see how.

"You always say that."

"Not always. I ate last night after you went to bed. Tonight, if I get hungry, I'll eat the sandwich or some of the other leftovers."

She sat back watching her son, praying he would grow out of his frailty. He was still so thin and weak. When he played, he sat. He didn't have the strength to run and race with the wind as other children did. Now, after lunch, he should play outside in the sunshine. There were a few others, children of the servants. She'd seen them. Brice was shy when it came to other children.

When he finished, she placed the uneaten food in her bag. "I've got to get back to work."

"You've been working all day. You could play with me instead."

Playing with her son was something she wished for with all her heart. "No, the wallpaper needs cleaning."

Her hands trembled when she thought of the man as well as her offer to him. Degradation clogged her throat. This was not what she wanted for herself. Reality clearly stated she had no choices left to her. Survival was of the utmost importance. If he asked, she would have to find a way to appear willing.

Her arms ached from the strenuous work. When she stood, her legs wobbled so hard she had to hold onto the table. The breath of air she tried to suck into her lungs stuck in the back of her throat.

Several hours later when she finished with all the wallpaper in the entrance, she kneeled down in front of her son. He was napping. Gently, she touched his shoulder before kissing him lightly on the forehead.

"Time to get up, sleepy head. We're going to the cottage. Do you think you can walk down the hill?"

She smiled at his sleepy-eyed look. Jenna certainly hoped he could walk. She knew she couldn't carry the boy.

"*Bien sur*, mama. I can do it. I rested."

His boyish grin made her heart lurch. He was such a handsome little boy.

Stepping back, Jenna helped him to his feet. Silently, they walked the distance down the hill. Brice skipped in front of her. All the while she thought of Gil's offer. Could not keep it from her mind.

She didn't know how to refuse him.

Telling him no was not an option.

Thoughts of his hands on her set a wild dance to her pulse while heat shimmied along her veins. The strange ache settled in her core. She didn't understand the reaction as she recalled all too well the feel of her husband's hands on her. Nothing Jacques did gave her pleasure or made her pulse pound. Jacques wanted a woman who would lie beneath him and not respond. At first she didn't understand. Months after they were wed, she realized he saw whores regularly. Jacques frequented brothels. For a wife, he didn't want a woman who would give herself willingly. So, she learned to lie still while he spent himself inside her. She was his vessel, nothing more. After Brice was born, thank the heavens above he left her alone. He had his heir, not that it meant anything now.

At one point in her life, she wondered about intimacies with a man. She wanted to learn what it would feel like to be loved. Since her wedding night, she no longer thought along those lines. To Jenna all thoughts of love were vanquished when she lay beneath her husband's fat rutting body. Not until she saw a mean-spirited, temperamental man with hard cold eyes did she think of possible pleasure at a man's hands.

Jenna didn't understand what drew her to a man such as Gil Allemand. His disposition alone should frighten her away. For some reason, her heart went out to him. There was something in his eyes when he was guarding his emotions. They were filled with hopelessness. She sensed the sadness simmering in dark, unreachable places. Wondered what caused the desperate, forlorn look that always hovered so very close to the surface.

Sucking in air, she forced her thoughts from that man who didn't deserve kind thoughts. He hated her boy. In Jenna's mind, there was no reason on earth for an adult to treat a child the way he did. Gil could barely stand to look at her son who did nothing to him to warrant such a reaction. She berated herself for harboring even one kind thought for him.

As soon as she stepped into the house, she unwrapped the leftover sandwich for Brice who stared at her with a look she didn't want to acknowledge. Just as Gil did, her son meant to confront her about eating. This was a conversation she didn't want to have with anyone, especially her little boy.

Before he could say anything, she spoke up, "I'm not hungry. I'll eat the meat and cheese left from this morning when I feel like food." The food Gil brought last night.

The man was such an enigma. One moment he did something nice the next he glowered at her son. She poured him milk that Gaby left on the table along with a note telling her it was fresh. She brought the milk from her home just for Brice.

Well, someone in Gil's household didn't despise her or her little boy. Jenna poured a glass of wine from the bottle Gil brought last night. She drank. It was sweet, wonderful. The *Cimaron* vineyards produced amazing wines. It settled in her stomach wishing for something more to go along with it.

While Brice ate hungrily, she heated water for her bath. The tub was small. She would have to stand in it to bathe nevertheless nothing seemed sweeter at the moment. Dirt and grime from the old mansion coated her body. Brice could have a bath in the morning. She didn't have the energy or the inclination to argue with him tonight.

Once Brice was playing in his bedroom, she bathed quickly. The water felt delicious on her aching muscles. She recalled a time when she could luxuriate in a hot bath until the water turned tepid. Quickly, she washed her hair. Dressed in the only other dress and shift she owned, she decided to leave her feet bare.

When she finished, she strode onto the porch to comb and dry her hair. The slight breeze would do wonders to dry the long thick locks that sometimes were the bane of her existence.

Colors from the setting sun danced on the horizon. The scent of crushed grapes filled the air. The harvest might be more plentiful than first appearance. It seemed Gil brought men to help at the new vineyard. As the men descended the hill to go to their homes, she watched intrigued by all the work.

She told him eight o'clock. That was when she put Brice to bed. Jenna poured what was left of the wine into her glass. If she drank enough, perhaps she wouldn't feel. It was almost that time now. She wanted to be numb.

Of course, he might not come.

What if he did?

Could she actually go through with what she offered him? Yes, if she closed her eyes and let him paw her it would be over before she could blink. That was what she was used to. It was what her husband did. Jacque never called what he did making love. She knew from the beginning all the man wanted was the heir as well as what he thought of as a respectable woman. At one time, she wanted to feel something, to understand the pleasure she heard about.

Would a man such as Gil paw a woman? Somehow, she suspected he wouldn't. For some reason, she was certain he would make love.

After tonight, she would no longer be considered respectable. She would be exactly as the people of the village thought her to be, a whore out for blood money. They would think she was after Gil just as they thought she'd been seducing her husband. They despised her, blamed her for their troubles just as they did her husband.

The memories gave her shudders.

"*Maman?*" Brice stood beside her, smiling. "What are you doing?"

"Watching the sun go to sleep for the night." *Waiting for the man who detests me to claim what I offered.*

Jenna pulled him onto her lap, tickled him until he laughed. "*Arret, maman*. I don't want to be tickled."

"Laughing is good for the mind and soul," she whispered as she stopped. "*Viens ici,* it's time for bed little one."

The words came out too quickly. At the top of the hill, she saw him. He stood unmoving, a dark shadow silhouetted against the dying sun. Didn't want Brice to know he visited. Didn't want him to know what she did to survive. Embarrassment flamed her cheeks, experienced the heat on her entire body.

Setting him on the porch, she stood then gave him her hand. Walked with him. She put him to bed. Hoped he would fall asleep before Gil stepped into the house to claim his prize.

As she sipped the rest of her wine, she watched his steady descent down the hill. His strides were long. As he approached, his features gradually came into focus. He was a man sure of himself and his part in this world.

For some reason, she thought he might not truly want her. Well, she was too thin, her breasts nearly nonexistent now with the weight loss. He spoke the degrading words. Thought perhaps he only meant to scare her away. If that was the case, nothing he did would frighten her so very much that she would leave the tiny bit of security she found here. It had been so long since she felt protected with a sheltered place to sleep. She didn't know why. Somehow, she did. It seemed, for the longest time, she had to sleep with one eye open.

When he stepped onto the porch, she stood, her knees threatening to buckle. Her hands were clasped in front of her as she tried to keep her trembling from him. Attempted to smile. "*Bonsoir.*" Despite her attempts at bravery her voice sounded paper-thin, wobbly as well. She inhaled on a shaky breath of air while she tried to swallow the huge lump stuck in her throat.

There was no smile of greeting, still, "*Du vin?*" he asked holding the bottle of a one-hundred-year-old burgundy in the air. "I'll pour. Did you eat your sandwich or did you give it to your son?"

The velvet strength of his voice touched her in a way she didn't understand. Censure was evident in his tone. He didn't like the fact she fed her son first. That was just too bad. The beastly man didn't have a say in the raising of her child.

"*Oui*, wine would be nice," she murmured as she sat back down refusing to answer the second question.

Most likely the man knew the answer. She wouldn't lie, nor would she change her way.

"You don't have to be nervous. I don't bite," he chuckled softly as if he thought that was a joke.

The brief smile changed his features. He should smile more often.

When it came to biting, Gil knew nothing, nothing at all. Jacque bit. Her husband seemed to delight when she cried out in pain. Everything about sex with him hurt in some way. Once a long time ago, before marriage, she thought there was pleasure in sex with a husband. She knew better than to still be so naive.

He touched her chin, turned her so she had to look at him. "You didn't answer my second question. Ah, but I do believe I know the answer. A woman has to live on more than just wine. Well, so, you won't save this for your son because he is still too young for the beverage. If you drink too much on an empty stomach, it will go to your head. Perhaps that's what you intend. Maybe I would appreciate that, a dizzy-headed woman." He held the glass of liquid to the ebbing light, swirling the contents as he seemed to look at her through the wine.

After he unwrapped more food, he sat back, his long arms settled across the chair, behind her back. His fingers toyed with the fabric of her dress at her shoulder. She felt the river of heat travel to the tips of her toes and back. When Jacques touched her, she felt cold. When Gil touched her, heat suffused her.

"I wasn't hungry. The sandwich, I can eat later if I do grow hungry." Her cheeks heated when her stomach spoke out something different than her words.

His laugher sounded genuine. When he smiled, gold flecks danced in his brown eyes. At the moment they weren't dark and frigid. No, the look in his eyes was warm, heating as he stared. "Eat. It's a meat pie. I've only one. Going to watch until the entire pie is gone."

To Jenna it seemed he was a man of a single purpose.

"Don't think I can eat it all. The pie is truly quite large. Most likely larger than my stomach."

She wondered if she postponed the eating long enough, he would grow bored and leave. No, she bargained for more here. She needed his approval, his acceptance so she could continue to work. Actually, she didn't know if she could eat the entire thing. Her stomach would most likely rebel if she tried.

He held it out to her. "Eat what you can. Has to be more than a small bite." He was studying her. Sounding hopeful he said, "Could you try for half?"

For a few seconds, she closed her eyes, appreciating the scent, imagining how it would taste. Her mouth watered. If she only ate half there would be some left for Brice in the morning. Half would have to satisfy Gil, because she wasn't about to leave her son with nothing to eat. Half the ham sandwich was still wrapped in the kitchen.

When she bit into the food, it tasted delicious. Her stomach grumbled. She tried to chew slowly. Tried to savor the taste. She was so hungry she could not cherish anything nor could she stop. Before she knew what happened half was gone and she was eating more. The groan of despair was far too real. Embarrassed, she set the pie down.

"Finish it. I know you can," he told her, his eyes mocking her minor defeat.

Before he said more, he sipped the wine, topped both glasses off. "There are two more in my bag. One for both of you in the morning, and Jenna, as long as you are here, as long as you refuse to leave, I won't allow you to starve yourself. Nor will I let your little boy starve, not that you would allow it either. There will be more than enough food for both of you. You need to eat your fill."

God, she wanted to believe him. She heard a tinge of admiration in his voice. Needed to see into his heart so she would know that he was a kind man. He would let her stay here if she gave herself to him. Her mind lingering on that thought, the rest of the pie tasted as if it was sawdust.

He refilled her glass as well as his. "Gaby will leave fresh milk for Brice when she comes to work in the morning. He will have a morning snack, lunch as well as one in the afternoon before you go home. If there is no dinner for you to take with you, I will bring some in the evening when I visit."

"Are you giving me the job?" She sounded breathless with anticipation even while she disliked her position. Wavering on the edge, not knowing, didn't suit her. What else was there?

"Don't know yet." His gaze traveled over her, lingered in various places. He sat back again, seeming relaxed while she was a ragged bundle of nerves. "I will have to see how this evening progresses. Now, won't I?" His smile didn't come close to being sincere.

"What do you want from me?" While she needed to know, at the same time she didn't want to know. Had to find some way to keep Brice from learning what she was doing with the mean man. The boy always understood far too much.

"Everything you offered me. Probably more. Don't want a woman who won't give herself in passion. So, if you plan to lie unmoving beneath me..." He swirled the contents of his glass before downing the contents. "You can plan on moving on."

She gasped, startled by his words. How did he know? "I don't know if I can do anything except that. Don't know how. What if I can't?"

All her husband ever did was hurt her. Unmoving was the only way she could get through the ordeal he called lovemaking. He never wanted her to be responsive.

"You will have to leave."

"I..."

Jenna ran her tongue along her bottom lip, staring into his cold fathomless eyes. They changed from the earlier warmth. She saw no passion just the emotionless dark recesses that he always showed. "We can't leave. I've nowhere to go."

Gil spread his hands before looking inside the cottage. "Do you think your boy is asleep yet? Wouldn't want to grab his attention while we play together."

"I need more wine."

"Whatever helps." He topped off her glass along with his. "I can wait. Not in a hurry to sample what you've offered. Not even sure if this is something I want. You'll have to convince me."

Silence hovered in the darkening night. Her thoughts dashing from here to there as she tried to find a way to avoid the ugly truth of what was happening. Convince him? How on earth was she supposed to do something like that?

"I'm not a whore," she whispered trying to sound forceful. "I don't have the slightest idea how to convince you of anything. I don't know how to seduce. My husband..."

"Never thought you were a whore." He picked up her hand, kissed the back then set it on his massive thigh, his hand over hers. "You were married. You're no innocent virgin who doesn't know how to kiss a man or what to expect from the evening of pleasure. So, why are you shaking?"

Ah, but she was pretty sure she had no idea how to kiss. What she remembered of kissing was hurtful and disgusting. For some reason she didn't think Gil wanted the same as Jacques.

He squeezed her hand. Slid it down to his knee then back to where it rested before. She never realized he was so big. Jacques was a small man in so many ways, physically as well as mentally. Without conscious thought, she pressed her palm against his leg. Realizing what she did, she yanked away her hand. As if doing so would give her courage, she fisted them.

At the moment, he didn't look at her with cold or warm eyes but with raw hungry eyes. She saw heat in the dark brown depths gold shimmered around the edges. A man never looked at her that way. Warm liquid heat, filled her, settled deep in her belly. A tiny sound escaped her.

"I would get this over with." Trembling, she tried to stand. "We can go to my room."

He brought her down to sit on his lap. His hand slowly, very gently stroked the curve of her hip then lower to travel back to where it began. When his lips brushed against the nape of her neck, she gasped as the mercuric sensation the slight touch evoked.

"Hurrying would be a travesty. Your offer would be invalid if such were to occur. You would have to leave in the morning. Loving should never be hurried."

Now his hand rose to just beneath her breast, hovered there for the longest time before returning to her hip.

Her breath caught in the back of her throat when he touched the sensitive spot. She swallowed what little moisture was there. This was so new to her. Heat pooled in private places while her stomach somersaulted. She reminded herself this was necessary. Her voice shook while she tried to speak. "Gil, please, I would get this over and done with before Brice wakes up."

He swore softly as his hand rose this time to lift her chin while he stared into her eyes. "Don't worry about the boy so much. Children have a way of sleeping through the loudest noises. Even if you scream out your pleasure, he won't wake." His thumb brushed across her lip, pulled on it until she felt the touch inside her mouth. Her eyes widened.

"Wh-what are you doing?"

"Your husband never kissed you, touched the sensitive spot here?" he asked as he continued his slow, evocative exploration. "Here too?"

"N-not like that. Is that a kiss?"

She was trembling so hard she was sure she would rattle right off his huge thighs. In truth, Jacques never kissed her, never caressed or stroked her body in any way. All he did was push inside her. He always hurt her. After he came to her, there would be blood on the sheets.

"Not yet although I mean to. In time, thoroughly kiss you."

She couldn't breathe. Her heart fought to beat. All rational thought evaded her. As he watched her, she swept her tongue across his finger. She jerked. "I'm sorry."

"Why?" he chuckled, his amusement evident in the golden shimmer of his eyes.

She had no idea why she apologized. No idea what he meant to do next. "Jacques never touched me like that. He did hurtful things. What about Brice? Are you sure he won't wake up?"

"Positive. Don't worry about your son. I'll make sure he doesn't hear your scream of pleasure."

His voice deepened seduced and coaxed. She'd never been seduced before or coaxed, just taken.

"I'll always worry about my son." She realized then what he truly said. "P-pleasure? Pleasure for a woman doesn't exist."

Beneath his breath he swore softly, cursed fluently in three different languages. "It does. I'll show you as soon as you're wiling. God help me, I hope it's soon." He stroked her neck with the callused pad of his thumb. "Why do you seem so innocent? You have a child. You must have done this a thousand times with Jacques Bonnet."

"Hardly a thousand."

He only took her to his bed when other options ran out. She conceived in the second month of their marriage, which was one forged in hell. "He gave me no pleasure, only pain..." After a lengthy pause, "As well as Brice. He gave me Brice. For that small fact, I'll be eternally grateful." She supposed for her son, the pain was worth what she received in the end.

~ * ~

Jenna's words of agony brought a sudden and abrupt end to Gil's lust. The promise of this evening died as he thought on the implications of her words. Pain? He'd heard the man was a rutting bastard. Angel's bordello in Bordeaux wouldn't allow him entrance because of the way he treated the women. From what Jenna just said, the rumor was most likely true. What hell did that bastard put her through? What her husband did to her was not his concern though. He didn't want anything permanent with this woman or any other one. Gil wanted her for the night as well as the nights to come if she remained at *Cimaron*.

Pushing away from him, distancing herself, she stood on shaky feet. Even the hint of a smile disappeared. Seemingly all business she began again, "As I said earlier, I'd like to get this over with if you don't mind. When the deed is done, you can go home for the night."

He bristled at her tone as well as her words. *When the deed was done?* Ignoring his previous thoughts on bedding this woman, "I mind. What if I don't want to leave your bed until dawn? Sometimes I like to stay with my woman."

He watched the pulse at the base of her neck as it beat out of control. Saw the narrowing of her eyes as she looked inside, either to check on Brice or to make sure the bedroom was still there. He couldn't be sure.

"Gil..."

His name wavered on her damp lips as she spoke so softly, he could barely hear. She swiped her tongue along the full bottom one leaving a dew-covered path of moisture behind. In the meager light, her mouth glimmered, begging for him to taste.

"Yes?" He held her hand in his while he tugged once more wanting to get to know her better before sex. It seemed for Jenna she believed getting it over would convince him to keep her here. If he had sex with this woman, it would happen more than once. Getting it over with would not happen. It was still a valid question in his mind.

"What is it you want?"

"To get to know you. I'd like that."

She was an enigma to him. For some reason he understood some of her pain. That fact didn't change anything for him. Jenna would have to prove herself agreeable to the sex between them before they made love.

She looked hesitant, unsure of herself. Lifting her chin, seeming to take on a façade of bravery, "What do you want to know?"

She appeared so innocent. He had to remind himself again that she'd been married. "Everything. Nothing. Why do you think there is no pleasure in sex?"

Ah, that was a good start. He supposed he understood some of the reasons. Jacques Bonnet must have been a horrible lover as well as a rotten husband.

Her bare toes peeping out from beneath her frayed gown appeared to fascinate her. He settled his hand on her ankle. Felt the shiver ripple through her then into him. Her ankles were small. He was tempted to run his hand up her leg, sample the silken flesh then see how she would respond.

"Do you actually want to know? Sex is good only for men. They take what they want. Give nothing in return." Her voice sounded bitter to him almost as if at one time she believed differently.

"Have you only known one man?"

That was none of his business. She could answer or not. Once again, he had a pretty good idea what the answer would be. It was too bad she had such a jaded opinion of sex. With only one man in her life, she had nothing to compare.

Women weren't expected to compare lovers.

Unless they were whores.

Gil wasn't sure he could be the man to change that opinion. It was one that seemed to be forged in steel. Jenna was the kind of woman who would expect more than just sex. Would expect love and a commitment of some sort.

Would believe marriage followed.

He couldn't give her more than a few lusty encounters. Well, he could manage as many as she wished for. Sex was the driving force behind his relationship with Jenna. Wasn't even sure if he wanted to pursue anything else. Something about this woman tugged at his heartstrings though, gave him dreams he thought long dead. Understanding was impossible. Since Elisa, he'd never felt drawn to a woman. With this lady as much as he wanted to ignore the sweet desire that rose in him when he looked at her, he could not.

He would have sex with her. After that happened, she would be out of his mind forever. Restlessly, she moved on his lap, unmindfully stroking his arousal with her backside. One finger seductively found its way up her leg to mid-thigh then down. She was as soft and silken as he imagined.

On a breathless note, almost as though she wished to say the opposite, "You shouldn't be doing that?" As if she had the strength to stop his advances, her fingers tightened around his forearm.

"Why? You did offer yourself to me."

He continued his attention, this time to her inner thigh, wishing he dared move higher. If he did, she would jerk away. He would lose her. He didn't want that to happen. Tonight, he meant to take this as far as he thought possible.

"It..."

She drew her tiny, pink tongue across her lip again. The wet moisture left behind was kissable. "It isn't proper. You touching me like that."

Keeping his laughter from erupting was most likely a good idea. Two years had passed since he laughed. "Hate to burst the bubble in that pretty little head of yours. What we're about to do in your bedroom is much less proper than this." He turned his attention to deeper exploration.

"I wouldn't know." Her voice cracked as he touched even softer flesh.

"Jenna, how many men have you slept with?" His fingers tightened on her leg, squeezed then released. He wanted the answer then he didn't.

"Why?" The deep huskiness of her voice told him she wasn't immune to his coaxing.

"Because it's important for a man to know what he's encountering when he's deep inside a woman. Need to understand what experience she has with the male of the species."

He refused to be used by her. Understood the raw hunger she so easily drew from him. Passion seemed to sweep between them from one to the other.

Jenna breathed deeply. He saw the quivering of her throat as the tiny rush of air traveled downward. Understood she didn't want to talk about her past.

"Do you truly have to know? Does it make a difference?"

He ran a hand along her arm. Watched as the sky darkened. A fox slipped past disappearing between the vines. The night creatures would show themselves soon.

"Yes, who you've been intimate with makes a difference in this transaction of ours as does honesty. I would have you tell me." Actually, who she slept with or how many men she'd been with made little impact on his decision tonight nor would it in the days to come. Her need for him did. He had the feeling he'd tell her once more that she needed to leave the chateau. Once again, she would show up at his home in the morning working her fingers to the bone. The cynical man that he'd become he suddenly needed to be something different. He wondered why he cared.

His hand around her waist tightened as he waited for the answer. His breath held in check within his chest. Just as he assumed, night sounds molded one into the other.

She waved one of her slender hands in the air as she stared into the distance. "Too many to count. Hundreds maybe thousands."

The sarcasm didn't get by him. She couldn't lie worth a damn.

"Liar..." he murmured softly, placing silken strands behind her ear. "You are too innocent to have slept with too many to count, hundreds or thousands. Why do you hide behind the lie?"

Her delicate shoulders lifted slightly. He found she still stared at her toes. "I don't know." She paused searching the skyline for something, he wasn't sure.

"Tell me."

"Because you think—believe I know what to do when you kiss me. Jacques never kissed me. At least I don't believe what he did was a kiss. Because I was sure you wanted me to have a past. You have this opinion of me. It isn't true, none of it is."

"Everyone has a past."

"He bit..." she told him.

"Biting is not so bad. Like this?" With the tip of his finger, he turned her so she looked at him. He saw warmth coupled with desire in her eyes. He did like what he saw. Knew it was too soon for him to take her to the bedroom. Slowly and ever so gently, he closed his teeth over her bottom lip, tugged, soothed with his tongue, bit down again, let the soft flesh slide slowly between his teeth before he waited for an answer.

Somewhere between 'bit' and 'like this', her body softened against his. She melted. He heard tiny ripples of sound evoking pleasure softly floating from her lips. Pulling away, he ran his finger along her jaw then lower. What he saw was raw passion turning her ice-eyes to deep warm pools of blue.

He waited, smiling at her. Understood she would be surprised to see him looking at her in that light. He tempered the grin he couldn't hold back.

Seemingly mesmerized, she touched her swollen lip. Her eyes seemed to be glazed over with the raw desire he saw within the crystal-clear depths. The breath she inhaled shuddered as it slipped into her lungs. "No..."

"No?"

"Nothing like what you did. He..." She stalled for seconds as he saw the shiver sweep through her with what must have been sordid memories. "He...hurt me. The things he did weren't gentle."

"I'm gentle?"

"So far."

"Always. Why did you marry the man?"

He knew he wasn't going to make love to her tonight, soon, though if she stayed, if he couldn't chase her from his land... First, he had to make sure she understood he didn't intent to commit to anything. especially marriage. If she came to *Cimaron* to garner a second proposal of marriage, the proposal would not come from his lips.

Her fingers wove in and out of her dress so hard he was sure she would rip the worn fabric. It was clear to him she didn't want to say the words that would tell him what he wished to understand. Another story waited its telling. He was certain he would have to drag the tale from her.

"Why?"

Gil heard the tiny gulp of despair in her voice. His mind spun with different scenarios even while he felt the subtle and slow breaking of his heart for this woman. Without definite knowledge, it seemed she was a victim of her husband's as well as a victim now at his hands. The last thing he wanted to continue to do was to make her his victim in the use of her body. Guilt swept through him. He understood how easily it would be to coax passion from this vulnerable woman. *Enfer!* If she stayed here, he would not be able to help himself from taking what she didn't understand she offered.

She sounded hesitant, nonetheless she was opening up to him. Her next words confirmed his thoughts. "My father owned a crumbling estate in the south of France. When Jacques visited, I guess he saw me. I don't remember seeing him. I wasn't very old then. My father told me he wanted me, was willing to pay top dollar for me. He sold me." Tears slipped delicately from her eyes along her cheeks. "I don't want to talk about what happened. It's in the past. Nothing will change."

He could put all the bad memories to rest. "Not my past." His voice turned to gruff huskiness. "What happened to you, at least for me is my present."

"They turned me into a whore. Didn't they?"

"No!" He stood. Set her on her feet. "You're not a whore." No one could turn this lady into a prostitute. He certainly wasn't going to do so because he was lonely. "It's time I go home. Make sure you're out of here in the morning." They both understood she wasn't about to obey his command.

She stiffened. Her knees were shaking while the delicate fingers he wished to kiss fumbled with the buttons on the gown she wore. A stiff breeze would have knocked her over. Even though he should walk off the deck then down the steps of the porch, he didn't. Instead, he watched her, mesmerized by the site in front of him.

Enticingly, her dress slid off her shoulders. The same fingers slowly unlaced the ribbons on her chemise. Both gown and chemise lay on the floor. His breath caught in the back of his throat as he stared at her naked body. He froze. Had to will himself to breathe as each scant breath tripped inside.

Raw passion flared.

In the gentlest voice he could summon, he said, "Put your dress on, Jenna. I won't be the man to turn you into a whore. You and Brice need to leave in the morning before this thing between us turns into something we can't undo, something we would both come to regret."

While he strode down the porch, he heard the broken sob behind him followed by another then more seemingly unending. More than anything he wanted to turn around, go to her, hold then ease the pain in her heart and soul. If he looked back, he would invariably go to her. Pull her to him. That one act would lead to recriminations as well as regrets.

No woman should be sold to a lecherous old man.

Even with those feelings simmering in his gut, he was not the man for the task. She needed someone who was strong, a man who wasn't a broken shell, someone who could give love to her son as well. She didn't need someone who only wanted sex with a willing woman.

Gil Allemand wasn't the man for the job.

Love for him no longer existed if it ever did. Once he wanted to believe in the power of love.

Jenna Bonnet would endure. She was a survivor. Gil wasn't at all sure how he knew this although he did. Thoughts swirling in his head, he walked through rows upon rows of vines, the making of his vineyard. Walked until his feet hurt, until exhaustion might claim him. He stood on the top of a hill, his view stretching forever in three hundred sixty degrees. Fresh grapes crowded the air with their scents. After all the harvest was upon them.

He would do well to stay far away from the slender waif who claimed the gatekeeper's cottage as her own, from the woman who would show up to work tomorrow despite his mandate.

She would continue to defy him.

He would allow her defiance simply because he didn't have the strength of will to send her packing.

His head pounded. He still lusted for her, his body still pulsing and hard from the sight of her standing naked in front of him. He wasn't sure how to will his body to forget the hidden potential the woman offered, what he craved to explore.

She wasn't willing.

He could have sweet-talked her until she fell into his arms unable to deny him. As a man well versed in the ways of sexual pleasure, he could have taken what he wished for. Could have used her so thoroughly she would have wanted to run as far away from him as possible.

Jenna Bonnet wasn't willing. He didn't have to remind himself of anything. All he needed was the knowledge she'd been abused most of her adult life. He wasn't about to add to the story.

Hands to himself would be his mantra from this moment on. He was a man thoroughly doomed. He knew if she remained here, he wouldn't be able to do that.

By the time he made his way back to the house, soft ribbons of sunlight could barely be seen on the lowest point of the horizon. He hadn't slept. Didn't know if he wanted to try. Wondering if he could grab an hour of sleep before the men would begin assembling to harvest the grapes, he strode up the steps toward his bedroom. He should not have spent so many hours wandering the countryside.

Gill fell on his bed, his arm across his eyes wishing he could wipe the sight of Jenna, naked and vulnerable from his mind. Hoped he could stop the pulsing lust he could not walk off. Prayed Jenna did not take his command to leave to heart.

He woke to melodic humming somewhere on the second floor. His heart lurched in his chest. Jenna was still here. Reality hit him in the gut. Because she stayed, he would have to make sure he kept his distance. Aloofness was for the best.

Reluctant to see her, yet curious he splashed water on his face to help wake himself then changed his clothes. He wandered through the hallway until he found her scrubbing the wallpaper in one of the guest rooms.

When she heard his steps, she stopped. Her shoulders stiffened. A grim line brought her lips together obvious she wasn't pleased to see him.

"Where's the boy?"

Her shoulders shook at the harsh tone he greeted her with. Today she wore the other dress. The fabric wasn't any better than the first one. He wanted to pull her into his arms, tell her all would work out for her. The right to tell her something like that wasn't his.

"In the kitchen. Gaby is giving him a snack. Are you just getting up?"

Her face turned a soft shade of pink.

"You care?"

He kept the grin behind his teeth simply because he didn't want her to see his amusement at his answer as well as her question.

"I didn't mean anything by that question. It's just that..."

"Just what?"

He stepped closer. She couldn't move away. Her back was already against the wall she'd been cleaning.

"You don't look as if you slept last night, at least not very much."

"Why do you say that?"

Unable to help himself, he wiped away a smudge of dirt from her cheek. So much for his good intentions, the moment he saw her they flew away.

She gasped at the contact. For a mother and once a wife, she certainly did have an innocent way about her, that never seemed to change.

"Dark circles under your eyes. I need to get back to work."

"Why? You've never been hired. Asked you to leave just last night. Did you forget so soon?"

"You don't recall that I've nowhere to go?" she queried as she tried to turn away from him. "Have to get back to work."

"As I told you, you don't work here."

"I tried to give you what you offered." Her voice shook. "You left. It wasn't my fault. I should not have to be punished because you refused to take the gift of my body."

He regretted her words almost as much as he wanted her out of his life. You're a damn fool, Gil Allemand. Lust still drives you. She would have given you what you wanted except for the fact you didn't let her.

She wasn't willing.

You can seduce her.

Enfer! He hated the voice in his head. His hands fisted before he willed himself to relax the tiniest bit.

"If you're going to toss me out, the tossing won't be easy. I'm not going anywhere."

"Could lock you out of the cottage."

"I'd sleep in the cart. You would have to drive me to the next village. Once you returned here, I would follow."

"You're a damn stubborn woman to stay in a place where you aren't wanted. Did you eat one of the meat pies I left or did you give them both to your son?"

At his question, she turned from him, hiding her face continuing to wipe the spongy bread on the wallpaper to clean it. "None of your business."

Her statement riled him. Felt anger bubbling up within. "As long as you're working here it's my business."

She turned then, one hand on his chest. Even through the fabric of his shirt where she touched him, he burned.

"I'm working for you?"

Her smile lit the room. The small gift bedazzled his senses.

He'd give most anything to see that smile more often. "Suppose you are. When you work for me, you eat. Want you downstairs at the noon hour. Gaby will make sure you put something in your stomach as well as the boy's."

"You going to check up on me?"

"Do I need to?"

"I'll be there."

~ * ~

After saying their goodbyes to their two children, Etienne and Elisa set out on their journey to visit with Gil. Elisa didn't have a single illusion that her friend of so many years would have vanquished his melancholy despite what her husband told her. Time wasn't going to cure Gil as long as all his friends and family overprotected him. To Elisa it seemed Gil wanted to be depressed, wished to wallow in despair. As far as she was concerned those emotions weren't healthy. For right or wrong, good or bad he was pouting as if he was still a little boy. He needed to get on with his life. If she could, she'd tell him to grow up to snap out of his snit.

The man had everything to live for despite the death of his son. Other people moved on with their lives after tragedy. As far as she was concerned, feeling sorry for yourself could only last so long. Gil used up his time. Hopefully this visit would help him see life was precious, not to be wasted.

"You're not going to meddle," Etienne warned as their carriage lumbered up the long driveway to the estate Gil purchased. "If you try, we'll leave. I promise you that. I'm not going to stand by while you make matters worse for my friend."

"Of course I am. He would do the same for me, as would you. Allowing a friend to waste away his precious life is not acceptable. If nothing else works, I'm going to shake him until his teeth rattle. If you don't like what is happening, you can go home."

"I'm sure you could try. As for me, I would enjoy seeing your attempt to stay if I choose to make you leave, knowing you would be better off at our house. Have you forgotten I'm bigger and stronger? In a battle of strength, we both understand who the winner will be."

His grin widened as it seemed he thought on the apparition conjured by his imagination. Remembered when she tried to dodge some much-needed discipline.

"Well," she paused as she stared at him.

She could do that to him. Meant to do the same if the opportunity arrived. His form of discipline didn't scare her. In fact, she relished it. This time she would give in to him sooner. There was no reason to prolong his attempt at discipline. "You could help sway your friend to start enjoying his life. Perhaps you need the proper incentive. I should see to your chastisement."

In a quick sure move, he pulled her onto his lap. His lips found hers in a hot driving kiss that promised so much more than he could give her at the moment. "You will do my bidding. There is no other choice since I am your husband. I won't allow you, *mon bijoux*, to meddle."

"As you wish," she shot out smartly as she grinned.

"Too bad we've arrived," Etienne murmured as his hand slipped down the corsage of her gown. He held her breast in his hand, swept his thumb across the hardened tip. I will find time later to better help you understand my wishes."

Breaths for Elisa came in short sharp gulps that left her in need of more. It took very little on his part to coax her to his will. She ran her hands along his forearms enjoying the play of his muscles as she caressed him. It would not be difficult to turn the tables on him.

"Too bad for you," she stared pointedly at the growing bulge between his legs. "At least I can hide what you've provoked. When we walk into the chateau anyone who cares to notice will know what you have in mind."

"They will think you a tart," he grinned, caressing her intimately.

"A tart who is seducing her husband," she murmured tossing her head back.

"We are both going to have to live with this until we have privacy. As you well understand, I'll make sure you don't forget how hot you are for me. Suggestive ways, many of which you taught me, will continue to inflame you until you can think of nothing else besides inviting me inside your precious warmth."

She leaned into him, slanting her head upward for another deep hot and penetrating kiss. He did have a way with his words. "What I do understand is that you will be feeling the same. You cannot think to stimulate me to a point where I'm begging for you without doing the same to yourself. Tit for tat, seduction goes both ways, Etienne."

"Such a cutthroat I've wed."

"*Non*, that is what you are. You've learned all your devilish ways at the hands of the French government. Whatever dastardly things I've learned, you've taught me. Before you came into my world, as you well know, I was an innocent."

Flinging his head back his laughter roared from his throat. "An innocent in wolf's clothing. *Mon bijoux*, I don't believe you were ever innocent. You knew your womanly charms from the moment you were born. You seduced me in the brothel when you breathily said my name from the foot of the stairs. From that moment on I was yours to play with. I was only a man."

With a punch to his chest, she meant to emphasize her point. "You left me for years and years. What do you mean you were only a man, a man who wields his power unconditionally and with no remorse?"

"We should not go over this simply because you neglected to tell me about your delicate condition, later that you bore me a son. As to my absence, you've no one to blame except yourself. You had multiple opportunities to enlighten me even keeping the truth of my son's existence from me when he was almost five and I stood on your porch expecting answers."

She waved her hand in the air. "We digress. Let's get back to Gil's untenable condition. We cannot allow him to wallow in self-pity for one more minute. It doesn't seem he intends to do anything but that."

At least in this instance they could agree to disagree. When it came to Etienne's son, she was entirely at fault.

The carriage lumbered to a slow stop. She looked to the porch leading into the home. The message they were intruding on his privacy should have reached Gil an hour earlier. Elisa supposed a greeting from him might be too much to ask. So, she was surprised when his long lanky form strode down the steps then opened the carriage door. Greeting her with a smile that didn't convince her of anything, he gave her his hand to help her down. Etienne followed.

"Thought you'd be involved with the harvest," Etienne said blandly. "Didn't think you'd be here to greet us."

"As you know, father sent his best hands to help this year. I've employed veterans from the village who are eager for work along with decent wages they were denied for too many years. There is little for me to do except oversee a very competent manager."

"Whatever rumors you've heard concerning the villager's wages as well as about the Count and his wife, they are all true," Elisa said bitterness in her tone.

She swept her gaze along the rows of vines as she strove for the right words to describe Jenna Bonnet. "In too many ways to count, his wife was worse than he was. All she wanted was to cloak herself in fashionable clothing and the jewels derived from what slave labor would buy."

"The men were not slaves. Everyone had a choice as to work or not. The men could have refused the offered employment and gone elsewhere," Gil said, "I remember my brief stint in North Carolina where I saw firsthand how slaves were treated. Despite the fact Jacques abused his workers, the men were far from slaves."

Elisa's words about Jenna seemed to startle Gil. "As to what I've seen over the last days, Jenna doesn't seem to be the way Elisa describes her. Not one instant of our brief relationship has she asked me for anything except to hire her. She meant to work as well as earn enough for her along with her son to survive another day. I don't know why I'm telling you all this."

"You defend two people who are not worth the waste of the energy you use to speak in their defense." Elisa remembered the times she'd seen the pair together, strolling the streets of Bordeaux. Always the woman was cloaked in jewels while the men who brought all the wealth were hard pressed to feed their families. Her husband spent hours in her mother's brothel *abusing the women*. That remembrance didn't give her a moment's pause. The forgotten memory sent her mind spinning in multiple directions.

At her words of distaste for the woman, Gil didn't say anything yet a strange expression crossed his handsome features. For a few seconds he looked to a window on the second floor. The simmer of his eyes hinting at something Elisa didn't quite understand.

"What brings you here?" he asked yet his lips were set in a grim line as if he thought on her words. "To meddle I assume."

"Just to make sure we cheer you up. You cannot continue to behave as you are wallowing in self-pity."

"I was doing just fine before you arrived. Don't need cheering up or company. In any case it's not possible. Where are Masson and Margo?" he asked as his attention still seemed to be directed elsewhere.

"Don't expect me not to try. We've been friends far too long for me to give up. It seems you played an integral part in my life when I chose to hide from the world. You did know what was best for me then." Elisa linked her arm in his as they started up the steps. She stopped. "What is going on upstairs that is drawing your attention?"

"Only been here a few seconds and already he's trying to seduce my wife," Etienne said blandly. "Yes, what is on the second floor? A woman? A lover perhaps? Maybe you've actually wrestled yourself away out of your despondency."

"Always did want your wife for myself," Gil said as this time his gaze swept to the front door. "Would never lower myself to seduce another man's wife."

"Gil?"

Elisa gasped air when she saw Jenna Bonnet standing on the porch as if she still belonged as mistress of the chateau. She looked to Gil who was staring at the woman with raw, hungry passion in his eyes. Elisa had no trouble recognizing the look. Etienne looked at her in the same light when he wanted her even when he knew he couldn't have her. Only a few minutes earlier in the carriage, he stared at her in the same vein.

Non, it couldn't be. It was though, "*Madam Bonnet*?"

Elisa now had more than one mission while they visited. She would find out what exactly that charlatan of a woman wanted from Gil.

"Do we have an empty bedroom that is clean?" Gil asked Jenna, his voice turned soft. "If so, show my friends to their room. If not, would you please make sure one is ready for them as soon as possible. Ask Gaby to put hot water to boil for their baths. Whatever they need see to them. After that you may go home."

Jenna curtsied prettily a look of amusement on her face. Elisa was stunned the woman would go beneath herself to work. It would do little good to discuss this woman with either her husband or Gil. Neither man was around during her reign of terror. Neither understood what she was capable of. At this moment they both looked at her with stars in their eyes. Even Etienne appeared dazzled by her beauty. How on earth would Gil resist? Elisa wanted to shake her husband then rattle Gil's brain until he gained some sense of reality where this woman was concerned. They both needed to learn the truth about her.

It was imperative she make certain Gil was made aware of the woman's lack of scruples. He shouldn't trust her. Elisa could tell by the way his eyes tracked her when she moved that he was drawn to her.

As the woman departed, Gil yelled, "Make sure you eat. I'll be down to see you later."

So, it was that way. She warmed his bed at night. Elisa knew Jenna would be after far more than simply bedding Gil. Jenna had to be after all she lost. Undeniably, Gil was her prey.

Chapter Three

At Gil's direction Jenna began to clean all the upstairs rooms. Her fingers ached. They were red and dry from all the soapy water she'd had her hands in over the last few days. It seemed she worked her fingers to the bone just to receive a roof over her head and a few meals. The long ensuing sigh was one of resignation.

What more could a destitute lady ask for, meals and a roof?

Perhaps a franc or two to help with minor comforts. A candle or two would be nice. New night clothes for Brice since he was outgrowing the ones he wore now. Her two dresses weren't going to last much longer.

Gil failed to come to the cottage the night before. Jenna wasn't sure if she was relieved or terrified. The woman, his friend, seemed to hate her, accused her of deeds that weren't hers. What could she expect? The woman would have no way of seeing into her mind or reading her inner thoughts. She'd never wanted to parade in the finery through the streets of Bordeaux. Never wanted to gain wealth at the cost of others. The flaunting of their prosperity was all Jacque's realm of pleasure.

This morning there had been little food left. Jenna fed Brice the two-day-old bread that had been in the basket. Last night she finished the wine from the night before while she waited on the porch for him. If he had not told her he would be down, she would have gone to bed.

She understood Gaby would feed Brice a good breakfast when she brought her son up to the chateau. Her stomach rumbled, waking her from her musings. She heard the chatter in the hallway. Prayed the lady would not come into the room to confront her.

She didn't want a confrontation.

One where she wouldn't come out on top. At the moment it was all she could do to remain standing. When she opened her eyes, she felt as if the room turned and the floor moved. With the hope her small world would stop spinning, she closed her eyes willing her body to steady itself, felt the floor rise up to meet her face. While Jenna thrust her hands out in front of herself to stop the inevitable fall, they didn't work. After that she didn't feel anything, nothing at all.

Time drifted by in a hazy fog.

She was cognizant of the flowing of air around her, of sounds in the home. Voices filtered through her mind. A clock chimed the hour. Somewhere below her she heard booted feet. Dreams filled her head. Thoughts of confronting Elisa floated within the fuzzy recesses of her head. There was nothing she could say that would defend her actions.

"Wake up!"

The sound of the harsh voice rattled her, sent her nerves spinning in desperate ripples to do just that. Hands on her shoulders shaking her didn't have the desired result. The splash of cold water on her face brought her to startling consciousness. Her breath rushed from her lungs. Beneath her chest her heartbeat froze. Slowly, she pushed herself from the floor, drops of water falling from her hair as well as her nose.

"I wasn't asleep," she was able to mumble, desperate to prove her point.

She didn't want Gil to think she was slacking.

"You fainted from lack of food. Didn't you eat last night or this morning? Do I have to feed you myself?"

She cringed at the tone of voice that greeted her. More than anything she wanted to do as he asked. Did he actually think she wished to starve herself? He didn't bring food last night. He forgot about her. Must have had better things to do.

Gil crouched beside her, his eyes blazing, anger simmering in the depths. She wished she could reach out to touch him. He stared at her with the raw hunger she'd come to recognize even while he seemed to condemn her for not eating. Unlike the days before there was nothing to eat. While she still had the twenty-five silver francs, she'd not had time to take the mare into town.

"No."

She stood, her knees shaking. He held her steady. Indignation rose to the forefront of her mind. She resented him for his insistence along with the fact she had no way to change her circumstance.

"I would eat if there was something to eat. In case you forgot, you haven't paid me yet. I would go into the village and purchase food. There's been no time."

"Gaby would have made sure you had food this morning before you worked. All you had to do was go through the kitchen. You're too stubborn for your own good. Now that you are here you don't have to starve yourself." He stood, jammed his hands through his hair. "What am I going to do with you?"

Before she could go back to work, he grabbed her elbow, guiding her through the room then down the servant staircase to the kitchen. All the time he was swearing.

"I'm not going to pay you because you've never been hired." He swore again as he pulled out a chair then motioned for her to sit. "You can't go into the village because no one would allow you to buy anything. Have you forgotten how people feel about you there?"

How could she forget when everyone reminded her? She didn't believe people would refuse her business if she tried to shop.

"Where is Brice?"

She looked to Gaby for answers. Jenna knew Gil wouldn't know where he was. Understood he hated her son but not why. He didn't have use for her either.

"The little sweetheart is out playing with some of the children. The workers, those who need to, bring their children here. He's having a great time. They've all had a morning snack. He's even talking with a few of the others."

She wanted to go outside to make sure he was doing fine and that he was all right. He didn't know how to play. Brice had always been with her. He'd never been around other children. When she started to rise, Gil's hands fell on her shoulders. He pushed her down. His scowl deepened.

"I understand all too well what you are up to. You're going to eat before you do anything else. Don't want you fainting on me again."

He motioned for Gaby to bring her whatever was left from the breakfast he shared with his guests. Elisa and Etienne drove into the village for the day.

"You didn't come last night," she told him accusingly, thinking none of this would have happened if he'd visited. She had no hold over the man. "You said you would."

He looked away for a moment. "I had other things on my mind. In any case, I had visitors, two dear friends. I haven't seen them for several months. We were catching up."

"If you're not going to bring food, you need to pay me. I've a son..." She wasn't sure what else to say to the man.

He poured coffee then pulled out a chair watching her. She fiddled with the butter knife. "You should go see to your guests. Go with them into the village."

"Why doesn't Elisa like you? I know she gave me some facts. Somehow, I'm not certain I believe her. From what I've seen of you, the details Elisa told me and what I see do not coincide."

"I'm sure she gave you an earful. Everything she told you was true. What she couldn't tell you was what was in my heart. If you must know the truth, the choices I was given were limited." She bit into the slice of bread that had no taste.

"Nonetheless, I'd like to hear your side of the story. Did you covet jewels and wealth? Did you like to parade down the streets in Bordeaux and show off your finery?" he asked as he heaped her plate high with scrambled eggs.

"You will believe what you will. I'm positive nothing I say will change your mind."

She bit into the eggs which tasted no better than the bread. The coffee was hot as it slithered down her throat.

"True. Didn't you ever hear the best offensive is a good defensive? You should try the truth with me," He placed two links of sausage on her plate. "As I said earlier, I want to know what was in your heart."

"I've done nothing wrong. No reason to defend myself."

She wondered how much of her life she would have to reveal to this man before he was satisfied. What was in her heart was private. If she told him, she would feel the humiliation again.

"Elisa says different."

He topped off her coffee before adding potatoes to her plate.

Bile rose in her throat. "I would save some of this mountain of food for Brice."

"Come here." He held out his hand, led her to the door where she saw her son sitting with the children eating apple slices. They each held a glass of milk. "You've no need to save anything for your son. He gets plenty of food. It is you who is slowly starving to death."

Etienne walked through the door. She wondered where his wife was. She thought they were in the village.

"We came back sooner than expected. Elisa has a headache. She needed to lie down."

"One of those times?" Gil asked as he remembered making the special tea for her, soothing her.

The headaches were excruciating for her. Like clockwork once a month she would have to take to her bed.

As if he knew something he shouldn't, Etienne frowned at Jenna. "For some reason my wife dislikes you." He poured a cup of coffee then joined them at the kitchen table. "I think Elisa is wrong about her assumptions where you are concerned. However, all the villagers seem to have the same opinion."

"I'm certain they do. Is that why the two of you visited the village this morning? To listen to gossip about me?"

She picked at the sausage with her fork. When she looked at Gil, it seemed he told her with the slow burn of his eyes they would stay here until she finished or did justice to what was heaped on her plate. Just thinking about her past caused her stomach to turn sour. Eating seemed impossible. She swallowed down the encroaching bile.

She tried to distract her thoughts with the truth. Perhaps this man would consider her story plausible. "Jacques paid them as little as he could get away with. Don't know what that has to do with me. I was simply another one of my husband's victims. Had no say in his business matters. He was in control, not me." She toyed and played with the food, pushing it around on her plate while her stomach continued its rebellion. If he wanted her to eat, he shouldn't question her at the same time.

"Rumor has it you paraded through the city arm in arm flaunting yourself," Etienne spoke softly seeming to search her eyes for answers.

"Do I believe that? Were there other reasons for your behavior? I'd like to hear what you have to say."

It seemed the man was giving her a chance to explain herself. She didn't believe she should have to do so. Jenna didn't think he would consider her truth valid. The evidence against her was too outstanding. "Only if you want to."

"Getting words out of her is more difficult than you could ever believe. She thinks to hold herself in the past," Gil said with a mocking tone. "She needs to eat then get back to the cleaning. She won't quit. Won't leave. Don't know what to do with her. I never hired her so I can't fire her."

Despite her headache, Elisa stood in the doorway, tapping her foot, her eyes blazing her disapproval. Jenna understood what the woman wanted to say to her.

Kick her out before she hurts you.

Jenna wanted nothing more than to escape in that oblivious unconscious state she'd been in earlier. She didn't have the words to defend herself to people who thought the worst. She wasn't sure if she cared any more. Once a long time ago, she believed actions spoke louder than words. Now, she supposed that to be true. Because Jacques made her do so, she did walk arm in arm with him. She did force a smile on her face. All the things the villagers said about her were true. Though, she didn't enjoy one second of the time she spent with her husband. For her the marriage was one made in hell.

By the time she finished half her plate of food, Etienne and Gil left. Elisa went to her room. Jenna drew in a long breath of air.

If he wasn't going to pay her, why was she laboring until her fingers bled? She decided that when those two left, she would find a way to get up to the third floor where she hid the jewels. If she'd had the time to sew them into the lining of her cloak before she fled, her life would be far different now. She knew where they were. If no one moved them, she could be in and out of the third floor room before Gil would even know she was there. When she found them, she would never have to see the chateau again.

The plan seemed simple.

A chance to go to the third floor came earlier than expected. Unfortunately, the sac of jewels was not where she left them. Perhaps they'd been sold and searching was a waste of time. She was bone-weary. It was time to go home to the cottage. An hour later, she found Brice. They walked home while she thought about her future luck. If she did eventually find the jewels, she could do exactly what Gil wanted. Leave. He would be happy.

That was the problem though. She liked living in the cottage. Brice was settling in. He looked forward to Gaby's morning visits. Had friends from the village he enjoyed playing with. She wasn't in a hurry to leave simply because her son for the first time in his life appeared happy.

Once home, she heated water. It seemed while playing with the children her son collected more dirt on his little body than she'd ever seen before. She bathed him then unwrapped the food Gaby gave them for dinner. She placed the second portion away for Brice's morning fare only because she couldn't trust her circumstances. She didn't know when Gil would force her to leave. Didn't know if he would show up tonight with more food and wine. She hated the inconsistency.

With his friends, Etienne and Elisa, firmly ensconced in his home, she didn't expect to see Gil this evening. Last night she waited up for him. Tonight, she wouldn't. Not for a moment did she expect him to grace her with his presence. Why did she think he might?

Because he said as much.

She washed one of her dresses then hung it up to dry. The dress was so thin parts of it ripped with the washing. It would not last much longer. After dumping Brice's bath water, she heated water for herself. Naked in the tub, she thought of the moment she bared herself to Gil. Her embarrassment at the memory heated the water anew.

He found her lacking.

Well, of course, he did. She was nothing but skin and bones, her belly sunken between her hipbones. Her stomach chose that moment to rumble. Until she came here, she didn't notice her hunger. Day after day she found ways to ignore the ache in her belly. Now that he fed her, she longed for more food.

Dressed in the old nightdress that once a long time ago wasn't threadbare, she walked to the porch then sat. With her bare foot she pushed the swing, watching the birds glide in the air. Heard the steady humming of the crickets. A chill swept across the porch. The scent of grapes filled the air. Harvest time, she always loved this time of year. She pulled the old quilt she kept on the swing around her shoulders then closed her eyes, soaking in the sounds of the land.

Gil sat down beside her startling her awake. His hand rested on her shoulder

"What...what are you doing here? I didn't expect you." She was breathless, shaking as she scooted away from him.

"Visiting with you."

He stared straight ahead almost as if his shoulder didn't touch hers.

"What about your guests?"

Truly she'd not expected him.

"Tired of the well-meaning lectures. Of friends thinking they know what's best for me." With a lift of his broad shoulders as if that answered everything, he continued, "It's late. They retired for the night" After pulling a bottle from the sac, he poured the wine he brought with him.

She wanted to know if he brought dinner and breakfast. Wished to know if he expected sex from her. Even though he rejected her two nights ago, he'd also told her he wanted her.

Jenna found she was tired of a lot of things too. Tired of defending herself to people who had closed minds. It seemed with Gil she didn't need to do so. He didn't ask too many questions about her past. Didn't seem to care what she did or didn't do with Jacques. All he wanted from her was her disappearance. His words were in direct contrast with his actions.

They found a strange way to coexist.

When he handed her the wine and looked at her, his gaze still seemed raw and hungry. Her body stirred to life. He seemed to follow her every move. "What were the lectures about? Or, if you don't care to share, that is fine too. I understand the need for privacy better than most."

Before he began speaking, he cleared his throat. "Elisa thinks I should get on with my life. Forget the death of my son, put the boy to the back of my mind. I can't do that. He haunts my nights as well as my days. She's adamant you want nothing more than to become my wife. To take from me and give nothing in return." He sipped, watching her, studying her perhaps for a reaction to his statement.

All she took from him was food in lieu of wages. "One marriage for me is enough, thank you. Don't ever want a man to own me or hurt me again." Often, she wondered why she told him things she'd kept to herself for so long. She sipped. The wine tonight was delicious. The food he was holding back would be even more pleasant when he decided the time was right to give it to her. It appeared he was waiting for something.

His soft chuckle surprised her. The fleeting smile changed his features so much she gasped.

"Is this what you are waiting for? You have this look in your eyes. A hungry look however the desire is not for me."

He unpacked the small carton he brought with him. As soon as the steaming potatoes filled with butter were unwrapped, the small porch was filled with the heady aroma.

She walked into the house to bring out plates, knives as well as forks eager to fill her stomach. For the duration, she hoped he wouldn't probe her with questions. She wished to eat without feeling nauseas.

"I've not wed anyone. Don't believe it's something I'd like although Etienne and Elisa are happy. Your marriage sounds as if it was a disaster from beginning to end. Though, I don't know very much about it."

The extra butter he put on the potatoes melted slithering over the sides. He scattered chopped bits of bacon and chives on the top. Her mouth watered.

"You don't believe in love?" she asked all the while hoping he wouldn't start questioning her. She did want to enjoy this meal.

"I didn't say that." He looked at her.

No, she supposed he didn't say nevertheless implied. She didn't bother to hide her hunger. Jenna bit into the potato smeared with sweet butter. It was more delicious than the wine. Her mouth full, she waved her fork in the air a million questions simmering in her brain. She wanted to learn more about his son and his wife. He never spoke of a wife nonetheless he had to have one. He just told her he never wed?

"Are you eating?" she asked deferring from her thoughts about the woman who sired his son. He hadn't wed her. The boy had been a bastard. Was that why he didn't like Brice?

"Yes, tonight yes. Etienne and Elisa are friends however sometimes they dare too much." He ate, watching her, the hunger still vibrant in his dark brown eyes.

She couldn't help the sarcasm coating her question. "Elisa will not stop probing. Now she wants to learn more about me."

"Suppose so." Gil stared out at the land, his thoughts appearing to be too private to speak of.

She wished she could become one with his mind, learn what he thought. When she was mostly finished, she set her fork on the plate. Jenna meant to delve where she shouldn't. "You know, you will never forget your son. The memories will be precious as well as priceless. In this matter, I do believe Elisa is right. Tell me about Lance, everything you can remember."

"*Non!*"

Ah, well, he visibly flinched when she said his son's name. His eyes turned dark with what she suspected was anger. Obviously, this wasn't something Gil was ready to share. Though his reaction was a good sign. When he turned his head from her, she was sure he would stay quiet.

"Maybe you would rather speak of Chantel. I know you will feel better if you speak of the mother. Why didn't you marry her? I'm sure she would have been a wonderful wife for you just as Lance was an amazing young boy. You wouldn't be down here with me if you'd done so. Perhaps you would have not bought *Cimaron*."

"Someone else would have bought the vineyard. It would not be yours."

"I understand that. What did your wife look like?"

Jenna didn't want to think of Chantel any more than she actually wished for him to speak of her. At best, her feelings for Gil were tenuous to fraught with confusion. She was surprised the mention of Chantel brought jealousy to the forefront of her thoughts. When he gazed at her,

her body reacted, stimulated by the simmering heat in his eyes. She never knew a man could touch her with his gaze.

"Her hair was dark, black as a raven's wing. She possessed green eyes that seemed too big for her face. They seemed to always question. She was sweet, submissive. Loved to give and receive pleasure."

It seemed easier for him to speak of Chantel than it did his son. Jenna couldn't help but wonder at the reasons why. If anything, she was the antithesis of this woman. Jenna knew she wasn't sweet or submissive. She understood she might have been that way six years ago before life taught her cruelties she never knew existed. Life with Jacques Bonnet changed her irreparably.

With a wistful expression on his handsome features, Gil gazed at her. The heat of his eyes swept over her, lingered in places then explored further.

Her body heated more with his ardent perusal. She realized she wore nothing beneath the old nightdress. Felt the sensitized tips of her breasts harden as his gaze rested where they touched upon the flimsy fabric. She gasped in a quick breath of air.

His grin had a way of chasing away the constant scowl lines on his face that aged him. She needed to turn his attention to something other than her woman's body. Unless sex would gain her permanent use of this cottage, she didn't want anything do to with it.

"What are you thinking?" Her voice wavered from her; so thin and weak she hardly recognized it.

"Need you ask?" Gently, almost reverently, Gil ran his knuckles across her cheek then along her neck. He let his fingertip rest on her racing pulse. It seemed he saw the terror in her eyes. He let his hand drop away. "I won't force you if that's what you're afraid of. Tell me..."

Jenna didn't think she would ever fear Gil. It wasn't Gil though that created all the tightening of her nerves until she was a ragged bundle of them, the thought of sex with any man did so.

"I told you I would do anything if you would hire me. I meant the words then as I do now. That makes whatever we do together, willing."

"So, the proposal still stands?" his query was soft.

To her ears the words sounded sincere as well as contemplative.

"You know it does. Now, however, I would allow you to do as you please with me for the permanence of the cottage. I wish for stability in my life. Brice needs the same. You still don't want me though, do you? I'm nothing like Chantel, the woman you loved. I'm not a sweet woman nor am I submissive in any way. I disobey you at every turn."

It seemed he was unnerved by her statement or was it a question? "Do you want me?"

Jenna wasn't at all certain why she pursued the topic. All along she meant for him to open up about his life. Now, it seemed, he was about to turn the table.

"One might say, my body craves release," Gil said as he once again looked over the rows of vines. "Sex with you could be nice, only if you are not afraid of me. If you give yourself to me, I will give you a woman's pleasure."

Bitterly she thought of her time with her husband. "That's all I meant to Jacques, a way to ease his manly parts. Oh, he liked to display me in front of people. Other than those two reasons he didn't care for me. He didn't like me, just as you don't. No matter how you phrase what you want, I don't believe a woman's pleasure exists."

She thought on all the times her husband pushed inside her, hurt her. If she cried out or protested, he would backhand her. Seemed she was destined to be a vessel for a man's lust, nothing more.

"Perhaps we shouldn't talk about this. I would have you willing or not at all. I'll never hurt you. You don't believe me. I don't know how to convince you otherwise except to show you."

Her laugh sounded brittle to her ears. "Convince me of something that doesn't exist? Not with words."

"As I just said, I could show you."

He picked up her plate and glass. Setting it aside he watched her for a few seconds.

Suddenly, she found herself sitting on his lap, his arms around her. She squirmed. "*Non...*" She had no way to refuse. If she did so, she might lose everything she gained so far.

"Do you say no to me? Give me a chance, Jenna. Let me show you how it can be between a man and a woman." Briefly his lips touched her ear feathered softly down the long white column of her throat just as his knuckles did earlier."

"You know I cannot say *non*. A promise made is a promise kept."

~ * ~

Gil made promises to himself, ones he meant to keep. In this instance, he decided to teach this waif-like woman about the heat of pleasure and passion. Yes, he would teach her all the different as well as the sweet possibilities that could happen between a man and a woman. Wanted her to know how she would feel beneath his hands as well as his body. Needed to hear the little, female sounds he could elicit from her with each evocative caress of his fingertips. Perhaps he could teach her about the heights he could send her to; maybe she would thank him sweetly.

"Did you know you decline my attentions every time your blue eyes darken with fear? No woman I can recall has ever feared me or denied me."

He was known as a playboy, a ladies' man. Not so much as Etienne nevertheless he took as well as gave pleasure readily. This woman eluded him. The more she stepped back the more he wanted her. It seemed to him she would take two steps forward then one back. At least he made progress.

Gil could tell by the way her light-brown eyebrows drew together she didn't believe him. Her chest moved visibly when she tugged in a long sweep of air. "I don't want to be afraid."

"Jacques caused you pain. I understand that. Sex between a man and a woman doesn't have to be that way. Shouldn't be." With tender concern he never felt with another woman, he moved still damp hair from her face, tucking the thick silken strands gently behind her ear. After he was satisfied, he followed with his lips, nibbling touching, caressing. When he pulled away, her breathing changed. The delicate breaths were soft and ragged. Visibly she was affected by his attentions. If he didn't miss his guess, at this moment fear wasn't the emotion touching her.

"*Oui.* He did."

"Want to talk about it?"

"Non."

"A woman of few words. I like that. Never did relish a chatter-box for a woman, a lover."

Before she had a second to say more, his lips closed over hers. Quickly, he swept his tongue along her mouth, hoping she would get the idea and open for him. He suckled her bottom lip, touched and explored, delved as far as she allowed. When she tried to inhale, she opened for him. He took wicked advantage of the moment. The kiss was hot and wet, drugging. The moment she relaxed into him, he understood he could claim her, make good on the offer she promised.

Inside her secret depths, she was dark and warm. She tasted of the sweet Bordeaux they drank as well as the sultry heat of a woman stimulated, needing a man to fill her with ecstasy. Only she didn't recognize the emotion. Despite the fact she was a mother, she was also more innocent than any woman he'd ever known. He desired her with a spiraling need he wished he could ignore. The more time he spent with her the more she burrowed beneath his carefully erected barriers. He cursed himself for his restraint while she offered herself to him.

What he couldn't tell her about Chantel was that he never loved the mother of his son. Couldn't tell Jenna that Chantel slept with countless men before as well as after she took him to her bed. He knew Lance was his son for two reasons. One, he'd been her only lover at the time when she would have conceived and the undeniable proof lay in the fact the boy had been the spitting image of him.

As his hands roamed Jenna's arms, she leaned into him, melted against him. Every feminine curve she possessed cried out to him to coax until she willingly gifted him with what he sought. He was surprised when she tentatively played with his tongue, danced and fenced as he explored inside her, touching her where he was certain she'd never been touched before.

When he pulled away, he meant to leave her to think about the kiss he wanted to deepen until it was so much more, until she would give herself over to him. Deepen until she would allow his exploration into more sweetly intimate places. As it was at this moment, she would still deny him entry because of fear. That frightened look he would see in her eyes couldn't be hidden from him.

Too bad Jacques Bonnet was dead. He would like to torture him as the man did Jenna.

He didn't understand why he cared so damn much. It had been so long since anything or anyone stirred his heart. For some reason this woman challenged him and defied him. At the same time, made him think of the future coupled with its prospects.

Within his arms, she trembled with the passion he expertly built. Her body arched begging for something he would give her in the future if she continued to ask. Not tonight. The small pert breasts that he was sure would enlarge once she began to fill out from the food he would bring to her pressed invitingly against his chest. His groan rumbled deep from within. Overhead the sky was startlingly clear. A soft breeze ruffled across the vines.

When she ventured from her lust-induced fog, she would, he was positive, feel the sting of embarrassment. Inside he chuckled. Felt a moment's easing of his heart. For a second, his thoughts were not centered on his son along with the terrible loss he always felt. At this moment, he spent a few seconds thinking of his pleasure.

Guilt forged its way into his head.

Slowly, she relaxed against him. Her head fit perfectly in the curve of his shoulder. To calm her, he stroked her back, touching upon each well-defined vertebra. He understood the vibrant need he induced inside her body. In time, she would look at him with passion filled eyes instead of fear. In time, she would be his for the taking.

Gil didn't understand why he ignored Elisa's warnings. If he was intelligent, he should never listen to the gossip. If he indeed possessed a modicum of good sense, he should dismiss the rumors and seek the truth. Deep in his heart, he didn't believe the stories to be true about this woman he held in his arms. The village people had degraded her good name. To his thoughts she was as innocent a woman as any woman could be.

"Gil?"

She moistened her lips with the small, pink tongue that had only a few seconds before been inside him. His body stirred to life by her kisses, was hard and ready for her as his member pulsed, throbbing with need that wouldn't be fulfilled tonight.

He wanted more. He placed his hand on her back, as she seemed to push away from him.

"What?" His voice was low, whiskey smooth, inviting further intimacies if she would say the necessary words.

"You kissed me?" Her voice held a wealth of wonder the softness creating mercurial heat.

Deep inside he chuckled. "*Oui.* That was indeed a kiss. Did you want another?"

He needed to ask her if she liked his kiss. Instead, he remained silent while he waited for her next comment, perhaps the answer to his question.

He watched her slowly swallow. Relished the rapid pulse at the base of her neck, knowing his kiss created the rush of blood. Her long slender fingers traced a path along his jawline. She appeared to be searching for something. He suspected it was for the words.

"I've never been kissed before." The pause was lengthy, "Yes, if you don't mind, I would like another."

His body tightened with the two statements. He wasn't at all positive how he meant to proceed with this revelation even though she didn't surprise him. "I'm going to do a whole lot of things with you that you've never done before. What would you like to do next?"

He did pull away as he needed a small measure of distance between them. Did top off the glasses with the Bordeaux he brought with him. Did watch her eyes for signs of fear or regret. He saw neither.

"I've no idea what you would do."

"That's my point. If you've never done something..."

He let his voice trail away as he thought on answers for her. Solutions he didn't intend to give verbally as he decided something new each night might be in order. Teaching her the ways of love would serve his purposes as well as hers. At least he hoped they would.

After he sat back, he tucked her neatly beneath his arm. Trailing a finger along her arm he meant to keep her slightly stimulated, hoped she would continue to feel the heat while her desire and passion increased.

"Gil?"

"What?"

"Before you owned the vineyard, you said you weren't around. Besides Paris where were you?"

"Working," he laughed softly. "Curious, are you? It seems I worked all the time. Never took time to enjoy life."

It was true. He had his dalliances. Still, he didn't enjoy his life. His gut churned while he thought of Lance, the way his boyish grin stopped his heart. How his eyes twinkled when he laughed.

"At what?" She pushed away from him, watching, waiting expectantly. Her lashes lowered slightly before she concentrated on him. "What did you do?"

"If I told you, I'd have to kill you." His voice was soft.

How many times had he used that phrase? It wasn't true. In this case, he saw her eyes widen for less than a second. She didn't believe him.

She hit him on the shoulder, her lips pursing. "You're lying. It's just a means to keep you from telling me the truth. If you were a gentleman, you'd tell me you don't want to talk about it instead of that outlandish declaration."

Gil thought for a few seconds. "Probably the most obvious statement you pointed out was that I'm not a gentleman. Don't know what gave you the idea I might be. A gentleman would never accept the blatant and seductive offer you proposed to me."

"You haven't accepted," she murmured, her eyes closing for a second. Pushing away from him, she strode to the railing. "Every time I've offered myself you put me aside. Why? I understand I'm not much to look at, however you are a man. Don't men want that all the time?"

"Sex?"

"*Oui.*"

He was glad they abandoned the topic of his work. In truth he missed the danger along with the excitement and the strange hum of energy the risk always gave him. Beside her, he enclosed her in his arms. Her back pressed against his chest. He turned her.

"Look at me."

She did.

To his surprise she touched her bottom lip with the tip of her tongue. She didn't understand how flirtatious the gesture was or how tempting. "I think I've told you several times. It's because I see the fear in your eyes. It's not there now. The fear, nevertheless I see questions. I refused because you aren't ready. You are very pleasing to look at. Don't forget that."

"Will you accept what I offer you?" she asked seemingly unable to hide the need.

"So, you are eager to become mine. *Non*, not tonight. To answer your earlier question, I worked for the government. Mostly I traveled to different parts of France on missions. Most of the missions were secret some were not. At times I was simply a messenger. Even though I would like to, I can't speak of them. I worked for the king as well as a government agency."

Her hands rested on his chest. "You're a spy." In those few words there were a wealth of questions.

"Was."

He felt the smile well up inside him again. She would be the death of him yet. The detachment he needed between them was narrowing.

"You quit. Was it because of your son?"

With the single word he withdrew from her. Felt the cold chill settle in the pit of his stomach. Never truly thought about the reason he resigned until this moment.

"*Non*, it was because I almost got the woman I believed I loved killed."

Gil never spoke those words before. Never told anyone how he felt. In his letter of resignation, he spoke of boredom of needing to move on to something new as well as more challenging. Time and again, he blamed himself for misreading the situation surrounding Etienne and Elisa. He never thought she would be so bold as to venture out of the protective environment she was encased in to defend her husband.

When he left them, he'd thought they were both safe. For the first time in his life, he understood the power of love.

He supposed that was when he realized she was so deeply in love with Etienne she would give her life for him. While he didn't want anyone to die to protect him, he longed for a love as deep and lasting as his friend's was.

"Elisa?" Her hands rested on his chest, toyed with the fastening of his shirt. "You still love her?"

He didn't think she understood what she did when her long, slender fingers found his flesh and caressed. She would not know how those few tentative touches stimulated and provoked to a fever pitch then evocative sensation rushing straight to his groin. This was not what he anticipated when he kissed her. Did not expect to be stirred this deeply by this woman and her story.

"*Oui,* thought I loved her. Discovered what I felt for her wasn't the same kind of love she and Etienne have."

At one time he wished for a woman who could love him that way. Now, he just didn't give a damn.

"It must be rare," she murmured while her hands danced across his chest, floating across the hard crests that stirred him profoundly.

His shirt was now open, hanging from his shoulders. Unable to help himself while not wishing to frighten her, a low groan rumbled from his chest. He clamped her roving hand to the center of his chest.

"Rare?" He wasn't thinking straight.

"A love such as they have is rare. Suppose that's why they don't like me. I could never give you what you want. I could never love you, give myself over to a man."

"Why not?"

He lifted her chin to better see into her eyes. They were filled with unshed tears her lashes spiked with glimmering drops. Sipping one that slid down her cheek, he tasted the salt.

"Don't believe love exists like that except for those two. Most couples just take what can be given to enjoy."

He tried to lighten the mood as he suspected she was in part right in her assessment of the situation.

"Neither do I. For your friends, I'm just going on your word that they love each other."

"Why do you cry then?"

The moment the words left his mouth he regretted them. At that instant, it appeared she withdrew into herself. Until this moment, it seemed they were beginning to understand each other, at least where she was concerned.

"There was nothing between Jacques and myself except hate. I despised the man. Was so heartily glad when I conceived and he left me alone. He loathed me because I didn't fit into the mold he wanted for his wife."

"Are you sure that's how he felt about you? He married you." He grimaced when her exploring fingers pressed across his nipples again. "If you don't stop..."

"I want to give myself to you. Wish to know if this woman's pleasure you spoke of actually exists."

He swept her into his arms. Carried her to the porch swing where he set her once more on his thighs. "Not tonight. Not until you're ready."

He hoped and prayed that would be soon. Rushing this seduction, he planned would do him no good. Even though she didn't know it yet, she was his. He wasn't about to let her go. Then why did it matter?

One handed he explored inside the pack he brought with him. Pulling out lemon tarts he offered one to her.

"You're changing the subject with food."

Her soft feminine laughter surprised him, pleased him as well.

"*Oui*, is it working?"

He certainly hoped a sweet delicacy would get her mind off seducing him. Inwardly, he laughed along with her. That was what she was doing. In her innocence she had no idea what those strokes with her tiny fingers could do to a man.

"I'll tell you after I've finished these two. They are delicious." She shot him a stunning smile.

He did enjoy watching her eat. Loved seeing the smile on her lips when she first bit into the food. She would close her eyes, a tiny smile hovering on her lips as if she tasted heaven. This sweet confection would help put something on her bones.

With her mouth full of the second tart, "Aren't you going to have one?"

"Would rather watch you."

He should go. He should leave before he took more than he wanted tonight.

"Gil, how did you meet Chantel? Why did it take you so long to discover your child?"

"Too many questions for now."

His gut turned cold once again with the memory.

"Truly, I understand if you don't want to talk about your past. I don't want to think let alone speak of things long dead. In my entire life, no has loved me. Don't know why my life would change now."

No one ever loved her.

"Not even your mother and father?"

He didn't understand. Sure as hell wanted to discover the truth.

"My mother died when I was too young to know. Father despised me." She spoke with such an indifferent tone. "I don't know why. Suppose he might have felt different about a son."

He found he'd been holding his breath while she spoke. His breath left him in a long swish of air before he began to speak. "Met Chantel when I was on a mission in the south of France. She was a widow. Supported herself by seeing men. They would pay her for a night of pleasure. Since I don't share my women, I was the only one paying for her favors. I wasn't careful or perhaps she wasn't. She conceived. As far as I know, Lance was my only mistake. In my eyes the boy was never a mistake. Wish I would discover another one."

"You paid for her to make love to you. Just as you're going to do with me, when I'm ready." Her long heart-felt rush of air from her moist lips surprised him. "Does that make me your mistress? Or your whore?"

"Mistress? I never thought about it that way. Neither, I'm thinking. Not going to pay you so you're neither." *All I do know is that I want her. She gives me something I've been missing for so long.*

She waved a small hand in the air. Her lips smashed together as if she thought on what he told her. "Doesn't matter. If that's what I am, what I have to do to make sure Brice always feels my love it will be what I have to do. Better you than the last man who offered for me."

"Last man?" His words stuck in his throat while his fists tightened.

The sudden need to hit that man filled his gut. "Who?"

"You wouldn't know him. I ran from him though. He was too much like my husband."

The small whisper of her sigh left him breathless with the need to protect and shelter this woman. Gil wanted to fight all the newly burgeoning feelings. Didn't know how.

"You did? You ran?"

With this new knowledge, he needed to understand why she made the offer to him. He sipped his wine trying to will his body to a calm he didn't feel. He wished he could put her statement to the back of his mind.

"*Oui*. As fast as I could. "

"You're not running from me."

Mon Dieu was he any better than the other man, any different from Jacques. He wanted her just as the other men in her life did, with no strings attached. She was beautiful, ethereal, waif like. She tugged at all that he knew of himself to look inside for something deeper.

"*Non*. I am not."

Her fingers nervously wrapped in and out of the gown she wore testing the fabrics strength.

"I brought you something else tonight."

He didn't understand why. Insecurity rarely played a part in his life. Now it did.

"Something besides food?" she asked, her eyes alight with anticipation. "What did you bring?"

He grinned, foolishly pleased with his attempt to help her. She would like the gift.

His voice gentled. She appeared a little girl in anticipation of a gift. He guessed she had not received many, "*Viens avec moi.*"

He set her on the floor then held out his hand to her. Without protest she accepted his hand. Within his large callused hand, hers was small, delicate feeling. She allowed him to lead the way down the porch then around the corner to the barn. Led her inside. She trusted him.

He lit a lantern. Held it up high. They stood in front of a small buggy. She looked at him, to the buggy, back to him. Questions rose in her eyes. Slowly, with this woman, his heart began to thaw. What exactly made him bring this means of transportation to her, he didn't understand. Deep inside he was terrified she would take it and run. He consoled himself with the fact she had no money. Here in the cottage, she had security. Brice was well fed. In the near future, he didn't plan on paying her. She would have no means to run from him.

She didn't say anything. Her eyes simmered changing into crystal shards. Instead of the warmth he expected she withdrew from him. He felt her withdrawal.

"Do you like it?" Hesitantly, he ventured the question prevalent in his mind.

She swept the small, pink tongue he wanted to taste again across her lip. "I don't understand why you would do such a thing. I haven't earned this."

"You told me you needed to go into the village. It's too far for you to walk. You don't have shoes that would make it there and back. If you tried, you'd wind up barefoot."

By his mind, she should be throwing her arms around him to thank him. Her lips should be atop his. At this moment, he should once more taste her sweetness.

"I can't pay you for this. The buggy is not something we bargained for. The last thing I want from you is charity."

She turned from him, back stiff, shoulders squared stomping back to the cottage.

His heart lodged in his throat. *The devil take you.* Startled by her reaction, "It's not charity!" he yelled at her retreating back.

His anger was about to erupt. Cold waves of fury swept through him. Her stubborn pride might well be her downfall.

Gil found her sitting on the porch swing, sipping her wine, another lemon tart in her hand. "It's an act of kindness."

He poured more wine while making a mental note that in the future he should bring two bottles. He didn't know how to convince her she should keep the buggy. He wasn't about to take it back.

"Charity. What do you want from me so I can pay for it? Was the kiss enough? Should I do more? Two kisses? Three? You've already snubbed the use of my body."

To Gil Jenna sounded bitter and tired.

He supposed she had every right to her bitterness. Life did not treat her the way it should.

Yes, he'd wanted more kisses. In the future would have more. "How should I know? Women!"

He jabbed his hands in his hair. Just when he was thinking he understood her, she turned on him her eyes blazing. He silenced her with the tip of his finger to her luscious lips. "I was trying to be nice."

"I've no money to go into the village. Well, I have enough to buy a few loaves of bread. Why should I spend what little francs I've left on food when you feed me? What do you want from me, Gil? Spell it out in terms I'll understand. Do you want me to clean another room? Do you want me to mend your clothes? You obviously don't want me in your bed."

He heard the sour tone to her voice. Didn't know how to change that tenor. He swept a large breath of grape scented air into his lungs. "You've earned enough coin to warrant the buggy for your use. I've never seen anyone man or woman work as hard as you do. Don't look at me that way." The look in her eyes had him sweating buckets. Her hands were clasped tightly beneath her breasts. If she didn't stop looking at him with her eyes blazing with raw hunger, he would surely sweep her off her feet and collect on that bargain between them.

"*Merci.*"

"Thank you? Thank you? Is that it?"

"For now, until you ask for something more."

"*Maman*? What are you doing?" Brice asked as he stood in the frame of the door.

His little boy voice sent waves of anger through Gil. Cold encased him. He withdrew into the hard shell that kept him isolated from his emotions.

Lance.

The sound of Brice's voice nearly brought him to his knees. Lance was dead, buried in the south of France. He would never hold him or kiss him again. He couldn't play with him or watch him smile and giggle. He couldn't bear to look at this little boy. The sight brought back memories he didn't know how to deal with.

"Use the damn buggy or not. Don't come to work in the morning. Can't bear to see you or your son."

Gil strode from the cottage. Once he passed the main gate leading to the chateau, he ran. Ran until his lungs gave out. Fled from the demons haunting his soul. Nothing he could do would keep him from seeing the boy's eyes fill with tears at his unkind words. He couldn't control his emotions when he saw Jenna's son. Nothing, nothing to do except run until the pain along with the memories could no longer control him. As it was now, they took charge of his life.

~ * ~

Elisa sat in the plush room above her mother's house of pleasure in Bordeaux, France. She came not just to visit with her mother but also to discover as much as she could about Jenna Bonnet. Etienne elected to stay home with Masson and Margo telling her she was wasting her time and that she needed to cease her meddling. Any fool could tell Jenna didn't have a mean bone in her body. The woman had been Jacques' victim just as the villagers had been. Her husband was content to believe that. She wasn't.

"You should have brought your children," Angelica spoke softly. "You know how much I love to see them. I miss the little monsters."

"This isn't a social visit or I might have done so. Besides you know how much Etienne is against the children staying in the brothel. He doesn't believe the time I spent here as well as in Paris was good for me."

Elisa walked around the room, content for the time being to allow her mother to direct the discussion. "Why don't you return with me? You can stay a few days or a week if you like. Visit the children. Torment my husband. Heaven knows he needs to be brought down a peg or two."

"A week in the same vicinity as your husband? Is there a death wish in any of this?" Angelica asked, her tone bittersweet. "As you well know I would not be the one doing the tormenting."

"You do understand he will do his best to stay away while you are there. He can always find work especially this time of the year."

Elisa felt a sudden violent need to laugh at these two. After all these years, they still didn't like each other. She wanted to believe they tolerated each other. At one time she hoped it was an act. Etienne assured her it was not.

"Etienne cannot forgive you the past. Believes you should have encouraged me to see him before he left on that last mission that kept him away from me as well as our son for almost five years. Should have made sure he was informed about his child. He resents so much of what happened, also blames you."

Angelica drank long and deep of the brandy she poured earlier. "He should have tried harder. If it had been me, I would have stormed the place. Would not have left until I got the answers I needed. Instead, he meekly tucked his tail between his legs and left."

"Ha! You know very well your bouncer would never let him past the front door. I gave him no indication I wanted to see him. He expected me to be upfront as well as honest with him. At your encouragement I was neither."

"Don't blame this all on me. You had time to inform him. You could have taken the initiative. You were a scared young lady. Right you are though, I should have done more for you." Her mother shot back. The words between them were always the same.

"I know," Elisa spoke softly. "The true reason I'm here is to find out what you know about the Bonnets. We could have the argument about my past again and again. We would never come to terms with futility of my defiance."

"Why? Why Jenna?" Angelica sat forward seemingly more interested in the conversation now that it wasn't about her relationship with her son-in-law.

"In my humble opinion, Jenna Bonnet is out to gain whatever she can by using Gil. At this point in time, Gil is vulnerable. You know that Gil bought *Cimaron*. She lives in the gatekeeper's cottage and works at the house. I don't trust her to have his best interest at heart. She wants to claw her way into Gil's life so she can find a way back into the chateau."

"Why should she? A woman who has a man's best interest at heart will lose her soul perhaps more. Women need to look out for themselves.

Gil's a big boy. He doesn't need anyone second-guessing his decisions. Let him take care of himself."

"Because Gil is an honest and straight forward man. Where she is concerned, he wears his heart on his sleeve."

"I'm sure the man is not that obvious. Gil doesn't strike me as a man who will allow a woman to take advantage of him."

"In other circumstances I might agree with you. He's been grieving the loss of his son as well as the woman he meant to ask to marry him. His grief is all consuming. If you saw him, you would understand where I'm coming from. Gil is not the same man we used to know."

Elisa knew he suffered had been until this woman entered his life. She wanted him to find a woman to love.

Not this one.

Never Jenna Bonnet.

"You afraid this woman will snap him out of his melancholy?" Angelica laughed softly as she watched her. "Isn't that what you want? So what if she worms her way into his heart. Worse things have happened. If he is happy, what do you care who makes him that way?"

"What I'm afraid of is that she will end up wed to him. When that happens, I've not a doubt in my mind she will take and take until he has nothing left, not even his soul."

"That sounds a bit harsh." Angelica's laughter sent a cold ripple of anger into Elisa's heart.

"I'm not wrong about this. You need to do something. You've always liked Gil. At one time you selected him to be my husband. Go talk to him. Tell him Jenna is not the woman for him."

"You want me to visit Gil Allemand? When I'm there and under his roof you want me to tell him what a conniving bitch Jenna Bonnet is?" Angelica asked, a strange twinkle in her eyes.

Air seemed to be sucked from her lungs. She understood her mother was telling her it would happen when hell froze over. Elisa stiffened her shoulders. "*Oui*, that is exactly what I'd like."

Her mother had a way of confusing and frustrating her. She didn't understand why Angelique wasn't more protective of this man she called friend.

"I would never do that to Jenna. She's been through far more than you would ever suspect. Been accused of things she had no desire to be part of in the first place. In my mind, Gil and Jenna would make an amazing marriage. They can heal each other. I like her. Respect her."

Elisa snorted. "She's fooled you too? I've a hard time believing that."

"Believe what you will. Jenna worked for me. She spent almost a year cleaning and helping wherever possible. She never prostituted herself even though she could have made far more money if she had done so. When she saved enough money to go back to *Cimaron*, she left. Jenna didn't know at the time Gil bought the vineyard. Neither did I. Had I known I would have helped her out more than I did. Would have loaned her the francs needed to buy little Brice's inheritance. When she owned the vineyard, it would not have taken her long to pay the money back."

"What do you know about her? I'm open to what you have to say." *Sort of.* "What did she tell you that gave you the impression she wasn't what she seemed?"

"The woman didn't have to tell me anything. I knew her late husband as well as her father. They were both hard men, unbending in so many ways. They were cruel. Deep down they hated women. Took delight in any small way they could hurt a woman. Her father sold her to Jacques. Jacques used her. The tale is simple."

"You've always had a jaded opinion of men."

"True."

"Not Gil."

"*Non*, not Gil. He deserves the best. Jenna possesses both the stubbornness to deal with that hardheaded demanding man as well as the beauty that will tug at his heartstrings. She has a kind heart. Her son is a weakness they will have to find a means to overcome."

"What are you saying?" Elisa studied her mother for a few seconds. With mockery in her words, she spoke softly. "You're matchmaking."

"Only stating the facts. What neither of them understand is that they can fill the hole in each other hearts if they give themselves the chance. They both need love, are desperate for it. I don't think Jenna has ever felt love. However, there is a great deal standing in their way."

"Jenna Bonnet is a gold digger."

"Time will tell."

"What is it you're not telling me?" Elisa was discovering there was so much more to this story than she expected.

"Jacques was kicked out of this establishment because he was too rough with the girls. Was told to never come back, that he wasn't welcome. As for her father, the same message was handed to him more than two years ago. Jenna has known nothing but abuse at the hands of men."

"The rumors?"

Elisa knew she had to learn more. Had to find some means to understand the strange tug at Gil's heart. She didn't think Gil slept with her yet. She hoped to end that possibility by giving him hard proof she wasn't good enough for him. Angelique was not going to be the source of that information.

"Gossip shouldn't ever be believed. What was said about her was laughable. If Etienne forced you to wear jewels and pretend you were happy parading around as if you were better than everyone else, is there any way you could stand in his way? Would you be pleased with your circumstances?" The question was a probing one.

Elisa found herself shaking her head as she thought of all the things Etienne demanded. None of them were harsh. All were meant for her safety. He held her to them. *Mon Dieu!* She recalled the time he threatened her with a child's punishment. Hauled her over his shoulder while she did her best to get away from him. If he wanted her to do something, even something she didn't want to do, she would have no choice.

"I see your point."

"Jacques Bonnet was a cruel son of a bitch."

Chapter Four

Unsure of the reception in the village, Jenna left Brice with Gaby. He would be fed all day. Would have the children to play with. When she hitched the buggy to the mare Gil left for her use, she swallowed her pride. Last night he'd been angry with her. Told her not to come to work. At least for one day, she decided she would take him up on the declaration.

Tomorrow, she would go back to work. Today however, she wanted to spend some of the silver francs on a treat for Brice. She didn't understand why she'd taken such umbrage with his gift. Becoming his mistress was not part of the proposition. All she wanted was work and a fair day's wage. The work she'd done. Had not received the fair day's wage.

She stopped at the *epicerie* first to see what types of groceries she could pick up that might round out the foods provided by Gaby. She wanted to bake her own bread. Needed to have fruits and vegetables for Brice to eat. When she stepped inside, she stiffened. The man standing at the front of the store clearly didn't want her in the store. The anger slashed across his face was perfectly clear. If he meant for her to leave, he would have to say as much.

"*Sors d'ici!*"

Well, he did tell her to get out.

Jenna wasn't going to leave before she purchased what she came here for unless the man forced her out. This was exactly the reason she didn't want to bring Brice with her this morning. She didn't want him to see the hatred. She ignored *Monsieur Garnier* as she wandered through the small grocery store. Thinking fresh bread might be nice for her son, she picked up flour and sugar as well as yeast. As she made her way, she put in her basket other items she thought might come in handy. There were oranges and lemons, a few apples. *Monsieur Garnier* followed her as if he thought she meant to steal from him.

"Of all the nerve," *Madam Tossaint* tapped her foot, her hands settled on her robust hips when Jenna walked by. "You don't belong here. You need to leave *Monsieur Allemand*. Leave him alone. You and your little boy are nothing but trouble. No one wants you here. Slut."

Her head held high, she stole a breath of air from the stagnant environment. If she had anywhere else to go... Again, she chose to ignore the woman. Her words hurt. Jenna didn't do anything to these people. Because of Jacques they all despised her. When she finished, she paid for the items. She had just enough coin left to purchase a pastry and a small piece of chocolate for Brice. Once more, when she entered the *boulangerie* she was asked to leave. With her head held as high as she could get it, her chin in the air she purchased what she wanted. Interesting though, the merchants didn't refuse her money.

The ride home seemed to take her forever, the seconds slowly ticking by. Jenna could not remove the hurtful words from her mind. Unsuccessfully, she tried not to replay them over and over again. Thinking of her son helped momentarily.

Get out of here!

Jenna didn't know why she thought she could wander into the village untouched. Thankful Brice was with Gaby, she let her shoulders relax while she tried to enjoy the slow drive back to *Cimaron*. The day was pleasantly warm. A soft breeze floated, swirling across the hills laden with vines. The air was redolent with the sweet scent of grapes waiting for harvest reminding her of a past she needed to forget as well as a future that still needed forging. Above her a hawk soared on the currents of air. Squirrels chattered happily in the trees while songbirds flitted from one branch to another.

As her mind wandered, she thought on Gil. After the last week or so, he wasn't as unfriendly as he had been those first two days. The man with the icy veneer seemed to tolerate her. His anger didn't surface as quickly. When he smiled, ah, when he smiled and his lips twitched with some unspoken humor, she thought her heart would melt. If she allowed him into her heart, he could change her life forever.

Gil still hated her son. She didn't care if he had a reason. In her mind, his reason just wasn't good enough. Nothing, no motive would be good enough to hurt a child the way he did. His actions weren't something she could forgive.

His kiss last night turned her insides to liquid fire. If he asked, she would have given herself to him, despite her fear. Truly, she didn't think the anxiety along with the terror would ever leave her. Someday he would ask to collect on her offer.

What would happen if she refused? She prayed nothing.

Gil's touch was nothing like Jacques. It was all she had to compare. Jacques never kissed her, never stroked her tenderly. Her husband never wanted her to respond to him. Expected her to lie beneath him, frigid and unmoving. From the few kisses they shared, she didn't believe that was what Gil wanted.

As she approached the gatehouse she looked to the chateau. On the top of the hill her old home stood proud and beautiful, formidable. It spoke of days long gone, at least for her. Spoke of a time when the aristocracy ruled this small portion of France. That all ended during the revolution. Before Gil owned *Cimaron*, the home always seemed so foreboding. Now, now she saw hope. Perhaps she was happy a man such as Gil Allemand bought the home. She would have never found the coin to pay the taxes that were ignored by her husband. Taxes she assumed went back several years. Jacques always believed he could circumvent the law. It seemed during her absence the law caught up to him.

Good riddance.

When she drew closer to the cottage, air rushed from her lungs. Her heart pounded erratically. Bushes around the small home were upended, their roots bare. Flowers were stripped. Muddied dirt was thrown at the home, puddled on the floor of the porch. Her heart stopped its beat for a moment. The breath she held for a second left in a sickening gasp of despair. She drove straight to the barn leaving the horse still tethered to the buggy. She would take care of them later. As she walked around the house, paint was spilled on the railings.

She touched damp paint. So fresh the mixture didn't have time to dry.

Her finger came away red with the wet paint.

Blood red...

"Non...!" Panic swept through her. Her knees trembled as she stared at the home, her home now. Why? She knew why as she fisted her hands. She wasn't going to run.

On the side of her house the same words the grocer used were painted in red, *Sors d'ici!*

Jenna's stomach coiled and churned. She fell to her knees, hands clasped in front of her. *"Non...Mon Dieu, non...Brice?"*

Her heart in her throat, breath held tight, she looked up the hill. He had to be safe with Gaby. Her son wouldn't leave without her. Quickly, she put the horse away, brushed the little mare then gave the animal water. With her skirts hiked nearly to her knees, she raced toward the chateau. She didn't know what she would tell Gil or her son. Wasn't at all sure Gil would be there. After all there was work to do. It was harvest time. They would be stomping the grapes soon. He wouldn't have time for her problems. He didn't want her here either. This would just serve to solidify his reasoning.

Gil had too much on his mind with the vineyard to be concerned about her or her problems. He might not care someone had violated the home where she lived. He would care. He had to care.

When she stepped inside the kitchen, Gaby was a comforting presence. Her hands were in soapy water, washing the dishes she'd used to make dinner. Contentedly, she was humming to herself. The room smelled of fresh bread. Stew simmered in a large pot. A pitcher of milk along with a plate of cookies sat on the counter waiting for snack time for the children.

"Brice?" she asked her voice trembling, frantic with need. "Where is Brice?"

Gaby smiled at her. She didn't seem to notice her terror. Nodding toward the kitchen door, she told her, "He's just fine. Outside playing with little Micah. Your boy is such a dear. He brought me a bouquet of daisies. Of course, the little tyke didn't ask if he could pick the flowers. Still, I appreciated them more than anything."

Jenna raced to the door. She looked through the opening. The site of him playing in the dirt made her laugh, made her weak with relief. She leaned her head against the doorframe closing her eyes for a blessed moment so she could soak in the sight.

"He will need another bath tonight," she murmured to herself. "Thank God for small favors." She wanted to deal with simple things such as baths as well as reading stories to him, not threats. It had been so long since she had a book to read. Sometimes she told him stories she remembered, fairy tales along with fables.

"Boys need baths every night. Now tell me what's got you so riled as well as tied up in knots. Never seen you such a bundle of nerves. Looks like you've run yourself ragged. Did you race all the way from the cottage?"

Her hand rested at her throat. "Nothing, everything, just needed to know if you saw anything today. I traveled into the village. Seems the trip was a big mistake. I knew they hated me, however..." Her voice trailed off with a quiver of despair.

"Anything unusual?" Gaby emptied the basin of soapy water. "I've been in the kitchen since this morning. Haven't heard or seen anything but the two lads playing. Earlier there was a little girl. She went home with her *papa* an hour ago."

"Do you know where Gil is?"

She didn't want to sound so needy but she was afraid to go to the cottage. Didn't want Brice to see what had been done. He would be afraid. There was nothing to do about it if Gil wasn't at the chateau to keep him here.

"Gil? He's about somewhere. Why?"

Why? It was unusual for her to seek him out. He always came to her. Brought her food. Her stomach lurched. Food wouldn't sit well in her stomach now. She forced down the rising bile.

"When he comes in for dinner, tell him I need to see him." She didn't want to be afraid. She had to go home. Needed to explain it all to Brice. In the process make sure he wasn't terrified. Perhaps there was some way she could turn the painting into a game.

"Whatever for? Is everything alright?" Gaby looked a bit worried. "What is wrong?"

Jenna knew her face must appear a death mask she was so

terrified. She didn't want Gaby to know anything. "Nothing is right. As soon as he eats...tell him. *S'il te plait.*"

She whisked from the kitchen striding quickly to Brice. She knelt down beside him while she tried to mask her fear. She kissed his forehead despite the fact she knew he would protest. "Time to go home, sweetheart." She hoped her voice was cheery.

"Do I have too?"

His question surprised Jenna. Brice rarely complained. This was a new side to him. It seemed he was growing stronger as well as more confident each day. Even though this wasn't exactly a complaint he was letting her know he wanted to stay right where he was. Jenna wished she could oblige.

"*Oui*, it is time. I've something to talk to you about as we walk."

She ruffled his hair knowing he would take umbrage at the motherly gesture. Would remind her he was too old for her to embarrass him in such a way. Today, she didn't care. Jenna meant to relish each precious second.

As they walked, she explained to him what happened. His brows drew together in a deep frown.

"Did the mean man do that to the cottage?"

She choked back, a whimpering laugh. *Non.* Brice's words caught her attention twisting her insides. She should have spoken to him more about Gil. Should have never allowed him to hear Gil last night. If she'd only sent him to bed sooner when he wandered outside.

"Gil? He didn't. He wouldn't hurt you or me. Even though he sounds mean at times, he truly is not. He lost his son, you know. He's hurting deep inside, just as you would feel if you lost me. In some ways I believe you remind him of his son. Your presence makes the hurt raw and deeper."

When they first arrived at the chateau, Gil did want her to leave. She was certain that feeling was in his past. If last night coupled with the kiss was an indication, he was warming to her.

"I don't believe you," Brice told her crossing his arms in front of his chest as if he tried to make the point with obstinacy. "He doesn't like me. I don't like him."

Well, that was simple. "You're welcome to your opinion as I am to mine. Gil would come right out and tell me what he thought. He had done so many times. Gil would never resort to this type of game."

Her son was right though. When it came to her son, he was damn mean, cold hearted. She found all kinds of ways to write it off. Despite his reasons, no child deserved this type of treatment. Gil still mourned his son. Might always misplace his values in his despair. She needed to shake sense into the man. Didn't know how to do such a thing.

"There was red paint in the cellar." His arms were still crossed in front of him. "I saw it the other day when Gaby let us play down there. Do you think someone from here did it?"

He was allowed to play in the cellar?

"Red is a common color."

One of the workers might have found the time to walk down to the cottage. Whoever did this was a threat to her as well as Brice. She understood what these people wanted. Unfortunately for them, she wasn't going anywhere. With no money to her name, she didn't have anywhere to go.

"I bought you a surprise from the village. After your bath you can have it. Gil gave me the use of a carriage along with a horse so I wouldn't have to walk." Jenna hoped her words would persuade him to a different line of thinking. She didn't want him believing Gil was a bad person.

After Brice ate his piece of chocolate, she baked a loaf of bread for their morning meal. He could have the pastry then if he preferred it. She put him to bed. Later that evening, she sat on the porch swing waiting and wondering if Gil would show up. Last night he left in such a black mood she couldn't be sure what his intentions were. Even her plea for him to talk to her might not be enough to drag him from his home.

Jenna didn't like thinking about or seeing the words she heard too often in the village. She wished she didn't need Gil to make this right. Wished she had a can of paint and could cover the horrible words.

Growing restless waiting, she worked on the plants that had been wrenched from the ground. "Such a ridiculous waste of time as well as energy," she murmured to herself.

She was dirty and tired. Her dress ripped in several more places.

She would have to mend it tonight or before she set off to the chateau tomorrow for work.

"What did you want to talk with me about..." Gil's voice trailed off as he noticed what she'd been doing.

Jenna turned to look at him while she wiped her dirt-smeared hands on her gown. Her heart stopped beating for a moment at his genuine look of concern. He felt something for her. Cold hard anger simmered in his eyes as he stared at the damage.

"I'll send my gardener down tomorrow to finish for you. Who did this?" He grabbed her hand tugging her around the corner of the cottage before she had a chance to reply.

"I..." She stumbled over a root. He swept her into his arms finishing the distance to the porch when he saw the rest of threats.

"*Sors d'ici...*"

He rounded on her his large hands on her shoulders. For a moment, she thought he meant to shake her.

"I don't know who."

Over the hours she'd been home, she thought strangely she'd grown used to seeing the words. They were only words. No one meant to hurt her just make her leave. If they wanted something to happen to her, there had been plenty of times on the ride back from the village. She was sure all they wanted was to frighten her.

Gil didn't say anything else. She watched his back as he strode up the steps to the porch setting the pack of food on the table by the swing then into the house. Slowly, she followed him wondering what she would find.

He pulled out the bath. Kettles filled with water for her were now heating on the stove. She didn't care if the bath was tepid. What she cared about was that he wouldn't be watching.

He was right.

She wasn't ready to become his lover.

"You should have found me instead of waiting for Gaby to give me your message." His tone harsh he scraped his hands through his hair. He appeared furious. "*Mon Dieu,* woman, you have been here all alone for hours."

"Nothing happened."

"You can't stay here by yourself."

"I'm not staying with you."

"Didn't offer that. You will come to the chateau."

"*Non!* I won't allow you to dictate my life. I'll lock the door."

"When you didn't come to work, I was sure you went into town. You used the buggy. Tested the waters there. They don't like you any better now than they did when you lived in the house on top that hill." He poured steaming water into the tub. Tested it then finished filling it with tepid water.

"I'll wait outside for you."

One of her concerns was just answered. Before she slipped from her dress, she watched him walk through the front door. Heard the soft squeak of the swing as he pushed it with a foot. She rushed to her room then pulled out her second gown. With quick strides, determined to make this speedy she strode back to the kitchen where the tub was filled.

The water was divine. Deliciously so. She couldn't linger. He might come to see what was keeping her.

She used the jasmine scented soap she purchased in the village for her treat. The soap would be the last unless Gil decided to pay her. When she stepped outside, his head rested on the back of the swing. His eyes were closed, arms crossed on his chest. For an instant she thought he might be asleep.

"Sit down, Jenna," his voice was soft, concerned.

He didn't open his eyes right away.

Another argument was not something she wanted or needed. She would do as she thought best. He wasn't going to make her remove herself along with Brice from the cottage. "What do you want?"

"I gather you won't move to the chateau." Now he sounded resigned. "I can't protect you if you stay here. Do you want your son to get hurt?"

That was underhanded. It seemed he meant to throw all the punches he could. "You know I don't. It's just that..."

He was a man. Didn't understand that only her pride kept her from... She didn't have pride any longer. Her offer was the lowest she ever sunk. "I can't."

"Don't see how your reputation can get any more sullied than it is at the moment. While I can't do anything to change that fact, I can protect you. No one can get to you if you're living in the main house."

"Don't care about my reputation."

Once she did, no longer. What people thought of her couldn't hurt her.

"You should for Brice's sake. He doesn't need to grow up hearing that his mother is anything less than pure. You will be their bad example." His words might end up haunting her.

"They will think I'm your mistress if I move in with you." She knew what he was thinking before he could say the hurtful words. She had to accept what her life turned into.

His broad shoulders lifted in a gesture that told her he didn't particularly care about her reputation either. "The villagers who come to work call you my whore, my pretty piece. Perhaps the term mistress is better than the term whore. What do you think, Jenna? Which would you rather be? My pretty piece or my mistress?"

"I'm neither."

"True, at least not yet. If you stay here, I won't be able to sleep at night worrying about you."

"You trying to guilt me into moving up the hill?"

Brice would never be happy living under his roof. She wanted this tiny bit of independence coupled with the security of knowing she made the decisions. It was something she never truly felt before.

"Just trying to keep you alive."

His fingers drummed on the armrest. He rose to pour wine before setting out what was to be dinner.

The stew smelled wonderful. Maybe for the duration of the meal, she wouldn't have to defend herself. He couldn't make her move back to a place that haunted her nights even while she wasn't living in the chateau. Sometimes the dreams she had were horrific. When she looked up the hill at the house, all she saw was Jacques on top of her, laughing, pushing into her, hurting her. She needed new memories.

"Do you have paint to cover up the writing? If you don't mind, I'd like to do that tomorrow," she asked.

"You didn't work today. You're behind. I've things for you to do at the main house." He spoke blandly with no emotion. "You don't have the time to paint over this."

"You never wanted me there in the first place. What difference would another day make?" She thought on the offer. Remembered if he wanted to use force, he could keep her from the cottage.

He wasn't that kind of man.

"I find I miss seeing you. Feeling your presence. Thought to have an afternoon snack today. There was no one to share it with."

She sucked in a startled gasp of air. "You miss me?" She was astounded at the revelation. She watched as his lips twitched in what might turn into a smile.

"Find that I do. Now, perhaps wine and food will help you see things my way. What do you think? If you drink enough, I'll be able to persuade you to the right course."

"You expect me to keep all this writing on the home? Let me get the paint and..."

He knifed a hand in the air. What once looked to be a smirk turned to a scowl. "*Non!* I'll send the gardener tomorrow as soon as you arrive with Brice. He will take care of the grounds as well as painting over the hateful words. Don't want you to worry about them."

"Gil..."

Once again, he slashed his hand through the air. "No arguments. I've things for you to do. Want you to clean the master chamber. The floors need scrubbing, everything else a good dusting. You can take the curtains down to the scullery. They need washing. I'll supply a more thorough list tomorrow."

"Are you going to pay me?"

She needed the money. Needed to be able to buy a few things. Didn't like the tone he spoke to her. She supposed he had his reasons. It still didn't sit well with her.

He was shaking his head staring at her as if he saw through her. "*Non*, not yet. There is still the accountability, the offer to consider."

Jenna bristled, furious with him. Angry he was so autocratic. The reasons made a great deal of difference to her. He never wanted to tell her why. "You're cheap, *Monsieur Allemand*. I've worked hard."

She stood, her fists clenched with the rage that seemed to be taking over her body. This resentment would do her no good. She inhaled as much air as she could suck inside her lungs.

Nonchalantly, he stretched his legs out in front of him. His position coupled with the expression on his handsome face was pure male arrogance. Before he spoke, he cleared his throat, "*Madam*, you have a roof over your head, food in your belly. What more is it that you want? You've come nowhere close to working enough to pay for the rent on this place you're calling home. If you moved to the chateau, I could rent the cottage. Make money instead of encountering loses."

She was standing over him, her nerves stretching to a breaking point. She hated to admit he was right. "I need to be able to buy..."

"Clothing for Brice? Noble endeavor."

"*Oui!* He's a growing boy.*"

"From what I can see, he has more than he needs. If you spend a franc on him, you're wasting your money. Let's see what you're willing to give. You could convince me in other ways." He spread his legs, his hand outstretched. "*Viens ici.*"

"You want to take me up on my offer now? Now, when I'm vulnerable and...and..."

He smiled. White teeth flashed behind it. "We will see. Remember, I want you willing. There is no force, no fear in your eyes. No hesitancy. Should we begin where we left off last night? A warm and very willing woman would be a pleasure. After that we can negotiate, perhaps reach terms that are more to your liking."

Mon Dieu, last night she'd been willing. Truly, she didn't know what she had to do to convince him she wanted him. He was right though. Simply because he was a man, she still feared him. Didn't think she could ever relax enough to forget the fear. She knew if he touched her intimately, she would shriek. He would withdraw. They would be no closer to an agreement than they were now.

She stood in front of him, between his muscled thighs. He held both her hands in his. His eyes raked over her, seeming to see what she was covering. He looked inside. "Are you sure your son will not intrude?"

"Surely you jest. If you don't do anything that would wake him, he will not venture out to see."

He rubbed gentle circles on her wrists. "You mean yell out my name when I reach my peak deep inside your velvet hot sheathe? Is that what you mean?"

Gently, he tugged her closer. From both sides, his legs pressed against hers.

She felt the warmth pour from him into her. He was a devil, a rogue. Unable to help herself, Jenna gulped air. She recalled the times Jacques would do just that. Blood drained from her face. "Jacques did that while he made me lie without moving beneath him. I couldn't..." Her voice was a thin whimper in the warm heat of the evening.

Gil swore in a language she'd never heard before. She supposed he knew a lot of different languages. He would have to communicate when he was in different countries. She wanted to know what he was saying now.

"I wouldn't do what he did. Wouldn't expect you to lie still beneath me. Would rather hear you howl with pleasure. Wish to feel your hips press against mine in your need. Would love to hear you scream my name when you reached the ecstasy, I could bring you to." He settled a finger over her lips. "Hush now, I know you want to insist there is no such pleasure for a woman. I guarantee you there is. All you have to do is trust me. Let me pleasure you."

Unable to help herself, she blinked several times. To Jenna, trusting a man didn't seem prudent. "Trust?" That was one commodity Jenna didn't believe she could deliver to anyone of the male persuasion.

"In time you will. Shall we proceed where we left off when we were interrupted last night?" He was stroking her arms, slowly coaxing her to agree with him. His sweet-talking, seduced her to places she never knew existed until he arrived in her life.

She'd been standing between his legs. Suddenly and quite jarringly she found herself straddling his hips. Beneath her she felt the pulsing, the quivering of the steel length of him, the part that would hurt her. His broad hands cupped her derrière, squeezing, creating a tempest of heat within. She didn't understand why. Without more seconds passing, he moved one hand to cup her breast. A thumb passed lazily over the crest, tantalizing and teasing repeating and repeating the simple movement until a tiny mewl of pleasure whispered from her lips until heat built within so torrid, she closed her eyes while letting the sensations build and build.

"It's not quite a howl or a yowl. The sound will do for now." His voice was whiskey smooth. He sounded pleased with himself.

~ * ~

Gil grit his teeth together while he tried to concentrate on Jenna and creating so much pleasure she would forget her past along with the terror Jacques single handedly created. Thoughts of anyone violating the house and grounds sent a tremor of fear through him. He wanted to protect her. She wanted her independence. If he could, he would shake some sense into her. In this cottage she had some tiny measure of independence.

At the chateau...

Well hell, at the chateau the villagers would know her for what they believed she was. What he yearned for her to be. His lover.

Tenderly, his hands ran the length of her spine and back down. She was in such a lush, ripe position, heaven sent for all his dreams. The scent of warm willing woman along with jasmine filled his senses, played mischief with his swelling desire. Tonight, he yearned to coax her one step farther then another tomorrow night. If he planned this right, it wouldn't be too much longer before she graced his bed with her beauty.

"If I paid you, you should start with something to wear for yourself. These dresses will not see too many more days. When I look at your shoes, well, let's not go there. Soon, all your dresses will be in shreds. Won't have to do much to sample the sweet charms you're trying to hide beneath gowns that are falling apart."

Slipping one hand through her hair, pins flew, clattering to the floor. Thick strands of silken hair slid through long fingers as he gently brought her lips closer to his. Her hands rose to his neck, rose higher as if to bring him closer to her. Her nails raked his scalp.

He smiled, pleased.

"*Embrasse-moi*," he murmured as he brought her so close their mouths nearly met. "I want you to kiss me. Can you do that? Kiss me?"

She moistened her lips, caught the bottom one beneath her top teeth, her striking blue eyes riveted on him. They shimmered with desire along with a small ripple of confusion. "Gil...I..."

"Don't tell me you don't know how to kiss me or perhaps where to kiss me is what has you in such a quandary. I taught you so well last night you wouldn't have forgotten. Do I have to fix this predicament?"

"*Non*, but..." She puffed out a tight bit of air before she traced a fingertip along his jaw.

Hours seemed to pass as he found he was holding his breath. Tentatively, she brushed her lips along his. He groaned at the first contact. She pulled back, her eyes wide.

"Keep going. Don't stop now. You've just begun." He didn't mean to show her how easily that tiny caress affected him.

Jenna was so hesitant he wanted to laugh. With desperation he never felt before when it came to a woman, he needed to taste her. Wished she wasn't so damn untried that he had to teach her everything. Perhaps he liked her this way, enjoyed the innocence. He couldn't ever remember bedding an innocent.

She wasn't a virgin.

No, but she was so damn unknowing of sexual pleasure his gut tightened.

The fact Jacques initiated her to the ways of sex was not a fact he wished to dwell on. He tried to close his mind to everything except the present. The sweep of her hot moist tongue across his lips delighted as well as enchanted created magic in an otherwise drab world. He could spend a lifetime enjoying this woman, coaxing her a delightful encounter.

When she pressed against his lips, he opened for her, caught the little mew of surprise in his mouth. She tasted him, explored enticing him to respond to take control. Enjoying this side of her, he held back, waited to see what she remembered. Kept distance between them until she tugged him closer. That was just the way he liked his kisses, a moist inferno of heated bliss. He returned the favor delving inside her hot warmth, searching out the deep scorching mystery that was Jenna. His hands ran the length of her spine then back. He wanted to keep kissing her until he stuck his spoon in the wall.

"Look at me," he whispered, hoping to see the passion in the deep blue of her eyes, not the fear. He needed to see desire so he could take this one step further on the path to her seduction.

Lifting her head from his lips, he stifled the groan derived from the departure of her warmth. Wished for the heat of her against him. She moved slowly, her hips rising to settle on him, stimulating him further.

He didn't understand how potent she was. After Lance and Chantel died, he drowned himself in brandy. Spent a year in Madrid while all he did was drink and sleep. One of the Spanish whores in the small inn where he stayed came to him one night. She used all her powers of seduction. The time she spent with him was wasted. She wasn't able to arouse him. With Jenna sex was different. The first time he looked at her he felt an intense surge of lust straight to his groin.

At that time in Spain, he didn't want anything except to join his son. Wanted to die. He probably would have if Etienne hadn't come for him, dragged him back. With help from Elisa and Angelica, they dried him out. They weren't able to give him a reason to live. Elisa and Etienne encouraged him to purchase this vineyard. He understood their hopes. He just didn't give a damn.

Now, this skinny woman with the determination of ten men found her way straight to his soul. He discovered he couldn't leave her alone even though at first he tried. In the present, he was counting the days until she graced his bed.

Gil found he needed to taste more of her. As planned, he wanted to bring this one step farther. *Mon Dieu,* if he still didn't feel the slightest hesitation, a glazing over of her eyes, he would be inside her right now.

He drew in a long deep breath of air. How long would it take to erase the damage that Jacques Bonnet caused?

Slowly and with gentle fingers, he moved the shoulders of her gown down her arms. The fabric was so thin the tiniest strain would rip the material. Watching as her breast were uncovered, he stared at the tightened pale pink crests tipping the white mounds that sill hid beneath cloth, material he intended to remove.

She gasped, startled as she looked at him.

"Need to see you. Is that alright?"

Her hands resting on his shoulders, her fingers tightened. Felt the bite of her nails through the fabric of his shirt. She was excited yet terrified as well.

In silent answer, she moved on him again, readjusted her body. Her eyes wide pools questioning him as he carefully pulled the laces that held the front of her chemise together. It seemed she couldn't look away as the fabric slowly loosened.

"Jenna...?" He waited for her to refuse him. Waited for a word or gesture of consent or rejection.

When the chemise was pushed aside, she sat back as if she wanted to give him a better view or distance herself from him. He couldn't be certain. Reverently, he touched her, brushed the palms of his hands across both hardened tips. The beautiful pink crests tightened even more. Despite the smaller size of her breasts, her nipples were large, more so when they tightened.

A sensual cry rippled from her telling him she liked this as much as he did. As he bent to take her nipple into his mouth, his mind unraveled. She tasted of endless nights of lovemaking, of sweetness everlasting. Her hips pushed against him while her fingers wove in and out of his hair. He pulled her skirt higher so the only thing between them were his trousers. Against him she was wet and hot. Felt the heat of her pour into him, tempting and stimulating until he had trouble thinking, could only react. Control was momentary, fleeting at its best.

Suckling her breast, he flicked his tongue across the turgid peak sucking the rounded globe deep into his mouth. The tiny sounds she made gave him good reason to continue. Still, she moved with a rhythm that was as old as time, primitive in nature so sensual he could barely suck air into his lungs. His hands cupped her breasts, his thumbs initiating small circles meant to coax and arouse.

With more regret than he could imagine, he slowly withdrew from her. Pulled the fabric of her chemise along with her gown together. He would continue farther next time they were together.

"Gil...? When she looked at him, he saw no fear only passion. "What? I..." she moistened her lips with her tongue leaving a dewy trail of moisture behind that he wanted to taste.

He lifted one eyebrow in speculation. Wondering if she understood how seductive that one gesture was to a starving man. "What?" he queried hoping for an answer to his liking.

"Are you stopping?" Her voice was shaking as well as her body. One trembling finger touched his jaw.

"Do you want me to?" he asked with masculine arrogance understanding what her answer would be.

"I..." She moistened her lips again then again in unconcealed invitation. "I'd like another kiss..."

"Would you now?" He watched as one more time she presented him with her tongue sweeping across her bottom lip in anticipation.

She nodded.

"Prove it to me. I don't want to see fear in your eyes. Don't want you to be afraid of anything we do together. I only wish for you to know pleasure."

Gil knew he'd like nothing better than to move her into the chateau. She could have the room adjoining his. She would be in his bed whenever he wanted her there.

Every night, perhaps even every day.

Once again, she settled on him, moved and caressed him without knowing how thoroughly she provoked him. Lust surged straight to his man parts. All he would have to do is unfasten his trousers. He'd be inside her sultry inferno. He would feel the soft velvet surround him, lick as well as kiss his steel-hard length. Together they could ride the tempest she created, the storm she generated within his body.

She bent toward him. Her breasts pushed and danced languidly across his chest. She kissed him just as he taught her, deep and hard, played with him. He responded with everything he could give without taking what he didn't believe she was ready for.

Tomorrow night when he came for her, he would teach her about true ecstasy. He would show her how wrong she was about what could be shared between a man and a woman. He would gift her with the ultimate pleasure. *A woman's pleasure.*

When she pulled away, her lips were swollen, her eyes slightly glazed. It was time for him to leave. He wanted her wondering what would come next. Needed her needing him more than ever. Perhaps he even longed for her to beg.

"I'm leaving now." Gil gently set her away. "Should we have another glass of wine before I walk back up that long road to my cold lonely bed? It would be much nicer if all I had to do was walk from one room to another. If you lived in the chateau..."

She pushed away, her eyes narrowing slightly. Determinedly, she repeated herself, "I won't move up there. You know that. Don't ask me to do, *s'il te plait.*"

"Is it me or the memories?"

He understood somewhat. Memories nearly did him in. They still ruled too much of his life. There was nothing at the chateau to remind him of Lance or his time before he found his son. The home presented a blank slate.

She looked down, studying her hands that were now resting against his chest. "Both," she whispered softly, her beautiful eyes shimmering with unshed moisture. "Both you as well as the memories. There is more though. You've shown me more."

"You don't want me to control you?" he questioned even though he could easily guess at the truth. "A man is always in charge. Even now, you've little say in your life. You take what I'm willing to give. It would be no different with another man."

She passed her small hands across his shirt. Beneath her palms she touched his nipples. As if she didn't know what she was doing, she looked at him with wide eyes.

"Little minx..." he whispered as he set her aside.

They were done here. His tortured male body couldn't take more of her gentle exploration.

Despite her marriage, she was the closest woman he'd ever made love to as being virgin. Most everything they did together was new to her. Everything, he amended. According to her she never knew pleasure at her husband's hands, only pain.

He filled the wine glasses. Handed one to her. His breath as well as his heartbeat turned ragged.

She looked at him again, sipped slowly while she seemed to want to speak, "Gil, I'm not afraid. You make me want to feel something. I'm not too certain what that is. I don't want to be numb any longer."

"Then you're ready to give to me what you offered that first day you wanted a job. Your body, you will hand it over to me? You will be mine?"

Despite the tiny, startled gasp at his harsh words she nodded while she stared at her glass of wine. When she looked at him again, he wasn't all that positive she meant what she told him. During the interlude when she was in the throes of their lovemaking, she didn't fear him. Now, when she had time to think, he knew she dreaded their eventual joining. Perhaps it was just maidenly uncertainties of the unknown. Perhaps not. She might not be able to chase the thoughts of her former husband from her head.

He brushed hair from her forehead, placed wayward strands behind her ear. "I promise you when we come together the experience won't be anything like you remember. Tomorrow, I will teach you a few delights that can be found at my hand. Delights," he reminded her, "not pain." He lifted her chin with his finger. "Do you trust me?"

"We are back to that? Don't know if I can ever trust a man. If I could find it in my heart to believe in a man's words as well as his deeds, that man might be you. So, perhaps in time."

Gil heard the truth in her words. If Jacques weren't already gone, he wouldn't mind sending him to hades for what he did to Jenna. Men like that should not be allowed anywhere near women, even prostitutes. "I will have your trust before we do anything together you might come to regret. Drink your wine. The liquor will help you sleep."

He understood his voice turned harsh. A hell of a long time might pass before she believed in him. He watched as she downed the liquid in one gulp, her eyes simmering when she looked back at him.

"I will be early to work. Perhaps someday you will pay me honest wages." Her voice sounded bittersweet to him. "If you paid me honest wages, I would definitely pay you rent."

The real world intruded in this magical fantasy they created. He wasn't going to pay her because he didn't trust her to stay at the vineyard. "Someday."

All the sweetness she shared with him vanished. "You will send the gardener to fix up my home. Tomorrow morning."

It seemed to him she emphasized the word home. He knew she was telling him in her way that she wasn't moving for him. He didn't want to leave her alone. "Yes, he will paint as well as plant the bushes that were torn up. You will lock the door behind me when I leave." These were not the terms he wanted to depart with.

Barefoot, she took the plates and glasses into the kitchen. He followed. For a few seconds, she leaned against the counter. He wanted to see into her mind. Needed to understand her thoughts, perhaps even her wishes. Wished he could sway her to his way of thinking. Too bad he didn't exactly know what that was.

Jenna closed the door to her mind. "When I think about what you did, the way you touched me and how I responded..." A soft exhalation of air parted her lips. For a moment only, she closed her eyes as if she relived the past moments they shared. "...I might find a way to trust you."

"Jenna..."

"I'm embarrassed. Wanton, perhaps. I would make a better mistress than I did a wife. God knows Jacques thought so little of me. All he wanted was the heir. Look what good that did."

"A woman in the right man's arms is supposed to be wanton. It's exactly how I want you, unrestrained and giving. There should be no room for embarrassment between lovers."

"You also want a mistress. You don't want marriage." She held up her hands stopping his reply. "I don't want marriage either. We've been over this once before. Nothing has changed in the last few days. Any man I wed would have complete say over my life as well as Brice's. I can't allow that. Never again."

"I'm not letting you go."

Still, the thought of becoming a surrogate father to her son twisted his gut into a knot he could find no way to untie. Anger at the injustices of the world filled his heart.

"Not until you've had your fill. Gil, I want your promise that you'll let me live here. Forever. I will always clean for you. Do other things if that is what you need."

What he understood about himself was that he didn't want her to leave. He also didn't want her to remain at the cottage. *Non,* he wanted her in the chateau where she belonged. A promise of that sort would be impossible.

The thought of forever jarred him. Pain at his losses turned to fury that she would defy him. That she would ask for something such as this. "I can't do that."

"You would kick me out? Just because you got tired of me in your bed, you know I've nowhere to go. I've no one to turn to, no family." Her words came out in a strangled sob her fingers twisting the worn fabric of her gown.

"*Non.*" He scraped his hands through his hair, his stomach turning sour. "I would have you live in the chateau. You would be more comfortable there."

"We've been over that, Gil. I won't change my mind. Promise me. *S'il te plait.*"

He didn't want her to beg. Needed her sweet compliance. "I can't promise you something so permanent. Neither one of us knows what the future will bring."

"We both understand what you want from me. At least once you take what I proposed, you can make that promise."

He was shaking his head. As far as he was concerned this evening was going from bad to worse. At this point, she wouldn't ever give herself to him. She would hold back until he gave in to her unreasonable demands.

He was angry, furiously so. "Go to sleep, Jenna. I'll see you bright and early in the morning."

"I detest what you plan to do to me, Gil Allemand."

"Little liar. You melted in my arms. I could have been inside you tonight, deep and hot." With his words, he saw her blanche, her face turning a pasty shade of death.

"It is what you do..." She sliced her hand through the air. "You will never understand."

Gil didn't wait for another retort or a question. With long, hurried strides he left the room and the house behind him. He felt as if he suffocated. Each breath he inhaled burned his lungs. He felt walls closing in all around him. As soon as he could find a way, he would move them. She was going to live in the chateau with him in the adjoining bedroom. For Jenna, he would even try to tolerate her son.

Demons bombarded him from what seemed like all sides as he rushed up the drive. He needed to find some way to retrieve the beauty of the night, to put the pain of his past behind. Now, as he walked, he saw images of his son. They melded with Brice. Tonight, when he closed his eyes, he couldn't tell one boy from the other. Brice was not his son, would never take the place of his most precious creation.

Lance didn't deserve to die.

Brice was sickly, barely able to do what all five-year-olds could do.

Unable to stop the horrific thoughts, he ran. Hell seemed to close around him. He was not the mean man Brice thought him to be. He was not a *tete de butt.*

Gil ran through the vines. Swiped at spider webs. Running was his only salvation. He raced the wind until his breath came in huge gulping sobs. Until his lungs ached and burned. Until he could no longer sip enough air to keep up the pace. Slipping to his knees, he let the tears fall. Sobs wracked his body. His chest heaved. He clutched his fingers together as tight as he could, hoping to keep thoughts of Lance at bay.

If he could give his life to see Lance running and playing again, he would. As it was, he had no reason for living.

Jenna...

Jenna gave him reason. He couldn't explain how this scrawny wisp of a woman could torment his thoughts so. She was a bright spot in his world he didn't want to let go of. Gil didn't understand. Didn't want to find a diversion that would keep the memories of his losses from him. He didn't deserve happiness.

Jenna...

She was just a woman, nothing more. All women were much the same. She didn't have anything he hadn't seen before. He loved women then he went on his way. No commitments. No promises. He didn't understand how she was slowly worming her way into his heart. Couldn't comprehend how much he wanted her.

Elisa believed Jenna was after his wealth. *Enfer!* Hell, he was in hell. She would have to marry him to get anything from him. She wanted the cottage...forever. He didn't want to believe she played him for a fool. Maybe nothing she told him was true. Perhaps she was asking him for the moon and stars. Did she lie? He didn't believe so.

I don't want to be married to anyone. Once was enough.

For reasons he couldn't fathom, her words ate at his soul, tore his heart into shreds. They haunted him night and day. To be wed to a man such as Jacques Bonnet, of course, once was enough.

He didn't love her. Couldn't love any woman.

He thought he loved Elisa.

His feelings for Jenna were different.

Far different.

~ * ~

Gil couldn't bear to return to the chateau. He did return long enough to pack a bag. Thoughts of traveling to Paris whispered to him. Thoughts of finding the *madam*, Margaux, then spending hours with whatever woman would put up with his melancholy. A woman who could ease the ache Jenna created so easily.

He settled for Bordeaux instead of Paris, Angel's place would have to do. Elisa's mother, Angelique, always had a soft spot for him. Had wanted him to be Elisa's husband, not Etienne. In the end, that would have never worked. Elisa didn't love him.

After seeing the two together, he understood nothing like that would come his way. Comprehended what true love looked like.

Until he met Jenna.

Until he knew a woman who's scent and sweet beguiling eyes brought him to his knees.

"You've come to talk?"

Angel waltzed into the room, a smile gracing her face. She was tall, regal as she if owned this small piece of Bordeaux. Her age didn't show at all. "About Elisa or the woman who my daughter believes is after your wealth. What's her name?" The *madam* placed a slender finger on her chin. "Jenna Bonnet? An intriguing woman, interesting, I suppose she is a thorn in your side, asking for so much from you."

"Jenna..." He sat down in a wing chair near the fireplace drawing his brows together in concentration. He knew what she would say. Needed to hear it firsthand. "What did Elisa say? Besides she thinks Jenna has anything but a pure heart. To tell the truth, I'm the one taking. Taking whatever pleases me."

Gil thought about the offer he'd yet to collect. If he remained at home instead of running away, he might be in the process of collecting at this moment.

"Do you want one of my women? A woman such as Jenna Bonnet couldn't compete?"

Angel studied him as if she could read his mind. Maybe she could. He would have to take better care with his expressions.

"You read my mind, almost. *Non*, I thought so at first. Now, don't know what it is I do want. She has me changing my mind with every breath."

He was drumming his fingers on the arm of his chair. Tossing back the full glass of brandy Angel poured for him, he stared into the flames, wondering what hell he'd fallen into.

Angel laughed, her soft chuckles grating farther into Gil's overstretched nerves. He understood what she was thinking. Angel was right. He wouldn't be able to perform. "The only woman I want is Jenna. I can't have her."

"Why? You said you were the one taking." Angel filled his glass. "Seems if she wants you, there's no reason not to do what comes naturally."

Naturally, Gil grimaced. It was all too damn natural between them except the fear in her eyes coupled with the presence of her son. Wherever she went her son was beside her. He wanted her alone with no burden. She loved Brice. He couldn't abide the sight of the little boy.

"Well?" Angel pursued the question.

"Jenna is afraid of men," he murmured all too easily recalling the look in her eyes. "We both understand why that is."

"Change it. I've heard, at least before you discovered a son, before he died, you are an amazing lover. My girls talk, you understand. You never left without seeing to their needs, their pleasure."

"Easier said than done. She has a son. A frail sickly little boy, every time I look at him..." He cursed himself for his feelings. He should never wish for one boy to replace another.

He did though.

"So, Jenna Bonnet, the object of your sensual desires comes with baggage you don't appreciate or contemplate how to get rid of. How drole? Imagine a defenseless little boy causing a grown man such torture."

"Don't see anything humorous about this. Tell me about Jenna. In your opinion is Elisa right in her estimation?"

He stood. Strode to a window overlooking the river along with the city. Watched the water move languidly between the buildings while sea gulls played in the breezes overhead. The sun was setting. Jenna would wonder where he was. He should have left a note for her. Told Gaby instead. Even if he rode hard, he wouldn't get back to the winery before late tomorrow morning.

"You wish to know if she's as Elisa has said. She's not. At least she didn't act that way while she worked at the bordello. She cleaned for me. You understand she didn't have a room here. Jenna had a tiny room in the worst part of the city. The hovel was all she could afford."

He turned, his head moving slowly, telling her he knew nothing about what she did in the brothel although he was certain she didn't sell her body. She was too damn untried too afraid.

"What did she do with her son while she worked?" He thought perhaps he could find a way to make the little boy disappear from his sight during the days. Except in rare cases, he wouldn't have to concern himself about the nights. So far, Gaby did an exceptional job keeping the boy away from this view. Gaby understood. Maybe he should pay his cook more.

"You do know we have other children to take care of while their mama's work. I designed a play area for the children. The children of the women who don't want to put them up for adoption play as well as learn there. It's quite progressive. Don't you think?"

Gil was surprised. He'd never given much thought to the women getting pregnant. They took precautions. He should have. Etienne and Elisa found themselves in that predicament. Of course, Elisa wasn't a working girl. Ah, he thought on that story.

"So, Jenna was forced to bring the boy here. I wouldn't think a mother such as her would want her child exposed to this type of life."

"She didn't want that for her son." Angel lifted her shoulders thoughtfully. "Not much of a choice when you have to weigh it with putting food on the table."

Gil noticed a hint of anger in Angel's voice. He stuffed his hands through his hair. "I..."

"You did. The children were never exposed to anything sordid. There is an entire wing of this home where no gentleman or ladies go, except for the employees who take care of the children along with me. This wing is where Elisa spent her days when she wasn't at the cottage."

"Brice?"

"A charming boy. I suppose you frightened him. When you scowl so darkly, I've thoughts of running and hiding. If you want Jenna, you're going to have to find a way to accept the child into your life. She is a doting as well as a very loving mother."

"I do want her. Not for a lifetime though."

His words ate at his gut. A lifetime with one woman? She already held a place in his heart, squeezing, hinting at pure, sweet bliss.

Once again Angel's soft laughter rippled through his dusty brain, he understood her laughter was at his expense. The sound angered him. He was in no better mood now than when he left Jenna the other night.

"You believe Jenna will give herself to you willingly." One of her light-blond eyebrows lifted in speculation.

"She made me an offer."

"An offer? Whatever for?"

This time he had to laugh at himself as well as his conflicting actions concerning Jenna. "Told her she couldn't stay in the gatekeeper's cottage. Told her she had to remove herself and the boy. Even told her I wouldn't hire her. She showed up at six in the morning working her little butt off."

"You threatened her."

"Well, that was what I thought I was doing. She ignored me. Jenna's a hard woman to threaten."

For the briefest time his lips twitched in amusement. He saw her on hands and knees scrubbing the floor. Remembered her as she swayed because she was so exhausted and starved she couldn't stay on her feet.

Recalled, too, the second when she fainted.

With him gone, Jenna wouldn't have anyone to bring her food. If Gaby didn't sit and watch her eat, Jenna would wrap up whatever food Gaby gave her for Brice. His stomach lurched. In two days, she would undo all he accomplished since she arrived. Why the devil did she insist on starving herself for someone who had more than enough to eat? She was crazy.

"An independent woman. I like that. Taught Elisa to be that way then it backfired on me when she chose Etienne over you. Maybe if I didn't want her to think for herself, she would have listened to me."

Gil grunted wondering, too, what he would want in a woman now that he couldn't have Elisa.

Angel swished her hand through the air staring pointedly at him. "Go home, Gil. Go to your woman. Tell her you love her. It's obvious to any blind fool that you do."

Love... He didn't think so. *Tender concern maybe. Lust absolutely.*

"I want her to move up to the chateau."

He would carry all her meager belongings on his back if she would agree. If she didn't agree, she would have to follow him, give into his wishes because there would be nothing of hers left in her home.

"She won't do it. You know what she would be called if she did your bidding. Do you want that? What you want for this woman you won't admit to loving is something to think about before you toss her life upside down. Unless you want to marry her, you should accept the fact she wishes to remain independent of you. You can visit her in the cottage. People will guess but they won't have proof."

"The villagers already call her my mistress, my whore. What

difference would it make if she moves in with me?"

He was a big boy. He knew exactly what it would make her even though he didn't want to think about the term that didn't fit her at all.

Angela's brows came together in a frown. "What little I know of your lady, she is no man's whore. No man's mistress either. One or the other, that's what you want to make her. It's not well done of you. A man should never have that kind of power over a woman."

"I didn't call her that."

"Your actions will turn her into your whore. If you do something like move her into the chateau, you'll regret your uncaring, selfish actions. I'm assuming she has refused your attentions."

"*Non*, she has melted under my expert coaxing. Although she won't admit to the fact, she wants me as much as I want her. She's afraid though. Afraid of a man's touch."

He laughed at his language, at his outlandish behavior. He wanted her kisses, needed more.

"Seduction is what you are using to coax. I'm not surprised she's afraid. You understand her husband was a mean son of a bitch. After he beat one of my girls so thoroughly, she almost died, he was refused admittance. Do you suppose he beat Jenna?"

"She hasn't mentioned it." The thought did, however, cross his mind several times.

"She's talked about other abuses, hasn't she?" Angela spoke further, the concern in her expression evident. "You have to treat her right, Gil. If you don't, you'll have me to answer to."

"Wouldn't have it any other way, Angel. Sexual abuse, yes. That's why she is afraid to be intimate with me."

"You must take tender care of your woman. She is more important to you than you will concede. Vividly, I see the love in your eyes when you speak her name. I'm guessing she has a tender spot in her heart for you as well. She would not allow you so close if she didn't. Go to her."

"Her son...he calls me a *tete du butt*."

Angel's laughter was very nearly a cackle when she heard. Her lips parted in a wide grin before she asked. "Are you?"

"Where it comes to the boy, most likely...hell, yes."

"Only you can change this. Only you can find a place in your heart for her son. Without that you won't have her heart. She'll run as far as she can. She will do what she always does, save the wages you pay her no matter how small they are. When she has enough, she will go to the next place."

"That's not very far," he mumbled.

Angel's words gave him more reason to deny her the money he owed her for her labors.

Chapter Five

Jenna slept in the next morning enjoying a moment she'd not had in so long she couldn't remember. She told herself Gil could rot in hell if he intended to order her around then out of her home. No way, no way in this world would she move to the chateau. Would not allow him to make her his whore.

He meant to work her fingers to the bone then not pay her. She deserved an honest wage. Deserved to be treated as a human being.

He didn't agree with her.

Well, perhaps he had a point when he spoke of the food as well as the rent for the cottage. She needed a few francs though. Brice was growing out of all his clothes.

"*Maman*, are you sick?" Brice tugged at the quilt covering her. He appeared worried, tiny frown lines creased his brow. "Don't you have to go to work? I'm hungry."

"*Non*, just lazy this morning, nothing to worry over. Gaby must have left milk and bread in the kitchen. She always does. Why don't you help yourself while I dress?"

She sat up stretching overtaxed muscles. This morning she was exhausted. Staying up late every night with Gil took as much of a toll on her body as did all the hard work. Gil had no idea how hard she worked. If he came by tonight for more kisses or more pleasure, he wasn't going to find her receptive.

Working girls need their sleep.

Damn, she wasn't a working girl. She labored hard. She was his employee not his whore.

An hour later she was at the chateau. Brice played in the yard with the other children. Gaby handed her a cup of coffee. Gil usually made an appearance when she showed up to work. She was late this morning.

Perhaps he had other things that needed his attention.

"Where is Gil?"

Jenna didn't understand why she asked. Didn't want a confrontation with him.

"Did you have that talk you needed?" Gaby asked as she peeled carrots.

She was acting as if she didn't care what was said but Jenna understood she must have heard about the carnage that was her cottage, the horrible writing on the house.

"We did." Jenna played with the spoon, stirring the cream in gentle circles in the cup.

She tried not to look at Gaby. The gardener was not at her place when she left. The horrible words were still on the wall of the cottage. The plants still uprooted. They talked about more than she was comfortable with. He wanted things from her she didn't know if she could give.

"Gil is gone. Left a note that he would be back tomorrow or the next day." Gaby seemed to watch her. "So, what did you talk about? Seems the two of you need to straighten out your feelings for each other."

Jenna bristled. As far as she was concerned, they wouldn't ever be able to come to terms with their feelings. There was too much between them. It wasn't any of her business. Nonetheless it might very well be. "A lot of things. Nothing." She lifted her shoulders in silent resignation. "Where did he go?"

"Bordeaux. Heard you went into the village yesterday. The people weren't pleased." Gaby's voice was somewhat harsh. "It wasn't wise to go without Gil. You're reputation..."

"Don't suppose they were, thrilled. They hate me. Wish me gone. Would have left when I discovered Brice no longer possessed his inheritance. Had nowhere to go."

Jenna didn't want to feel sorry for herself. She did. She slowly sipped the hot coffee, thinking about last night, remembering the way his caresses aroused. "Suppose you heard what happened. Bordeaux, why on earth would he go there?"

After their conversation the night before she'd been unsettled.

Understood he left angry with her.

Neither her son nor his was a topic he would talk about.

Neither was her staying at the cottage.

"What I understand is that you were threatened. Those people, for whatever reasons, believe you've bewitched Gil. They haven't flat out called you a witch but..."

It seemed Gaby didn't know what else to say. Her brows were creased with worry.

A witch.

Jenna gasped startled by her pronouncement. She never set out to do anything where Gil was concerned. If he hadn't been such a butthead that first day, they probably would not have said more than two words to each other. "I'm...couldn't bewitch that man if I tried. He's so...desperate...filled with melancholy and hate. Sometimes when I talk to him, I get the feeling he wishes he could be with his son. He wants to die."

"You're not far off the mark. Your being here has changed him though. You've given him a reason, a purpose to live. So, in some ways I can agree with the good people. You challenge him to think about life rather than death. Perhaps you have bewitched him. I watch him watch you, his eyes hungry with longing."

Jenna didn't want to be anyone's reason for living or dying. For that matter, she didn't want him to watch her with hungry eyes. "I don't see how you can say that. He still doesn't like me. Gil despises my son because he isn't Lance."

Jenna wondered at Gil's coaxing ways. Admittedly, he told her he meant to seduce, teach her that women could find pleasure from sex. Well, he told her she would be delighted. Why would he want her? He had no reason to treat her so gently.

"Do you know why he went to Bordeaux?" She was curious but was also afraid of the answer. What she did know was that he wouldn't be going to Chantel for a sexual encounter. If he needed release, he would go to the brothel there, to Angel's place. From the few weeks she worked at Angel's establishment, she knew Gil had ties there. From the way he spoke about Elisa...

"To Angel's place." Gaby confirmed her thoughts. "He thought I should know if anyone needed to find him." Clearly embarrassed, Gaby looked away when she told her.

"Angel's place..."

The words stung. Knowing he wanted sex with someone else hurt. She wanted to curl up and die. Humiliation raced through her at an alarming pace. "He wanted to go to one of the ladies who entertained men?"

Jenna didn't like the way her voice quivered when she asked. Didn't like her feelings either.

"He did have a favorite there. Used to spend a lot of time with the one woman as well as at Margaux's place in Paris. Men have needs." Gaby's last words were matter of fact.

She could have fulfilled those needs. Gil Allemand wasn't going to touch her again. To Jenna, the day passed slowly. Waiting was agony. Gaby made sure when she left for home that evening she would have dinner along with breakfast. One day turned to three.

She felt the smoldering intensity of his presence before she saw him. It seemed to her, he hovered over her. In his bedchamber, she was hanging the freshly laundered curtains. His heat emanated into her. Valiantly, she tried to keep thoughts of him touching another woman in the way he caressed her from her mind. With her arms raised, her fingers hanging on to the rod, she was helpless.

He settled his hands around her waist. She felt the brush of his lips across her nape. "Would you like help? All you need do is ask."

His hands rose higher, touching beneath her breasts. She wanted so much more.

"If you would leave me alone, this would be much simpler." Jenna found she was very nearly out of breath, gasping to inhale the air in the room. His bedchamber.

"That's not going to happen." His voice was husky, smooth with the desire she was coming to recognize.

"I cannot stand here forever with my arms over my head. Either help me or leave."

He did help. The curtains were hung. Now...she didn't know what to think or do. She finished everything that was on his list when he rode out to be with another woman. If he wanted her tonight, she would send him home. She wasn't a consolation prize.

He would have some major explaining.

You're a silly woman, Jenna Bonnet if you think the likes of Gil Allemand will explain anything to you. He believes he owns you.

That damn offer solidified his thoughts. You did tell him you would do anything. You're lucky he's given you time to adjust to your fear.

"I'll walk you home." His hand settled on her shoulder, turning her. "Why are you angry? Did I do something wrong?"

"I'm not angry." No, she was furious. "It's your imagination. If you walk me home, you will have to be with Brice. I understand how you feel about my boy."

Jenna wasn't about to let on she was angry, furiously so, because he was with another woman. Nor did she want to confirm her jealousy.

"He's going on a sleep over with Gaby and her little girl. You've no need to worry about him. He'll be safe and sound while we explore each other further."

"What!" She wasn't at all certain she heard correctly. He was assuming too much.

"He's going home with Gaby." Gil was the epitome of calm certainty. "You've nothing to worry about. You will have me all to yourself. That fact should please you."

She couldn't think of anything except his arrogance in assuming a father role to a boy he couldn't tolerate. "How dare you! You had no right to arrange something like that without my permission."

He lifted his shoulders while he rocked back on his heels. His mouth twitched as if he was amused at her. Leaving a small amount of distance between them, "Believe I've every right, *Madam Bonnet*. You work for me. You are here at *Cimaron* at my whim. Have you forgotten your offer so soon? Could hardly collect on your proposition with your boy at the cottage. Well, you could stay here at the chateau with me. My bed is large. We would have the balcony for ambiance. You did tell me you would do anything if I let you stay at the cottage."

"I said I would do anything if you gave me a job."

"Gave you a place to call home. You owe me. Perhaps if all goes well, I can collect tonight."

"You would not force me."

"True."

"I tell you now, tonight it would be force. I'm not willing. I'm angry, more than angry with you."

Damn, she said too much. He would think she was jealous or worse missed him. She did not.

"Angry? More than angry?" One perfectly sculpted eyebrow arched in speculation. "Because I left? Perhaps we should explore this further. The reason for your anger intrigues me."

She turned from him unwilling to allow him to see her eyes. "Of course not. I was glad to see you gone."

The soft rumble she heard left her drowning in misery. He would see through her lie. She was miffed he changed the subject from Brice to her. Furious, he sent her son to another's home for the night without even asking her. Like everything else he did, he wouldn't allow for her opinion.

Gil Allemand would always do what he wanted.

He touched her chin with a finger, lifted it high. She saw into the dark depths of his eyes. He wouldn't let this rest. Wouldn't allow her to get away without answering. She didn't have to speak true.

She could lie.

He would see through it. She was terrible at lying.

"I think you are jealous. Gaby would have told you where I went. Did you think I was with another woman? Is that why you're fuming?" His knuckles drew a gentle path down her neck. "I wasn't. Not that who I sleep with concerns you or affects what we do."

The grin showing his even white teeth infuriated her more than she could imagine.

"I wouldn't care if you were with a dozen women all at once."

Her lashes lowered. She didn't have to see the humor in his eyes to know it was there hovering on the surface. Once again, she gave herself away. He would understand all she felt.

"That would be quite a feat even for me."

This time he wasn't bothering to hide his laughter.

"I'm sure you could manage if you put your very agile mind to the task. For someone as experienced as you..." she murmured, still furious with herself. Showing him her feelings was not something she intended. Jealousy was a trait she never experienced before this.

"You can lie to yourself all you want. I for one understand more than you want me to believe. Those nights we spent together at your cottage left you with a hunger you didn't understand. It's time to change that so you know a woman can have pleasure as well as the man." Once more he gently ran his knuckles down the side of her face.

"I told you I'm not willing."

She spoke so softly she wasn't even sure herself if the words actually left her mouth. Jenna knew he could make her feel different. Could with a tiny coax, have her dissolving in his arms.

"I will change that." Slowly, his mouth lowered to meet hers.

Jenna caught the scent of mint on his breath as well as the musk of the man. Oh, she did know that in a matter of seconds not even minutes she would melt into a puddle at his feet.

"*Non*...you cannot. Won't allow that to happen."

The words were whispered if she even said them. She sighed as his mouth opened then pressed against hers. Sounds of the small pond and its waterfall filled her senses. His lips were hot, wet. They enticed her to become something she wasn't. Jenna found no defense against everything he asked of her.

"I already have. Give me your tongue, sweet Jenna. Play with me, coax me to a point where I will not let you down. Explore my man's body as if you can't leave me alone. Remember who I am."

She didn't understand what he meant. How could she let him down?

"Gil," she sighed his name into the warmth of his mouth.

The sound rippled between his lips then into his mouth. He felt the heated whisper meld with his breath.

"That was exquisite, Jenna, my name on your lips. You are wonderful. Later you will howl with your pleasure. I will make sure to bring you to a point of ecstasy you've never known."

Jenna still didn't believe that was possible. However, she did like his kisses. The way his lips felt against hers, the moist warmth along with the magic. When he caressed her breasts, teased them with his hands and mouth, she liked that too. Felt the quickening where she always knew pain before. She supposed she would like just about everything he did. It was all so new to her. If this could last forever, she wouldn't be disappointed.

He kissed her again and again, hot, wet sultry kisses then gentle coaxing kisses that left her wanting more, so much more. Jenna didn't wish to think of other women with him. Didn't want to think of anything save this very moment. A tiny sound of desire rippled from her throat, a purr then a soft mewl. She couldn't deny the man anything.

His large calloused hands around her pulled her closer. He slipped them downward, pressed her so close she felt his hard arousal next to her belly. For the briefest moment she was reminded of her husband. A moment later it seemed nothing but the image of Gil filled her senses. Jenna forgot her past. Forgot everything except what was happening to her now. Her future was all that mattered.

His lips now hovered slightly above hers. The sweet scent of mint mingled with the man. "We're going to eat first as well as drink some of this vineyard's fine Bordeaux. I want you relaxed, pliant in mind as well as body. This will be slow tonight, filled with whatever your heart wants. Shall we walk to the cottage or would you prefer to stay here? You understand what I wish for."

Yes, she knew what he expected. Staying at the chateau wasn't possible. If she stayed for one night, it might turn into two or more. She would be his piece of muslin then. Now, she would end up his mistress, a kept woman. For some reason one title over the other sounded better.

"The cottage," she told him, as his hand settled possessively on her waist, squeezed, moved up then down sending shivers along her spine.

"I've sent dinner ahead of us. You will eat until you can't eat another bite. I've a feeling there was not much that went into your mouth while I was gone."

Once again, he squeezed her waist. His hand roamed higher then back. With the gestures he sent a message. "You don't have to answer."

During the short walk to the cottage, she let her mind drift. Tried to recall the amazing sensations he so easily evoked. Tried to tell herself he needed to be accountable for the woman he saw at Angel's place. She was brought back to the moment when one palm of his hand grazed a tightened crest.

The magic.

The enchantment.

He was a fantasy she might have dreamed of as a little girl. A girl who, once upon a time, did have dreams as well as hopes. Two men single handedly destroyed those dreams. She had nothing left now.

She wanted Gil more than anything else she'd ever wanted. Yearned for what he told her he could give to her even if it was for only a short amount of time. Yes, she wanted to feel pleasure, a woman's pleasure. He told her what they would do, would be delightful. She was a widow. So, her actions should not matter so much.

Jenna didn't know about the delightful part. Nonetheless she was willing to try, beginning to believe in his sincerity. Eager to learn more about Gil Allemand.

When they reached the cottage, dinner was set on a table on the porch. Crystal glasses held wine. The plates were covered to keep the food warm. The aroma was heaven sent. She knew the food would be delicious, the wine the same.

"Do you know what we're eating tonight?" she asked as he pulled out a chair for her.

She sat, appreciating the gesture. It seemed a lifetime ago she had anything this nice. For an instant, she closed her eyes feeling as if he courted her.

Foolish notion.

"Baked salmon, tender red potatoes, corn picked from the stalk. I believe Gaby told me there are fresh tomatoes as well as cucumbers from the garden. She made berry tarts for our desert."

His grin widened. The sight gave her heart a small lurch.

Her mouth watered. Gil was right. She barely ate while he was gone. She was so very hungry. She wanted to stuff everything in her mouth at once. Gaby always made lunch for them but dinner was not served as he had been doing. She always wrapped half of her lunch to save for Brice's dinner.

"Taste the wine," he told her as they sat down. "We've enough to last the night. If we wish into the morning. If you don't want to work tomorrow, I'll excuse you. If I keep you up all night, you won't have the strength to wield your duster."

"What...?" she shook her head. "Never mind."

Discussing the outcome of her proposal was better left to another time. For now, she wanted to eat this meal then see what else he planned.

Between bites of the delicious food, he asked, "Tell me again how you ended up marrying Count Bonnet? It seems I need a retelling of the tale. When you discovered the type of man he was, why didn't you tell him no."

"I couldn't tell him no, even then I had nowhere to go. What if I don't wish to recount it again? It's painful to think about."

The salmon was delicious as was everything else on the plate. "Why don't you tell me how you entertained twelve women all at the same time?"

She watched him beneath lowered lashes. Was amazed when she recognized a slight flush brush his face.

He leaned back, stretched his legs out in front of him. His arms were negligently crossed in front of him. "The women were indeed delightful. It wasn't so much what I did. I was a pawn at their mercy. They played my man's body as if I was finely tuned. They seduced so thoroughly; I could never speak let alone tell anyone *non*."

Well, she deserved his teasing. Didn't understand why she brought the subject up again. The moment the scandalous tale left his lips, she knew he was lying. Heat rushed to her face. *Well, you started this to avoid the other topic.* "Played you, did they? What does that entail? Perhaps you can teach me."

Where did that question come from? It seemed she was digging herself a grave that might be difficult to climb from.

His manly grin stretched nearly across his entire face. "We can explore all the details after you finish your wine. I would take each specific touch, kiss, one at a time. Play with all the parts that will make you howl your delight."

He was smooth, deadly smooth. "What if I say *non?*"

The smile vanished only to return a moment later. "The offer...seems I'm ready for my first installment. I want you, Jenna. Believe I've made that abundantly clear. We've put this off too damn long. You cannot say no any longer, not that you have the last time I was with you alone right here on this porch. You wanted me too. You didn't wish for me to walk away."

Eyeing him critically she sipped her wine, her heart beating erratically. "Perhaps I need to know a bit more about how to play with a man before I commit to this delight thing you talked about."

She was playing with fire.

She knew it.

He knew it.

For some untold reason she couldn't stop herself. His gaze settled on her lips where the crystal touched then lower to her breasts. He cleared his throat before he continued. "Jenna, if that dress gets any more worn everyone is going to see your sweet charms. Don't believe I like that. They are mine to see, no one else's. Will have to do something about that. Since you will soon be my mistress, it's my obligation to see you properly clothed as well as fed."

She stiffened in the chair. A small portion of her wine sloshed from her glass. "*Non!* You won't buy me clothing. I won't have it. The food is one thing, the cottage as well..." She couldn't allow him to steal any more of her pride.

"After tonight you'll have no say."

"I won't wear what you buy me."

"You'd prefer to go around naked? I won't have that. If you persist in this notion, I'll burn everything I've not paid for," he told her, lips twitching as if he was seeing her naked. His gaze rested on her breasts before slipping lower.

"You know I wouldn't prefer that. Because you don't pay me, I can't buy anything."

"Only because you would spend every franc on your son."

With the word son, his voice grew harsh. The only way she put off the inevitable tonight would be to bring up either of the two boys.

She couldn't do that even though she understood his healing

would only begin when he could speak of his son without withdrawing into another world. "I have two perfectly good dresses."

"As well as perfectly good shoes."

Seemed he wasn't going to let this go. "You know my shoes are..."

"With no soles?" he queried.

Leaning forward, he stroked her neck rested on the pulse at the base. Traced her collarbone, "I will take care of you. You've nothing more to worry about."

Her heart sounded a frantic beat with the barest of touches from him. She wheezed a tattered breath of air. "Haven't finished my wine."

"Doesn't matter. We'll drink it later. It's time for your education to continue."

He set her glass on the table before he pulled her into his arms. Before she could swallow a gulp of air, Jenna found herself straddling him just as she'd been several nights ago. Beneath her he was hard. The pulse of his desire so close to that part of her that seemed to long for him sent a raging tempest barreling through her.

Without her consent, terror rolled into her throat ripping away all the past wonderful sensation she knew from his hands. All she could think of was her husband and the hateful way he drove into her. "This," she pushed on his chest, "this is what I was afraid of. Tonight, you're not giving me a choice. Tonight, you're going to force me. Always before I felt as if I said no, you would stop."

He pressed his forehead against hers. "No force, sweetheart. Just delight. Give this a chance. I promise I will take great care where you are concerned. Rest assured if you do tell me to stop I will."

She tried to scurry from his thighs. He held her fast. Her eyes were wide. Moisture filled them. "What if I cannot do this?"

"I will make sure you can. Trust me," he murmured softly as his lips and teeth descended along the column of her neck, nibbling, tasting, sucking gently.

~ * ~

"You were just with other women," she reminded him, as he

nimbly played with the fasteners of her dress. "You told me twelve at one time. I understand you were teasing, however..."

If he didn't take care, the dress would be ruined. While he slowly removed the flimsy barrier between them, his mouth found hers. He played with her lips, nipping, tugging so she would open for him. The scent of her toyed mischievously with his senses. Sweet Bordeaux hovered on her lips inside the sultry heat of her mouth. She had no idea how much the innocence of her actions brought his passions to a boiling point.

"I've not been with anyone except you, sweetheart. Not even one woman at Angela's tempted me." he murmured as he slowly unlaced the ribbons holding her chemise together. Watched mesmerized as the fabric fell open revealing her sweetness while tempting. He cursed. The promise to teach her the delights a woman could experience before he made love to her weighed on his mind. He didn't know if he had the patience and the strength to resist her charms. All the while he'd been at Angel's he wanted her, needed relief. Any other woman wasn't going to do for him. Even tonight her innocent promise of sensual delight might not be his.

"You said..."

"I teased. Only thought of you while I was away. Can you say the same?"

He hoped she missed him because he missed her. She was a poison in his heart, one that could easily dissemble him. A woman never affected him this way, not even Elisa.

He sensed her discomfort. Wondered that she might have longed for him but was unwilling to give him such sway over her feelings. He understood she didn't want to be vulnerable.

"You were not...you didn't pay for favors...?" Her fingers wound through his hair, as she seemed to pull him closer.

So close to her breasts the sweet scent of jasmine floated to him in fiery ribbons. He nibbled and kissed along the valley between her breasts. Held a smile back when she moved, her breasts swaying so very close to his mouth, inviting him to give ardent attention to them to suck each one deep into his mouth.

"Only wanted you," he murmured as his mouth touched gently on a hardened peak, his tongue flicking across the flesh. While his hands skimmed along the length of her bared leg.

He explored, coaxed as he slowly discovered her. The sightseeing continued as she purred and arched, unwittingly beseeching him for more then even more.

"Do you understand what you do to me? I want to tell you *non*. Need to tell you that I'm a good woman. Want to explain to you the proposition was given because I was desperate to have a roof over my son's head. Yet..."

"Yet?" Biting gently where his lips had just tasted, he waited. She was wanton, an aphrodisiac to his tortured soul. If he allowed it, she could heal him. He reminded himself he didn't want healing.

"You are nothing like my husband."

Thank God. "How so?" He lifted his head to see her more clearly. Her eyes were huge pools of crystal-blue jewels. Perhaps he didn't want to know. She never truly wanted to speak of the count.

Jenna closed her eyes, her hands toying with the laces on his shirt.

He grinned.

"I don't want to answer that." Her soft murmur coupled with her roaming fingers delighted him.

Once again, he rose over her, his mouth descending to capture hers in a hot, wet demanding kiss, one that would leave her with no doubts as to the outcome of tonight's games.

He lifted his arms when she tugged his shirt from his trousers. "Take if off."

He needed desperately to feel the tips of her breasts against his chest. His imagination was playing havoc with his feverish body.

After she did, she set her hands on his naked flesh. She pushed a small distance from him as she thought to look at him. What she didn't know was how provocative the movement of her breasts was. She wouldn't understand how a man could grow harder than steel looking at her. He didn't think she understood just how attractive and inflammatory she was. Now, he knew firsthand the taste as well as the texture of her body. Before the night was done, he would learn more, sightsee over the rest of her. Would learn her more intimately than she would have ever imagined. The hell he'd been living in before she arrived at the cottage lessened with thoughts of this woman. Jenna plunged unwanted into his life. Now she was tenderly changing his living hell to heaven.

She brushed her palms across his chest again and again as if amazed at something she was discovering. "You're so different." Closing her eyes, she paused. "He never let me touch him. Had to keep my hands at my sides."

Christ, he didn't want her thinking about that bastard now. Wanted all of her, her thoughts everything all to himself. "Thank the saints above that we are so different. If we weren't, we would not fit together the way I've planned. You would not be the enchantress to me that you are."

He slid his hands along the length of her legs while she toyed with his nipples. It seemed they fascinated her. He knew he taught her well when she bent over to taste them with her tongue.

He groaned deep in the back of his throat. Felt the depth of her purity to the bottom of his soul. A momentary bout of guilt gave him a moment's pause. An instant after, he reminded himself he had nothing to feel guilty about.

Jenna offered herself to him.

Sliding his hand along her charming backside, he squeezed silken flesh, remembered how she called him a butthead. She squirmed on him clearly aroused, obviously needing something more, something she never experienced. He didn't have to touch her intimately to know she was aroused as the heat as well as the moisture of her seared through his trousers.

Moving cautiously, understanding this was uncharted territory, he moved one hand to her belly, the other lower to cup her intimately. Her lashes flew open, her lips forming a small oh. "Gil...?"

"Easy, sweetheart. I promise you will enjoy this as well as the way it will make you feel. Relax, don't tense up on me."

"Is this part of the delight you spoke of?"

She squirmed again as his thumb touched upon the small, velvet pearl between her honeyed folds. Her petite body arched and coiled as if trying to receive more.

"It is."

His lips found hers again as he massaged and caressed, tantalized and delighted. He didn't want to give her a chance to realize exactly where his hand found purchase. Rippling sounds of pleasure filled the warm fall air around them. The heady scent of her woman's honey floated around him.

She squirmed, arching against him, her small breasts thrusting toward him so close he brushed across each one with his mouth. Heard the soft sighs of pleasure he elicited from her. She could not deny to finding heaven this night in his arms.

With great caution he pushed one then two fingers inside her velvet core. It didn't seem to him she noticed this new invasion. Her hot sheathe licked him with fire, kissed his fingers with her innocent response. Christ, he wanted to bury himself deep then deeper still inside her. Wanted her to ride him until they cried out their pleasure. Recalled too vividly that he promised that would come another time.

Perhaps not, maybe tonight would be the perfect time to finish her introduction to carnal pleasure.

She was moving to the pace he set. He felt the slow ripple of her desire slide along his fingers as her walls convulsed around them, shattered through her until she reached the turbulent peak she sought. She was frantic, wild with her need.

"Gil...! Oh God, Gil...*mon dieu.* What is this*?* "

Her pleasure was ecstasy to him. He played with her body until her cries of pleasure began to wane. Until she gasped in a deep breath of air. Until she let her head fall against his chest.

With his free hand he soothed her, touched her along the length of her spine until she began to relax more fully. He felt the flutter of her eyelashes against his flesh. Relished the sweet feel of her breasts as they moved against his chest.

Jenna was truly his now. For her there was no going back.

She would understand that fact by morning.

"Are you delighted?" he couldn't help but ask as he brushed damp tendrils of hair from her forehead. "You were a delight to me."

When she looked at him, what he could see of her was flushed. Her eyes were wide as if in disbelief. Though it seemed she accepted this new truth he helped her create. She closed her eyes for an instant. Swept her tongue along her swollen lower lip.

"I..."

She swallowed, sipped new air before answering. Didn't seem she could do so. Closed her eyes for another moment then it seemed to him her gaze riveted on his naked chest then lower. She would see the bulge in his trousers. "I imagine what you did was more than I ever thought possible. You should understand I didn't believe you."

"Delightful? Hmm...are you a believer now?" he queried again as he refused to let her continue to change the subject.

Didn't want her to get away without admitting what they did together was indeed delightful maybe more than just delightful.

This time she looked out over the vines before she returned her attention to him. "I suppose so."

It didn't seem she wanted to admit to anything. Perhaps she believed she would be giving him the upper hand if she did so. Where Jenna was concerned, he cemented the position just now.

"Say the word, Jenna," he coaxed hoping she would give in to tender encouragement.

She was shaking her head although a slight smile danced across her features. He was sure he would have to do more coaxing as well as sweet-talking before she would admit to anything she'd denied for so very long.

He touched his thumb to her slightly swollen lips. Swollen from his attention. He ran it across the moisture left there from his kisses again then one more time. "Pure delight, at least for me it was. Did you know your eyes glazed over as you reached that pinnacle only lovemaking can bring you to? I didn't even have to ask you to open your eyes. A man enjoys seeing his woman's eyes in the throes of her passion."

Biting her lower lip. "Delightful," she admitted her voice soft yet husky with her newly found desire.

Gil decided he couldn't wait another night to seal her offer. "Good then, now we can move on to the next step. Are you afraid of me?"

He knew she no longer feared him. Understood she might lie. If she did, he would call her out. Now that she understood what they needed from each other, there would be no more lies between them.

He watched her swallow, saw the hesitation. Didn't see it as fear. "You embarrass me. Challenge me with things I've never felt before or believed, expected. *Non*, I'm not afraid of you. I'm terrified of what you do to me. How easily I let you have your way when I'm determined not to do so."

A man well pleased by his mistress' words; he kissed the tip of her nose. "That was exactly what I needed to hear. I don't want you to be terrified of your honest passion."

He swept her into his arms before grabbing the bottle of wine as well as the crystal glasses from the table.

"What are you doing?" She sounded hesitant, a brief note of fear in her question.

"Challenging you. I'm taking you to bed, Jenna girl. Don't need your clothes for what we are going to be doing. We are going to make love then sleep together, perhaps after that we will make love another time. We will drink more wine then some more just because we can. I believe I mentioned it earlier. You won't be going to work tomorrow. I might want to make love to you all morning too."

"What if I don't want to go...?"

He laughed softly knowing what she was speaking of, refusing not to let her back out of the commitment she made to him. Not now, not when he understood how much she wanted him. "To work?"

He placed the glasses along with the wine on a bedside table before setting her on the bed.

"*Non*, to bed with you?"

"Ah, Jenna, don't lie to me. I know you want that delightful pleasure I just treated you to again and again.

"Lift your hips, sweetheart. There." He removed the dress, leaving it pooled on the floor. He stood back to look at her. She was so damn beautiful. She stole his breath. She was filling out quite nicely. In another month with his tender care, she might be back to normal. "If you told me something so ludicrous, I'd have to call you out, label you a liar."

Gil found he was impatient. Never felt that way with a woman. He sat to pull off his boots. When he stood to undress, he did so looking at her. Quickly, he disrobed. He waited a few seconds before sitting on the bed next to her.

"You're naked," she whispered, her voice soft and a bit pouty. "Your... I never..."

"Hush." That was something he didn't need to hear. "As far as we are concerned, your late husband no longer exists in your memory. I will take his place there. Believe I've thoroughly purged him from your mind. At my hands you experienced what should happen between a man and a woman. All I want you to think about is you and me. Can you do that?" He chuckled softly, "As you are naked. I believe it is the way I prefer you. Now, my sweet darling, I'm going to make love to you."

She moved in his arms as if to push him away yet a small sound of pleasure rippled from her. At the same time, she murmured in his ear, touching the lobe with the tip of her tongue. *"S'il te plait..."*

"I won't hurt you." He proceeded to show her exactly what he meant until once more she cried out his name.

Gil never believed a woman could be this giving. Her passion rivaled every woman he'd ever known. He never experienced such strong hunger in a woman or this raging desire. Never, still he thought of the women in his past he bedded. He never cared for any of them so considerately and so tenderly. Perhaps before Jenna he never cared at all.

In his arms, Jenna was sweetness coupled with innocence. She possessed a fire he never felt from another woman. Jenna brought all his possessive instincts to the forefront. *Protect and shelter.* Her cheek was pressed against his chest, her hand resting on his belly. If she dipped her fingers a small amount, he would be instantly hard.

They made love twice.

Each time better than the last.

Dozing, he found himself suddenly awake, instantly alert. A strange eerie sensation stole through him. He heard the chanting. Felt a sense of foreboding curl deep in his belly. The words were the same as the scribbles written on her house that the gardener, just yesterday morning, painstakingly painted over. His insides coiled. Quickly, he rose then pulled on the trousers that he hastily discarded a few hours earlier.

"Sors d'ici," was the chant. *"Sors d'ici...sors d'ici..."*

Outside her window, the sky glowed red and orange. Sparks flew upward. Shadows danced behind the people surrounding the house. Flames lit up a cross planted on her lawn.

She was sitting up now, pushing hair from her sleepy eyes. The sheet fell around her waist. She pulled it up to thoroughly cover her.

"Gil?" she questioned, suddenly seeming more alert. "What is happening out there?"

"Get dressed. Do it quickly. I want you to stay inside. Whatever you do, don't come outside. I will handle whatever it is these people want. Defuse the anger, at least I hope I can do that." Hoping on one foot then the other he was deftly pulling on his boots.

His gut turned over. This was exactly what he feared after her ill-advised trip into town. These people would stop at nothing to have their way. What they wanted was for Jenna to leave, to put so much fear in her head she would never be able to stay.

What they didn't know is that he wouldn't allow her to leave. If she did so, he would follow then bring her back. Shirtless, he stood on the porch, his hands fisted in defiance.

"Jenna is not going anywhere." His voice was loud, commanding. "All of you go home to your families. If you do so, I'll forget you were here to terrorize an innocent young woman." Because of the fire, warm air wafted across the porch. The people were shadows with no faces, no way to name any one of them.

The chanting ceased. "The woman has bewitched you." A man with a fisted hand yelled at him.

"Put a spell on you otherwise you wouldn't want her to stay."

"Jenna has my protection. Anyone who wishes to challenge that will be destroyed. I won't have her or her son harmed in any way. Terrorizing a woman you believe to be alone and vulnerable is the cowards way. She has no way to fight your hatred."

"See, you wouldn't be saying those things if there was no spell."

"She wants the chateau back."

"The only way for her to get her wish is through you."

"Jenna Bonnet is a witch."

"*Sorciere...sorciere...sorciere...*" The person in charge began the chanting putting a megaphone to his lips to be better heard. His fist pumped in the air. The chant changed back to the original words.

"*Sors d'ici...sors d'ici...sors d'ici.*"

Leave here.

If he had his way, never.

He felt her presence before she placed a hand on his back. The lightest touch the briefest encounter yet he still felt her fear. He told her to stay inside. Her presence would only serve to rile these people farther.

"Go inside, Jenna," his voice was a hushed whisper. He needed for her to obey him. His voice exacting, he continued, "You should not be out here."

The flames crackled on the dry wood, rising higher and higher into the sky. Sparks flew into the dawn air. He would have to convince her to move to the chateau. There was no viable choice for her.

"She's a witch. She'll burn in hell. You along with her if you continue to give shelter."

Frustration at the stupidity in front of him sent his anger to a boiling point. "Jenna is no witch. It is superstition and no crime," he spoke severely wishing he could make them understand they spouted nonsense. "Go home all of you. Take care of the needs of your families. If you wish to continue to work for me, go home. I see those of you out there who help tend the vineyard. I won't tolerate this betrayal. Go home. I will see to Jenna. As I told you, she is under my protection. If she is hurt in anyway, I will seek out the man or woman who did so and see you prosecuted. If I have to do so, I'll call in all the government agents I know to help."

Together they stood, watching as the crowds slowly began to dissipate. Gil's body shook with fury. There were words of disapproval about his presence in her home along with comments as to Jenna's spells. There would not be a witch-hunt.

Well, he thought in some ways she might have cast a spell, bewitched him. She was certainly like no other woman. Because of Jenna Bonnet he found something to think of other than his lost son. When he did recall Lance, the despair and grief wasn't so intense. He understood that was because of Jenna. Slowly, she was claiming a piece of his heart.

Gil wished he could accept her son. When he looked at Brice, raw and bitter despair ripped through him tore at every part of him. The sensations wouldn't go away.

"Are they going to come back?" she whispered still standing behind him, her fingers digging into his shoulders as if he was her lifeline.

"Thought I told you to stay inside." His voice was gruff as he wasn't accustomed to having his orders disobeyed. "I can't protect you if you disobey me."

"This was about me. Felt as if I needed to be outside, to know what was happening. Do you think they will keep this up or is your threat enough to stop them?"

"Continue," he paused thinking about all that happened. "Their attempts to get you to leave might be subtler. Who knows? I'm not taking chances with your life. It wouldn't be wise for you to go into the village by yourself."

In the morning, he would send a message to Etienne then one to a few friends in Paris. He still had connections there with the agency. Still knew men he commanded who would drop what they were doing in order to come to his defense.

"What are we going to do?" she asked as he turned, pulling her into his arms.

Against him, he felt her shivering, the tensing of her muscles. He didn't want her to be afraid.

Ah, but she wasn't going to like what he meant to tell her. She would protest. This time he wouldn't give her a choice. Not after he held her so tenderly, not after she turned to liquid fire in his arms. She would do his bidding because there simply was no other choice.

Jenna would follow his instructions, not willingly, nevertheless she would come along because he would give her no options. Stubbornness kept a woman alive only so long. After that she would have to rely on him. She could not protect herself.

With a heavy breath of air leaving his lungs, knowing she would argue, "You're moving to the chateau." He watched as her beautiful eyes sparkled and darkened with the onslaught of her anger.

"*Non*, I'm not." Her chin set in obstinate determination.

A sight he knew all too well in the short time he'd known this woman.

"*Oui*, you are."

"Gil...you cannot make me." Her voice faltered, as it seemed she understood he could do just that. "Please, I would not be branded your whore."

"It won't be so bad, sweetheart. It's obvious to anyone who is not blind as well as deaf that you cannot stay here...alone. If you live down the hill, you won't have my protection." He put major emphasis on the single word alone. He wouldn't want her staying here even if she wasn't alone.

She turned away from him as if she meant to leave or perhaps do his bidding. He thought he saw the wheels in her head turning. Could almost hear the word *whore*. Didn't think she would take well to directives coming from him. He didn't care. She would obey for her safety as well as Brice's.

That wasn't how he felt about her. To him she was a loving gentle woman, one who wore her heart on her sleeve. She shouldn't be branded. He wanted to cherish as well as safeguard every fragile bone in her delicate body. The hell of it was she didn't want his protection. If she were a whore, he wouldn't have any of those emotions seething inside.

She stood by the bed, moving the sheets, pulling them up then the quilt covering it. He watched a bit amused as she made the bed. Next, she plumped the pillows. Moving trancelike she continued into the kitchen, setting a pot of water on the stove to boil.

Jenna wasn't going to make this easy for him. He stood behind her. Removed the pot. He placed his hand on her shoulder.

"You can't make me."

The words sounded desperate to convince him. She understood he could do just that. He would do so if she defied him. Even with her defiance she understood she was about to lose this battle of wills.

"We are going now. I'll send someone down to collect your things. You will be safe from your holier-than-thou neighbors." He held her by the shoulders, staring into the startling blue depths of her eyes. "If you want to continue to breathe, if you want to live without fear, you have no choice."

"I didn't cast any spells."

"I know. If you had, I would still want to keep you with me, would still need to protect. You have woven yourself into my life, the threads run deep."

As he thought earlier, there was something about her that was finding a way into his jaded heart. It had been so long since he looked forward to anything.

Now, he looked forward to seeing her. Looked ahead to relish the next time they made love. As if she generated something inside, he found he needed her as much as he did his next breath.

"I want to stay here," she persisted, her hands now on her hips as she stood defiantly in front of him. She placed the kettle on the stove.

Merde! Took it off again. Without more being said, he swept her into his arms. "We are going to the chateau now. No more games, Jenna. I don't want to spend all my time worrying about you or arguing with you over this."

He left his shirt on the floor in the bedroom. He cursed as he started up the slope realizing he should have donned his shirt. This outing was premature. She wasn't going anywhere that he couldn't catch up to her.

He set her down then walked back to the bedroom and finished dressing.

~ * ~

"Mon Dieu!" Etienne paced the drawing room of his home his fists tight at his sides. Gil is in trouble. He wasn't surprised the problem involved the Bonnet woman.

Elisa watched wide-eyed along with a smile as if she understood what bothered him. "What has you so on edge?"

"He cannot mean to keep the woman at his home. Is he a fool? She will be ruined. I thought he would take her feelings into consideration. I never thought Gil to be so selfish. His arrogance knows no bounds." Etienne harbored a soft spot for Jenna while his wife found her to be self-centered as well as after whatever Gil would give her. "It's too much."

"What is too much?" Elisa asked in a soft voice as if she wanted to soothe his boiling anger. "You need to let me help. Tell me what is going on. I can be your sounding board."

"The things that are happening to Jenna. She doesn't deserve any of the nonsense going on at the chateau. The victim should not be punished."

Etienne paced, knifing his hand through his hair. He was beside himself. If it wasn't nearing ten o'clock in the evening, he'd start out for *Cimaron* right now. If he didn't know his wife would insist she come with him, he'd rise before dawn and leave.

Elisa didn't like Jenna. Would end up being a thorn in his side if she accompanied him. She might also become the voice of reason in this endeavor. While Etienne agreed Jenna had to live in the chateau for the time being, he didn't agree with how Gil treated the situation. He felt certain Gil moved her into his bedroom not a guest room in another wing. Servants talk.

"What has happened to set you off like this?" Elisa words stopped him cold. "You don't usually react so violently."

"The villagers have accused her of witchcraft, of casting a spell on him. They burnt a cross in the front of the cottage among other vile things. The nerve, the very nerve..."

He would have to explain. Would need to assuage her curiosity. After pouring them both a generous glass of wine, he sat down. "I..." he drank deep before speaking. The vintage was one of their best.

"I'm going to *Cimaron*. You're staying here with the children."

He drank again as he tried to figure out the best way to tell his wife why he planned a sudden trip to see his best friend, also why she couldn't go with him. She would be angry with his arrogant command. He should have thought this out before issuing the order.

"The hell I am." She grinned at him all sweetness and light. Lashes lowered it appeared she waited for the explosion.

It didn't come. Etienne knew when he would lose a confrontation with his wife. He wasn't about to start a conflict he couldn't win. This wasn't something he had the will to fight her on. As far as he was concerned, he was doomed to let her tag along. She would get her way simply because he had no explanation to convince her otherwise. "You don't like Jenna. In any case, you would be a distraction I don't want. Your opinions would differ too much with mine."

"What else happened at *Cimaron?* There has to be more. You said the villagers accused her of witchcraft. Isn't that enough?"

Etienne knew the battle was lost as well as the war. Elisa would have her way in this. He couldn't deny her. "A lot of things. None good. Perhaps I can tell you while we go there. Gil says he needs me as soon as possible."

"Tell me what has you swearing and pacing." Her voice was still sweet and charming. "She always was an enigma to him. At this moment she placated his stretched nerves."

Well, why not? She got her way without even the tiniest scuffle.

"I suppose one could say three things happened, major things to have Gil calling in his friends for help. Even sent to Paris for some of the men who were under his command. Jenna is in trouble. Part of the reason is because he now has her living at the chateau."

"The witchcraft?" Elisa asked one eyebrow arched in speculation. *"Oui."*

"They believe she cast a spell on Gil. Perhaps she did." She lifted her delicate shoulders as if she thought it might be true. "He is not acting rational."

"You know as well as I do there is no such thing as witchcraft. It's all superstition. As for rational, well, he's behaving as a man infatuated with a woman will behave."

She smiled at him, waiting as if they had all day for more information, much of which he didn't have. He wanted to be up by dawn. Elisa never had trouble getting up that early.

"Are we taking the children?" Her voice was still sweet, still soft, cajoling.

"Non." For some odd reason he needed for her to yell. He needed an outlet for his explosive emotions. She was just far too calm, too serene.

"You want to leave as soon as possible. I don't suppose we have a choice. We will have to take them."

"Non."

This time she lifted both eyebrows. The look in her eyes asking him what he intended if he wasn't taking them while he still wanted to be off by dawn. "You need to be sensible."

"I am sensible."

He hated it when she lifted eyebrows at him. Disliked the fact she thought this out better than he did. He still didn't want the children there, for Gil's sake.

"You must stop coddling the man. He will have to come to terms with the loss of his son sometime. The sooner the better as far as I'm concerned." Her knitting needles were flying. She swore as she examined the piece. "Now, see what you've done? I've dropped a stitch."

What I've done?

They should get back on track. "First," he tried for patience he wasn't feeling when he wanted to be on the road. If he could go by himself, he could ride. He would arrive hours sooner. Now, he would have to take the carriage. The children would slow them.

Heaving a long draught of air into his lungs to compose himself, "It seems Jenna went into the village. From the few inquiries we made while we were there earlier, we understand their feelings for her. After her short visit, they damaged the house as well as the grounds around them. Told her to get out. "Next," he went on, "a few of the men decided what happened was not enough since she didn't leave. They burned a cross in front the house. Luckily Gil was there. It appears he was caught staying the night with her. That's not all though. As I said earlier, they are calling Jenna a witch. The anger is escalating. That's why Gil is calling in favors."

"That's not acceptable," she spoke softly once more. "What happened then? You said Gil spent the night? Suppose he has fallen madly for the woman. A charm or a spell, I won't put that past her."

"You're joking. I know what you're about. It won't work. She's not a witch, as well you know. It would not do him well if his best friends spread the rumors. We both know the government does not prosecute witchcraft because it's made a statement that witchcraft doesn't exist. Those statements would never stop an unruly mob. They might even become bold enough to storm the chateau." Etienne was beside himself with worry for the both of them. In a heartbeat this situation could go from bad to worse.

"He's moved Jenna and the boy to the chateau, hasn't he?" Elisa asked seeming to take this all-in stride. "That was not well done of him." She held her hand up obviously to stop his rebuttal. "I understand the options were limited. So, you don't have to clarify things to me. The act, although necessary, will label her. While I don't like or trust the woman, she doesn't deserve what Gil is doing to her. For some reason Gil is not thinking straight."

In any case, he meant to explain more thoroughly even though she made a point of telling him he need not do that. "He couldn't leave her to fend for herself. They might have tarred and feathered her."

Elisa rose, slowly walking to him. She wrapped her arms around him, pulling him closer as she kissed him. "Etienne," she whispered close to his ear, "I understand more than you know. You've such a soft heart. Be careful."

Lord, the scent of her was sweet. He wanted her almost as much as he needed to leave this instant. He touched her lips with his tongue. Settled his hands around her derrière as he tugged her closer. The kiss was hot and wet, filled with passion predicting what would come next if he allowed the sensual dance between them to continue. If only he had the time.

When she pulled away, "Go now, my tender lover. I'll follow with the children. You don't have to concern yourself."

He kissed her again, wished he dared take her standing and against a wall. She would not have liked that. Perhaps she wouldn't have cared. *"Merci,"* he murmured as he strode from the room.

"I will pack for you."

Chapter Six

Mon Dieu, this was not what she expected when she woke this morning to witness an angry mod in front of her home. Gil carried her all the way to the chateau then up the steps. He didn't stop until he set her on his big bed in the master chamber.

Jenna didn't voice her opinion of his high-handedness since she understood quite clearly she'd be speaking to a wall. He needed to comprehend the fact he had no right to order her except when she was cleaning, working for him. He overstepped.

"This is where you're sleeping," he told her before he turned and left.

"Like hell!" fists clenched tightly she spoke to his back.

Didn't think he heard. Would have expected him to confront her, perhaps make his point clearer. Instead, he continued on his way. Now what? She wasn't going to stay in this room all day. He took her from her house without bothering to collect her shoes or anything else.

He should listen to her. Should hear her thoughts on the subject. She understood why he was so determined to have her live here. Still didn't change the facts. She didn't want to be here in his bedchamber. He needed to understand that tiny yet important fact.

Instead of sulking she rose, wandered through the well-appointed room trying to adjust to his bossiness. Dark burgundy curtains hung from the large window that looked over the gardens. She slept here with Jacques. The thought brought goosebumps to her arms. Everything was different. It seemed Gil didn't keep anything that was her husband's. She was relieved at that. Jacques used gold draperies, gold quilts. She cringed at the extravagance. Gil's taste ran simpler. The four-poster bed was cherry. It was large. She giggled thinking his feet would not hang over the end as they would if he kept Jacques' bed.

He would insist she sleep with him.

The adjoining room had been hers. When she walked inside, nothing was changed. Her favorite colors were the light blues. It surprised her this room wasn't different. She wandered. Picked up a figurine of a unicorn. It had been one of Brice's favorites. She set it down.

Jenna did not want to relive the past. Here she was though. She cleaned the master chamber the day before never taking a moment to think about sleeping on that huge bed with Gil. At the time, she didn't intend for it to happen. Had never thought the villagers would go to such lengths to frighten her. Their intimidation was so obvious.

This happened so quickly the thought nearly stole her breath from her lungs. One moment she was independent, living in a cottage with her son, the next she found herself moved in with a man who...

She wasn't sure what Gil thought of her. Didn't understand why he sought her out. She was hardly beautiful. He called her scrawny, all skin and bones. She bared herself for him. He turned away uninterested. Found her lacking. This was all so confusing.

After last night, she wasn't sure if that changed.

It seemed he wanted her. He made love to her tenderly as if he cared about her as well as her feelings. All the while he taught her things about her body.

When she entered Brice's old room, the décor was also unchanged. She supposed her son would sleep here again. Wondered too if Brice remembered the room. He'd been three when they left, stole away in the dead of the night.

"You found the boy's room."

The booming harsh voice behind her startled her. Her heart seemed to leap to her throat. Gil still didn't want anything to do with her son. "Well, I hoped he would be close to me."

Gil carried the basket with their few belongings. He set it in the room. "Everything in here except one dress is his. I'll have to fix that. You cannot continue in this sacrificial vein."

He watched her with hooded eyes.

She bristled, anger growing inside at an alarming rate. Control of her life slowly vanished. "How so? I'm not going to wear anything you purchase for me. I won't allow you to buy my favors. Working is still the only...if you paid me, I could buy my own things."

"*Non.*"

"*S'il te plait,* Gil."

He stepped forward gently caressing the column of her throat, allowing his fingertip to rest where her pulse beat out of control. "In a few days you will have nothing to wear. What do you plan on doing then? It might prove interesting to me, however..."

"If you would pay me services rendered, I could purchase a new gown," she retorted. It was difficult to hold her ground with the heat of his big body so close to hers.

"Services rendered? Interesting thought. Perhaps I will."

He ran his thumb across her lip, once then twice. Her body quickened. Heat instantly flared. One touch from him created turbulence inside.

Jenna stepped back, refusing to let him have his way with her. She made it so very easy for him. Where he was concerned, the backbone she wished for was nonexistent.

"Cleaning, for cleaning," she insisted.

When she stepped away, he countered with a step closer.

"Of course, for cleaning, what did you think I would pay you for?"

His hands were exploring, touching her arms, her neck. He bent close. His breath whispered against her lips. "Would never pay you for your bed play. You are still too inexperienced for me to pay you. We can change that you and I. With practice you might even be payable."

"*Non,* Gil, don't."

She pushed away from him even while her fingers were rising to his neck so she could pull him closer. She wanted that kiss he seemed to be suggesting would happen sooner than later.

Where he was concerned, she should have more willpower. Her unruly body wanted those sensations he introduced her too. When she felt the light, subtle brush of his lips across hers, her knees began to buckle.

It seemed all that kept her upright was his hands on her waist, pulling her closer, coaxing, wheedling things from her she shouldn't give. She knew better. He teased her mouth with his teeth along with his tongue.

Heat and tempest entered into her, filled the emptiness she felt for so long.

His hands fell away, his gaze hungry and raw raked over every part of her. She felt the power of the man, the confidence. Could not fight it even if she wanted to do such a thing.

"Tonight, Jenna. We'll have dinner together then see what transpires. I ordered a bath for you. Gaby has lunch in the kitchen waiting for you when you are finished bathing. If you need me, I'll be in the cellars working. I don't want you to lift a hand today. That's an order."

"Tonight? What am I supposed to do until then?" Her heartbeat quickened at the thought of tonight with him. "I can't just sit all day."

"Whatever you like. This is your home now."

She laughed softly thinking how absolutely wrong that notion of his was. "I would earn my keep."

"You will."

He was succinct. His answer left no doubt in Jenna's mind what he wanted from her as he glanced at the bed then back to her. She would earn her keep on her back. All that she was along with all that she'd ever wanted to be protested.

You offered yourself to him. He is merely collecting on that suggestion.

Moisture clogged the back of her throat. He was treating her no better than her husband. He wanted her for one thing only. The problem was, she couldn't deny him. As soon as he touched her, she was his. Indeed, in order to put food in Brice's stomach, she told him she would do anything.

"You don't play fair, Gil Allemand. You told me I wouldn't be your whore or your mistress."

"Perhaps a lover," his voice flowed from his throat heavy with desire. "The name one puts on what we do together is not important in the scheme of things. I want to lie with you at night while I do sweet things to your body."

"It's no different."

"I don't want you cleaning. Don't want to see your hands raw and red from the soap. Don't want you so exhausted you fall asleep immediately after you put your son to bed. After your bath and lunch, you can help Gaby plan the menu for the week. I'm sure you've experience with that sort of thing. You can oversee the women from the village I've hired to clean as well as serve us."

Her stomach coiled into a hard knot. Fear sizzled. "From the village?"

"They will be here tomorrow. You may compile a list of duties."

It seemed he saw her fear. "They..."

"The women will be paid handsomely, nothing to complain about. If they don't want to work under your supervision, they will be dismissed. You will be the mistress of the house."

She sipped air at the use of the word mistress. "You want me to befriend these people who hate me? I find that notion absurd."

She found herself shaking her head in disbelief.

"Never befriend. It's a job for the ladies, Jenna. Nothing more. The women will be employees. From what I've heard the money will be welcome. It will also give you the opportunity to redeem your character in their eyes."

Just as he did earlier, he left her. His long-booted strides beating against the floor then down the steps leaving her to wonder about her sanity as well as his. Perhaps they were more suited for each other than she previously thought.

The hot water was heavenly. Jenna couldn't remember the last time she had a bath in a tub this size. The jasmine scented soap must be left over from when she lived here. She relaxed until the water turned tepid. She finished quickly before dressing in one of her old, very-worn dresses. When she looked in the mirror, she realized how much of her showed. Even with her chemise one could clearly see the outline of her nipples.

He was right about her gowns.

She didn't have anything else. Her other dress was worse. There was nothing to be done about her clothing, as she had nothing else to wear. She hurried down the steps then into the kitchen.

Gaby had her hands in bread dough. She looked up puffing a stray lock of hair from her eyes. "Well," the woman said a question in her voice, "Brice had a fine time at my place last night. We ate and played games until bedtime. Your boy is outside now with his friends. He's a wonderful lad. Suppose you know that." After a slight pause, "What did you do?"

To Jenna's surprise there was no censure in Gaby's voice even though she was sure the woman knew what happened. At the moment, she didn't want to speak or think about what went on. She should give what she allowed Gil to do considerable thought, "Thank you. It was kind of you to take him for the night on such short notice."

"He's a pleasure to have. I understand though, *Monsieur Allemand* never sought your permission. I'm not going to ask what happened with the two of you between yesterday afternoon and this morning. Not my business. However, doesn't take someone with the sight to understand by the way he devours you with hungry eyes when the two of you are in the same room to guess."

At Gaby's words heat flooded her face and warmed her to her toes. Nothing was ever going to be the same for her. Everyone knew what they did together last night. All knew he moved her into his home and his bed. She had to find some way to live with this fact.

She tugged in a deep breath hoping for the courage to go on with the day as well as the conversation. "Your right of course, he did not ask. Seems he makes plans without consulting anyone who might be involved. It wasn't well done of him. Just as he moved me into the house, he never thought to discover my feelings. Made the decision in the process gave my concerns no consideration."

"Everyone is talking about where he put you. Was that without your permission also?"

Where she slept wasn't Gaby's business. Well, it would be best if she told the truth. "Yes and no, the story is long and boring. I said something I shouldn't have when we first met. I was desperate for him to hire me."

"Desperate mothers often take desperate actions they wouldn't if a child wasn't involved. If you ever decide to trust me with the yes part of your answer, I'll be a good listener. Learned a long time ago where men are concerned not to pass judgment on the woman involved as well as expect them to do what they damn well please. I'm sure you were given little choice if any at all in the matter."

"He was highhanded." Jenna admitted thinking she gave him the means to do so.

Gaby snorted before she chuckled softly. "You're good for him though. Since you've been here, I've seen him smile more. He even laughed about something this morning. The only time I see the man fall back to his melancholy ways is when he runs across your son."

"It's because he lost his son, lost Lance."

She didn't want to give the mean-spirited man reasons to be the way he was nevertheless deep in her heart she understood. Jenna also comprehended some of the pain he felt. The thought of losing her child stole her breath from her.

"He thinks his son's death is his fault. Believes if he'd been there for the boy, he wouldn't have been caught in the fire with no way to get out. More than likely Gil would have lost his life trying to rescue the boy."

Jenna looked at the sandwich wishing she were hungry. She was until the last topic. She ate what she could then pushed the plate away from her. Gaby looked from her to the sandwich as if she was pretending to be Gil.

"I ate what I could. It was good, very good."

"You are getting a bit of meat on your bones," Gaby laughed softly. "I suppose a man would appreciate that."

Jenna wanted to ask her what was so funny. She didn't dare, afraid it had something to do with the way Gil stared at her. When he did, she felt the heat, saw the raw hunger in his eyes.

"When Gil left, he said I was to help you plan the meals for the week. Do you have any idea why? Seems you do well by yourself. Doubt if you need me. Believe he was trying to give me something to do besides clean."

Jenna understood it was said just so she could occupy her time before she had to give services. Despite his order not to work, she was tempted to pick up the duster. Sitting idle was not something she wanted to do.

"Seems he's going to have some company in the next few days. Heard the men he invited could help with what happened last night. Before he arrived here, the owner of the vineyard, he was a spy."

A spy?

She wanted to ask if it was to help with the villagers or her lack of moral values. Didn't dare do anything of the sort. She had no regrets. If confronted with the same situation, she would make the same bargain.

"What do you know about last night?"

Her heart seemed to be beating wildly out of control in her throat. The burning cross terrified her. She was just happy Brice hadn't been home to see it. She thanked her lucky stars Gil went behind her back giving permission for Brice to sleep over with his friend.

"Do you truly want to talk about this? Did tell you I was a good listener." Gaby seemed to speak sincerely from the heart.

"Non et oui."

"Love a lady who knows her mind like the back of her hand. Well," Gaby paused to take a good look at her, "you're as white as a sheet." Her eyes narrowed. "I know he spent the night with you at the gatekeeper's cottage. Knew what he intended when he had me deliver the meal to your home. Heard when he confronted the mob, that he wore only his britches along with his boots. Seems a man who has been sleeping soundly, naked too, would put on the barest necessity when he left the bedchamber. Learned you joined him on the porch wearing only that scrap of a dress. Am I right?"

Jenna could do little except nod as she spoke. What Gaby said was the solemn truth. "I wish I could say otherwise."

"Madam Bonnet! Madam, s'il vous plait! I have to talk with you."

Sounds of a scuffle outside along with the woman's words caught their attention. Her heart suddenly raced.

"What is it?"

Jenna along with Gaby found their attention directed toward the door. One of Gil's men physically restrained an older woman. With her hands, the lady batted at him. Tried to kick him several times until she panted for air.

"Let me go!" the woman cried out, clearly distressed by the man holding her.

Once more she tried to wriggle away from him.

Jenna approached the door, curious before she looked to the man then the lady. "What do you want? Do I know you?" Jenna thought she recognized her.

"Just to talk. I'm sorry about what happened to you. Please, this is important. I won't take but a moment of your time."

The elderly lady stopped struggling while she seemed to wait for an answer.

She was looking at the man holding her while she ran her hands along her arms. "I'm fine. I'll talk to this woman."

"Can't do that. I've strict orders not to let any of the villagers get by me."

"Truly, that's commendable. I'd like to talk to this woman to discover what she wants with me."

When the man didn't appear to be giving ground, "You can stand in the corner. This woman appears harmless to me."

Jenna turned to Gaby, "Will you get the lady some tea. Maybe some of those berry tarts that taste so good if there are any left?"

Gaby nodded.

The man let the elderly lady go.

Jenna could tell he didn't want to do so. She understood his loyalty was to Gil. Even though the woman appeared harmless, Jenna's stomach churned.

"Merci," she said then sat down as Jenna pointed to a chair. "I appreciate your taking the time to speak with me," she paused, "more than you will ever know."

This all was so absurd. The woman wouldn't be able to harm a fly. Her dark brown hair was sprinkled with gray. The stoop of her shoulders told Jenna she had trouble walking without hurting her back. The light blue of her eyes was glazed over with fear.

Jenna pulled in a long draught of air preparing herself to proceed. "What brings you to *Cimaron?"* Jenna pushed the sugar and cream to her. "Help yourself."

While she attended to her tea, the woman began to speak. *"Ma petite fille,* she is very sick. The doctor says she doesn't have long to live. I thought perhaps you could..."

Jenna bristled, thinking, after last night she had a good idea where this was going. She didn't want anything to do with casting spells. "Who are you?"

Jenna knew her voice sounded overly harsh. Once the realization blindsided her, she was furious.

When the older lady looked up moisture clouded her eyes. "*Madam Macon.*"

To Jenna it seemed the woman held her breath, waiting as if in anticipation. "Now, tell me again why you are here. Don't waste my time. After the events of the last two days, I've little to no patience."

"She is dying. There is nothing the doctors can do for her. I thought...well, thought perhaps you could do something for her."

The woman's tea cup rattled on the saucer when she tried to pick both up.

Jenna slashed her hand in the air. Her stomach rolled, nausea threatening. *Je ne suis pas une sorciere. Truly, they believe I can cast spells.* She set her hands in her lap while she tried to come to grips with what the woman was telling her. Her hands clasped so tightly they left nail marks on her palms. "Let me get this straight. You want me to cast a spell over your granddaughter so she will live?" Jenna asked not knowing whether to laugh or be appalled.

She was horrified anyone truly believed in witchcraft or that she was capable of something so ridiculous.

"If you don't mind, I'd appreciate it so much." The *madam*'s voice was weak, barely audible above the thundering of Jenna's heart.

Unshed tears pooled in her eyes spiking her lashes with the drops.

"I cannot do that." Jenna's voice was soft. She hoped there was a firmness about it that would dissuade the lady from attempting to convince her. She could not fathom any of this. "I don't..." She swallowed air.

"Won't do it?" The woman visibly bristled, her chin went up, her back stiffened. "You cast a spell so the man will fall in love with you. Now, you won't help a dying child. You are even more despicable than they say. I defended you when everyone said you were a horrible person when they cast aspersions on your character." She spit on the floor before wiping her lips with the back of her hand. "You are even worse than anyone says."

"I think you should leave," Gaby said while she nodded to the guard standing in the corner. "Remove her now."

"*Sorciere!*" the lady shouted. "You are nothing but a witch!"

"No, wait." Jenna reached out a hand to her. Her stomach churned in fear. "It's not that I don't want to help your granddaughter. I can't. I'm not a witch. Spells, charms, incantations, they are nothing I understand. I have no power as you suggest."

"That's not what the villagers say." Once again, the lady stiffened with visible anger. "All I want is for my beautiful granddaughter to live."

The woman seemed determined to continue this charade. Jenna defended herself again. "I don't care what they say. It's all superstition. Nonsense. The villagers don't know me."

The lady held out her hand imploring her, "Come with me. You can meet my granddaughter. Perhaps you will change your mind when you see how she suffers. Poor thing cannot even get out of bed. She sleeps most of the day and barely eats."

This situation was bittersweet. If she gave in and visited the child, Gil would be furious. In any case, there was no reason to do so. She was so very sorry. There was nothing she could do to ease the pain of loss or heal the sick. *"Desole, je ne peux pas aider.* There was no spell cast upon *Monsieur Allemand.* He doesn't love me. Most of the time he doesn't even like me. I've no control of how he thinks or feels."

Just wants me in his bed so he can collect on our agreement.

"The *monsieur* would not take a woman to bed he doesn't think he loves. He is a gentleman, unlike..."

"Unlike the woman in his bed who the town believes is after all he is worth. I assure you I am not. Nor am I a whore."

Brice lost his inheritance. Now, all she wanted was what was rightfully hers.

"That is not what I meant. You're right. If I cannot make you see things my way, I should leave. If you change your mind, send a message to the bakery where you bought the pastries the other day."

"Yes, the place where the proprietor ordered me to leave. Did he also paint the words on my home?"

She would help the woman if she could. Would do anything for a child. It didn't matter that others would run her out of the area. If she could cast a spell to save the little girl's life, she would do so.

Damn the consequences. Damn anything Gil ordered her not to do.

Once again, Gaby nodded to the guard.

"It's alright I'm leaving." *Madam Macon* said as she slowly pushed away from the table.

Her heart breaking for the older woman, Jenna watched as she shuffled from the kitchen then down the steps. "I don't know what I did to make people believe I'm a witch. I know what they say about Gil. It's not true. Do you believe me?"

"Don't believe it's too early for a small dram. What I do know about you is that you are an innocent. You've been abused by men your entire life." Gaby poured them both a glass of sherry. "Drink up."

"Merci," Jenna murmured softly downing the liquid in a quick gulp. It seemed the alcohol had the desired effect. It was delicious.

"In time the people will forget. Don't know what you can do to speed things along. You must know also that everyone who has known *Monsieur*, comprehends he is different now that you're here. Sometimes superstition is difficult to dismiss. She wants her granddaughter to live. Thinks you are her only hope. What can a person do to change that?"

~ * ~

With his trusted men on route, Gil felt a moment of relief. Before he sent for the men, he didn't know how much he missed the life. He would never go back in the field though. Too old, he mused, for that. Didn't feel as if he still wanted the excitement of bullets blasting toward him or running and riding hard. He enjoyed his life a bit more sedate than it used to be. Although directing the men once more was heaven to his soul. As Drake Montgomerie did from his home, he could set up a command center from the winery. He would not have to live in Paris. All legitimate business could take place right here.

Despite the difficulty in doing so, he needed to put his past behind him even though he would never forget the memories he held for his son. Needed to forge a new life. Jenna ignited a spark he thought long extinguished. He hoped work that he loved along with Jenna would help him come to terms with the loss of his son.

The pain still existed. It would always be there deep in his heart.

Gil supposed this new feeling of worth would end if he couldn't rid his mind of the ever-present memories. For months now, he felt stifled. His life was stagnant. At times he couldn't breathe. When Jenna came to live at *Cimaron*, everything changed. Somehow, she gave him a purpose, challenging him in ways he didn't understand. Jenna was determined, stubborn to a fault. She found ways to defy him by doing exactly as she pleased. Surprising to him he allowed her disobedience. In fact, most of the time he enjoyed watching the stubborn jut of her chin while she went against his direct command. No one did that, no one except Jenna.

That was it. She contested every thought in his head. She made him think about Lance. Made him remember the good times. Forced him to talk about his son. Well, he conceded, he didn't do much talking. However, the encounters did force him to put his misery aside, to remember the laughter they shared. She made him laugh. He discovered laughing felt good. As days passed the pain didn't seem quite so intense. She was finding a way inside his heart.

Except when he saw Brice or heard him. Just this one thought caused his gut to clench. He hated himself for his thoughts toward her son. Despised the fact he wished their sons could change places.

Etienne should arrive soon. His friend seemed to harbor a few good thoughts about Jenna, unlike his wife who had little toleration for her. Elisa was wrong about Jenna. He didn't believe she was after anything he could give her. Sexually they shared a strong bond. Gil didn't think she liked him. No, after what he did this morning, she most likely despised him. He would have to find a means to alter her mind. What she didn't understand was that he had no choice except to bring her to the chateau.

To his bedroom though?

Jenna thought only of her son, never of herself. He intended to revise that fact. Everything she did was to make life easier for the boy, including starving herself. If she hadn't found him, she would most likely be dead now.

What would have happened to Brice if she died?

She was so damn tenacious. He grinned. Thoughts of her in his bed tonight, heated every solitary part of him. If she hadn't offered herself to him the first day they met, he wouldn't be dreaming of bedding her now. He probably wouldn't have given her a second thought. Even though she hurt herself, he admired her loyalty to her child.

At first, he didn't mean to collect on her offer. When he saw her naked even though she was nearly skin and bones, he felt raw desire sweep through him to land in his manly parts. Now when he watched her that same desire surged intensely.

He wanted her now.

Right this instant his body was ready. Lust surged into his groin.

He spent most of the day with the workers. The grapes were abundant. It would take days and more days to pick them all. The stomping of them would begin. Sometimes the men and women involved would make a game of it. They would sing and chant. When he was young, this time of year had always been a little magical.

Gil wasn't too astonished when Etienne walked through the front door that evening. While he understood his good friend would race here, he was shocked to see him without his wife.

He slanted one eyebrow considering the situation, "Elisa didn't want to come? Was it something I said?"

Etienne slipped his jacket off, hanging it on a coat stand. "Brandy? I'm a thirsty man. It's been a long hard ride. I'm exhausted."

First things first, Gil poured them both a drink. They sat in the drawing room. Etienne set his head on the back of the chair, closing his eyes.

"Been riding since I got the message. This tastes good. Did Gaby make anything I can sample before dinner? I'm a starving man. It is almost dinner or have I missed it? Where's the reason I raced here?"

Gil nodded to one of his new employees to get something from the kitchen. "That's a lot of questions. Let's start with the most important at this moment. I'm sure Gaby has a few things that would tide you over until the evening meal."

Gil understood his friend would race here. Still, he waited for answers. It wasn't like Etienne to leave his wife. Perhaps it wasn't like Elisa to allow him to travel without her.

After a few minutes, Etienne sat up, drank long and deep. He set the empty glass on a nearby table. His gaze hard, eyes narrowed. "What is Jenna to you? Before we do anything that can't be undone, you need to tell me. Is she important to you or just a piece of muslin?"

"Cutting to the chase and you've been here less than ten minutes. I assume you feel the question is important."

Gil didn't know what Jenna was to him except she was more than a convenient piece of muslin. He knew he wanted her. Understood she was going to stay with him for as long as he could convince her to do so. Forever, if he had his way.

Forever?

"I wouldn't ask if it wasn't critical. Unlike my wife, I like *Madam Bonnet*. However, I do agree she wants something here. Do you know what that is?"

"It's not me she wants," Gil was quick to say while he was thinking of her responsive body beneath his. "Jenna hasn't mentioned anything. I do suppose she returned for some reason. If she did, she hasn't divulged it yet. Well, she did believe Brice would inherit. Didn't know her husband lost the vineyard do to back taxes."

"Did you truly believe she would come right out and ask you?"

"Don't know what I believe. All she cares about is her son."

"You've made love to her, I presume. Brought her into the chateau for whatever reason I'm not going to guess. She is no longer independent of you. The villagers will name her your whore. At least in the cottage she could be your mistress or lover. People would never really know the truth. This one act changed everything. Changed her life."

"I want her."

"She doesn't want you? I find that hard to comprehend when she allows you into her bed. I understand she's willing. You would never force a woman," Etienne spoke as if he understood more than he possibly could.

"Once in my bed, I seduced her. If that is willing, I'm not sure. Jenna didn't tell me no. Why the third degree?" Gil found he didn't want to answer personal questions.

In a sense he did force her. Well hell, she offered herself up on a silver platter. He accepted what was offered nothing more.

"Trying to figure out how we're going to defend your woman. Ah, food," Etienne picked up some cheese and meat. Closing his eyes, he chewed. "This is delicious."

"Jenna Bonnet is not my woman."

He protested too much. She was his for now anyway.

"For the time being she is. She sleeps in your bed."

Not yet. She would tonight though. He looked forward to the interlude. "She works for me. Helping to spruce up the old chateau so it's as good as new." He didn't like lying to his best friend.

"On her back?" Etienne asked blandly as if he didn't care one way or the other while he picked up another delicious morsel off the tray brought to them.

"Cleans," Gil corrected.

Didn't he just this morning order her to do nothing. A few hours ago, he caught her with the duster in her hand, attacking the shelves and books in this library.

"Until the other night when you slept at her place. Until today when you moved her into your bedchamber." Etienne's dark brown eyes bore into him. "Now, she works on her back. Is that what you want for her?"

Didn't care for the direction of Etienne's questions. He tried to resist her. What a lie. Truthfully, he wanted her the first time he looked at her naked body. Lulled her into the seduction by taking tiny steps in her coaxing. Had done admirably well at deluding himself until three nights ago. Now, all he could think about was Jenna Bonnet. It wasn't just his lust for her. He found her tenacious personality endearing in so many ways.

They were both crazy. Found their flaws were compatible in too many ways. It seemed to Gil she understood his grief. She was the only person who did. He found he could talk to her. She told him what she thought.

"The villagers are calling her a witch. Say she cast a spell on me."

Gil wanted to laugh then cry. This was loony. The villagers shouldn't care about him one-way or the other except that Jenna returned expecting her son to inherit.

"You called in some of your men?" Etienne asked as he continued to feast on the delicacies brought into the room.

"I've been corresponding with the ministry. Decided to continue working on the inside, a role I would enjoy. Going to set up a command center from here. We're going to begin by putting down the notion of witchcraft in this small area of Bordeaux. With the government behind my efforts, dousing the notion of witchcraft will prove easier."

"*Bonsoir*," Jenna entered the room. "I'm here."

Both men stood. Etienne held her hand in his, kissed the back. Slanted her a genuine smile that made Gil jealous.

She sounded angry with him. He chuckled. He enjoyed her anger as much as her sweeter side. Although she was angry with him more often than she was sweet. When he made love to her...ah she was very, very sweet.

Beneath the tenor of her voice Gil heard what she wasn't saying. *As you commanded.* He did order her here. He was obeyed. Told her he needed her here with him even though he didn't know Etienne would arrive so soon. All he wanted from her at the moment was to spend a peaceful interlude with her.

"Thank you, Jenna. Was it too much trouble? Too taxing for you?" Gil asked watching her.

She pretty much did as she pleased today, defying him at every turn. Now he wanted to hear about her visitor. Gaby told him what she thought. A different perspective would be nice.

"Etienne," she nodded, her smile only half there. "Where is Elisa?"

"Suppose you're waiting for my wife to pounce. She'll be along sometime tomorrow I'm guessing. Depends on the children." Etienne stared hard at Gil. "I was in a hurry. The children would never have been ready at dawn. Elisa understood I needed to leave the moment I read your missive. You would have done the same for me."

There was a wealth of information Etienne wasn't sharing. Gil would find out later what Etienne hid.

"I was wondering. Need to stiffen my back when your wife arrives. She thinks I'm after what Gil can give me." She smiled sweetly at him. "How can that be? Gil doesn't even like me."

"I can give you a great deal." Gil was thinking about the sweet nights.

She must have been too. She flushed a sensual shade of pink giving rise to carnal thoughts in his head. Jenna understood exactly what he meant.

"When pigs fly," she murmured softly while she found something about her feet fascinating.

"Oh, *ma cherie,* sooner than that," he laughed keeping his gaze locked on her. "For now, I need you to tell me about this woman who visited this afternoon. Gaby gave an interesting rendition, as did my guard. He was chagrinned at disobeying my orders. Had to tell him it wasn't his fault. My man assured me it wouldn't happen again despite your sweet cajoling."

"You know about that."

Again, she stared at her feet, at the horrible shoes she wore.

"My men don't keep anything from me. Gaby is loyal. Where you are concerned, well, I made sure I would learn the moment something happened. My men are also competent."

"I've no privacy."

"None," he agreed with her eyeing her critically even though the tone of his voice was light. "I'm going to know everything you do including when you disobey me. You cleaned this room. I specifically told you weren't to work for me."

He saw the narrowing of her eyes. Knew she thought all he wanted was to have her in his bed. Wouldn't deny the fact that he did want that.

"I need the francs." She sounded emphatic then she lifted her delicate shoulders in an indifferent shrug. "I was bored."

Mon Dieu, he needed to find something for her to wear. He rose then picked up a small blanket that was draped over the back of the sofa.

Without further comment he placed it around her shoulders, making sure the material covered her bosom. After that was accomplished, he proceeded with the questions. "What did the woman want?" Gil persisted not wishing to remind her he was not paying her, didn't intend to pay her.

Jenna scowled at him.

Etienne smirked. Gil didn't care.

"You know who she was as well as what she wanted. Your men spy on me. I don't have a moment of peace." Her chin tilted up in a tiny show of defiance.

He enjoyed it. Loved it when she stiffened her backbone. The challenge took his mind away from his son.

"Want your perspective."

This was important to him. The need to protect her overwhelmed him at times. He couldn't keep her safe even from herself if she didn't tell him the truth. The thought of losing her terrified him.

"Can I have a drink?"

Ah, she was trying to put off the inevitable or perhaps her mouth was dry from fear. She might need fortification. Maybe it was all of the above.

Etienne poured her a glass of brandy before Gil granted permission. Not that he would deny her drink. Still, jealousy erupted. "You don't need to ask for a drink or food. I hope you understand that."

Slowly she sipped, looking at him over the rim of the glass. Her lashes were long and dark against the paleness of her face, her eyes brilliantly blue. She played him perfectly.

After some time, she set what was left of the brandy down. She looked at him. Her lashes fluttered a couple of times. Her smile was slow, beguiling him until he wanted to howl. How did she so easily set him on sexual edge?

"What was it you wanted to know?" Her lashes fluttered then daintily rested for a moment on her alabaster cheeks.

"*Madam Macon*?" He wanted to nudge her a bit without giving too much away. "Don't understand what she couldn't have wanted from you. She walked all the way from the village. Her purpose must have been important."

He sensed a change in tactics. She cleared her throat before she tilted her chin rebelliously. "The lady believed me to be a witch. That's all. I'm sure it's enough. It's what the men shouted last night at my door, in my yard."

She was shaking now, her shoulders trembling. The insolence she showed earlier vanished.

His door.

His yard.

He wanted to remind her of the facts. Stopped cold though as he also wished to know what she wasn't telling him. "That isn't all though, is it?"

He drummed his fingers on the armrest of his chair. This woman could try his patience to a boiling point. Etienne grinned as if he enjoyed the moments here.

"She's much like my Elisa. Sometimes I find I have to drag every word from her mouth. Even then I don't ever know if she's told me all that's in her mind," Etienne smirked.

"Jenna is nothing like Elisa," Gil gritted out wishing the woman would tell him what he needed to know instead of remaining quiet. "What did *Madam Macon* want you to do? I'm sure it had something to do with spells."

For too many seconds to count, Jenna withdrew into herself. When she looked up, she was calm, so serene, Gil wished he could shake her. "Why don't you tell me? I'm sure you know the answer to your question," she said softly, no anger in her voice. "You've been informed. Interrogating me is not going to garner you any more information."

"Jenna does have a point," Etienne said chuckling as if he remembered something. "You do know almost word for word what transpired between the two women."

His fingers continued to drum with frustration. More than annoyed, he leaned forward, "Correct me if I'm wrong. Feel free to tell me your version if I waver. Yes, you're right. Gaby as well as my guard you convinced to let the woman inside told me what was said. Getting to my man was not well done of you. You could have been hurt. I assure you, it won't happen again."

She nodded.

"The truth finally. Go on." Speaking the order, he should have been giving.

Etienne roared with the laughter it seemed he'd been holding back for the last half hour or so. Gil shot a glare at him that should have withered him in his chair. It didn't. The man clearly enjoyed this altercation.

"The lady wanted you to heal her granddaughter. You refused, a wise choice by the way. If you went along with the woman and the girl died, there might not have been anything we could have done to save your sweet hide."

He heard the startled gasp of air. The need to pump caution into her was prevalent in his head. She just didn't listen to reason.

"I would never give anyone false hope especially a child. I would think you understood that about me. Besides, I've nothing to fear. It's illegal to persecute witchcraft in France."

He ignored her blind mentality when it came to crowds of people bent on a mission. "Tomorrow we'll go into the village together. I want to show them who you are along with the fact that you don't hold any power, magical or otherwise over me. Etienne can come along as well as the man who was supposed to keep the woman from you this afternoon."

She stiffened her back. Her eyes darkened, "I don't want to go. Have no reason to put myself in harm's way. Won't be paraded around for anyone's inspection. Isn't that what Jacques used to do to me? Now, you mean to do the same."

"Nothing will happen to you. I want everyone to see that you hold no magical powers over me. You've cast no spell. I'm a sane rational man." It seemed the events of that night impacted her in more ways than he could comprehend. Perhaps, the burning cross did generate more caution in her.

"I agree with Gil. It's important to show our strength," Etienne said thoughtfully as if he'd given this notion great consideration.

"I'm not strong," she was quick to say.

At least she recognized that fact. She was fragile and weak. Needed the protection he could give her.

It took all his strength to say the words. "We will find a special treat for your son."

"A bribe...?"

He lifted his shoulders before sipping the brandy in front of him. "Whatever it takes. I'd get you something too if you would accept." He held up his hands to stop her reply. "I know you'd refuse. A new dress, perhaps..." He wanted to buy her things, especially a dress that didn't show all of her body to every man, woman, and child.

She colored prettily as his gaze rested on the blanket covering the worn dress. As he pointed out to her before, it was very nearly see through. If she wasn't thoroughly covered by the blanket, both he and Etienne would be able to see the outline of her nipples. He was sure they hardened at his ardent perusal. He grinned knowing what he imagined would not be what Etienne saw.

"I would purchase one, a dress, if you would pay me."

Etienne seemed to be enjoying this conversation as well as the show she presented to him before he covered her. "Pay her for what?"

"Cleaning," she shot out before Gil could tell him about the outrageous offer.

"If you recall, I never hired you."

This conversation bored him. He wasn't about to change his mind. Besides, their intimate relationship was none of Etienne's business.

She flushed hotter. Pursuing this conversation would make her more uncomfortable. In front of Etienne, he didn't want this to go farther than it had already.

"You didn't. I know. You allowed me to work though. Thought you would pay me eventually," she told him, her tiny fists clenched tight, her eyes blazing ice blue fireworks.

It appeared she wanted to hit him. "Tomorrow after breakfast we'll make a day of it. Gaby can pack a lunch. We'll eat in the common area in the village. We will show everyone you have no unearthly powers over me."

"Don't understand why the people of the village think the sins of Jacques Bonnet are your sins as well," Etienne said tapping his finger on his chin. He eyed her critically.

"It's because," She ran her tongue across her lips, "he liked to dress me up. Bought jewels for me to wear with the money he didn't pay the men who worked the vines. He paraded me in front of the people here as well as in Bordeaux to show them that he was the better person because he possessed a great wealth." She tugged in air. "I hated it. Didn't want to be any part of the show, just as I don't want to be part of your little spectacle tomorrow. Men!" She slammed her fist on her leg.

"What can we do to change that?" Etienne asked sympathetically. "It won't be easy, you understand. Feel as if Elisa has an open mind. Even she thinks you're a conniving woman."

"Don't believe I care what people think about me. Just want to be left alone with my son. May I go now?"

Gil nodded, understanding Jenna wouldn't join them for dinner. She would put Brice to bed. He would have to make sure she had dinner tonight. Later, after he finished speaking with Etienne, he would see to her stomach as well as other things.

"Don't forget..." Gil slanted her a heated glance, pointing his gaze at her mouth then lower.

He knew she understood what he was asking of her. If she wasn't in his bed when he retired for the night, he would retrieve her. While she lived in the chateau, he wasn't going to sleep alone.

"If you don't want a child from her, you best take precautions," Etienne warned seeming to understand the silent exchange between them.

It might be too late.

~ * ~

Etienne knew Gil took advantage of Jenna. Gil told him they slept together. By the heated exchange he just witnessed, Jenna would be in Gil's bed tonight as well as every night after that but for how long? Evidently, she promised him something that first day he came upon her by the gatekeeper's cottage. He understood part of the story from that first time he visited. Would like to know what the offer was although he was certain it had something to do with granting sexual favors.

What Jenna understood now that Gil moved her into his home was that she was no longer cleaning but working on her back. Gil should be ashamed of himself. Etienne never saw him treat a woman this way. He couldn't comprehend the reasons for this abrupt turnaround.

Although...

One didn't have to spend more than a few seconds in the company of those two to see the sparks fly. They both watched each other with raw heated passion dancing in the depths of their eyes. More than once, Etienne caught Jenna staring at Gil's mouth. The same could be said about Gil. If he wasn't gazing hungrily at Jenna's soft lips, he was focused on her bosom. The two could set fire to a room if given half a chance.

It might be a rocky path but Jenna and Gil were meant for each other. Etienne was certain time would ease the problems with the villagers. Jenna had Gaby for a friend. Even though *Madam Macon* was willing to plead her case with Jenna thinking she was a witch, he thought the woman might come to appreciate some of Jenna's finer qualities.

Up early the next morning, he strode through the kitchen, giving Gaby a quick kiss on the cheek. "Where is Brice? What have you got to eat? I'm famished." He rambled off questions having to laugh at himself as he did so.

He wanted to get to know the boy. Needed to see what about Brice sent Gil into his melancholy of despair. From everything he heard the boy was nothing like his son Lance. There should be no comparisons. Perhaps the feelings were no longer desolation. Last night when the boy's name was mentioned Etienne saw anger flit across Gil's face.

"He's outside playing with my girl along with the other children. Before you go see to him, sit down and help yourself."

Etienne grabbed a piece of hot bread already slathered with butter before stepping through the door. While he didn't know the children, he recognized the boy that must be Brice. He was smaller than the others seeming to hold back from the group. Jenna told him he was recovering from an illness that nearly sent the boy to an early grave. He was still frail. With one look Etienne understood why she was so concerned about the little tyke.

Truly, Brice was nothing like Lance. Gil's boy would have been in the middle of the fray directing everyone, ordering them around. As his father would be doing.

Etienne chuckled at his thoughts. Even as a lad Gil was the leader. Nothing changed over the years. It didn't surprise him that Gil wanted to continue the work with the French ministry. Over the years while he was playing at spying, Gil worked his way to the top. He was trusted and respected. Men liked him. His decision-making was sound.

He walked to Brice, hunkered down so they were at eye level. "You're Jenna's boy? Am I right?"

"*Oui, monsieur.*"

He appeared to want to run, bony knees wobbling, narrow chest heaving frantically. His gaze darted to the scullery door. Gaby stood watching. She nodded as if to say this man's all right. He looked up, his features grim, "Are you a *tete du butt* like *Monsieur* Gil?"

Etienne couldn't stop the low rumble of laughter erupting. "*Non,* I'm not. I've a little boy about two years older than you. He will be here soon. Perhaps the two of you would like to play. His name is Masson. I have a little girl we call Margo."

"How old is she?"

"Turned one. She's walking and gets into a lot of mischief just like her mother. Perhaps you can watch her and make sure she doesn't hurt herself."

Ah, but she was a lot like Elisa. She would run them a merry dance if he didn't learn to discipline his children. As it was Elisa had to do it all, the discipline that is. He contributed in other ways. He'd rather play than scold the duo.

"I would like to meet your children."

"I will make sure you do so as soon as they arrive unless the hour is too late," Etienne promised brushing the hair from the boy's forehead.

"I'm sleeping in my old room," Brice offered, a quick smile flitted across his face. "Don't remember it. *Maman* tells me the bed chamber is just the way we left it."

"We are going into the village, your *maman*, Gil and myself. Is there anything you'd like?"

"Could you get *Maman* a new dress? She needs one. I can see through hers. I think that's why the mean man stares at her all the time.

He won't pay her, so she can't buy one."

Ah, even the innocent children notice things like that. "It would not be appropriate or I would." It was up to Gil to make sure she was clothed. He could give her the coin while on the way to the village. In that case, he could also make sure she purchased clothing for herself.

"That's why the other kids call *Maman* a whore. It's because the mean man gives her things he shouldn't."

Well, Etienne didn't think Gil gave her anything, at least not yet. She had the label because he moved her not only into his house but also into his bedchamber. The servants would gossip. There was no way to stop that from happening.

The label would stick if Gil didn't do something about the description imposed on her soon.

Chapter Seven

Jenna went to bed in her room that evening, understanding Gil would most likely make sure she slept with him. It seemed to be a pattern. Tonight, was no different. She woke up in his arms. Before he made love to her, he would always ask, *"Coucher avec moi, cherie?"* Sweetly he kissed her, coaxed her until she was breathless with need and he was deep inside her giving her every pleasure until she screamed his name.

He would laugh. Would remind her she wanted him. It was no use for her to shy away. If he had to carry her to his bed every night, he would do so.

She gave up whining about her plight. She discovered she adored him even though he taxed her patience. Would accept what he asked of her until he tossed her from his home. That time would come. It was inevitable. When that happened, she would have memories, bliss-filled memories so unlike the ones she had with Jacques.

Dreading the morning's outing, she searched for some way to get out of the trip. As she told them last night, she didn't want to find herself paraded in front of anyone, least of all those who hated her to such an extreme they would burn a cross in front of her home. The vile act brought too much of her past memories into the forefront. The only thing she could think of to do was claim she was sick. Gil would see through that ploy with ease. She wasn't a good liar.

She knew she had no choice in this except to refuse. If she did so, he would pick her up then put her where he wanted her. Damn, but he wouldn't. The phrase one always had a choice didn't apply to her not in these circumstances. Perhaps by telling him she would do anything, the word negated any other possibilities.

When she woke, he was gone. Her breath caught in her throat as she thought she might have luck on her side. She didn't. A few minutes later he strode through the door with a tray of food, hot coffee as well. Her mouth watered.

"You look disappointed to see me. Ah, *Cherie*, you thought since I was gone you wouldn't have to go into the village. You thought wrong, must know I wouldn't change my mind."

"I hoped." She caught herself, looked to the food then him. She was famished. "I don't want to do this." If she told him enough times, was it possible he would listen to her? No, probably not.

He laughed softly, his eyes twinkling mischievously, "I understand your fear. Appreciate it too. You should be weary. Today, with my men along with Etienne you've nothing to be afraid of. I see the fear in your eyes. What can I do to chase the terror away?"

For the longest time she stared at the food on the tray. She sipped her coffee. Wanted to distract him. When she looked up, her focus was his lips then lower to his crotch. She'd not thought to seduce him so easily as she watched the bulge in his trousers grow. Her gaze flew to his eyes.

"Ah, *Cherie*, we do have time for what you're so blatantly asking for before we leave. Etienne wanted to walk through the vineyards, peruse the grapes, speak with the workers. He believes his well-practiced eye will be informative for me. I agreed. Even now he's walking with your son who seems to like him much better than he does me."

Her focus snapped to her coffee cup. She scooped butter onto the warm bread, watched it melt.

"You want to...now?" She gulped air.

Her blatant suggestion was not meant to be taken seriously.

"You did offer." He strode to her grinning devilishly. "Your eyes tell it all."

"I have to eat." Jenna found herself groping for a way out of this even though she would much prefer to be with Gil in bed than in the village.

"That you do. Finish the bread then we will engage in other pleasures until it is time to leave. The lunch Gaby made is bountiful. Would feed at least four men so you will have more than enough food for the day." He sat back watching her. "I do believe I'd like you to wear that old shawl of yours. That dress shows way too much of you for my liking."

She nodded as she chewed slowly. He needed to order someone else around. "I would stay here and help Gaby with the menu." A menu that was so precise it didn't need work. "If Elisa and the children are arriving this evening, I need to make sure their rooms are ready for them. There is a wealth of things to do."

He grinned.

She sipped her coffee, trying to think of anything that would keep her here. Her mind seemed to be filled with cobwebs.

"I'm famished," he told her as he rose then extended a hand to her. "For you, *Cherie*."

"Gil, please..." A thin layer of air shifted inside her. "*S'il te plait, I...*"

"If you say no, I'll leave. I don't believe you will though." He pulled her into his arms. His lips found hers in a shattering and very hot kiss. The intimate contact was one that left her breathless and wanting.

His hand deftly undid the buttons. Carefully, he slid the fabric down her arms letting it pool on the floor by her feet. She was naked. Her chemise fell into the garbage only a few days earlier. It would not be too long before she had nothing at all to wear.

Kissing and stroking her he swept her off her feet then to the bed. She could not say no to him. Her body responded so thoroughly and sweetly to his gentle and enchanting caress, she trembled with the pleasure, seeking the ecstasy she knew he could give. Before she could deny anything, he was deep inside her. Just as he wished, she cried out his name as her body shattered in his arms.

Afterward, his love play was always soothing. Her head rested on his chest, her eyelashes fluttering there. His hands stroked her gently in a way that was not meant to seduce or coax. One fingertip lazily traveled the length of her spine then back. She reveled in this time with him. It was bliss-filled. She imagined he loved her. Imagined this might last a lifetime.

Wished it would last into eternity.

The serenity was over when he chuckled then swatted her playfully on her derrière. If you don't want Etienne to find us in this state of dishabille, we should dress."

She pushed away from him, gazing into the depths of his eyes. "I don't want to go." She would tell him her feelings until there was no reason to say the words.

His long-suffering sigh told her she protested one too many times. It seemed to her he bit back a curse. Now he was frustrated as well as annoyed. She walked away. Found her dress then slipped it over her head quickly fastening it. Finished with her shoes.

"I'm ready." She wasn't. What else was she to do?

Dressed, he wrapped her in his arms. "It will be good. I promise we won't parade you as you think we intend. This is an outing, nothing more. We will purchase a few items, talk to some of the villagers. I will show them I care for you. This is all for appearances that will be good for you."

In his own way Gil did care for her. She should appreciate that fact. She no longer believed he disliked her, only her son. They could have nothing together as long as he felt the way he did about Brice.

"It will not be that easy to sway their minds." If she understood the fact, Gil should also.

"I never thought it would be. Time will win out. Trust me. *Viens, Cherie.* It is time to go.*"

Another order.

Gil slipped his fingers through hers as they walked to the carriage. The vehicle was nothing like the little buggy he loaned her. This was large, comfortable inside. His family crest was blazoned on the outside for everyone to see.

She never knew Gil was a count.

The steps were down. He helped her inside then he sat beside her, Etienne across from them. His arm rested across the top of the seat behind her. Even though Etienne was in the carriage with them, he toyed with her hair, slipped his fingers across the back of her neck. Enticed her in every way. She shivered with fragile emotions needing to be denied.

She wished she could bat his hand away. With hooded eyes, Etienne watched them. Heat rushed to her cheeks. Perhaps if she closed her eyes, the inferno tumbling through her would vanish.

It didn't.

Etienne cleared his throat.

Gil's hand rested possessively on her shoulder. Even in front of Etienne he claimed her. At least he wasn't toying with her now. The conversation between the two men droned in her head. She wasn't part of it even if the words were about her.

The short ride to the village lasted forever. Jenna was sure he told the driver to go a roundabout way.

Their first destination was the village store. She found herself sandwiched between the two men. She should have felt protected. Instead, it seemed they placed her on display. One of the guards walked ten feet behind them. Jenna didn't think for a moment Gil expected trouble. The guard was a precaution. Gil was a cautious man.

Gil purchased a few things she didn't think they needed.

"Bienvenue," Monsieur Garnier called out. "Can I get you anything?"

"Were you with the people who burned the cross at my gatekeeper's cottage?"

The question startled the man. Blood drained from his face. The man, undoubtedly, was there.

The inquiry made her gasp. Shock at his audacity rippled through her. She clutched his arm. Gil didn't hold back. The man held a hand up as if trying to deny the fact. He fumbled with his words before he finally admitted that yes, he was there.

"You called Jenna Bonnet a witch," Gil continued in such a calm voice Jenna wasn't at all sure how he would proceed. "Told people she cast a spell on me. As you can clearly see this woman is no witch. She can't cook let alone make a potion. Even it was true, which it is not, do I look like a man who could succumb to a witch's spell?"

Garnier's ashen color turned pasty. If the floor rose up to swallow her, she would be happy. No, he wasn't parading her. He was in the process of making a valuable point.

At her expense.

Was it?

The man stiffened, seemed to regain a small modicum of composure. "Jenna Bonnet is your whore. You shouldn't display her around town as if she is a respectable lady fitting your status. None of the good ladies here want to be anywhere near this woman."

She cringed at the words even though the man spoke true. Callously and with no thought to her, Gil made her his whore.

Gil cleared his throat, dark eyebrows drawing together as he seemed to be thinking about what he would say next. "The lady had to move into the chateau because you along with the rest of your kind created a situation that wasn't safe for her to live without protection in the cottage. I would not be the gentleman that I am if I allowed her to live by herself with the threat of her life on the line. Jenna Bonnet is no whore, no more than your wife is."

The man managed to look sheepish. Jenna didn't think any progress was made. They continued on to the other shops in the village. The discussions proceeded the same way.

At the bakery and despite the harsh look from Gil, *Madam Macon* approached her again. "You've changed your mind? I hoped and prayed you would do so." Her voice sounded so hope-filled and wistful. "She grows sicker each day. She won't live much longer."

Jenna strove for the right approach to the older lady. "I'm not a witch. No potion that would cure your granddaughter exists. As Gil told *Monsieur Garnier*, my cooking skills are so bad I wouldn't be able to create a spell. For your granddaughter's sake I wish I could." That was the truth of the matter.

When she spoke, Gil's fingers tightened on her elbow. The encouragement was minimal but gave her strength.

As a silent thank you, she smiled at him.

On the common area, Gil spread the blanket then set out the food. "You did well today. I'm proud of you."

Somehow his words sounded condescending. "Nothing was accomplished as well you know. They still believe me to be a witch as well as your whore." She sounded bitter.

This was his fault. Well, no it wasn't. It was Jacques deeds that set these events into motion.

"Don't ever want to hear you say that about yourself. You are not a whore," his voice turned harsh. He knifed a hand through the air before he gently lifted her chin with a finger. "You are not a whore."

Well, Gil might be in denial. She wasn't. She was his whore for the duration. There was nothing she could do about the label. Every night she was in his bed. In return, he gave her a place to stay along with food to eat. There was nothing else to say about her situation. The way he treated her was the exact definition of a whore except he didn't pay her with coin. In fact, now that she wasn't living in the cottage her payment was meals. Didn't quite seem enough.

Etienne served wine as well as the meal. He didn't speak at all, just watched them, a strange light in his twinkling eyes. She sometimes wondered what he thought he knew that no one else did. The food and wine were delicious. Still, he didn't say anything.

When Etienne rose, Jenna was ready to follow suit and vanish from this horrible place. More than anything she wanted to go home to be done with this travesty.

"Sit," he told her his voice soft. "I promised Brice a small surprise. I'm going to get him a *bonbon* or two, some chocolate. I assume he likes the sweets."

She paled before she looked away. Gil enfolded her hand in his. "A long time ago he ate chocolate. I'm sure my son will love the gift."

"Ah, you didn't have the francs to spend on chocolate. If you'd rather I didn't..."

"*Merci*, he would love the sweet treat. You are a sweet man to think about my son."

Jenna slanted Gil a look as she thought of his lost son along with his feelings about her. In time she would have to leave. How to do that, leaving him went beyond her wildest imagination. If Gil never paid her, she would always have to live at the chateau.

She had to find the jewels.

They were hers, gifts from her late husband. In her mind, she paid dearly for them, gave her soul to the man who took her pride.

After Etienne disappeared into the shop, Gil set his hand on hers. "I would not give your son the wrong impression. Nor will I allow you to think so poorly of yourself. Do not allow these people to give you a label such as that."

"You still expect me in your bed each night. You refuse to let me work at an honest job. Isn't that a whore? You don't even give me the considerations you would give a mistress." Her heart pounded so hard she thought surely it would jump from her chest.

"Jenna, what is so wrong with that. You love my attentions. To be in my bed with me is a little piece of heaven for both of us. Your body doesn't lie to me." He ran his finger along the column of her throat, letting his finger rest on her pulse. "You're hungry for me at this moment. If I wanted, I could make love to you here and now. You wouldn't protest."

"I'm not going to deny the truth. Doesn't mean I don't loathe myself for the feelings I'm having. For what I'm allowing you to do to my body every night." He was so right. She'd never been able to tell him no, to deny him, even when she knew she should.

He chuckled as he continued the slow coaxing of her body. She understood he planned to reinforce his words with his actions, the assumptions of an arrogant man who was well versed in the ways of love.

He poured her more wine. "Drink up," he told her, his smile growing wide as she frowned at him. "You're beautiful when you're angry. Your eyes flash, change color while a soft pink color stains your cheeks."

She had the sudden urge to toss the wine in his face. It seemed he read her mind far too easily.

"Don't do it, Jenna."

His warning didn't catch her by surprise. She was more surprised that it came so late.

"Do what?"

He would have to spit it out if he meant to stop her. She knew the act would not be prudent. If she gave into her whim, she would most likely end up with the remaining contents of the bottle poured over her head. She needed to challenge him, as she was far too easy.

"It would be a waste of good wine to toss it in my face."

"Do we have to stay here longer? You made your point. Not that it did any good. They all still harbor the same feelings."

"Until Etienne returns. Once home, you may, if you wish see to the children's rooms. I'm sure Elisa will arrive before the evening meal.

Will you be joining us?" He knew he didn't need to ask.

Certain he asked to be polite. "You understand why I won't. I'm not going to sit through such a stilted affair. Not going to eat with someone who despises me, thinks the worst."

"You'll be in my bed when I retire." His words were not a question.

"No."

She turned away from him, understanding he would be angry if he had to fetch her.

She didn't care.

"Perhaps, in that case, I should show you what happens when you disobey." He sounded all serious business.

"I'm not one of your men. Don't take commands from an autocrat. I've given you everything you've asked for."

"That could be left up to interpretation."

Suddenly, she found herself pulled into his arms. His mouth pressed hotly against hers sent a myriad of emotions tumbling through her. He would make his point. She would receive more censure from those they spent the day trying to change their minds about her.

His warm hand settled over a breast while his other hand slid up her leg. "No, Gil...please not here. I cannot bear to think of the repercussions."

"Will you be in my bed tonight?" He pulled away, his large hand still rested possessively on her thigh. "Will you? Before I stop, I want your promise." His eyes darkened until they were very nearly black.

"Do I have an alternative?" her voice wavered.

She didn't want to give into the blatant seduction.

"Yes, if not in my bed in the chateau, then I'll have you here and now." Gently, Gil touched her cheek, ran his knuckles down the column of her throat.

"Tete du butt," she murmured pushing away from him.

She continued toward the waiting carriage, heedless of the fact he followed her. He would strive to elicit the promise she was unwilling to give. If he gave her no reprieve from this, she would lie.

"Jenna." His hand rested on her shoulder turning her to face him.

For a moment she thought she saw remorse in his passionate gaze. The moment vanished as if it never existed. "You're right about me. I know what I want and that's you. Neither am I accustomed to being defied or challenged in any way."

She swallowed trying to form the words. "You always get what you want."

"I do, Jenna. Best you remember that fact. Stop fighting what we both hunger for. Promise me you'll be where you want to be also."

She had to keep fighting. Pride kept her believing in something that would never exist for her. Gil would never be hers. He would remain elusive and untouchable.

"Can't do that." She called his bluff. Gil was not the type of man who would embarrass and humiliate her to such a degree as to make love to her where anyone would see. He would not take her on the green like a common slut. "This one time you're not getting your way, Gil Allemand."

"We will see."

He helped her into the carriage. They stopped in front of the sweet shop. Etienne popped into the vehicle.

"Thought the two of you were leaving me behind." He opened the sack for Jenna. "Pick one out. A sweet for a sweet lady." Etienne glanced at Gil an all-knowing smirk on his face.

"That's a lot of chocolate," she said, amazed, "thank you."

He lifted his broad shoulders. "Don't know what hell Elisa went through bringing the children here all by herself. Want to have something to placate her with when she arrives. These chocolates along with a full bottle of wine as well as my man's body should do the trick quite nicely." His was a lazy grin.

"Ah, a man who knows his woman's heart." Gil laughed as his fingers dallied with the hair that escaped the bun on Jenna's head, challenging her still.

He didn't know her heart. Instead, he toyed with it. She decided tonight after they ate dinner she would search the third floor room a second time. There were still several trunks she didn't get a chance to look through. Maybe with luck she would be able to find the jewels. Luck, unfortunately luck abandoned her a long time ago.

"What do you think is my heart? Assuming your words were about me."

Gil didn't know her, didn't know her greatest fears or what she wished for. He assumed things he shouldn't.

He bent low. Despite Etienne's presence he touched his tongue to her ear. "Me. I am your heart, Jenna. I will give you my man's body to play with any time you like."

His words hit too close to the truth. She didn't want to be so vulnerable. Didn't want to love him. He saw through her or he guessed. In any case it didn't matter. When she found the jewels, he couldn't keep her in his bed or the chateau. She would take Brice and leave. Where she would go, she had no idea. As far away as possible came to her mind.

When they passed by the cottage, she stared at the home, her home for a brief few days. The memories there would always be sweet. Looking at the porch as well as the swing sent her mind spinning. Memories bounced through her head. Thoughts of her first kiss with Gil as well as the night he made love to her.

Across from them, Etienne's eyes were closed. He wasn't asleep, just giving Gil carte blanch to do whatever he wanted. Gil took wicked advantage of the opportunity.

"Do you remember the first time you made love to me?" His teeth nipped along the back of her neck. His tongue followed suit.

She sipped air, struggling to keep her emotions under control. "Beast."

Yet, she leaned into his caresses, needing more, needing Gil. The carriage lumbered up the hill. Beneath her shawl, his hand cupped her breast, stroked the hardened crest.

He teased and taunted her body to his will.

"Promise me you'll be there?" he asked again as if she would change her mind and fall prey to the sweet-talking.

Well, he wasn't doing much talking, sweet or naughty. This was a blatant seduction of her body and mind.

"I cannot." She sighed into his mouth as it covered hers, molded over the contours.

His lips were hot and wet, leaving a trail of moisture and heat.

"You must. While I wouldn't have made love to you in the village where everyone could see, I've no qualms about here in the carriage. Etienne will keep his eyes closed.

"We are here, Gil. You've no time."

"Ah, but *Cherie*, I don't have to get out of the carriage with you even though it has ceased to move."

"You wouldn't."

"I would."

~ * ~

"I promise."

"Why do I get the feeling you're lying to me?"

He knew the truth of her words. She would make promises then make an excuse to belie that same vow. "I fancy I will have to retrieve you from your room again tonight."

His was not just a feeling. He understood her lie for what it was. Fear. He didn't understand why she wanted more than what he could give. He gave her his man's body, also treated her to a woman's pleasure. She enjoyed the wild ecstasy they created together. What more was there?

Smiling sweetly at him, it seemed she ignored the presented question. Etienne left the carriage with a nod coupled with an omniscient smile.

"We are alone, finally alone." His voice was husky smooth yet gruff with desire too.

When she started to leave, he drew her back until she sat on his thighs, his hand around her waist, rising slowly to cup a breast. He meant to pursue this until he had a real promise.

"Don't want to be alone with you, Gil. You take advantage."

"Always."

"Gil, *s'il te plait.*"

Beneath his hands he felt her tension. Understood she was not going to give a real promise no matter what he did.

"I can prove you lie." His words were gentle.

All he wanted was a promise she would be there for him.

"Gil, not now, not here." She pushed away rushing through the carriage door then into the chateau.

Well hell, he had been so positive she would give into his wheedling even though his actions were anything but subtle. He could have stopped her. Could have gone after her so he could prove his point. Etienne poked his head into the carriages open door.

"Walk with me."

To Gil's ears Etienne's request didn't sound like a question, more of a command. He nodded, stepping from the vehicle to walk. His hands behind his back he waited for the ensuing lecture. Etienne had a soft spot for Jenna, no doubt about it. This discussion wasn't going to be pleasant simply because he couldn't deny he'd been obnoxious. Would never deny that where Jenna was concerned, he had ulterior motives.

"You can get your way more often with sweetness," Etienne told him once they were yards from the house.

"Mind your own business. Remember when everything wasn't sweetness with you and Elisa."

Reminding Etienne was not well done of him. Those five years were hell for Etienne.

"No reason not to learn from my mistakes." He held up the bag of chocolates purchased for his wife. "Want to have a pleasant evening in bed with her. I've missed Elisa."

Gil grunted. "Don't need bribes to enjoy Jenna in my bed."

Jenna made it perfectly clear. She didn't want what he was giving her. He couldn't give her anything else. Marriage was out of the question.

"Did you consider protection for her?" Etienne's questioned stabbed him in the gut. "As untried as she is, she would never have thought about it."

That also was not Etienne's business. With Jenna he never considered protection. Couldn't think when she was beneath him, or straddling him when he was deep inside her sultry warmth. Lust ruled his poor man's brain.

"I see you haven't. What are you going to do when she conceives your bastard?" Etienne's pointed question shook him to the core. He hadn't given that a moment's thought. He knew better. Never in his entire life had he forgotten to protect the woman he was with. Chantel was different since she always used protection.

At the moment there was no answer for that other than take care of the child. "Haven't thought that far ahead."

"Will you treat the child as you do Brice?" Etienne asked blandly. "As if he doesn't exist? As if he's dirt beneath your shoes."

"*Non!* Why would you think something so absurd?" He would love his child, give the child all that he could.

"A bastard?" he questioned as if that fact would make a difference. It seemed Etienne persisted in his interrogation. "It's a valid question, Gil. One of the reasons a man considers the feelings of the woman he cares about. Pride is one of the few things a woman has she can call hers. You've taken all that away from Jenna by demanding her presence in your bedchamber. In a matter of a few weeks, you've reduced her to nothing."

"She wants to be there." He defended his actions.

"Are you certain?"

They walked for minutes in silence. Etienne's words tumbled around in his head in a frustrating deluge. Gil considered himself a man of principal. Etienne was right. He would have to make decisions concerning Jenna if she did carry his child. Marrying was out of the question. Letting her go held the same status in his mind.

The woman he cares about.

"You should let her go. At least allow her to make up her mind about how she feels about you. If she chooses to stay in your bedchamber, then it makes no difference. If she chooses to leave, you will have to accept her decision."

"Don't need or want a lecture from you."

"Even though you know I'm right," Etienne persisted.

"Let it go."

Gil started for the chateau, retracing his steps. He didn't hear Etienne behind him. Good, he needed time to think about his actions. Didn't like the implications Etienne suggested.

All he understood about Jenna Bonnet was that he couldn't let her go, at least not yet. Wouldn't ever let her go if she conceived his child. A wave of giddiness summersaulted through him. He couldn't breathe, his imagination conjuring a boy, his boy. His heir.

Lance was a bastard. Chantel didn't seem to care. Jenna wouldn't either. He would make sure they were both taken care of for the rest of their lives. He could give Jenna security, a stable life where she wouldn't have to worry about surviving the day. He would give his son or daughter his name. If a son, he would make him legitimate. There were proper channels he could go through.

Once inside the house he looked for Jenna. Couldn't find her. Gaby didn't know where she was. None of the servants could direct him to her.

Gil sat down in his office with a glass of brandy. Everything Etienne told him simmered deep inside, his head pounding. Jenna might be increasing now. She didn't seem to care that he took her without a thought as to the repercussions of their lovemaking. If she didn't care, he didn't see why he should. If she mentioned it, they would discuss the possibilities.

Perhaps she didn't understand. Of course, she understood. She was a mother.

He needed to find her now. What if she left? Brice was outside playing. He'd seen the boy when he returned from his walk with Etienne. She wouldn't leave without her son.

She couldn't flee his presence even if she wanted to do just that. She didn't have one franc to her name. He'd made sure of that. Not too much longer she wouldn't have anything to wear. The gown she had on today was beyond thin. A stiff breeze would rip it apart. He wasn't going to pay her for that single reason. He wasn't going to give her the means to run away from him.

Selfishly, he needed her in his home, in his bed as well. He wouldn't force her. Never had he forced her. She could cry foul all she wanted. When he touched her, she turned to liquid in his arms.

Gil strode through the first floor searching the rooms. She wasn't on the first floor. When she went missing, he would usually find her in the kitchen with Gaby. He told her to prepare the rooms for the new arrivals. That was most likely where she was.

Gil headed for the second floor. She wasn't to be found. This wasn't like her to disappear. A person had to be somewhere. A slight scuffle above him gave him pause. Why would she go to the third floor? Perhaps the noise was his imagination.

He found her bent over a trunk, her adorable backside endearingly in the air. Heard her curses as she tossed items onto the floor. As he leaned against the doorframe arms crossed in front of him, he continued his ardent perusal of her backside, a very nice backside. Imagined her skirt around her waist. He would be deep inside her. What was she up to? Obviously, she searched for something.

When she didn't notice his presence, he cleared his throat. She stiffened then slowly stood. Her eyes flashed angry sparks at him. This was something he meant to get to the bottom of. Why was she angry with him unless it was still about his high-handedness in the carriage?

"What are you doing, Jenna? You will tell me now." He pushed away from the door, strode to her. Peered into the trunk. Looked into her eyes. "Is there something you want to tell me? Or explain?"

"Forget it."

She started to walk around him. He held her arm, swinging her around until she was flush against him. His hands settled on her waist. "No, Jenna."

"I'm going to your room to wait for you," she spoke as if that was her intent.

Gil knew better. "Good try." His lip curled in amusement. "Care to start over? Don't suppose you do. Let's start over anyway. What are you looking for?"

"My long-lost cousin," she snapped at him.

It didn't seem she was receptive to the truth. They would stay here until he learned what she was doing. "Did you find him?"

"Her."

He didn't know she had any living relatives. Didn't believe she did. This was another lie. "When you were starving why didn't you go to your cousin? I'm sure she would have helped you out."

"She was in the trunk."

Jenna shook off his arm striding from him. Her back was stiff her chin tilted into the air.

Gil let her go, watching the gentle sway of her skirts as she walked. He was so very intrigued with her. She would bedevil him from here into eternity set his life into tempestuous waters. He didn't think she would be with him that long. The thought of living life without her wasn't something he wished to give consideration to.

Somehow, Gil couldn't see his life without her. The same feeling, he had for his son.

He heard her light tread on the steps. Listened as her door opened then closed. It was then he followed her. When he was inside her room, he spoke. "Be in my room tonight, Jenna."

Casually, he leaned against the door. His arms were crossed.

"If I'm not?" She stood in the middle of her room, fists clenched tightly the image fascinating.

What was in her eyes even more so? "I would see you stay in my room during the day also."

It was a threat he didn't know if he could carry out. If she had nothing to wear, it would not be too difficult.

"Go to the devil." Her chin tilted upward.

"I can lock you out of the adjoining room if I choose."

Her chin tilted regally. It was a position he usually quite liked. Today, he detested her inflexible nature.

He thought at this time he might be in hell. "In my room, Jenna. Tonight. Don't want to fetch you again. Naked. Ready and willing to be in my arms. There is no other way, *Cherie*."

Gil did want her to come to him, give everything she was, her heart as well as her soul. Wished she would make the first move, touch and caress him without coercion. Ah, she did give of herself. The offering just wasn't enough.

He thought on Etienne's words. The time to deal with a possible pregnancy was not now. If he had his way, she would bear him a son, a daughter too. She would learn to ignore the villagers. She wasn't a whore or a witch. She was important to him.

His gut coiled. He didn't like the thoughts festering inside. Didn't like what his actions did to her. Hell fire, he had no choice in any of this.

He'd never before been on such tenterhooks that he didn't understand his mind. She told him she would do anything. Her statement was for her son. He managed to take complete advantage.

He assumed the upper hand because he wanted her and in some elemental way needed her too. She filled a void in his empty life. In so many different ways she made him whole. Hell, she also gave him a reason to live.

When she strode from the room her fists clenched so tightly he was sure her nails grazed her flesh, he knew she would disregard his wishes again. His mind wandering, thoughts of her first and foremost in front, he found himself in the drawing room.

Chaos abounded.

It seemed while he was gone Elisa along with the children arrived. Margo toddled around the room discovering everything in reach with one pudgy fist in her mouth. Masson laughed at his sister while Brice trailed along behind the infant gently taking the objects from her then setting them back where she found them. This wasn't a scene he wanted to get used to even though he imagined a son of his own.

Margo finally gave up. She sat on the floor, tears in her eyes, sobbing loudly. Gil assumed for attention. Brice sat beside her. Offered her his wooden horse. With that accomplished, Margo gurgled happily, immediately sticking the head in her mouth.

The boy spoke to her in soft low words. Margo smiled at him. The one tooth she owned showing delightfully with her grin. It seemed amazing how she could go from sobs one moment to happy laughter the next. Until the moment he heard Elisa call Jenna a whore, his attention was focused exclusively on the children. He cringed at the label. The description was solely his fault. Before he could rise to her defense, Etienne spoke up in Jenna's defense.

"Jenna is not a whore even though Gil is trying his best to turn her into one," Etienne protected her while he was still trying to get his wits about him. "His selfishness is astounding. He listens to no one's good advice."

"Gil should be tarred and feathered," Elisa said furiously her eyes seeming to spit nails she was so angry. "He's no right to keep her in his bedchamber even though I'm certain she is willing. She wants everything he has to give. Wants his money along with this vineyard. While I don't like seeing a woman labeled because of a man's actions, if any one deserves it, Jenna does."

Gil's head swam as he listened to his two friends analyze his life as well as the woman he kept upstairs.

"Our dear friend, Gil, has given the woman he adores nothing. She doesn't even have anything decent to wear. Although I'm sure it is because Jenna refuses to accept his charity. Her actions speak loud and clear that she doesn't want him to give her anything. She doesn't want to be his mistress or his whore. Jenna has few options."

At the word "adores" spoken in his name, his head jerked up. *Adores. Did he?*

"He doesn't adore that woman. She is simply using her womanly charms to blindside him. He's still in mourning, an easy conquest. Jenna Bonnet takes advantage of the poor man at every opportunity. There isn't another woman he would install in his home."

Poor man. Install in his home.

"This poor man seduces and charms as if he is Casanova except Casanova used protection." He shot Gil a pointed look. "He has given her few opportunities to refuse him anything. If you would take the time to listen, you would know he gives her ultimatums she has no way to counter. In any case she is just like you, she cannot ignore the man just as you cannot ignore me. You turn to liquid in my arms. If you would watch them when they are together, you would come to realize Jenna adores him also."

Elisa tossed a pillow at him. He ducked striding toward her as if he meant to retaliate. "If Gil is Casanova, what am I?" He mused as he hovered above her.

Those were his words not Elisa's. He pulled her so she found herself flush against his body. His lips so close to hers Gil felt the need to turn away.

"Chopped liver, duck liver to be exact." She spoke primly, her eyes flashing at Etienne, daring him to kiss her.

Etienne growled low in his throat, "Chopped duck liver...?"

Margo let out a howl. Brice was there for her, giving her a piece of bread to eat. She cooed softly smiling at the lad as if she was already in love.

Etienne laughed then roared, his attention stolen from Elisa. "Brice will make a good big brother to the babe your Jenna most likely carries as we speak. Don't you think?"

"She is increasing?" Elisa sounded appalled. "She will have a death grip on you if that is the case. How can she do this when she knew you were still mourning your loses?"

Have his baby? Didn't seem either one spent too much time caring about a possible pregnancy. It was possible however still unlikely. They had not been sleeping together that long.

"Your husband is trying to rattle my nerves as well as my disposition. Jenna does not carry a child."

"Is it working?" Etienne asked still unable to stop laughing. "You cannot be sure. You've done all the necessary things for her to conceive. Done nothing to prevent conception."

"Hardly."

"If the woman is increasing, something needs to be done before she lays claim to everything you own. You must see your solicitor so you can get something in writing." Elisa pulled Margo onto her lap. The babe protested, her arms waving wildly seeming to want Brice's attention instead of her mother's.

"Bri..." Margo said, her chubby pint-sized hands reaching out to the little boy.

"Our little Margo has good taste in men. It seems she goes for those who can give her what she wants," Etienne said blandly as he watched the blood drain from Elisa's features.

If he didn't miss his guess, tonight Etienne was going to need the entire bag of chocolates he bought this afternoon to placate her. Elisa didn't look as if she was pleased with her husband.

"It's time for Brice to come with me."

Jenna entered the room in her threadbare dress. Just as she had done on the outing, she wore the shawl.

Gil watched her, his mind festering with all the thoughts and emotions that tumbled through him today. Both Etienne and Elisa gave him things to think about. A babe in her belly, *mon Dieu* but he hoped it was true. He found he wanted to be a father.

He was sure Jenna would not be pleased. So far, she said nothing. He counted the weeks they'd been together, slept together. Three. That was no indication. Everyday she'd been in his bed. He'd been deep inside her. Eventually, his seed would take root. Letting her go was impossible.

"I want to stay," Brice complained. "I like playing with Margo. Do I have to go to bed so soon?"

Jenna bent down so she was eye level with both children. "It's time for us to spend some time together. *"Viens avec moi.* You will see Margo in the morning, play with her then."

"Promise? If she wants, she can keep my horse."

As if she understood, Margo cuddled the wooden horse close to her precious face.

"Oui, of course you can play," Jenna said softly as she led Brice upstairs.

Watching her, his heart beat loudly beneath his chest. Jenna was a beautiful woman in so many ways. He didn't want to fall in love. He thought he might be doing that very thing.

For the longest time after Elisa and Etienne retired for the night, Gil sat in the drawing room sipping his brandy. He didn't want to go to his room. Didn't want to have to fetch her again. Gil needed Jenna warm as well as willing waiting in his bed for him.

He understood he challenged her, made her do things she thought were wrong. She didn't want to be forced. Sex with her was better the first time when she gave herself more freely to him. That was in the cottage he allowed her to live in. Was when she held her independence to her heart. When she wasn't known as his whore. Well, she was but it wasn't the same.

"Enfer!" he mumbled, his hand landing hard on the nearby table.

That was the hell of this situation. Everyone had an opinion as to who she truly was. No one knew her strength as he did. No one watched her battle to save her child. She gave all her food to the boy until she was virtually starving. He comprehended everything she gave up for her son.

His admiration grew. She was courageous.

He supposed it was time to find out if she obeyed. The hell of it was, she was the only human who ignored his orders. She did it with alacrity. Jenna Bonnet was not afraid of him. It wasn't as if she respected him either. She had no reason to do so.

Actually, all he knew about Jenna save the short history she elaborated when they first met was that she turned to liquid fire when he made love to her. He kissed and stroked her until she was frantic and wild with need for him. Gil downed the last of the brandy he was drinking. For a few more minutes, he stared out the window thinking of the night to come, his hopes as well as his fears. The moon was a slender slipper in the dark, velvet sky. Stars littered the blackness. He stood, stretched. With a great gulp of air, he started up the steps toward his bedchamber.

He stopped on the landing. His lashes fluttered closed for a moment as he imagined Jenna waiting for him in his bed. Despite the fact he wanted her compliance more than anything, he wished for it simply because it would mean she cared about him. He understood she would never surrender. Would not easily go to his bed. Perhaps she meant to fight him every step of the way. Fighting him might be her way of making sure he understood she was not his whore or his mistress. *Non*, but she was his lover.

Her fight was subtle though, non-combative.

With slow pronounced steps, he made his way down the long hallway. When he stood in the doorway to his bedchamber, his breath caught in his throat at the sight of her. Half his wish came true. She was in his room. Sound asleep on a wing chair in front of the fire.

He watched her. Saw her breasts move gently with each breath. She had removed the shawl. The outline of her nipples along with the curve of her breasts was very evident now as was her woman's mound. She should not be allowed anywhere outside this room attired as she was. Around her as well as the chair where she slept dresses were scattered. There had to be at least five.

Careful not to wake her until he was ready, he moved to her. Held each gown up for his inspection. It struck him these were hers from the previous time she lived at the chateau before she ran for her life. Each was fashioned from the finest material. It seemed though she chose dresses more suitable for work than the role he orchestrated for her. Jenna was mending them, or perhaps refashioning them so the dresses would fit her. She was slenderer now than she'd been before.

What role is that, old fellow? Am I going to admit I've turned her into something she isn't?

He stole a smidgeon of breath from the air. It wasn't enough to soothe the knowledge he might have done that very thing, turned her into a woman she didn't want to be. Perhaps her son was correct in his assumption. Maybe he was a mean man.

Overcome with different sentiments, Gil knelt beside her. Gently traced the line of her jaw, feeling a wealth of emotions rise within. She moaned softly, nestling her head against his hand.

So many times, she did that very thing after they made love. Tenderly, he kissed her forehead, her eyes, brushed his lips across hers. He cupped one breast in his hand, running a thumb over the hard crest as he watched her slowly open her eyes. That sleepy-eyed looked was always his undoing. Without conscious thought her hand rose to touch his chin.

"You're not in my bed, *Cherie*." *Enfer*, he'd not meant to say that.

She met him halfway. That act had to be good enough for him.

The sleepy-eyed look vanished as quickly as it appeared. She stiffened. "I meant to be. I fell asleep. If you would go away then come back in a few minutes, I would be where you commanded."

Commanded.

He supposed he deserved that from her. Ah, but she deserved more from him than orders. Holding up one of the gowns, "Is this what you were looking for in the attic. Don't understand why you couldn't tell me though."

Reluctantly, it seemed she nodded. By watching her, Gil caught the distinct impression she hid something from him. Jenna was not good at lying. She nervously ran her tongue along her lips before she looked away.

"These are...were mine. I didn't think I needed to ask permission."

Even though her body stiffened in rebelliousness he saw the

apprehension. "What are you afraid of? I'm not a monster."

Maybe he was. He'd refused to pay her, refused because she would have the means to buy something to wear. Nonetheless, she found some of her gowns upstairs in the trunks. The discovery defeated his intentions. He'd hoped she would find herself totally naked and unable to leave this room.

Her soft smile was hesitant. "Not sure I'm afraid. Thought you might deny me the gowns. Gil, I've nothing to wear. This gown I'm wearing gave out when I was tucking Brice into bed this evening. Unless you want me wearing nothing at all..."

It seemed she left the sentence hanging for him to fill in the details. He kept his laughter shuttered when she realized what she said.

Her statement was thought provoking. The image was definitely something he envisioned numerous times. Understood when the last gown was no more, she would be confined to the two rooms.

"*Non,* I wouldn't want that for you. I see you are taking them in." He held a blue and white day dress up as if inspecting it. The gown was suitable for her daily activities. As the dress was now, the bodice would gape open, as the shoulders would slip down her arms. The gown would do little to conceal her womanly charms.

Jenna studied the gown on her lap before looking to him. "They are too large for me now."

"Much too large," he agreed watching her reactions. "You're a very slender woman. Do you mean to sew these all tonight?"

"I was passing time until you returned. With so much to do I did not want to crawl into your bed prematurely."

He stood. Held out his hand to her. "*Coucher avec moi, Cherie.* You can finish these in the morning." Still, he held his hand toward her, inviting her to come sleep with him.

"I have your permission?"

His gut coiled. She shouldn't feel as if she needed his permission to do anything. Yet she did.

~ * ~

Elisa argued about Jenna and Gil's relationship with Etienne half the night. She knew exactly how to hold Jenna accountable while saving Gil from her. After hours of heated discussion, Etienne finally agreed with her. For some reason her husband believed in the woman. He would discover the truth about Jenna Bonnet this very afternoon.

Jenna stepped into the sitting room adjacent to the room Gil gave his friend. "You wanted to see me? I don't see why. We've nothing to speak about."

Elisa did. Jenna didn't appear to want to see her though. *Bien,* she should be afraid. All *Madam Bonnet*'s carefully laid plans to snare Gil were soon to be put to rest. Today, Jenna would show her hand. There would be nothing left for her at *Cimaron*. She would no longer be able to claim innocence. This was all for Gil's good.

"I did. I've a proposition for you. Tea?" Elisa queried, as she didn't wait for an answer.

Elisa handed Jenna a cup. Jenna looked at her, weariness in the shadowing of her eyes. "I would rather you tell me why you called me here. I'm not in the mood for niceties."

"You can guess why you are here. Are you in a rush to be sent on your way, revealed for the money-grabbing woman you are? Gil needs to see you clearly." Elisa spoke to her sweetly.

When Etienne suggested he accompany her during this confrontation, she told him no. Elisa was afraid her husband's soft spot for this woman would get in the way of the truth coming out.

Elisa wanted to free Gil as soon as possible. This was the only way she could think of that would divulge Jenna's true nature. She meant to offer Jenna something she wouldn't be able to refuse.

With shaking hands, Jenna set the cup on the table. She clasped her hands in front of her. Her chin tilted up as if she prepared herself. "Get on with it. What is your plan to set him free? Seems I'm the wronged party here even though I understand you won't see it that way."

"It's very simple my dear. I will give you the means to leave the chateau as well as Gil behind. I know you don't care about the man. You are after so much more, nonetheless I'll make it worthwhile."

"What is that? A means to leave him? I've no money, not one

franc."

"You do now, at least if you will accept this tiny offer. I've twenty thousand gold francs for you."

Elisa held her breath while she waited for the answer. She marveled at the way Jenna could manipulate as well as lie. She managed to lose all color from her face.

"What's the twist?"

Jenna tried to pick up the cup. Defeated she sat on the chair leaving the cup where it rested on the saucer.

"The twist? So, you are interested. Thought you would be. Doesn't surprise me either. Although my sweet husband was certain you wouldn't be attracted by the bribe. He believes the two of you are in love."

"As you said, let us get on with this." Jenna's chin tilted higher, her back stiffer.

Elisa was now more positive than ever her ploy would be a success. "If you accept the francs, you will leave here within the week. That will give you time to say your good byes as well as organize your affairs. You will promise to never return or seek out Gil again for whatever reason. I want you out of here by the end of the week. That gives you five days to make plans. I see you've come by a new dress. Did you finally allow Gil to purchase clothes for you?"

For the briefest moment, Elisa was certain she saw a sadness flash on Jenna's face. The next second, she thought Jenna might refuse.

She didn't deign to answer. "I will take the francs as well as agree to the conditions." Her voice was stiff, hard as she accepted the proposal.

It didn't sit well with Elisa that she was right about this woman. Until the second Jenna accepted the proposition, she wanted this. Now, she wished she were wrong. She wished she never offered the money. She did see a spark between them when they were together.

"Five days. Don't say anything to Gil or the deal is rescinded."

Elisa handed her the note for the francs. It was written to the bank in Bordeaux. The funds were more than enough to see her along with the boy settled comfortably until the boy turned of age and could then take care of his mother.

The small sound of despair she heard then saw in Jenna's eyes as she walked from the room stopped her for a moment. She was doing the right thing even though Etienne didn't believe the same way. Etienne told her Jenna would never leave Gil. Would never accept the bribe.

She did and that was that.

Etienne must have been watching. Grinning, sure of himself along with his assumptions he was in the room.

"Well?"

"She accepted." Elisa saw the muscle in Etienne's jaw twitch.

"I'll be damned."

Chapter Eight

The following days were bittersweet for Jenna. She knew now, more than ever before, she had to find the jewels because she wasn't going to accept the money Elisa offered for herself. She had a better use for Elisa Dubois' francs. She would never accept tainted money, blood money. It seemed all she had left was her pride. She wasn't going to let Gil or his well-meaning friends tromp it into the ground.

This time it was her pride at risk.

She spent every possible moment searching the third floor rooms for the jewels. Frantically, in her mind she went over every possible hiding place. In the evening she was always in Gil's bed, naked and willing. Jenna found she needed to savor every moment she could grab with him. Each night was a countdown to the day she would leave him.

Falling in love with him was not something she planned or wanted. His feelings for her didn't change. He still wanted her, lusted for her. Every night he made love to her as if it was the last time. He didn't love her.

He didn't know. Couldn't know in a matter of days she was leaving to never return.

Elisa would never tell him what transpired in that room. Jenna didn't know if Etienne learned what his wife did. In any case his knowledge wouldn't matter. As soon as he discovered the truth, that she took the money, he would be on his wife's side. Her one supporter in this strange charade would become another enemy.

Brice spent his days playing with Margo. It seemed the two were inseparable. Brice would miss the little girl when they left. Once more she would find herself forced to uproot her son. He never asked for his beloved horse to be given back to him. It was his only toy. Brice always said Margo needed it more than he did. Told her he was bigger now and didn't want the horse.

It was on the second day after Elisa's offer and her acceptance that Gil found her rummaging through a trunk of some of Brice's cast-off toys. She found a few favorites of his they didn't have time to take the first time she left this home. He was too old for them now. One was a doll he cuddled with every night. She pulled it out, hoping perhaps Brice would have something to gift Margo with when they left. The gesture would make him feel better because Jenna didn't have a doubt in her mind that Margo would cry.

"I see you're still rummaging through old things. What are you looking for now? If you need more gowns, you won't find any in there. If you're looking for your lost cousin, doubt if she's in there either."

Gil's languid yet amused voice shook her from her reverie. She had been deep in thought, absorbed by a past most of which she longed to forget.

She jumped, startled by his appearance. Something she hadn't expected. He was supposed to be outside overseeing the harvest. Her hands clasped beneath her chin, she turned swiftly. She'd been so lost she didn't hear his approach. He was always quiet. He had this ability to sneak up on her.

"Of course not, these are some of Brice's old toys." Jenna tried for indignation.

Searching here had been foolish at best. He might draw conclusions better left unsaid. She tugged in a deep breath of air as she watched him slowly uncross his arms.

"Nothing he would want to play with now that he's older."

His calm words had this way of infuriating her when he spoke of her son. She always felt as if he degraded Brice. Her son was who he was. He would never be like Lance, strong and capable as Gil always implied. Gil would always belittle Brice or turn from him.

"Don't suppose he would," Jenna agreed while she tried desperately to keep her simmering emotions in check. She cleared her throat from the moisture clogging it before she spoke again. "Margo might like some of these things. They were Brice's when he was about her age."

His amused chuckle didn't go unnoticed by her. "The baby has more toys than she knows what to do with. Besides, the doll is the only thing here I see that a girl might appreciate. What's the real reason, Jenna? You can't fool me. I know there is something else, another motive."

She lifted her shoulders slightly not appreciating the interrogation. "Curiosity as to what was left behind?"

"Curiosity?" He bent over the chest, examined a few items. Put them back inside. "Looks like garbage to me. The toys you've left on the floor are no better. What's the real reason?"

"Nostalgia."

She attempted another motive he might accept. The moment the single word left her lips she knew he would continue to question. He was intent on discovering her truth.

"Keep trying." His lips twitched in seeming amusement. "While you are at these lies why don't you tell me why you've obeyed my wishes the last couple of nights? You've been in my bed just as I dreamed. You've been passionate, more than willing."

"Forget it."

She didn't know what to tell him that he would believe. The truth certainly would never work. He would never imagine she loved him. If she told him she was leaving in a few days, that would negate the money. Keeping the secret was imperative.

"Don't want to forget anything. These have been the best damn nights of my life, *Cherie*. However, you don't do anything without a purpose." He stepped in her path when she tried to move around him. "Why?" His hands settled on her arms.

She lifted her shoulders. "Like the way you kiss."

Once again, she tried to move around him.

His fingers tightened their hold. He blocked her path. His eyes bored into hers, commanding without saying anything.

"You liked my kisses from the first one. I still had to fetch you from your bed then bring you to mine. You were trying to make a point that you weren't my whore. Now, you've turned yourself into what you would deny."

His words were too harsh. After Elisa's assumptions coupled with her proposition, the single word was too much. "Bastard!"

She slapped him hard. His head jerked back. A bold red handprint on his face was her reminder she lost her temper. This wouldn't do at all.

Rubbing his cheek, "Suppose I deserved that. Didn't mean to hurt you. I'm not going to quit here until you tell me the truth. What are you looking so diligently for, Jenna?" he paused seeming to wait for the right words to come to him. "What you don't seem to comprehend is that I've never thought of you that way. None of the labels fit you. You're not my whore or my mistress. I've come to care for you a great deal."

Care, not love.

"I need a glass of wine, on second thought a bottle. You can have your own bottle if you feel the same."

She was on her way, striding past him. This time he let her go.

"Does this mean you're willing to talk?"

He started after her, close on her heels then continued the conversation.

She needed to tell him at least part of the truth. The jewels were hers. She didn't think he would deny her them just as he didn't deny her the gowns. He would if he understood she was using them to leave the chateau behind forever.

Jenna stopped, turning to him. He nearly bumped into her. "Can we go somewhere private? Don't want Elisa to overhear anything that's said."

"Etienne?"

"*Non!* Neither of them."

"Interesting, however he doesn't seem to have that soft spot for you any longer. Perhaps you could tell me what you did to change his mind about you. It's possible Elisa finally convinced him of her feelings."

"Forget it. Elisa didn't change his mind. I did. There is nothing more to be said about that. Etienne will never defend me again. He's knows better."

They stopped in the middle of the long hallway. The stairs loomed in front of them. She looked longingly at them wishing the conversation was finished.

"So." He slowly rocked back on his heels keeping his gaze riveted on her. "Let me get this straight. We will need two bottles of wine, one for you, one for me. You will tell me what you search for in that moldy trunk of Brice's toys. After that you will enlighten me as to why you've become so biddable at bedtime, not that I've any complaints. Maybe, you will also explain what you did or said to create the dislike for you in a man who always found something good to say about you."

"*Oui.*"

Oh god, she could tell him only so much. Certainly, the truth about her willingness in bed was not part of those truths. Could not tell him she loved him. Had always wanted to be in his bed, willing. Needed to savor the few remaining moments with him so she could hold them close to her heart for the rest of her life. Could not tell him she agreed to leave him as well as the chateau behind for the sum of twenty thousand gold francs. How could anyone have so much money they could offer another person so much to vanish from their life?

She wasn't even so much as disappearing from Elisa and Etienne's life but from Gil's. That thought left heaviness in her heart she didn't want to acknowledge now that she only had a few days left with him. She meant to cherish every moment she could find. In the end, he would wonder why. After she left, he would figure it all out. Elisa would make sure she told him about the francs. Gil would understand she wanted the money more than she wanted him.

With her hand firmly held in his, they made their way to the cellar then to the back where the best vintage wines were waiting to be sipped. She didn't want to sip. She needed to down the entire bottle in a gulp. The last few days had been too harrowing for anything else. Now that she decided to explain what she searched for, her nerves were a tangled mess.

After two bottles of Bordeaux were procured, they stopped in the kitchen. Gaby always left sliced ham along with cubes of camembert and brie that would go nicely with a baguette for a late night appetizer if one wanted to indulge. It seemed Gil had that very notion on his mind. He piled a tray high with food. The afternoon might indeed run into the night. A fire blazed in the hearth casting warm golden shadows on the walls. He set the scene. The atmosphere, one of romance, gave her heart a gentle squeeze. She did want to savor every moment of her last remaining time.

After candles were lit, he poured.

He set a small plate of food in front of her tempting her grumbling stomach.

He lifted his glass; a broad smile slanted across his handsome features. He was so tall, his shoulder's broad. "To us, Jenna. I want you in my life for a long time. Forever if possible."

That was what she also wanted. It wasn't to be. While she tried to memorize his face, guilt coiled in her stomach. The food she ate seemed to seethe inside her belly with turmoil. She swallowed the bile threatening. Downed a strong portion of the wine.

Blood drained from her face.

"You look as if you saw a ghost. Did I say something wrong? What is it? What has you so bothered you've turned a deathly shade of white?" he asked her, a puzzled and concerned expression creasing his too handsome face.

Jenna understood this was not going to be easy. Somehow, she needed to figure out a way to school her features. "Nothing is wrong. Everything is right."

She sipped again. The wine settled her overanxious nerves even while it pooled heavily in her stomach.

Everything is wrong. Nothing is right.

"You're sure. You don't look well. Should we put this conversation off to another time?"

Oh god, yes. *S'il te plait* another time later, much, much later. If she never had to explain anything to him it would be too soon. She didn't want to talk. Can we just go to bed didn't seem appropriate at the moment. That was what she wanted. To be held in his arms. She only had a few nights left.

He ate. Watched her as the seconds ticked by seeming to wait for her to begin the conversation.

Jenna drank more wine. It was delicious sliding down her throat as if it was water. She breathed deeply, calming her rattled nerves the best she could.

As she inhaled a long draught of much needed air, she saw a small tick of amusement on his lips. If he understood what was actually happening here, he wouldn't see anything humorous.

"More wine?" He was solicitous, seemed to have a never-ending supply of patience while all she could do was sit quiet while she slowly drank the entire bottle. Falling asleep because of the wine would hardly suit her motives here today.

"*S'il te plait.*"

She couldn't put this off much longer. Oh God, oh god, how could she tell him any of this.

He sipped. Set his glass on the nearby table before he stretched out his legs. Unlike her he appeared relaxed, oblivious of the time slipping by. "I've got all night if that's what you want. Why don't we start with the reason you searched through the toy trunks?"

"Good idea," she said too quickly.

When she didn't say anything more, one eyebrow launched itself toward the heavens. "Go on."

Nervous energy entered into her with more and more intensity. She swept her tongue across her lips. Couldn't help but drink again. She fiddled with her fingers.

"Well..." she began.

"Well?"

He didn't sound angry or impatient. Perhaps he truly thought they had all night. He reached over to take her shaking hands in his. His were warm. When he traced gentle circles on the underside of her wrists, she needed to forget everything except him. Melting inside at this moment was not an option if the conversation was to move forward.

"D-don't do that." Her voice shook while all of her cried out for more.

"Why?"

"If you keep that up, we'll never have the conversation."

She was still shaking, trembling with emotions as well as fears. She wasn't going to give anything away. Reminded herself she had to find the jewels. If she didn't tell him, he would find her searching the attic again and again. She needed to know now if he would deny her access to the third floor and her explorations.

"I'm not going to stop touching and exploring the parts of you I love, the parts that respond to my caresses. You will just have to find a way to deal with this."

"The trunk."

She sipped the wine again, this time trying to adjust her mind to the horrible thoughts he might have when she told him.

"The trunk. The toys. You bent over with your sweet derrière in the air. An interesting sight, almost gave into my baser needs. If I ever find you that way again, perhaps I will."

"Yes, well, I was looking for something."

He laughed softly almost as if he was trying for caution in his responses. "I thought as much. Truly didn't think you were purposely attempting to seduce me in that manner. Although it did have that affect, nonetheless, I was able to control myself."

"Control yourself?"

"Don't believe we've ever made love in that fashion." He baited her. She had no idea what he meant by his words.

She thought her eyes were about to cross. "In what manner?"

"From behind you, me deep inside."

Her eyes did cross. She licked her lips. "You can do that?"

He laughed out right then at her bafflement. "If we ever finish this interesting *tête-à-tête*, we can go back to the third floor. I can show you."

"Show me...?"

"After you tell me what you were looking for along with a couple of the reasons why you are so eager to be in my bed. Maybe why your staunchest supporter now calls you the enemy."

"Oh..." Her heart forgot to beat for a moment. She would have to figure out how to tell him certain truths without revealing it all.

"We can start with what you were looking for."

"You're not going to like this. Don't know...was looking for something that was mine when I lived here. If I found it, would you let me keep it or would you claim it for yourself?"

Her question was no longer hypothetical. It was very real. If he would claim the jewels for his own, in the process deny her possession of the stones there was no earthly reason to continue to search.

"We won't know until you tell me."

His hands were clasped on his belly, his gaze focused on her. The smile he sported a few minutes ago vanished. This time his voice was harsh or at least to her ears the words sounded that way. She didn't want him to be angry. He would be though.

She inhaled let the breath out quickly before sucking in another large bite of air. "We know that, well you know, everyone knows that Jacques liked to parade me in front of whoever he could find. He wanted to show off his wealth and prosperity." She closed her eyes trying to will herself to continue.

"What does that have to do with your search in the toy trunk?" He seemed patient while he sipped again.

"Jewels, I was searching for the jewels I didn't have time to take with me when I ran." She studied her feet, the floor and the rug, anything to keep from looking at him.

"That wasn't so hard."

It was terrifying. "Will you allow me to keep them?"

"Don't you have to find them first?" He leaned forward his smile still not apparent. "Why do you want to find them so badly?"

His voice was harsher now, more so demanding an answer she didn't want to give. He knew she would want to use the money they would bring her to flee.

Now, he did sound angry. Jenna supposed he must have guessed why she would search for them. He must understand she wasn't pleased with the living situation she found herself forced in. Didn't appreciate the labels attached to her name.

"Because they are mine."

"Try again."

She lifted her shoulders trying to shrug off her reasons. Telling him the truth was simply out of the question, yet she could tell him part of it. "I could pay the villagers back for the labor they were barely paid by my husband."

"Were there a lot of valuable jewels?"

She nodded before she understood what he was asking. "There would be a substantial amount left over."

The truth was easier to deal with than lies and half-truths. Besides the time it took him to figure everything out was minimal. He would guess soon if he hadn't already made the assumption.

"What would you do with the rest of the money? Would you wear the rest of the jewelry?" Frown lines creased his forehead. His eyes drew together. "Don't want you wearing anything I haven't given you."

"You know what I would do. Doubt if I have to spell it out."

Her heart pounded desperately beneath her ribs. She wiped her sweaty hands on her dress.

"I shouldn't allow you to continue your search. However, I will. I want you with me because here is where you want to be. If you have the funds to leave me, well, then, your heart will be revealed."

It would not, nevertheless she couldn't tell him that.

"This revelation most likely also tells me in a roundabout way why you've been so willing and warm these last few days. Drink your wine, Jenna." Gil stood, striding around the room, his fists tightened, shoulder muscles clenched.

He was angry, furiously so. She knew he would be.

I came to your bed willing and warm as you asked because I love you, Gil Allemand. No other motive brought me into your arms.

She couldn't tell him that either.

"Is this the reason Etienne is also angry with you? Because he understands you're leaving me?"

He handed her an explanation that was part truth although the assumption wouldn't tell him everything. She nodded, certain her despair was evident in her face. Her eyes welled with moisture.

"He thought we were in love," Jenna told him, the emotion was one sided at best. "If I leave you, it means he was wrong."

"You aren't in love with me. You're eager to leave as well as get on with a new life away from the chateau and everything I hold dear."

She tilted her chin telling him an undeniable truth. "The way you feel about my son. The way you treat him, I could never live with that. You want to keep me here until you grow bored. Gil, I deserve better than this conduct. There hasn't been one man in my life, including you who has treated me better than the dirt beneath their shoes."

"That's not true, Jenna..."

He stopped. Scrubbed his hand across his face.

It seemed he could not deny that he treated her poorly. The proof was in the way he dealt with her on a daily basis. He was an arrogant bastard. "You have not done anything to harm me except steal my pride from me under the guise that your actions would keep me safe. Set me up in your bedchamber as your plaything."

It would be best for her to sever all bonds between them. It was the only way she would survive after she left.

~ * ~

I've loved you, Cherie.

"You can look for the jewels. If you're so desperate to leave me, I will help you find them. Be it known to you, it is not what I want." As the meaning of her words took root his body trembled with a burning need to shake sense into her. Leaving here was the worst possible course she could take. He didn't like to believe she would feel happier if she weren't with him.

She was safe here. He could protect her. On the road, on her own, she would never be protected. She would always find herself looking over her shoulder. Would always have men with propositions she would decline whenever possible. What would happen when a man refused to take no for answer?

What would happen when her funds ran out? She would be faced once again with starvation. She would give all that along with all she possessed to her son. Moisture threatened to fill his eyes as well as clog his throat. As he tried to think with a clearer mind, he pushed the moisture away.

He couldn't let Jenna leave. She would stay here with him. The trinkets weren't where she put them, one of Jacques' relatives must have found the jewels, used them for whatever they could gain. Maybe Jacques found the jewels. Sold them then used the funds to help support his habits.

Rumors abounded that in the end the man was addicted to opium. If that was true, no wonder the chateau along with the vineyard failed to provide the monies *Monsieur Bonnet* needed to pay his taxes. As Jenna told him, her husband was also addicted to ladies of the evening. He was kicked out of Angel's brothel. He must have found relief in some of the seedier establishments.

"Gil?" Jenna placed her hand on his shoulder. "What is it?"

He didn't want another surprise tonight. Couldn't tell her how much he was afraid for her. He wondered then how much Elisa played in this sudden decision of hers to leave. Tomorrow, he would confront the woman. He no longer cared if he'd once thought he was in love with Elisa. After all these years, he finally understood why she never returned his feelings. Their love wasn't to be simply because the love wasn't there for either of them.

It took Etienne five long years to come home to the woman he could love for the rest of his life. Gil prayed now that it would not take that long for he and Jenna to settle their differences.

"You are certain of this decision?" he asked hoping and praying she would change her mind. If not that, maybe he could find a way to influence her to stay with him.

He could not. All he could wish for was that the jewels would not be found. If she didn't find the stones, she would not be able to leave.

"More wine?" he asked trying for a lighter note on this day of revelations that left him floundering.

Lowering her lashes before she looked up, "More wine would be nice. I feel as if I've been beaten over the head with a sledgehammer. Relieved, though, to have all this out in the open."

Gil thought those words summed up his feelings also. When he looked at her, he suddenly realized all was not in the open. Still, she held herself back. Kept something important from him. There were unspoken truths yet to be told. Perhaps, she told him only what she felt absolutely necessary, half-truths, partial truths. Before she found her ticket away from here, he needed to discover what she wasn't telling him.

Etienne was his first stop, Elisa his second. Jenna would never fully be his unless he found a way to love her son as well.

He knew that.

She told him so. He didn't need to be hit over the head to understand that important fact.

The thought widened the chasm in his heart. He held out his hand to her, hoping she would put all this to the side then come to his bed again. Her hand in his was cold. He understood just how the fears she dealt with affected her.

Well hell, maybe he didn't understand anything.

When Jenna nestled into his arms, her tears wetting the fabric of his shirt, he understood the real possessive need to right whatever wrongs happened to her. If he guessed correctly, it was two days ago. That was when everything changed. Elisa told him they would be gone in five days' time. His stomach rolled.

He ran his hands along her back. She lifted her face, gazing into his eyes. "Love me, Gil," she whispered softly, the breath she stole from the air brought her breasts pushing against his chest.

Just as always, she melted sweetly.

Just as always, his body hardened in anticipation.

He wished these moments with her tonight would last him a lifetime. Understood they would not. Prayed for a divine intervention. God seemed to have abandoned both of them. If his guesses were correct, he had three more days and nights with her. For some reason he couldn't be positive about, there was more fueling her departure than just the lost trinkets. She couldn't afford to leave unless she found the jewels. Once again, his mind twisted to Elisa and Etienne.

The source of francs had to come from the Dubois. Etienne would roast in hell if he discovered his longtime friend had a role in this. Jenna was a survivor. If either one of his friends offered her the financial resources to leave, she would take the funds then run. He didn't blame her. Indeed, in too many ways to count he was proud of her.

She suffered two years with nothing except her wits along with the few francs she could earn. If she accepted money, Etienne would believe her to be the money-grabbing woman Elisa thought she was. At least Elisa never believed she was a whore. The woman understood that label was his fault.

That evening their loving was bittersweet. Afterward, he held her in his arms, soothing her as she held back tears. Tears he understood now were because she was not going to be here in two more days.

She wasn't going anywhere.

The night passed slowly. She slept. He did not. Gil watched the day gradually lighten as the sun rose. Reveled in the soft play of Jenna's silken locks against his chest. This was how life should be. He had the means as well as the motive to keep her here in his bed.

If she bolted, he would follow. He would track her to the end of the earth if necessary. Hell, he'd even follow her to the moon if that were possible.

He left her asleep, dressed then made his way downstairs to the kitchen where he grabbed a bite to eat.

"When are you going to do right by Jenna and marry her? You know you want to do just that," Gaby asked a bit of irritation in her voice. "She's a sweet lovely girl. She doesn't deserve the insults she receives."

Gil choked on the bite of scone he chewed. "I'm working on it."

Christ, but this wasn't what he expected from his cook.

"You understand something is happening. This household has been turned upside down the last two days. You need to get to the bottom of what is going on before it's too late. If you don't, you'll have too many regrets. I know your friends are behind this. Whatever this is." Gaby shook her big wooden spoon at him looking as if she meant to rap his head with it.

"I've every intention. Going to start with Etienne. Thought he was a friend." Of course, Etienne would believe he was doing what was best for him. He wasn't. Etienne wouldn't know he loved Jenna. Now that he knew her, he didn't think he could live without her.

"Should start with the lady. She's the catalyst in all this. If you'd marry Jenna, none of this would be happening. She's getting ready to leave. I can feel it in my bones. You know that don't you? Do you want her to run away from you? Thought you had more backbone. Thought you would fight for what you wanted."

He pulled up to a stop on his way out the door. "Why do you think she's leaving? Have you heard something I should know about?"

"No."

"Then...?"

He needed to understand more of this. Wished to find a way to get ahead of this situation before he looked up and she vanished. How dare Elisa set something into motion that would affect him so profoundly without telling him about it.

"Know so because of the way Jenna's been acting, all melancholy and wistful. She tears up at the slightest word. She's spent time wandering over the property. Even walked down to the cottage. She sat on the porch swing for the longest time. At first, I thought you might have relented. You know, given her and the boy permission to move back in."

"I would if I thought it was safe for her to be alone. Nothing has happened to change the minds of anyone who condemns her."

"You should look to your guests if you want to know the source of her despair. Never seen her look so sad not even when she first arrived here and she was starving herself. If you let her go, in no time she'll be feeding everything to her son. She'll be nothing but a rack of bones."

"Gaby, keep an eye out for me. Believe from what little she's told me she'll be gone in two more days. Might even be sooner. You wouldn't know anything about jewels that have been hidden?"

She paused her hands deep in bread dough. "Didn't work for *Monsieur Bonnet*. From what I saw when he was the lord here, Jenna didn't wear a lot of jewels unless she was out with her husband. If there are any left here, I'd be surprised. Heard his relatives stripped the place bare of anything valuable. The *Monsieur* might have sold them because of his addiction. Might have given them to his ladybirds to pay for services rendered."

That is what he thought also. "I'm going to talk with Etienne. If he can't shed some light on this, I'll have to see Elisa."

"You go. Get to the bottom of the drama before you're seeing your bed empty. Now, I know you love Jenna. Do what a man should do. Tell her before it's too late. Don't let that little lady get away from you. We both know she is good for you. Gives you reason to laugh. Never seen you happier." Gaby punched the dough as if giving emphasis to her words. "By the way, you need to figure out how you can love that son of hers." Gaby was shaking her doughy finger at him. "Even if you tell her you love her, she's not going to want to stay with you if you keep treating Brice as if he doesn't exist."

Well, he told himself, probably deserved what Gaby lectured him about. He did want to feel different about the boy. Something intangible kept getting in his way. How the hell did Gaby know he loved Jenna? He didn't even know that until last night. Thoughts of her leaving brought the sentiment to the forefront again.

Gil found Etienne in the drawing room. He was playing with Brice and Margo. The look on his friend's face when he walked in sent him more information than he needed.

Etienne looked guilty as hell.

"You, along with Elisa could have let us figure this out for ourselves. You didn't have to meddle. It wasn't well done of you." After pouring them both a brandy he sat down by Etienne.

"Sure you want to do this with the boy where he can hear everything? Hell, she wasn't supposed to say a word to you. She promised. Masson, take Margo and Brice outside to play."

"Jenna didn't say anything. I guessed. You proved my point just now. What was it you and Elisa did to Jenna to cause her to make plans to leave me?"

The brandy burned on the way down. When Etienne greeted him with a face that said nothing, gave nothing away, Gil understood he guessed right. Etienne was too good a spy to give his emotions away.

"When you finally discover the truth, you'll appreciate the fact we saved you from her claws. Elisa was correct in her assumption that Jenna is after all you have, as well as all you are. Simply put, I was wrong. Couldn't let the woman hurt you."

"As far as I'm concerned if she asks me, she can have anything she wants. I don't intend to deny her."

In the short time Jenna had been with him his feelings changed more than he'd ever thought possible. Oh, from the moment he saw her, he wanted her, lust ruled him. Even as thin as she was that first afternoon, there was something about the woman that called his name.

With great alacrity he fought his feelings. Told himself it was hunger. Told himself that he'd not had a woman in so long any female would serve his purpose. Now he understood she was fascinating, intriguing. She gave him reason to laugh.

"In a short time, you will feel different." Etienne told him. "If you love her, you will understand she doesn't have the same sentiments as you do. It's best you get over this sudden infatuation, sooner than later."

"Jenna cannot afford to feel or to care for anyone except for her son. Every man she's known has treated her poorly, including me. I intend to change that."

He did by asking her to marry him. He could change all that went before.

"Including you...is that what has you so blind you cannot see what is right before your face? Jenna is a brilliant actress. She blinded me with her smile, her seeming genuineness where you are concerned. There isn't an honest or sincere bone in her body. What you see is all a an artfully constructed sham."

"I'm not blinded. I pray she is not acting. In any case, it doesn't matter. I intend to marry her as soon as she will say yes."

"You best hurry with your proposal."

He couldn't hurry. Had to first find a way past his feelings for Brice. The children were playing outside. When he watched the way Brice took care of Margo, Gil knew the child had a good heart. He comprehended his problem. Brice was not Lance, never would be. He had to come to terms with that.

Elisa stood in the doorway listening. Gil wondered how he ever thought himself in love with her. Ah, he had no idea what love felt like back then. He was just enamored of her, all that pale white hair.

"What have you heard?" Etienne rose to usher his wife into the room.

She waved her hand in the air, "Enough, nothing. You cannot mean to wed that woman."

"In the end it will all be up to Jenna. Yes, she is the woman for me. I've known since that afternoon when she begged me to hire her. When all I wanted was to wallow in self-pity and despair, she woke me up helped me feel again. I'm almost whole now because of Jenna."

In this instance, all he had to do was convince two people he was not such a bad sort. Jenna would be easier than the little boy.

"Did she tell you what she accepted?" Elisa asked as she picked apart the scone. The bread fell in tiny pieces on her plate.

"She's told me nothing. I'd hoped one of you would enlighten me. Doesn't seem Etienne meant to do so. How about you?"

"The telling is up to Jenna. She promised not to say. If she does, our offer is forfeit," Elisa said, her voice so very soft.

For a moment Gil thought he detected a trace of guilt. It vanished as quickly. "Doesn't matter. I won't let her go without a fight. Don't understand why all this is a secret."

Inside Gil seethed. His friends betrayed his trust. Elisa offered Jenna something she couldn't refuse. Without either elaborating he had a good idea. They would tempt her with the one thing she needed most. Money.

Most likely enough francs so she would not want for anything for a long time. Etienne had the resources. Elisa had the gall. For the time being, he couldn't stand to see them or talk to them.

He strode outside.

He stopped when he saw Brice playing alongside Margo. Masson was there too, however, he didn't seem concerned with the little girl. Brice doted on her. If he thought she was doing something that might get her into trouble, he would head her off. Truly, the site endeared the boy to him. Despite his efforts to the contrary, the anger persisted. No matter how many times he told himself it was not Brice's fault Lance died, he could not bring himself to care about the boy.

Leaning against a tree, arms crossed, he watched them until he could watch no longer. He pushed away from the tree intending to find Jenna. When she wasn't anywhere to be found at the chateau, he strode down the hill to the gatekeeper's cottage.

She sat on the porch swing, her head tilted toward the sky. He couldn't help but watch her. Tearing the truth from her would be difficult if not impossible. When he reached the porch, he continued inside, rummaging in the kitchen. There he found one of the bottles of wine he brought to the house the first night he made love to her.

With two glasses in one hand, the bottle in the other he joined her on the swing. He didn't ask if she wanted anything. Both glasses were full as he handed her one. All he wanted was to talk.

"Do you remember our first time?" he paused hesitating.

For the first time he could remember, he was unsure of himself.

She sipped then nodded. "It's too early for wine. You know that don't you?"

"Never," he told her softly, his heart pounding. "It's almost noon."

"Are you plying me with wine so you can have your wicked way with me?" She smiled a bedazzling smile at him.

Gil heard the tiniest bit of humor in her voice. "Don't have to use wine, *Cherie*. All I have to do is touch you."

He ran a fingertip down the column of her throat, gazed at her as she shuddered with the contact.

"You will not..."

"Do as I please?" he asked laughing as he sipped the wine watching the darkening of her eyes. Knew the very real need to pull her onto his thighs then into his arms. He wanted her to straddle him again. Needed to feel the hot moisture centered in her.

"I was trying to enjoy the warm sunshine. Attempting to listen to the sounds of autumn."

"Are you succeeding?"

Broaching the topic of Elisa and Etienne's machinations would ruin these few moments for both of them.

"Not now. You interrupted."

"Because I'm here? Hmm..."

His hand rested on her thigh, squeezed lightly knowing he could take this as far as he wanted.

"Because you are here. You test and challenge me. While I want to push your hand away, you know I won't."

"Gaby tells me you've been reminiscing, going places we've been as if you want to remember. When are you going to the village?" His question surprised him as much as it seemed to surprise her.

She gasped in a breath of air. When she turned to confront him, he saw the truth in her eyes. What he guessed was written clearly for any fool to see.

"You are not to go there by yourself. I won't take you. After what Etienne thinks you've done, he won't lend a hand."

"The only control you have over me is where I sleep."

The stubbornness in her voice set him on edge. He couldn't watch over her every second of every day. Perhaps for the remaining two and a half he should do just that.

"Going into the village will not be safe."

"I understand. It's something I have to do," she told him her voice soft.

Concern for her rose higher. Fear next. He wouldn't allow her to risk any silken part of her. Giving into her need he agreed. "If you must go, I'll take you."

"I don't see how that will work. I've need of privacy." Turning she touched his face with the palm of her hand. "You have to trust me in this."

"I will drive you wherever you wish. Will wait outside if you're thinking of visiting *Madam Macon*." He knew he guessed right when her eyes widened. "She is the only person you could possibly have unfinished business with in the village."

Her back stiffened, "*Tres bien*. You can take me. However, you will wait outside."

"Only if she is in her home. If she at the store I will insist that you let me accompany you."

"Nothing has happened since the cross burning. Your show of force the other day must have had an impact."

"When do you want to go?"

"Now would be a good time."

Reluctantly, he put the bottle of wine away. Holding out his hand to Jenna, he waited, holding his breath.

~ * ~

Jenna didn't understand how Gil guessed so much about what was now happening in her life. Without her telling him anything, it appeared he could read her mind. She supposed that ability must make him excellent at his first chosen profession. Etienne told her he was exceptional.

216

Two nights was all she had left with him. Even if she didn't find the jewels, she would have to leave. She gave her word. Once Gil learned she accepted the francs, he would no longer want her. The knowledge she came so close to love tore at her heart, ripping her apart.

Today the scent of autumn filled the air. The grapes were almost all harvested. The weather would turn cold soon. The outside air was not too cold. Still, she felt the cold to the bottom of her toes. Protecting Brice at any cost, yes, she had to figure out how to do that.

Jenna decided she would return to Bordeaux. Angel had been good to her. She could work there at least until Elisa told Angel what she accepted from her. If she was lucky, she might make it through the winter before her luck gave out.

Luck. Hah!

It was so elusive. She didn't know how to find it, let alone hang on to it.

Gil pulled to a stop in front of *Madam Macon*'s home. Jenna prayed the woman was there. She might not have the opportunity to return.

This time her luck did hold. The elderly grandmother answered the door. "*Madam Bonnet*? You changed your mind? I'm so glad to see you. Come in, come in."

"I wondered if I could see your granddaughter. I cannot cast a spell or weave any magical potion that might cure her. I don't have that ability. All I wanted was to tell you...to tell her that I hope and pray she gets better. I brought her a doll." Nervous, her hand shaking, Jenna held up the doll that at one time was her son's favorite. "She might like to play with this. Brice liked the doll when he was her age."

Madam Macon moved away from the door. She smiled yet it seemed bittersweet. When Jenna looked over her shoulder at Gil, she saw his frown. He nodded as if to tell her she could go on ahead.

She smiled back at him then followed the woman through the house to the bedroom. The little girl was on the bed, her face ashen. A soft smile parted her small lips as her lashes fluttered open.

"*Bonjour,*" she said softly. "Who are you?"

"A friend of your grandmother. I brought you something." Once again, Jenna held out the doll for the little girl's inspection. "It was my son's a long time ago. He's too old for it now. We both thought you might enjoy playing with it. He used to call her Lillian. I'm sure he won't mind if you give her another name."

The girl nodded, *"Merci,* Lillian is fine. I wouldn't want to confuse her,*"* she said even as she looked as if she would fall asleep at any second. For a moment, Jenna held the girl's hand in hers. Icy fingers began to warm. Her eyes fluttered open. She smiled again then she was fast asleep.

Jenna's heart broke. For so long she'd been afraid for Brice. His health had been so fragile. She wished with all her heart she did have the power to heal. She did not.

"Viens," *Madam* murmured. "She will sleep now. It was nice of you to bring her something. She has so little. We don't have the money to buy her gifts."

As they walked through the shabby home Jenna turned, hoping the woman would not look on her gesture as charity. "I've also something for you, to use to help the sweet child. Perhaps you can use this to take her to Paris. There might be a doctor in the city who can heal her. If I could, I would. I hope you understand that."

Madam Macon opened the envelope. Jenna held her breath, hands clasped tight beneath her chin as she waited.

The woman gasped. Seemed to read the letter two or three times. "Is this a dream? Twenty thousand gold francs?" The woman's hand was clutched to her bosom. *"Merci, merci,* may God be with you. I will take her tomorrow if her parents will allow me to do so. I will tell them it is your generosity that might save her life."

"You too, may God be with the child. I will say prayers for her speedy recovery."

Chapter Nine

Two days later, Jenna waited until Gil left the house. She prayed he would be involved with his work long enough she could get a few miles from the chateau before he realized she left. There wasn't a moment that passed by that she didn't doubt he would come after her. In any case, she'd done her part. Etienne and Elisa could rest assured she would not return unless forced. Gil knew nothing about what his friends did. It would remain so.

For some reason, she didn't believe Gil would force her home. After she left, his two friends would tell him about the money. He would be furious. All the trust they built together would vanish with the truth. Gil would believe the worst.

"Why are you crying, *maman*?" Brice asked as they loaded the buggy. "I wish we didn't have to leave. Did the mean man make you?"

No, it was the man you liked, the man you adored who is giving me no choice.

She meant to take the buggy and horse he offered for her use. He never rescinded the gift. So, this small act could not be considered stealing. He would have done so if he'd known what she was about. The only mare she arrived here with would never make the journey nor would the wagon. The trade wasn't fair. No, but it was just.

Jenna placed their belongings in the back. Gaby knew she was leaving. She made a lunch as well as a huge dinner for them to take with them. Gil's cook gave her a lecture that singed her ears. The words made no difference. Gil would throw her out when he learned the truth. Leaving would occur now or later. She couldn't bear to see him furious with her.

Shaking her finger, "You will not get far down that road before *monsieur* comes to find you. You understand that fact now, don't you? This is a waste of precious time, both yours along with his. You should stay put. Tell him what happened as well as why." Gaby told her when she handed the basket to her. "Where do you think you will sleep tonight?"

She didn't know. Wasn't looking forward to the cold ground. The buggy was big enough for Brice to sleep in, not for both of them.

"I will find an inn. I'm sure I can work for a meal and a bed."

She understood all too well what most proprietors wanted from her. They wanted her to work on her back. If that happened, she would move on until she had no strength to travel farther. There must be one man in this world who didn't want her for his pleasure.

"You and I both know what will be asked of you. If you weren't so beautiful, the men would give you work in the kitchen or serving. It's a shame that man of yours didn't have the courage to come out and tell you how much he loves you. To marry you, it would have solved all your problems, his too."

"Gil?" she coughed knowing Gaby was wrong. "He doesn't love me."

No, he is just like the others. He wants me in his bed. For her, the difference was that she wanted to be in his bed. She'd been willing to sell her reputation, her body, for that very purpose.

"We've got to leave." Jenna gave her a quick hug. "If I get the chance, I'll write. Know that I plan to ask Angel for help."

"Elisa's mother? He'll be after you as soon as he returns from the village," Gaby said, shaking her finger one more time. "He'll catch up to you before you have time to reach the first inn."

"Most likely. Luck has always eluded me," she murmured as she opened the door to leave. "When he learns the truth, he won't want me back."

"That's just not true."

It was but she'd never convince Gaby of that.

"It will be your lucky day if he finds you before you have to spend the first night under the stars and on the cold ground."

All of Gaby's words echoed in her head as she sent the little buggy in the opposite direction of the village. It wasn't anything she didn't think of herself. The road led straight to Bordeaux. If all went well, it would take two nights to reach her destination. She could ration the food to last that long. She could go without food for two days. She'd done it before.

Her stomach growled as she tried to ignore the rumbling. Brice would be just as hungry.

Every time she heard the beat of horse hooves behind her, she pulled off the road to hide in the trees. Every time the horse and rider passed by her heart lodged in her throat and her breath quickened. She didn't know if she was afraid he would find her or afraid he would not.

She bordered on hysteria.

After several miles passed behind her, she pulled off the road. In a secluded spot she handed Brice a half sandwich made of ham and cheese. Gaby packed enough milk for the evening meal since it wouldn't save. At the bottom of the basket there were three bottles of *Cimaron's* finest Bordeaux.

Jenna couldn't help the small giggle erupting. It was just like Gaby to put something in the food basket she couldn't give to Brice. After opening the bottle, she poured a small measure into a cup.

"Are you only going to drink wine?" Brice asked, his little voice sending a shiver of guilt down her spine. "Don't you need food too?"

Brice had been safe at *Cimaron.* How did she allow Elisa to drive her off?

It was, she decided, stubborn pride. Even when she accepted the francs, she knew she would give them to the little girl. She loved Gil. Would never take money to leave him. In all honesty, she believed with all her heart she would find her baubles. Jenna's baubles, she laughed.

"Wine for me, ham sandwich for you. We won't make it to the inn tonight. There is only an hour of light left. Suppose we can make our beds here. What do you think?" She ruffled his hair getting a sharp look in response.

The floor of the glade was moss-covered. Tall trees would give some shelter in case of rain. A stream ran close by. They had all the amenities of home.

"I think we should go back to the chateau. I don't want to sleep on the ground. Margo will be sad if I don't tuck her in tonight. She gave me back my horse."

Ah, well, those were almost her sentiments except for tucking Margo into bed. She knew she'd like nothing more than to have Gil crush her against his broad chest as well as take her to his bed.

"We can't go back. *Maman* did something for a special little girl. Because of that we cannot return to *Cimaron*. I promised to leave."

No, she sold her soul then lost her heart. Those two trampled on it as if her feelings meant nothing.

"I didn't make a promise. You could leave me there."

For a few seconds she couldn't breathe. "You would rather live with the mean man than me?"

"I didn't mean it that way. I just miss Margo. Maybe someday I can have a little sister."

"Margo is going to her home tomorrow. She doesn't live at *Cimaron*."

Jenna couldn't keep the moisture from clogging her throat when she looked at the sadness on her son's little face.

"I want you to be with me at *Cimaron*. *Tete du butt* is never around me. Stays as far away as he can. He won't bother us."

Well, that couldn't be. She closed her eyes for a few seconds trying to tally all her options. At the moment the only plan was to sleep here in the forest, beneath the stars. "You can sleep in the buggy."

"What about you?"

The buggy is too small for both of us. Gaby made me take extra blankets. I'll sleep on the ground."

The cold earth certainly didn't appear inviting. Her only possibility for a night of sleep seemed to stare coldly at her.

It wasn't long before the sun disappeared. Jenna leaned against a tree trunk gazing at what little she could see of the road. She heard Brice moving around in the buggy. Heard the little sounds he made in his sleep. Wished she could feel and hear Gil lying next to her.

Finally, she slept.

It wasn't the sun that woke her the next morning. The sun vanished with the new day. A soft drizzle coated the land. The blanket was soaked through as was she. The shivers wracking her body consumed her. She rubbed her hands along her body trying to gain warmth then gave up.

After shaking out the blanket, she woke Brice. They took care of their needs. She gave Brice the second half of the sandwich along with a few slices of apple. They shared water from the stream. For now, there was more than enough food left in the basket until they reached the first inn where she prayed, she would find work. If not, they would move on to the second inn. There was plenty of food for Brice.

The morning passed much as yesterday afternoon. With each sound of hoof beats they hid in the surrounding trees. Her breath of relief when she saw the inn faltered for a moment. Here, she wouldn't have to give anything the proprietor asked for.

She wouldn't have to sleep with this man.

There was food enough for another day. Sleeping could be done anywhere. Although nice, a bed wasn't a necessity.

There was no job here. No way to give Brice a bed or put more food in the basket.

This second night was spent outside. Brice stopped thinking of ways to convince her to return to *Cimaron*. He fell silently morose.

When the second inn appeared on the horizon on the next day, she lifted her chin, determined to do whatever was necessary. The basket of food was empty. The bottles of wine consumed.

Her stomach growled.

"Stay here until I come for you." Jenna kissed Brice on the forehead.

Chin held high she marched to the inn. Inside wonderful scents of baked bread and stew filled the air. Tears hovered in her eyes. This time, if she didn't make it to Angel's, she might die. What would happen to her little boy?

"I'd like to speak to the proprietor," she told one of the serving ladies. "Is he around?"

"There's no work here unless you want to go upstairs." The woman moved on, carrying the loaded tray on her shoulder.

Jenna asked two more women. Was greeted with the same answer. Why was it so hard? All she wanted was to make enough money to shelter and feed her boy.

Outside she sat on the step, her head in her hands. Unshed tears hovered in her eyes. The sun was setting on what would be there third night away from *Cimaron*. Brice was still in the buggy. Maybe she would earn enough if there was just one man. She could close her eyes then pretend the man was Gil.

She understood that would never work. She didn't have one idea how to survive something like that. Doing nothing was not a choice. She had to feed her son. As soon as she...as soon... Oh god, oh no, she couldn't...

She had to do just that. Standing, pushing her shoulders back, she strode inside. Once again, she asked for the proprietor. This time she was directed to the man who owned the inn.

"I need to earn money, enough for food and shelter for the night for me as well as my son. We'll be moving on tomorrow morning."

One night in hell, she could do it. Had to do it.

"You'll have to work all night. Your boy can sleep on one of the chairs over there." He nodded.

"All night?"

"How much do you think you're worth?"

Jenna grimaced. She didn't know. She had no idea except Angel's girls made a lot of money. Thought one man would be enough for what she asked for. Never believed she would have to do this more than once.

"Go on upstairs. One of the girls will show you to an empty room. You've got it for the entire evening. I'll make sure anyone who comes in looking for a new lady finds you." He paused a moment seeming to study her. "Do you know what you're doing?"

Nodding her head, she told herself it couldn't be too difficult. She could pretend the man was Jacques. She could float away into oblivion while he...

This is for Brice. For Brice...

She followed a woman up the steps. Once inside the room, she sat on a chair facing the door. There was no light. The first knock sent her heart pounding. It was the woman who showed her inside. I'm Bettina. You can call me Bet. My room is next door. If you need anything let me know."

"Bet..." Jenna wanted to tell her she'd never done anything like this before. Needed to tell her she didn't know what to do.

"You're new at this? It shows. Why?" Bet set two candles on a table before she lit them. "Suppose it's none of my business. If you have questions though, feel free to ask."

Jenna lifted her shoulders. "I have to feed my son. He's downstairs, sleeping in the common room. I wouldn't if I had another choice."

Bet sat down with her. Took her hands into hers. "We have some time. The customers wanting us don't come in for a few hours. As I just told you, if you have questions, I'll be pleased to answer."

Jenna filled her lungs for the first time since she set her course. "Don't know if I can do..."

Bet interrupted, "If you like, I'll tell you a little secret."

She nodded, "A secret to get me through this would be nice. Do you cosh them over the head?"

Bet laughed. The sound was delightful. It took some of the fear pooling in her gut away. "That would be something one could do. The act would get you kicked out of the room. Charles wants to keep his customers happy. Wants money in his pocket."

"The secret?"

"I dream of other things. Like to see fields of flowers. Whatever makes you happy think of that. The men are usually so drunk they don't notice if you lie still. They don't care. Do you have sponges?"

"Sponges?" Jenna blinked. She had no idea. Her eyes widened in confusion.

"They will keep you from getting with child. I brought you enough for tonight. They're ready. Put one inside you before the man comes into the room."

"That will stop..."

"Yes, now, I'm going to bring you some food along with a bottle of wine. Charles did ask me to see to your needs. As I said, Charles wants his clients happy so they'll come back. If you're lucky, you'll get a clientele. You won't have to entertain all the new men unless for some reason you want to do so."

Clientele?

In minutes Bet was back. "I gave your son food as well as a glass of milk. He will be fine for the night. One of the serving ladies agreed to keep an eye out for him."

"Merci."

They ate together. An hour slipped away then another. Bet left. Jenna tried not to think about her son or Gil. It was useless.

No one came to the room. She fell asleep, her neck skewed painfully against the chair. Sunshine slanted across her face. She jerked awake. Brice was asleep on the bed all tucked in, covers up to his chin.

A breakfast tray sat on the table in front of her. Nothing happened. There were no men who came to see her. What did that mean? The knock on the door surprised her.

"It's me, Bet. Let me in. The strangest thing happened." Bet waltzed in, poured herself a cup of coffee.

Groggy, Jenna sat up. Holding a finger to her lips, she motioned for Bet to whisper.

"Brice is asleep. Don't understand how he got here or the breakfast." Dumfounded, Jenna looked from Brice to Bet. "Do you know anything?"

"Some man paid for the entire night, food and all. Said you were to be left alone. He would talk to you in the morning."

"I didn't have anyone..." Jenna wasn't sure what to think. "A man paid... He didn't collect?"

"That's just the thing. He purchased a room down the hall for himself. Didn't want your services. Said he'd make amends in the morning. Told Charles he had to talk to you."

"Gil..." He found her. Gaby had been certain he would track her down. Apparently, he did so.

"You running from a man? I can get you out without anyone noticing. A woman who doesn't want to be a whore shouldn't have to be one."

"Do you want this life?" Jenna couldn't believe any woman would want to sell herself to men."

"Don't you worry about me. Do I have to get you out the back way or not?" Bet finished her coffee with a smile.

"If it's who I think it is, he won't hurt me. If he finds me gone today, he will just keep looking for me. I'm shocked it took him this long to come after me." With a heavy sigh, "If he discovered the truth, I'm surprised he came at all."

"Oh, he's been looking for you the last three days. He came here three nights ago, asking about you. It was late. He looked as if he'd been run over by a thundering herd of horses. Gave the descriptions of you along with your boy. That's why Charles was so quick to hire you. He was sure a man wanted you. Might pay top dollar to get you back. Seems he wanted you real bad. Charles was hoping to be paid splendidly if he kept you here all safe and sound."

"Maman?" Brice sat up rubbing his eyes. "Where are we?"

"At the inn where we stopped last night. You're safe."

Bet stood, glancing to the boy then back to Jenna. "I'll leave. You two eat up. If I'm right, it won't be much longer before you meet your benefactor. I hope this is the man you're expecting."

He would know the truth by now, perhaps not. If he did, he would be furious. She didn't understand. Why the devil was he here?

"I'm hungry. It smells good," Brice said as he slipped his legs over the side of the bed then made his way to the table.

Bet leaned over then gave Jenna a quick hug.

"You never answered me. Do you want to be here, Bet?"

Bet was shaking her head as she slowly moved toward the door. *"Non,* but it doesn't matter any longer. This is who I am. Charles treats me well. I've a roof over my head, food... What else could a girl ask for?"

Her laugh didn't sound genuine to her. The sound was filled with many different emotions.

Tears for Bet filled Jenna's eyes. Jenna didn't believe this was the only place she could be. If she could, she'd contact Angel. The *Madam* always helped those in need. Bet seemed to be a woman in need of a new direction in life. Angel could give that to her. She wasn't in a place to ask for help from anyone.

Turning her attention to her son, she helped with a plate of food. Goodness there was enough here to feed an army.

"You have to eat too, *maman*. We can't save all this unless you eat some. Promise me."

Her son was beginning to sound a lot like Gil. What he told her was true. At the moment her stomach didn't want food inside. Bile rose all too swiftly. She prayed she wasn't sick. The last nights were cold. Rushing she reached a bowl before she lost the contents of her stomach. She rinsed her mouth with water then drank some of the hot coffee that arrived with the meal.

She felt better. Smeared butter on a huge piece of warm bread that was halfway to her mouth when the knock on the door reverberated in the small room. The sound gave her a start. She dreaded seeing him again. It would have been so much easier if he just chose to let her go. Didn't want to explain anything.

Still, she knew she should be thanking Gil. If it weren't for him purchasing the room for her, she would have entertained men the night through. Bending her head, she covered her face with her hands. Tears filled her eyes.

With no hesitation the door pushed open. Gil stood framed by the opening. She clenched her teeth waiting for the recriminations, the anger. He must have discovered the money she accepted from Elisa and Etienne. Must know she left because of the promise made to them.

He followed her.

His feelings for her were possessive, nothing else. He wouldn't have trailed after her if he knew the truth. The Dubois would never say anything. They wanted the secret kept. There was no one else who could inform him.

"Jenna, we need to talk."

Talking wouldn't help. "I don't believe we've anything to talk about." It was true. She took the money offered. He would know she didn't love him enough to say no to twenty thousand gold francs. A sob caught in her throat. She vowed not to let him see her cry.

"I know everything." He stepped inside, slowly closing the door behind him. For a few seconds he leaned against the hard wood. "Brice, I need to talk to your mother. If you go outside, you'll see Gaby. She'll take you back to *Cimaron*. Don't know when your mother and I will arrive.

Rest assured we will come home. I've a little convincing to do before that happens." He stepped away from the door, pulling up a chair when he reached the table.

Brice looked to Jenna. She nodded. "Gaby is here? Did she tell you where I was going?"

Gil shook his head as he poured coffee. "Gaby was loyal to you. If you keep having a yearning for running away, I'm going to have to do something about that. If she told me, you wouldn't have starved yourself for three days. I would have found you the first night."

She swallowed. He understood her better than anyone. He looked for her. If he knew everything, "Why are you here?"

~ * ~

Gil stood in front of his best friend since they could toddle along. His fists were clenched as he tried desperately to contain the anger welling up from deep inside. What they did under the guise of friendship twisted his gut, ate at him. With one foul gesture, they sent her away. Without money she would starve herself.

"The two of you meddled in my life for the last time. Jenna's life could be in danger while the two of you sit here with smug expressions on your faces thinking you've done something that would help me. You seem pleased she left. I would think my feelings might mean more to you than the pats on your backs you are giving yourselves."

Gil turned to face the window afraid he might lash out at Etienne. His fury rose to a flashpoint before he found a means to control himself. His hands clasped behind his back, he rocked on his heels. It would take more than these few seconds for him to calm down. Anger simmered to explosive levels.

"She accepted blood money. Obviously, she doesn't love or care for you," Elisa told him her voice soft yet determined. "We wanted the best for you. Since you refused to see what was right in front of your face, I felt you needed proof."

"She also promised not to tell you," Etienne tried to defend himself. "She took what was offered with the assurance you wouldn't find out. She's exactly what Elisa thought she is, a jaded tart."

Gil whirled, his fists now clenched by his sides. He wanted to lash out. "Jenna didn't speak a word of this to me. What she did do was go into the village. I drove her because I feared for her life if she went by herself."

"Why?" Elisa didn't seem concerned despite what should be his very apparent anger. "How did you find out about the bribe?"

Etienne had the good grace to school his features seeming to understand something was very wrong. *Bribe?*

"Why did she go into the village? Or how did I find out?" Gil parroted the questions.

He slashed his hand in the air frustrated beyond endurance, fear for Jenna all-encompassing. He needed to bring his woman to the chateau. "I'm going to find Jenna, bring her home where she belongs. I want her here then I expect both of you to apologize to her. After that, I don't want to ever see you again."

Elisa played with the folds on her dress, a sweet angelic smile on her beautiful face. "Don't understand what we need to apologize for. We did nothing wrong."

"What did Jenna do with the twenty thousand gold francs?" It was Etienne who figured out something was deadly wrong. "Why is she in jeopardy? If she has the money, she also has a ticket to anywhere she wants to go."

"Were you here when she left?"

Gil paced the room. He felt caged in, needed to ride hard until he found her. The time he spent here with these two fools was wasted time. He tugged in air then more air as he fought the simmering emotions.

"Doesn't matter. The fact remains she has left the chateau."

Etienne rose, "I'll go with you. She must have headed for Bordeaux. If Jenna doesn't have the twenty thousand gold francs, who does?"

Gil's heart pounded hard, every nerve stretched thin. "*Madam Macon* has the blood money. Jenna gave it to her so she could take her granddaughter to Paris. The little girl is sick, dying."

"*Madam Macon* wanted Jenna to cast a spell to save the child,"

Elisa murmured as if she finally understood what he wasn't telling them. "Jenna isn't as we thought, is she?"

"I was right about Jenna. I'm glad about that." Etienne stuffed his hands through his hair. "Although I'm not happy about your plans that I took part in."

"*Oui*, Jenna took the money. *Oui*, just as you requested, she didn't tell me. Now she is out there somewhere with Brice alone and unprotected with not a franc to her name. Gaby gave her a basket of food. She won't eat it. Jenna will give everything to Brice."

Gil hit the wall with his fist. Desperate for Jenna and fearing for her, he started to the door.

"If it's any consolation, I'm sorry. Go, go find her, bring Jenna and Brice home. It's obvious you love her." Elisa stood her hands clasped tightly in front of her. "I will be happy to apologize, Gil. We want what is best for you."

Gil turned on her, all his fury directed at this woman he once thought he loved. "Don't you think I might know what is best for me?"

Etienne brushed a quick kiss on Elisa's forehead. "We will bring her home."

The pair left. They rode hard, stopping at the first then the second inn. Both places they left word of the woman and boy who might arrive looking for work. Gil guessed she would head to Bordeaux. Guessed she would go to Angel's place to seek help. Once before Angel gave her aid. From his visit there, Gil knew Angel respected Jenna, thought the best of her.

He wasn't going all the way to the city. Finding her before she starved herself to death was most important. They stayed the first night at the second inn. After that they traveled backward to the chateau.

Etienne found the spot where she and Brice slept the first night they began the journey. It was close to the chateau. In their haste they must have ridden past believing she would have traveled farther. He fought the emotions surfacing. Wrestled with the image of Jenna and Brice alone and afraid. Battled the realization of what she would have to do to survive, if she ran out of food.

The second day taking more care they still missed them. Jenna did a remarkable job hiding herself.

"We will find them. What then? Will she return with you?" Etienne asked as they rode up to the second inn.

"Hell if I know. She can't keep going when she has nothing to her name. The food Gaby gave her won't last her until they reach Bordeaux."

It was the evening of the third night. The day before he paid for a room for her at the inn. Explained to the innkeeper his intentions if she arrived. Told him not to mention him. He would speak with the lady in the morning. Told the man he should give her anything she needed. He would pay for everything.

There were topics the two of them needed to discuss. One was marriage. The other was her son. If she refused marriage, he could be more stubborn.

Now, he stood in front of her closed door, wishing he had the composure to knock on the door then take her into his arms. He did not. Instead, he made sure Brice was fed then taken to the room for the night.

He ordered breakfast. They would talk in the morning.

Charles assured him Jenna had food to eat that night. All Gil wanted was to pull her into his arms. Tell her he was proud of her. *Enfer*, all along he expected her to take whatever Elisa offered.

Before he settled in for the night, he sent Etienne to retrieve Gaby. They would arrive in the morning. He would keep Jenna here as long as it took for her to understand her choices.

Jenna was a survivor.

Morning dawned. Once again, he stood in front of Jenna's closed door. The air he tugged in seemed stagnant and frigid. As he reached for the doorknob, his hand shook. As a spy for the French government, he'd been through more harrowing and dangerous experiences. Gil had no idea how he was going to convince Jenna to marry him.

Brice stood in their way. He didn't love the boy. While he wouldn't hurt him, he would do everything in his power to give the boy everything he needed or wanted.

Lance...

His son's image seemed to fade a little with time. Since Jenna entered into his life, he no longer despaired of living. Sunshine... Jenna was the sunshine in his life. She gave him hope when he had none.

The door opened. A woman left the room. She stopped in front of him. "Are you the man who paid for the room? Treat her right. She doesn't want to do this, you understand. She's not like me."

"Want only the best for Jenna. I love her," he murmured as he stepped through the door.

No, despite what he did to her in the name of lust...she didn't want to whore for anyone including him.

"Jenna, we need to talk." His voice was brusque.

He watched her cower slightly when he spoke.

"I don't believe we've anything to talk about. Everything has been said. You need to go home, tend your vines. Find some woman who is worthy of you."

"I know everything." He stepped inside, slowly closing the door behind him. "Brice, I need to talk to your mother alone. If you go outside, you'll see Gaby. She'll take you back to *Cimaron*. Don't know when your mother and I will arrive. Rest assured we will come home. I've a little convincing to do before that happens."

Gil never felt this insecure in his life. He played spy for so long. He was arrogant and presupposing. His two greatest loves until he met Jenna were excitement and intrigue. The game was of utmost importance. His life had always been his to live with all his heart until he lost his son. This woman singlehandedly brought him back to life. It seemed it had been so very long since living held any appeal.

Brice looked to Jenna. She nodded.

"Gaby is here? Did she tell you where I was going and why?"

Gil shook his head understanding there must have been promises made. "Gaby was loyal to you. If you keep having a yearning for running away, I'm going to have to do something to change that woman's loyalties. If she told me the moment I returned home, you wouldn't have starved yourself for three days. I would have found you the first night."

"Why are you here?" Jenna drummed her nails on the table while she waited for his tale. "If you know the entire story, you can't possibly want anything to do with me."

One part of him wanted to make her wait for the answer, the other did not. He supposed it was the sleuth in him that wished to prolong the moment. Anticipation in the reveal, "Ah, now we get down to the nitty-gritty. I've more than one reason. First, we should eat. This discussion will be much better on a satisfied stomach. I for one am famished. Since you've been starving yourself, you are also hungry."

His nerves seemed to vanish with each passing second. It appeared he regained some of his confidence as he witnessed the scene unfolding and could see to its end. While he was certain Jenna loved him, he had to proceed with caution.

Unable to help himself, Gil watched her eat; counting each time her fork passed her lips. He grinned when she finally set the utensil on the table then folded her slender hands in her lap.

"Satisfied?"

"Believe the question is, are you?" Sitting back in the chair, he stretched out his legs ready now to proceed with the verbal dance they were going to play before all would be settled between them. "Now, why don't you tell me why you left with no money, not one franc to your name? I didn't think you would sacrifice yourself for a promise."

Heat swamping her face, she looked away, plucked at the fabric of her gown. "Didn't realize they would have told you what I did. Thought you would be furious. Prayed I would find work before we ran out of food."

"From past experience you should know better. You're too beautiful. I'm surprised the proprietor of the first inn you passed didn't give you the same opportunities as Charles. What would you have done if you had to entertain a man last night?"

Well hell, he didn't want to go there. Didn't need the answer to the question. The only answer she could give.

She made a little face. Gil was positive she would not have gone through with the deed. Certain she would have refused then been kicked out. It would have taken her at least two more days to reach the city.

"I—I would have gone through with it. Bet told me to lie in the bed then imagine something beautiful. She told me the customers didn't care if I acted like a corpse."

At her words he wanted to strike out while at the same time shake her until she understood how foolish that could have been. The breath of air he held, swept from him. It would not be wise to take his fury out on her. She was, after all, the victim.

"I'm heartily glad then that I arrived here before you were forced to give yourself to some man who wanted you only as a vessel for his lust. Perhaps we should dispense with this part of our discussion. I don't want to think about what could have happened to you. I'm certain you don't want to talk about that particular aspect either."

"I don't. You said you knew everything. What does that mean?"

He wanted to see her smile again. Needed to shelter her in his arms, kiss her senseless, kiss her until she whispered his name. Didn't know how to do all the things he wanted.

"*Oui,* when I took you to visit *Madam* at her granddaughter's home, I was certain there was some reason other than the fact you were concerned about the little girl. I know you wished at one time you could cast a spell that would heal her. *Madam* asked as much of you. That's why I was not at the chateau when you left. I went to find out for myself the real reason you visited her."

"You..." She moistened her lips. "You went there. She told you about the money."

"The money but not the promise to leave. *Madam* would not have known about the bargain you made with Elisa."

He followed the movement of her lips wishing he dared do the same, needing to sweep her into his arms then show her how much he wanted her. He was terrified for her as well as proud.

"*Madam* was more than eager to share the facts. She was so excited while making preparation for the trip to Paris. Since we never found the jewels, I knew you had to get the money from someone."

"Elisa..."

"I confronted them after I returned. Etienne was pleased to hear you were just as he expected. It seems he began to doubt his ability to read people, heaven forbid." He leaned forward no longer relaxed, taking her hands into his. "Etienne is the best agent I've ever known with that particular ability. That specific attribute is his pride and joy. He was utterly devastated that his wife proved him wrong about you."

"I made the two of them promise to be at the chateau when I returned with you so they can apologize. As far as I'm concerned it can't be too soon. They stuck their oars into our business where they didn't belong."

"Yes, well, I don't want to see either of them ever again and that would be too soon. Don't need an apology. If I return with you, nothing will be different. Nothing between us will have changed. The two of them, well, at least Elisa will still believe I'm not good enough for you. It's a daunting task to have to always prove myself to the people who love you."

"We both know I'm not good enough for you, *ma cherie,*"

"It's not what they will believe," she continued on in that vein, despite his effort to change her thoughts.

"They are two of my closest friends. We need to get this travesty out of the way so we can go on with our lives. Besides, I want them at my wedding even though I did tell them that after the apology I never wanted to see them again."

"Wedding?"

She was sitting up straighter, her chin higher than usual. The hand holding her teacup shook, the cup clattering on the saucer as her face turned ashen. "Who?"

"I think you know who I'm speaking of. We are going to be wed as soon as possible. Hush," he held his hand in the air, attempting to stop her from denying him. "We've no other choice left to us. I want you in my bed every night. Marriage is the only way I know of that I can keep you where I want you."

He cursed his words. He'd said nothing of love just lust. She shouldn't accept this half ass, selfish proposal.

"I cannot." She looked away from him seemingly unwilling to look him in the eyes. "You understand it's not possible. The people who work for you will never accept me as your wife."

With his thoughts he jinxed himself. "I understand this is happening too quickly. You need time to figure things out. There is no time. You could even now carry my child. My child will not be born a bastard."

Once again, he went about this in the worst sort of way. He should tell her he loved her. The sweet words might help smooth the way for him. Feelings of love were not the same as committing to her with the words. First, he needed to learn how she felt.

"You hate Brice. I understand you won't have to adopt him. How can I marry a man who cannot give my son the love he deserves? Wouldn't that be worse?"

"*Non*, I do not hate or despise the lad. It's just that I've trouble being around the boy."

This was the sticking point. He was nothing like Lance. The two boys were complete opposites.

He knew it.

She knew it.

There should be no comparisons.

"You would be expected to be a father to him. That would mean loving him. You despise him." Her words were fast in short puffs as if she sought air.

It seemed to him she ignored what he'd told her a few seconds ago. "*Non*, I do not. Do not despise anyone. It's just hard for me to be near him. His presence makes me remember. I will work on it." With a sweeping gesture, frustrated beyond anything else, "You cannot possibly think to return with me, to sleep in my bed, without benefit of marriage."

"It worked before. I was actually happy in your bed."

She studied the floor, her lashes lowered. She sounded defeated. He understood she must want this as much as he did. If not for the boy, this would be easy. Marriage to her would be inevitable.

"Look at me, Jenna."

He placed a finger beneath her chin, lifting, encouraging her to meet his gaze. "You don't want to continue in that fashion any more than I. We have to figure something else out."

"There is the cottage. I could stay there. You could visit in the evenings, bring a bottle of wine." With shimmering eyes, she stared into his. Once again, "There is the cottage."

"The villagers still don't like you. They will take issue with any arrangement we have except marriage."

When the gossip mill began to churn and the good people learned of the money she gave to the child, their hearts would change. He didn't want to encourage that sentiment, at least not until he had her promise of marriage. Didn't want her living in the cottage away from him. He needed to know she was safe, secure as well. Needed to know she was his.

"Their hearts might change with time." Her voice sounded wistful yet discouraged as well. With a breathy sigh it seemed she gave up all pretense. "Probably not. They hated me so thoroughly I doubt if there would be room in their hearts to come to a different conclusion about me."

She didn't believe what she just told him even though he did. "If you lived in the cottage, they would just have a different label for you. Nothing would be altered in your life."

He didn't want to make things worse. He needed to convince her his way was the only one.

"Mistress. I understand." The note of dejection was now more evident than ever before.

"*Oui.*"

"I don't want to be a mistress, yours or anyone's."

"Of course not, you should be a wife, my wife, the mother to my children. You should be cherished."

Loved as well. He would love her with all his heart. After Elisa wed Etienne, he never thought to be asking a woman to spend her life with him.

"Brice?"

"We will figure that out. What I mean to say is that I will find a way to deal with my flaw."

He meant every word. What he didn't know was how to do so. How to finally get over the loss of his son so he could accept another one into his life.

"I have to think. This is too important. You have to give me time," she murmured softly.

"Time is something we don't have. Can you think on your way home? Charles has made up a lunch for us. We'll stop one time between here and the chateau to spend the night. Don't want to ride through the darkness." He held out his hand to her.

When she accepted, he thought that to be a good sign.

~ * ~

By the time they reached *Cimaron* all Jenna's nerves were frayed and what was left was stretched to the limit. Gil was charming, suave as well as debonair. She'd never seen him quite so enchanting. She was so in love with him she couldn't think straight. The fact that he didn't care about the deception even applauded her for taking the money surprised her.

She had been so certain he would hate her for betraying him, for betraying what they had together. When she left a few days ago, she'd been almost certain she would never see him again. Although a tiny part of her prayed he would come after her, rescue her from herself. Now he asked for her hand in marriage.

He asked her to marry him.

With all her heart she loved him.

If not for Brice, she would have said yes in a heartbeat. She had to be a mother first. Had to think of Brice's needs before hers. On the way back, Gil begrudgingly told her she could stay at the cottage until she made up her mind about his proposal. The concession surprised her.

Now, in the cottage, she was dressing to confront his friends to await their apology. By giving their money away, she supposed she deceived them too. Her stomach churned. If truth be told, she'd not been feeling well for several days now. Maybe more if she thought back. She knew she carried Gil's child. Would have to tell him soon. Of course, he expected this. Had to have known what they did would result in this very thing.

When she told him, he would insist then insist again that they wed. She understood he would never want a bastard. He said as much in the short discussion they had the morning before.

Neither did she want a bastard. She inhaled a long deep breath of air. Her life changed then changed again. She wondered if she'd ever have control over the things happening to her. Didn't want either of them to suffer. No matter her choice, for marriage or no marriage, both her children would live with the decision.

Gil strode arrogantly onto her porch promptly at ten o'clock the morning after they arrived home. Just as he said he would last night, he would expect apologies from his friends. Would also expect her to agree to marriage.

When he stepped through the door to the cottage, he stood tall and straight. The crooked grin she loved so well swept across his lips. He looked carefree. She wished she could kiss him then pull him into her arms. Wished she could give him everything he desired.

Since he rescued her, he hadn't touched her. She missed the closeness of him, the warmth along with the tender concern. Supposed the list could go on pretty much forever. If she said no to him, she would miss all that for the rest of her life.

"Are you ready?"

Gallantly, Gil held out his arm for her. His eyes beckoned to her, spoke of good things to come. She prayed that was true.

When she slipped her hand in the crook of his elbow, he placed his possessively over hers. His touch was warm and comforting. She needed that security only he could give. He was so grand, broad shouldered, tall and lean of form. He was a formidable man. Everything he did, it seemed he excelled at. When he held her in his arms, she melted completely. With a look in his deep brown eyes, he could bend her to his will.

"*Non*, never ready for this. I would like them to go home. Would love to never see either one again even though I understand they were your friends long before you met me."

"They both owe you an apology. I'd like to say especially Elisa. Etienne had as much a role in the power game they played with you since he doubted you, doubted himself. He should have convinced Elisa of your true nature. Should have never allowed her to take control."

When they reached the main house, chaos reigned. The children...where were the children? The adults seemed to have lost all thought process. Except for Masson, it seemed the children vanished.

Elisa sat on a chair, her arms wrapped around herself rocking and moaning, seemingly unable to move.

Etienne was nowhere to be seen.

Elisa sat up, straitening her hair. Copious tears slid down her cheeks. "Etienne is on his way to Paris. He's following the only lead we have. He bade me wait here for the two of you. I want to search. Need to do something besides sit and wait. The children are missing, Margo and Brice," Elisa said between soft sobs of despair. "Someone from yours and Etienne's old life found the children. At least that is what we think. Will it never end?"

"How do you know?"

Elisa held up a piece of paper. "This. Read it."

He did quickly then handed it to Jenna. Before she could finish, he was out the door. Jenna dropped it. She raced after Gil, her heart pounding.

"Brice!" she cried out. His name vanished in the grape scented air.

Chapter Ten

Gil's heart lodged in his throat when he read the message. Margo and Brice had been playing outside. Masson was reading nearby propped against a tree. The kidnappers must not have seen Masson or they would have taken him too.

It was Masson who raced inside with the news. Because of Masson they knew the direction the men took. They weren't headed to Paris. They were in a black carriage with no ensign, no markings to identify the lumbering vehicle. The road they took led to the coast. Ships could be had. If they reached a port before them, the children could end up anywhere.

Masson did an admirable job describing the men. One was tall and very thin. His hair was golden while he sported a well-waxed mustache, one that curled on the ends. The other was normal in height, however he was stocky and possessed a barrel chest. His hair was brown. Both men were dressed in frock coats, white lawn shirts beneath and dark trousers.

The only good thing about the destination was that it couldn't be reached in a day. Riding hard, Etienne and Gil would have time to waylay the carriage before it reached the port.

Gil waited for two of his men to catch up with him. He didn't understand how these two men who stole their children could think to outrun horses. Maybe they were after something besides the children. Perhaps it was a trap set up for the soul purpose of doing away with him, Etienne as well. His role in the ministry was no secret. In the future, he would have to take more precautions. Future thoughts would not aid him now.

"Etienne along with your man, Gabe, set out after them. They rode hard and are not far behind the carriage. Our men should intercept the carriage before nightfall. They each had a second mount. We'll find the children."

Gil nodded as he thought of Jenna. His own heart lodged in his throat. What was she feeling now? He ran out of the drawing room before he could give her the reassurances she would need. Grimly, they followed the trail left for them.

"It's me they want. I'm sure these men see Etienne as a bonus. We will have to look out for an ambush. Hope Etienne and Gabe have come to the same conclusion."

Gil's heart in his throat he watched the farthest end of the road in hopes of finding Etienne along with the children.

Nothing was said for mile after mile. By the time they saw Etienne, the sun was low on the horizon. The golden orb would set soon. A carriage was turned on its side. Horses that drew the carriage were tethered to the side. Gil had not expected an accident to end the fearful chase. He closed his eyes, a silent prayer sent heavenward for the children.

Etienne scrubbed his hand down his face before he spoke. His expression grim, "The children are not inside. The driver is dead. Another man inside is injured. Has a broken leg. I've sent a messenger to the village for a constable. They should be here soon. I believe at least one of the kidnappers escaped. The culprit we apprehended won't speak. He seems to be mute."

"The children? You said they aren't here. Where...?"

Gil understood they were missing. His heart thundered with fear for both Margo and Brice. The remaining kidnapper either fled with them or they perhaps were able to escape. If they did get away, they would be alone in the dark without food or anything to keep them warm. The children would be cold.

"There is no sign of either one. Gabe is searching the woods. I stayed here to inform you. We should go opposite ways. Let out a yell if you find anything."

Etienne jabbed his hands through his hair, his breath whistling out of his lungs. Frown lines etched his features.

Gil turned to his men while he attempted to remain calm. "Start a fire," he said to one. To the other man, "Go back to the chateau. Get food and blankets from Gaby. Tell Jenna she can bring the buggy. She will want to be here when Brice is found."

He vowed they would be discovered soon, alive as well as healthy. The search would not end until that happened.

"Elisa and Gaby can come too," Etienne said as he stared at him as if he'd said something wrong.

It wasn't his place to give Elisa permission to join them. Wasn't his place to forgive yet either. Perhaps all of this happened because they'd been made vulnerable by the machinations set about by Elisa. Maybe he was grappling to assuage his guilt.

Gil wasn't going to tell him Elisa wasn't welcome. She was also missing a child who would need comforting when found. The kidnapping wasn't her fault. It was the damn job. In his melancholy, he'd forgotten about the dangers. Forgotten he had enemies. In the future, he would have to take more care. He would make sure he had the manpower available to him to keep Jenna and her son from harm. As long as he stayed in this line of work, there were no guarantees. He had second as well as third thoughts about staying with the ministry. Bottom line, it was how he wanted to spend his life.

Something else to discuss with Jenna.

For now, the present, the children had to be brought in safely. They would be hungry and tired, scared too. Both would need and want their mothers. Inviting one without the other was not well done of him.

The sky was darkening. Stars were beginning to appear. Gil closed his eyes for a moment, breathing in deeply the scent of the forest. He pushed his way through bushes. Tree limbs hit him in the face. There was no path to follow as he scouted in a different direction from Etienne.

"Brice! Margo!" he called out, afraid the boy wouldn't answer because he was the 'mean man' the *tete du butt.*

Better than he'd ever thought possible, he now understood Brice was a little boy. He was Jenna's son. He had to open his heart to the *petit garcon,* after that love him with all his heart. *Mon Dieu*, Brice was a little boy. He deserved his love. The child did nothing wrong.

Pride got in his way, damn stubborn pride. Unable to give up thoughts of his boy overshadowed what life should be about. He'd been so self-centered he didn't see beyond the end of his nose. Lance would never want him to despise or ignore another child because of his memory. Gil knew that fact beyond any thoughts, good or bad, he harbored for Brice.

The search dragged on, hours upon hour passed by. Gil went back to the makeshift camp. Gaby was standing by fire as was Elisa and Jenna. It seemed for the moment they mended their differences. The fire blazed warming the air around them. He wished he strode into the camp with the children in tow. Prayed for their safe return. Tears slid down Jenna's cheeks. He pulled her into his arms for a quick hug.

"We will find them," he whispered.

A huge pot of stew bubbled over the open fire to be soaked up by the bread Gaby brought with her. Lanterns were lit giving the base camp a glow that in any other circumstances would be cheery. Jenna wrapped her arms around him hugging him close. Hoping to give comfort he ran his hands along her back.

"We will find them. Margo and Brice will be fine." Gil prayed his words would come true. "As soon as I eat, I'll search in the other direction. They have to be close. Margo is so tiny she could not have gone far."

"I want to go with you," Jenna said, her hand settling on his chest. "I have to. They will be cold and hungry. What if you call his name...?"

"...and he doesn't answer because he's afraid of me? The thought crossed my mind more than once while I was hunting for them."

When he first encountered the boy, he'd been unable to keep his anger in check. Could not change his feelings at the time to save his soul. Jenna placed her hand in his. He felt her fear, knew the terror to be real. He felt the same horror. She could lose Brice tonight. The thought so bitter it brought tears to his eyes. *"Viens."* With you by my side, we will find those two. He could not allow himself to think otherwise.

With lanterns held high, they walked through the brush, pushing branches aside along with cobwebs from their faces. They moved on calling out their names over then over again until exhaustion hung on their shoulders beating them down. Beside him she sobbed. Taking a moment to rest, he crushed her in his arms. Pulled her close, her head resting in the hollow of his shoulder. He knew she was exhausted. "We have to stay strong," he murmured softly, hoping to give encouragement. She nodded as they searched anew.

"Brice! Brice! Margo!" Jenna called over and over again.

They heard others calling his name, Margo's as well. High overhead a sliver moon barely lit the darkness. A brisk wind chilled the air. The night grew cold too quickly. What did he expect? This was harvest time. The nights were always cold. They wouldn't have a blanket, nothing to keep them warm no food, no water. The children would be terrified.

"Are you cold?" He brought Jenna close.

Her shivers frightened him. He heard the chattering of her teeth. "I need to take you back to the fire."

"*Non*, the children will be colder. Before we came to *Cimaron*, Brice was always asking me if he was going to die. He will be thinking the same thing tonight. We had so little food. He'll think for sure his fears are coming true. I have to stay with you until he's found, until Margo is found. I won't abandon the children."

When Jenna stumbled, he held her tighter. When her tears slipped down her cheeks, Gil brushed them away with his fingers. Hope vanished as the hours continued to mount. The darkness hindered every effort seeming to swallow everything whole. It was so black there were no shadows. Time was against them as it gradually slipped by. The horizon slowly began to lighten.

"You have to sleep. I'm taking you back to camp," Gil told her, hoping she would take his advice knowing she would argue with him. "When the sun comes up, I'll come for you. You can search then."

She was shaking her head. "Can't do that. You need sleep as well."

"Hush, you won't be any good to that boy of yours if you are too exhausted to hold him, to ease his fears. Two hours, that's all that's left before sunrise." Before she could agree or disagree again, they were at the camp. He fixed a place for her to sleep. Gil held up two fingers. "Two hours. Sleep, *ma cherie,* get some food in your belly. You'll be ready when I return for you."

When he set her on the bedroll near the fire and covered her with a blanket, she didn't have an objection. Jenna pulled the blanket over her. Hesitantly, Gil tucked the fabric around her. He watched as her lashes fluttered across her cheeks. He was sure she'd be asleep in seconds. For Jenna, the last few days were exhausting. Smudges underlined the hollows beneath her eyes.

Gil grabbed a hunk of bread then started out again. Still, there was nothing, no clues as to where the two *enfants* might have travelled. Nothing changed. He was beside himself with worry and fear. Two hours seemed an eternity.

Dawn found the sun shining on the camp. He prayed the children would be discovered soon now that it was light. When he returned to camp, Jenna was up sipping a hot cup of coffee and eating. She appeared ready to start out anew. Once again, he stopped long enough to pick up a slice of bacon. He would eat again after they found the children. Etienne as well as the other men had been in and out of the camp throughout the night. Gaby kept hot coffee simmering on the fire along with food for the volunteers.

"Now that we can see we'll have better luck. Brice will be in your arms before you know it."

To his ears, his promises seemed hopeless. He was certain they didn't sound any better to Jenna.

No longer was he sure they would be located in time. The entire night they were alone in the dark and cold. They would suffer from the cold more than the empty bellies and lack of water. The thought of wild animals terrified him. They were walking now, searching again.

"Brice!" Jenna called out his name over and over again as she steadfastly moved through the thick growth.

"What's this?" Gil held a small piece of fabric to the light. He spotted another a short distance from them then another. They followed the trail left for them. The clues would have been missed in the darkness. No one would have seen the scraps of cloth.

"The fabric your finding is from Brice's jacket. He left us signs of their journey." She paused to breathe in a long needed deep breath of air before quickly stretching kinks from her back. "At least he wore a jacket. They'd been playing outside. Their clothing would have been warm."

"You have a very smart boy. Because of these clues, we will find them."

"I'm terrified, Gil. I've never been so afraid."

"Call again. Keep calling. Finally, we must be headed in the right direction," Gil whispered softly, after all this time discovering a reason for hope.

The brush grew denser, the canopy of trees thicker. "This place reminds me of the spots where we always stopped to spend our nights, out of the way, secluded from the road. Where it was safe and people wouldn't see us. Where if it rained, we would have some small measure of protection."

"It's why I didn't find you when I searched." He understood now why he missed them. She knew how to cover her tracks, hide herself away from possible trouble.

They broke through into a small moss-covered glade. He heard Jenna's gasp of air at the same time he saw the children.

"Oh, god, oh god, Brice, Margo..."

Arms open wide Jenna rushed to the children wrapping her arms around both, hugging them close to her heart, tears of happiness cascading down her cheeks "You're safe. You're alive." She moved them a short distance away looking them over, picking out sticks and leaves from their hair.

"*Maman*? You found me. I tried to leave a trail for you."

Brice's little voice was the sweetest sound he'd ever heard. Watching Jenna reunite with her son gave his heart a jolt. He looked upon Brice in a new and very different light. Brice was Jenna's little boy, so very important to her just as Lance had been important to him.

"You did well," Jenna said as Gil hollered that the children were safe.

They would be at the campsite soon. Everyone would be able to relax. He watched as Jenna ruffled his hair. This time Brice didn't object.

"I got a blanket from the carriage," Brice told them tilting his chin upward. "Margo was cold but we wrapped it around us so we stayed warm. Told her we would be found. We didn't go that far away."

"I see that you did. I'm very proud of you. You were very smart.

We've got to get the two of you back to camp. Are you hungry? Gaby has food frying for you and Margo. Some bacon, I believe, perhaps pancakes too."

"We had food, a little bit," Brice pointed to a small bag that was empty now. "I took it from the carriage when we left. It's not stealing, is it? I knew we would have to eat."

With tears in her eyes Jenna was staring at him. All their prayers were answered. "*Non*, not stealing. You were very smart to think of things you would need then bring them while you were running from the bad men who stole you."

"Why did you go with them," Gil asked, suddenly wondering why these two would leave the safety of the vineyard.

"They offered us *bonbons*. I knew better but I couldn't stop Margo. She's just a little girl. She needs protection," Brice told them his face as well as his voice solemn.

Crouching down so he was eye level with Brice, he asked, "Can you walk?"

Moisture clogged Gil's throat. Tried to clear it away. He suddenly realized he loved the little boy with all his heart. Jenna loved him so much he couldn't help himself. The boy was part of the woman he loved. He wondered how he failed to see that fact before now.

Brice nodded. Jenna clasped his hand in hers while he scooped Margo into his arms.

"Brice, save..." Margo said as she touched one drop that was sliding down Gil's cheek. "Save...feed too."

Gil wondered about the look the two shot each other. Brice did save Margo. Because of that they would have a forever bond. "Did Brice eat?" He couldn't help but ask.

Margo shook her head. Brice reached up to take her hand in his little one. "Not hungry."

That was what Gil would have expected. At her son's words Jenna closed her eyes, breathing deeply. He saw the agony flash across her face then the pride in her son. The little boy was a true hero.

Gil was certain he knew what she was thinking. He realized the example Jenna set might have saved Margo's life. The sac he showed them was not large. There couldn't have been more than a slice or two of bread inside. Brice was a boy any man could be proud of, could be proud to call his son.

When they were close enough to camp, they yelled, "They're found. We found the children." Gil's remaining men called out the good news as they went after the ones who were still searching.

Gaby and Elisa arrived first. Margo was handed over to Elisa. It wasn't too much longer and Etienne strode into the camp.

A couple hours later, the children were at home. They were bathed, fed then tucked into bed. Gil poured a brandy for Etienne and himself then wine for the ladies. He sat back, stretched out his legs, staring at the flames leaping in the fireplace. His life changed. Jenna changed it for the better.

He reached out for Jenna. She came to him with a soft smile on her face. He understood her relief. She sat down beside him. He kissed her tenderly on the lips, looking at the stairs as if he expected to see Brice.

First though, before she decided if she wanted to go to the cottage or stay here, he wanted an apology from his friends.

They had been so wrong about Jenna Bonnet. The pair should realize that fact now. They should be more than willing to admit they were wrong.

It seemed Elisa understood what he wanted. She broke the silence. "Jenna, I misread you from the beginning. You've got to understand that I saw you shaking up Gil's world. You were altering him. He was different. I was afraid you were making his life worse not better. Instead, you were exactly what he needed to make his life whole again. I was wrong. Can you forgive me?"

"In a good way you changed, *mon ami*," Etienne agreed with his wife. "I'm truly sorry that I played a part in this travesty. I should have relied on my intuition instead of listening to my wife who can be impulsive as well as short-sighted." He looked at her, fondness clearly showing in his expression.

"Set in motion by me," Elisa said. "I won't deny it. I also won't hesitate to tell you how wrong I was. As I jumped to conclusions without knowing the facts, the trouble began and ended with me. I've this need to protect those I love from harm. Etienne is right about me. I can be impulsive. Of course, if I wasn't we probably wouldn't be together now."

"It was that night in the Paris brothel," Etienne said. "When you whispered my name from the middle of the staircase."

"It was," she murmured.

"Will you accept our apology," Etienne asked, a great deal of remorse held tight in his voice. "We still want to be asked to the wedding."

"I haven't..." Jenna looked at him. Her eyes were telling him yes without the words. "I haven't decided yet."

"So, no wedding plans as we speak?" Etienne asked, an elegant dark eyebrow arched upward.

Gil wanted to hear her accept his proposal in private not in a room filled with people even though they were good friends. This was between them, no one else. "As Jenna told you, she hasn't decided. In any case, I do believe I would like to speak with Jenna alone. As is usual we've a great deal to talk over before plans can be made for a binding ceremony such as a wedding."

"We are off to bed. Elisa and I will give the two of you all the privacy you will need. Tomorrow we will leave for home. I do hope that if you decide to tie the knot, you will forgive our indiscretions and invite us."

"If you want to stay downstairs for a while, it's fine. I'd like to take Jenna either to the cottage or upstairs to my suite."

So many motives and plans swirled in his head. He needed Jenna on so many different levels. First, he'd have to start with his new feelings for her son. She might not believe his opinion changed so quickly. Knowledge the little boy faced death because of his occupation, would have to be the catalyst that would convince her.

"The cottage? You would let me go to the cottage?" she asked seemingly startled. "That would be nice, but..."

"If you like," he smiled, sipped the remainder of his brandy.

It would not be hard to make love to her first then explain later. When he could have gone to her at the inn, he chose not to do so.

"I would, except I can't leave Brice here. What if he wakes up and he can't get to me? The cottage is too far away."

"My suite of rooms?"

Patiently, he waited for her to agree. After all, he had the rest of his life with her. He wasn't going to quit until she said yes. He could be extremely patient when the need arose.

No matter what happened she would not go to the cottage. She might choose a different room to sleep in. He doubted that. She would sleep with him tonight. He would coax her sweetly until she agreed to his way of thinking.

Her lashes lowered, fluttered softly against her cheeks. If he wasn't mistaken, the gesture was flirtatious. Without showing his delight, he held out his hand waiting good-naturedly.

Upstairs in his suite, he'd set the stage. The fire crackled. Two bottles of wine were set out. A plate of Camembert and Brie along with a sliced baguette waited for them in the room. There were apple slices too. Gaby lit several candles lending aid with her romantic contribution.

"I would like to check on Brice first," she told him, her voice soft held a wealth of expectation. "After that we can talk about our future."

Gil was certain she wanted him. Sex had never been a problem between them. It was the other things, the miscommunication, and her son that caused her distress where it came to agreeing to his proposal. In the beginning neither wished to marry anyone. He waited while she walked to the door. She disappeared inside for a few seconds then stepped into the hallway.

He arched an eyebrow. "Everything fine?"

Oh, but he wanted to pull her into his arms, kiss her senseless. Needed an affirmation to his marriage proposal first. Among other things, he wanted to tell her how he felt about her, how she transformed his life. He hoped she would have something positive to say about him.

"*Oui.*" She looked down for a moment before she met his gaze. "He sleeps soundly. I don't believe he will harbor ill effects from his adventure."

Her eyes shimmered with what he'd come to know as passion. Her desire always ran hot and true. When she ran a fingertip along his jaw, she trembled, her eyes darkened with the passion he'd come to recognize.

I love you, Jenna.

Once in the room, she stopped. Her fingers rested on the fasteners of her dress. "You have seduction in mind?" There was a smile on her lips, a soft chuckle he thought he heard. "We haven't talked. I haven't accepted yet."

He liked it when she told him 'yet'. "You will."

He lowered his head to hers, felt the whisper of her breath against his lips. Mint scented air met him. Briefly, he touched her mouth with the tip of his tongue. She leaned into him as if asking for more. Reveled in the quick heady response.

"You're so sure of yourself, Gil Allemand. You are arrogant."

She danced away from him, teasing. She stopped at the window to look outside.

He walked close to her. Peered out the same window to the same picturesque scene. That same silver slipper of a moon looked down on the earth as it did last night. The same one that helped them search for the missing children. He would always remember that night with fear. Would remember the morning when they discovered them in the small glade with joy. He rested his hands on her shoulders, massaging. Her muscles. They were much too tight for what he planned. He would have to do something about that.

"Wine?" he asked as he stepped away from her, hoping to ease the tension he felt in her delicate frame. Understanding his intentions were part of it.

"You know I want some," she murmured, stepping toward him. "When you saw the moon were you thinking the same?"

"I'm certain I was. That was one of the worst nights of my life. The night turned to morning."

"We found them alive."

He couldn't help but remember the night Lance passed from this earth. "I'm forever thankful they were alive. I'm so relieved you did not have to suffer his death."

"You truly mean that?" Once more there were tears in her eyes. "I want to believe you've changed toward Brice."

~ * ~

"The moment I saw Margo curled up sound asleep in Brice's arms, my heart did a quick flip-flop."

"Flip-flop?" she asked sounding for a moment amused at his use of words. "You saw them together and that one image caused you to stop despising my son?" She sounded incredulous.

Nonetheless, her gaze remained fixed with his.

It seemed she waited for answers, for something more she could hold onto. He began as he refocused on his feelings. "I understand how strange that might seem to you."

"*Oui.*"

He sat down on one of the two chairs facing the fire. Peered at the flames over his glass. For several more seconds, he stared at the fire still searching for the right words. The arguments to convince her were too important. He let out a long breath of air, "It does to me, too, sound strange. I wondered how I could reverse my thoughts so quickly."

"As do I wonder the same. It is hard to believe that perhaps you are saying the words you want me to hear. That this is all contrived so you can coax an agreement from me."

"Your thoughts could be the case. They are not. Truth is I was slowly changing before that encounter in the forest. Your time with me at the vineyard seems to be healing my heart."

"I want to believe you," she told him. "It's dastardly hard."

"How long have you been at the chateau, a couple of months?" he asked, his gaze riveted on her.

She nodded then downed her glass of Bordeaux. She poured more then settled back into the chair, curling her legs around her. She pulled an afghan around her shoulders. "Closer to three, I suppose."

"Do you remember when you first saw me with Brice?" The last thing he wanted was to bring up that day. If he meant to convince her he changed, that day would have to be relived.

She choked on the wine left in her mouth and throat. Coughing, she sipped again. "I remember."

Yes, he understood. She most likely would never forget what he did, the things he insinuated. "You called me a *tete du butt*. I deserved the title. Shouldn't have treated Brice the way I did. Do you know why?"

"It was about Lance, wasn't it? What you did to my son. He was terrified. Brice didn't deserve what you did." Now she sounded as if she wasn't certain.

"In part. You learned very quickly I didn't want you around me either. I was surely mean spirited as well. Deserved all the wretched names the two of you called me. All I wanted was to be left alone to die." When he looked back on those years, he spent feeling that way, he was infinitely grateful Jenna blasted her way into his life.

"At the time you were my only hope. I was stubborn to a fault, always have been. In this case I didn't want to die. Most assuredly didn't want Brice to die. Was willing to do anything to keep him alive. There is more you should know. I never made that offer to anyone else. There were men who wanted me. I refused them all. Except for Jacques, you're the only man I've known intimately."

Gil soaked in all she said, felt intense emotions stumble into his heart. "Stubborn to a fault, I'm glad now that you were so immovable."

He remembered all the glances she shot his way. She disliked him yet on some level she didn't understand at the time, she also wanted him.

"Why?" her voice was soft, her eyes twinkling at him.

Mayhap she was beginning to see his change of heart. "When I first saw you, I was terrified. Even though you were reduced to skin and bones, I thought you were the most beautiful woman I'd ever seen. I was sure you would somehow wrench me from my melancholy. If you did that, you would also rip away all the walls I put up around myself."

At his words, her mouth seemed to gape open slightly. Crease lines marred her delicate forehead. "Beautiful? Me?" she asked again as if in disbelief. "No one has ever called me beautiful."

Amused, he chuckled softly at her response. "It must be the stupid men in your life. Etienne thought the only reason I was attracted to you was your beauty." He was quick to say. "Told him when you were around me that I felt again. When I met you, something snapped inside me. Ever since that moment, I've been healing. Yes, walls are coming down."

"Jacques always complained I was too thin. That was before. It seemed to me he disliked everything about me. I was too quiet, too shy. I never smiled. My breasts were too small. I was too tall." She let out a long sigh. "Don't suppose you want to hear all that."

"I don't. It's not the way I think of you." He held her hands in his, the color of his eyes darkening to almost black. "You're beautiful to me. Every part of you is also adorable. Don't care what any other man thinks. As far as you're concerned my opinion should be the only one that counts."

"Merci." She closed her mouth. Her small body shuddered as his thumbs worked circles on her wrists.

"Those first few days when you insisted on coming to work even though I refused to hire you, it was all I could do to keep my hands from exploring you. I would see you bent over scrubbing the floors. Your pert little butt high in the air. Would watch you polish the banister. Without a corset your breasts would sway enticing me to do more than watch, the tips pushing against the fabric of your thin gown. Wanted to taste you, investigate every part of you."

"You had a strange way of showing me how you felt."

"That was because I understood if I gave you encouragement you would...you would become part of my life. Deep down I didn't want that. Didn't want to ever feel joy again. Pleasure after I allowed Lance to die was never to be part of my life. I felt only guilt."

"It didn't take you long to assert yourself."

"That was because you offered to do anything. Your offer gave me reason to discover for myself what exactly you would give me. How far you would go to stay here at the chateau. I took advantage simply because I meant to continue feeding you, visiting you in the evenings. You understand I also didn't want you to die. I couldn't bear the thought of you leaving. If that happened, my life would be empty again."

She reached out to touch him. "I don't regret anything you took because you gave as much in return. Until you, I'd never been loved. Perhaps I took advantage of you, your kindness."

"That's not possible. I created a situation you couldn't live with. I treated you as if..." He couldn't say the word.

For a moment, he looked away. At the time he didn't care. All he cared about was Jenna in his bed loving him, making him forget the awful pain. The people who should have been her friend called her a whore as well as a witch. It was untenable that he created the situation she found herself in.

"I found a way. You must understand I wanted you. I'd never felt loved by anyone let alone a man. You don't love me. You did however cherish me with your caresses, the way you touched me, kissed me. I couldn't say no to you. Didn't want to in any case."

"Will you marry me?" He asked too soon. He understood that when he saw the change in her features, the rapid schooling of the emotions, which were beginning to show. They were just now beginning to understand each other.

Well, hell he was a fool.

"Don't rush me, Gil. You've given me a mountain of information to hash over. I don't know if I can trust myself to make a commitment."

"Come to bed with me. We can talk more in the morning." He looked to the bedroom then back to her, his grin spreading across his face. "Is it too soon to make love?"

"Too early in the evening. The hour isn't late enough to go to bed although I'm exhausted. The day has been more trying, my emotions blustering out of control. You've got to remember; I almost lost my child today. You of all people will understand."

That was something he would never forget. "More food?" He picked up the tray, sweeping it beneath her nose as if that would tempt her. She did choose a few things to eat. Sitting back in the chair she closed her eyes, seeming to savor what she put in her mouth. She pulled the afghan closer.

"Brice gave all his food to Margo."

He saw her response to that bit of news when the boy shared the intriguing piece of information this morning.

"He did. Wonder where he got that idea?" Gil asked as he tried to tamp down a tender smile.

"You know where. I wasn't pleased when I heard him say the words. When I had time to sift through my emotions, I was proud."

"He is going to grow up to be a strong man."

It must have been the tone of voice he used more than the words he said. Jenna finally looked at him as if she believed his earlier announcement.

"Just as Lance would have been," she murmured seeming to search his expression.

"*Oui*, because Brice has an amazing mother. Hopefully, he will have just as amazing step-father."

"You truly believe that about my son. You want to be a father to him?" Her words were whisper thin, a soft caress in the dimming light.

It wasn't a question Gil detected but a statement. Everything she asked of him was true. "I do, Jenna. I believe I love that little boy almost as much as I love his mother. Don't think I could love anyone or anything as much as I love you."

Her hands rose to cover her face. He saw the rapid pulsing of her breaths as she tried to drag air into her lungs. Gil was afraid he overstepped his bounds once more. He didn't want her to cry. Needed to see the smile on her face that he so loved. Too few times he'd seen it.

When she looked up, she wore a different expression. "When I first saw you dragging Brice by his collar, I wanted to kill you. That was all I could think about while I held my breath waiting for you to let him go. Knew if I succumbed to my anger, I would hang. Understood too that even then I needed you in order to survive."

"At the time I wished you would kill me. Maybe that's why I acted like a *tete du butt*," he said as he tried to forget those days. "There were several times I was so serious, I put the end of my pistol between my teeth."

She gasped softly as he recounted those haunted days he barely lived through. The pain so real it could still bring him to his knees. He didn't want her pity. What he told her was simply a fact about his past.

He couldn't fire the gun. Couldn't allow anyone to mourn his death.

"I'm glad you did not do it," she said softly. "I..." her words were stopped by his kiss.

His lips touched upon hers, warm and tender. She sipped air as she opened for him, accepting everything he gave.

~ * ~

She pulled away, touching his lips with a fingertip. "I need to tell you things too."

Jenna wasn't at all sure why she put him through this torture. She understood the telling of his story would be painful. She also knew the moment they found the children whatever animosity he felt for Brice vanished. She knew by the change of expression on his face.

Since that moment, the way he looked at her son was different. The pleasure was hers when he admitted the truth. Now, she had a decision to make. He asked her to marry him. More than anything she wanted to do just that.

I love you.

"What is it?" Gil questioned, touching her neck gently with the back of his knuckles, smoothing them along her flesh. Heat swept within.

"If you can treat Brice as your son, I will wed you. I understand even though your feelings have altered, to raise another man's son is a great deal to ask of any man."

She wanted Brice to have a father, a real father. If he refused, she didn't know what she would do next. She couldn't stay here.

He grinned at her, the lopsided grin she loved. By the darkening of his eyes, she understood he didn't want to talk. No, he wanted to make love. He placed his hands on either side of her head. "If you will allow me to do so, I would like to adopt your son."

She was stunned by his offer. Had never expected those words of commitment. "What did you say?" she asked needing to pinch herself to make sure she wasn't dreaming.

"You heard me right. I'd like to adopt Brice. He can keep whatever last name you want him to have. It's up to you."

His lips warmed hers once more, slipped across her mouth, touched upon her nose then her eyelids as he tenderly closed them. He found his way back to her lips, opened them, swept his tongue past her teeth to delve hotly inside. He kissed her again and again. Hot slick with moisture, he left her breathless with the need he created so easily.

Gil's hands touched upon her shoulders, rested there for a moment. He poured more wine. Sat back as if he was a satisfied man. The broad grin on his face told her nothing about what he was thinking.

He offered her wine.

More food.

She wanted him. "What is it?" she finally asked, wishing he would be more like himself.

Jenna wished he'd make love to her. By now he should at least have her clothes lying on the floor, his following.

"You need to eat more." His laughter warmed her while she remembered those earlier days.

"Why do you say that? You know very well I haven't starved myself for at least a day." She wondered if he knew she was carrying his child. No, she told herself it was too soon for him to realize. She wasn't showing at least not very much. Her breasts were larger. He hadn't touched her there for a day or so.

He laughed harder. "You have to make up for the days you did without food. One or two meals will not do the trick."

"Incorrigible man," she mumbled as she ate the plate of food he handed her then drank the wine. It was delicious. "Satisfied?"

"For now."

For a few seconds, silence surrounded them. Except for the crack of the fire and his deep breathing she heard nothing. Jenna continued to drink her wine, wondering what he would do next.

Finally, "Gil? I don't understand."

"What?" He leaned forward, gently touching her neck, running his finger along her collarbone then lower to trace a path across the tops of her breasts.

"Do you want me to do or say something?" Truly, she had no idea what he wanted, what he waited for.

"*Oui, cherie.*"

"You wouldn't mind explaining to me what you're waiting for?" Breathless from the gentle contact, she wanted to yell at him.

"A man shouldn't have to ask twice."

She swallowed the wine left in her throat, finally understanding what the man waited for. "I don't recall you asking anything."

Oh, she did though. She remembered the hasty marriage proposal. She wanted something a bit more romantic if she was going to say yes to this man. He wasn't going to get away with this.

"Liar." He smiled as he continued his tender assessments.

His exploring fingers found her ear, touched then traced the path back to her jaw and neck. He would coax and sweet-talk all he wanted. She wasn't about to give in to the seduction before she had what she wanted. Well, she would give into the seduction. What she hoped was for him to get down on one knee. Do this proposal thing the right way.

"*Oui, voulez vous coucher avec moi maintenant?*"

"Want your answer to my question, *cherie*. Not that I don't want to take you to my bed. Sleep is the last thing on my mind."

"You understand what I meant." Her words came out in huff.

She was tired of the word games. Tempted to back down and tell him what he wanted to know. Darn it but she needed him to initiate it without prompting from her.

"Of course I'm still waiting."

Perhaps he was too obtuse to comprehend what she wanted him to do. Maybe he didn't have a romantic bone in his body. Pigs might fly before he got down on one knee.

He told her she was stubborn. She yawned. "I would like to go to bed. Guess I'll find a room down the hallway, closer to Brice's room." She stood watching his expression change from happily condescending to angry.

"When you go to bed tonight it will be in my bed." His voice was husky with passion.

"*Oui*, I understand what you want. What you want is not what I want." Well, she could be angry too.

"You don't want to marry me? I thought after...after what we talked about you wanted..." it seemed he couldn't finish his thought.

"I do, you stupid man. It might be selfish of me. I want everything. Need for you to do this right. When I married Jacques, I wasn't asked. Father handed me over to him as if I was goods he sold, which he did."

"Do it right?" he asked sounding to Jenna's ears as if he didn't have any idea as to what she wanted.

She stood; her hands fisted. Perhaps the foolish man didn't. "I'm not going to give you an answer to your question until you do this the right way. I want to remember your proposal fondly. Not the way you blurted it an hour or so past. Just as the answer needs thought so does the question."

She started from the room, back straight determined to outlast him. He stepped in front of her. Jabbed his hands into his hair, leaving it charmingly disheveled. Unable to stop herself, she smiled. Wished to run her fingers through his hair.

"Blasted woman. Tell me what you want. I'll do it just to end the torture."

For a man such as Gil getting down on one knee might be tantamount to begging her. He didn't beg. If he wouldn't do it exactly her way, could there be a compromise?

Jenna blinked back the moisture forming in her eyes as she turned away. She didn't want Gil to see her cry over something so ridiculous as a proper wedding proposal. *Enfer!* This was going to be her last wedding. The only one she entered into as a willing participant. She would never marry another man. There would be no other opportunities. She didn't want to look back on the proposal and have regrets.

"You're crying?" He sounded stunned. "Truly, Jenna, I want to make you happy. Know now the answer will be *oui* if I ever figure out what you want me to do. Why don't you tell me?"

"Needed for you to think of it yourself."

She turned from him, thoughtful about what he told her. Understanding she should tell him yes and forget all her dreams. She could not. Just as she wanted a real wedding, she wanted a real proposal.

With a shrug, she gave up. "You will not like what I'm going to say. I understand that. So, wanted you to figure it out on your own. If you did so, I would know you weren't being forced. Now, you will do it just to make me happy."

He grinned seeming to misunderstand what she tried to tell him. Gently, he ran his thumb along her lips. "It's what I want, to make you happy. Try me. You won't find out if you don't ask."

For a moment Jenna looked down. When she finally grew the courage to look at him, she swallowed hard. "I want you to be romantic. To propose as if you mean it."

"I did mean the words. I don't understand the romantic bit. Wasn't I..." he stopped then seeming to recall his hasty question. "Well *non,* I guess not."

She gulped air, "Would you get down on one knee? Would you ask that way, holding my hand as well as a ring?" A sob tore from her as she slipped her hand from his, racing to the window. "I understand if you don't want to."

There were no sounds for several seconds. She watched the night sky, the stars twinkling brightly. When she felt his hand on her shoulder, she jumped, startled by the contact.

He turned her, a smile reaching his eyes, flashing his even white teeth. "You should have said something sooner." He appeared pleased with himself. Slowly he got down on one knee. Her hand now in his, he brought from behind his back a small box.

"Jenna, you are the most beautiful woman I've ever known. I need you with each breath I take. I want your son to be mine as well as yours. The child you now carry will have my name."

She gasped. So, he did know.

"Is that why you want to marry me?" she blurted before she thought it through.

"*Non,* foolish woman, I want to wed you because I love you. If I didn't, I would make sure our child carried my name. That isn't the case, Jenna. Will you marry me?"

He opened the box to uncover a beautiful solitaire diamond ring.

"It's huge," she murmured softly.

He laughed, finally seeming to understand he proposed the way she needed him to do so. "I hope you say that about other things you see tonight too."

Her eyes widening, she stared at him. Comprehension arrived slowly. When she realized exactly what he meant the heat of her discomposure flushed her cheeks.

"Well?" he asked while he slipped the ring onto her finger. "Did I do it right?"

"Maman! Maman!"

The cry shattered her into a thousand tiny pieces. Changed the moment for forever. She didn't answer. They both rushed from the room. Brice walked slowly down the long hallway. Sobs wrenched his body. When he saw her, he held out his hands to her.

"Maman..."

She pulled him into her arms, carrying him to the suite of rooms. Jenna sat down with Brice in her lap snuggled next to her. His head rested in the crook of her shoulder. Gil sat in the other chair, studying her over the top of her son's head.

"Oui," she mouthed the word then looked at her ring.

He smiled back while she rocked Brice soothing the little boy with murmured words that didn't mean anything. "Was it a bad dream?"

Brice nodded, clenching his wooden horse close to him. "Thought I was going to die for real this time."

"You don't need to worry any longer. All will be fine. You're not going to die."

It seemed an eternity before Brice was fast asleep again. Gil carried him to his room. Jenna tucked him in, smoothing the warm covers around him.

She leaned into the warmth Gil offered. Her back to him, his arms wrapped around her. His hands were clasped over her belly. She wondered how he knew so soon. Oh, he mumbled a few things. She meant to ask when she got the chance. Perhaps he would enlighten her.

Back in Gil's suit she laughed softly, suddenly no longer tired. She did want him to make love to her tonight. That could wait.

"Should we finish the bottle of wine?"

"The second one?" he asked while he nodded his head. He poured, watching her yet he didn't hand her the glass right away. "I believe, *Madam Bonnet*, I would like a proper acceptance of my marriage proposal."

"What would that be?" she teased.

"The words I've waited so patiently to hear."

"They would be..." Swirling her wine in the glass she watched him over the rim. She stared at his lips thinking of a kiss.

"You know."

"Oui, Monsieur Allemand Je t'epouserai."

"Kiss me," he murmured softly.

Epilogue

The balmy day was perfect for a fall wedding. Colorful leaves adorned the trees. Rain the night before cleared the air, leaving behind a brilliantly blue sky. Gil inhaled a deep breath. When he held out his hand his fingers shook.

Etienne laughed while he clapped him on the back. "It will all be over with before you can blink two times. After that you will be well and truly married. Jenna is a beautiful woman. I knew it from the first time I spoke with her."

"Even my hands are sweating," Gil grumbled as he wished he would see Jenna walking through the doorway. He tried not to think of all that happened all they went through because Etienne lost his confidence in his ability to discern a person's true character.

She didn't have anyone to give her away. He wrote her father on the off chance the man would come. When she discovered what he'd done behind her back, she was furious. Why shouldn't she be? The man sold her to her first husband. He apologized profusely.

If her father agreed, he would have had to find the words to tell him he wasn't wanted. She refused to allow Etienne to walk with her because of his part in Elisa's scheme. Jenna also refused to have Elisa stand up for her as a bride's maid. It seemed Jenna still held a bit of a grudge, perhaps a huge grudge.

At the last minute she decided her son would walk with her down the aisle and Gaby would be her bridesmaid. To Gil, it seemed unusual she had no friends. The only person from the village who attended was *Madam Macon* with her granddaughter. Bet, the woman from the inn, attended. She accepted the position as head housekeeper. Bet decided Angel's place in Bordeaux would not suit when she was given another option.

Because she was able to take her granddaughter to Paris with Etienne and Elisa's francs, she was able to see a doctor who knew what was wrong with the little girl. Her *petite fille* was no longer going to die.

His men along with their wives or in some cases girlfriends attended. He spent the two weeks before the wedding setting up his office as well as his means of communication at the chateau. Guards were placed strategically around the vineyard as well as the little cottage where they visited some evenings.

Music caught his attention. Finally. Etienne nudged him. "Just think about the night to come. The thought will vanquish those nerves you are having."

Yes, if he did that, he'd forget what he was supposed to say. He moved a bit to ease the tension building in his groin.

Damn Etienne.

Gaby appeared. She was beaming. From the moment she and Jenna met, Gaby must have loved her. She'd been shocked and very pleased when she was asked to be a bridesmaid or perhaps, she was the matron of honor since there were no others attendants.

When Gil first saw Jenna, his breath caught. For a moment he thought his knees would buckle. "Beautiful." Only Etienne and the minister heard his whispered word.

Her gown was made from white lace. It was the first gown she allowed him to pay for. Her long blond hair curled around her shoulders. Her lips were full, moist, waiting for his attention. He made sure she wore something borrowed, blue as well as new. Brice appeared handsome in his new suit. He held his mother's hand as they slowly walked down the aisle. The boy beamed at him. It seemed Brice didn't have trouble forgiving him his prior indiscretions.

"You still want go through with this?" Etienne asked with an all-knowing smirk on his face

"Do you have the ring?" Gil shot back.

Etienne chuckled, searched his pockets. "Ah, for a second, thought I might have lost it."

"If that happened you would have another Allemand who would not be able to forgive you. As it is at the moment only Jenna holds a grudge."

When she stopped in front of him, her smile was soft. Briefly, she lowered her lashes. As she looked at him again, he saw the desire along with the passion in her eyes. The ceremony passed in a blur. They both said the words, he loudly, she softly.

The priest pronounced them husband and wife. He kissed her.

Their lips touched gently. He deepened the kiss, touching her with his tongue. She leaned into him. He would have forgotten where they were except Etienne nudged him then cleared his throat.

He heard the applause. Tucked her hand onto his arm. As man and wife, they officially started their lives together.

Later that night they sat in the master chamber. He sipped champagne. She told him it didn't taste good to her. Gaby made her lemonade instead.

"Are you happy? I carried you over the threshold without you asking. Although I had to ask every woman," he held up his hand, grinning from ear to ear, "*Oui*, even Elisa what customs I had to make sure I did so you wouldn't be disappointed or angry with me. I wanted today to be perfect for you."

She laughed at him. He enjoyed her laughter.

The sound left him light-headed. Perhaps it was the champagne or a combination there of.

"I appreciate all that you did. I need you, Gil. With all my heart I will always need you in my life and Brice's. I love you."

He settled his hand on her slightly rounded belly. "I love you too. This child will need both of us."

"I will spend my life, needing you in every way possible." Then she mused, "Needing Gil."

"*Non, besoin de* Jenna," he murmured as he took the glass from her hands. "We will finish this later." He kissed her softly then with all the desire he felt for her. Their life would be filled with love and happiness. He looked forward to living. While the pain of losing Lance was not vanquished, it seemed he could now control the desperate feelings of loss.

Coming Soon by the Author
at
Rogue Phoenix Press

Just for Michael
Bad Boys Book Twelve

Chapter One

Virginia, July 1833

On this hot, windy day Clare Carter-Brown watched the sleek clipper until the white-tips of its sails were no longer visible. The vessel carried her sister along with the rest of her family. She pulled in a deep breath of the tangy Atlantic sea air savoring the moment. This was her home. Her sister and her husband were gone now, returning to their home in England. She was by herself. Nonetheless. she didn't feel alone. The affinity she had for this land went far and beyond the normal. The feelings traveled deep into her heart and soul. From the moment she left Virginia seven years ago Clare, knew she would return someday. America was in her blood.

Clare twirled, her skirts flaring out around her ankles showing more than was appropriate. She didn't care. Let the world think what they wished. Sophie thought she didn't know what she would do with herself. She did though. Link helped her with the promise he would never tell Sophie until she prospered. Following her dream, that's what she would do. He simply gave her the money she would need to get started. He helped her with other aspects too.

Mayfair Racing and Stud Farm.

Sophie believed wholeheartedly she would return to England by the end of the summer. She wouldn't. Link Stewart supposed she would stay at Leslie Hall, his family's home. That wasn't going to happen either.

Her intention was to march right up to Mayfair Hall then stake her claim to her inheritance. It was hers. Well, it would be in three months when she turned twenty-one. Link wasn't going to hold her to his wishes. She never promised him. When her uncle, William Brinkmeyer, passed on to greener pastures five years ago, Mayfair was turned over to her loving care.

She could barely stand the anticipation, the excitement of it all. Mayfair was hers. Beneath her ribs her heart thundered with eagerness. So excited her palms sweated. While it was true she wouldn't turn twenty-one for another three months, she felt independent. As her guardian at this moment, Link held all responsibility for the estate.

Link wasn't here. He was an ocean away, at least he would be soon. She did have his approval as well as monetary support until she started making a profit. Link Stewart, her brother-in-law backed her. He believed in her every bit as much as she believed in herself.

An agenda written in her head loomed at the top of her mind. There was so much to accomplish, so much planning. Clare walked away from the dock immersed in her thoughts. This area had not changed in the seven years since she was in Virginia. She walked past the alehouse where the men gathered to gossip. Hot toddies came to mind. Her brother-in-law used to spend time here so he heard all the rumors first hand. Most of them concerned her sister. Sophie had been known as the town harlot. She wasn't though. Enough of those antiquated thoughts. They were best left alone. Drudging them up would serve only to depress her. Only the small-minded people of the town believed the rumors. Well, perhaps not. Even Link believed those tales at first. Not much time passed, however, before he had second thoughts about Sophie.

So lost in reflections about the past, she walked right into Michael Flannigan. Michael was the manager of Mayfair Hall, all its properties as well as the slaves she meant to free. When she did so, she would have another strike against her where the townspeople were concerned. What she didn't comprehend as of yet was how Michael felt about slaves. She also didn't know if he would stand in her way when she took over the management.

"Hello," she said as she looked up into incredibly green eyes that reminded her of the soft moss in the glade where she used to spend a wealth of her free time when she was in England. She smiled hugely at him.

"You should pay attention to your surroundings," he told her, his hands resting gently on her shoulders. His smile was bold as well as arrogant. He offered an arm, "Where are you headed to now?"

The way his hands felt when he touched her sent shivers throughout. She stepped away, unwilling to give over to the certain pleasure he made her feel. He kissed her once. She liked it. After that she decided kisses between them couldn't happen. The sensations were way too much for her to consider. Those same sensations left her week kneed and breathless.

She didn't like it.

"We have a great deal of issues to discuss, Mr. Flannigan." She meant to keep the relationship between them business, nothing else.

"Mr. Flannigan?" Michael arched a dark red eyebrow that was indeed perfectly sculpted. With that single action, he questioned her on a level she didn't understand.

"Yes." She meant to continue here as she planned. Giving into his charming ways was not going to happen. She was sure he could seduce easily enough as she'd heard a few rumors concerning him.

"Michael," he murmured close to her ear. "Call me Michael."

His breath wafting across her sensitive flesh reaffirmed her need to keep this business-like. She stepped away, sifting in a staggered breath of air. Once again her knees felt weak. The man was too potent for her.

"Mr. Flannigan," she insisted as she suddenly realized he wasn't going to easily concede to her wishes.

She heard the breath of air he heaved into his lungs while she also saw the frown lines creasing his forehead. Clearly, he was displeased with her stubborn insistence on using his last name.

"Michael," he told her again, sterner this time. "Mr. Flannigan is far too formal. Besides it makes me out to be an old man. Here is Duster," he said as they stopped in front of one of the horses that would make her stud farm a success. His mount, Gypsy, was tethered next to her stallion. He was also from fine lineage. "I'll follow you to Leslie Hall. Did you know your trunks were deposited in the master chamber in Mayfair Hall?" He paused to look at her as if trying to discern her thoughts. "Ah, you do know. What should I think about that?" He slanted her a half-smile that made her stomach churn in a curious way.

Clare didn't think for a second he was asking her if she meant to take up residence in his bedroom hence sharing the bed. However, the look on his face was something she couldn't fathom. She wanted to see inside his thoughts.

"You will move into the manager's cottage behind the plantation. It was one of the issues we needed to talk about. I would prefer to wait for this discussion until we have an office where we can speak privately. Perhaps we can curtail the discussion until we arrive at Mayfair Hall."

"No."

"You don't have a choice, Mr. Flannigan. I'm not conversing with you until there is privacy." She found the calm serenity she wanted to proceed with was vanishing. The very look in his eyes challenged her.

He flashed even white teeth, his smile telling her she was wrong about that. Of course, she understood he could refuse her request. Well, indeed what she asked for wasn't a request. Her words were meant as a command.

She had the control.

He wasn't in charge.

"We will see." His large hands on her waist he tossed her atop Duster as if she weighed nothing at all. She wasn't tiny so why was he able to do that so easily? Why did she feel so helpless when she was with him? He meant to take charge. She wasn't about to allow such a thing.

Helpless was not a feeling she needed or wanted. Nor did she want to feel week-kneed or have her stomach turning somersaults when he smiled at her.

The next half hour they rode along the river in silence. She could think of nothing to say that wouldn't start an argument. The few times she glanced his way he looked straight ahead, crease lines on his forehead. What he was thinking was imperative for her to comprehend. It didn't seem he meant to enlighten her.

Pushing thoughts of the upcoming confrontation out of her mind for the moment, she let her mind wander to more pleasant avenues of thought. With the sun shining brightly, the heat kissed her face. She wanted to remove the hat. Thought better of it before she changed her mind.

Defying fashion along with good sense, she untied the ribbons so the hat dangled on her back. He slanted her a look, a fat grin on his handsome features. Heat rose to her cheeks.

Damn and blast, she didn't want to enjoy his smile or even the twinkling green eyes of his. She tilted her chin before nudging Duster to a faster pace. Wind sifted through her hair until nearly all the pins fled the strands. She headed the horse along the banks of the river. He followed behind her, the sounds of Gypsy's hooves loud.

They passed Leslie Hall then turned toward Mayfair Hall. Michael didn't say a word nor did she. Explaining herself to her manager about where she meant to live was not part of the manager's job description. She would have to enlighten him as to his new duties.

She was displacing him from a place he called home for the last five years. In his situation, she would be angry too.

He would understand he would have to move in three months if not today. They reached the newly furbished stables that would house her pride and joys. Her horses. Duster was a descendant of Fearnought who was a big bright bay horse very nearly sixteen hands high. Duster was of his size. He would be the stud of the Mayfair Hall Racing and Stud Farm. Duster filled a major portion of her dream.

She and Link discussed this in length. Neither wanted to own slaves. At Leslie Hall most of the slaves were now freed. Leslie Stewart, the Duke of Southcliff, Link's older brother, didn't wish to have any part of slavery. Link conspired with his friends as well as his business associates to find the perfect stud for her new adventure. This wasn't actually an adventure it was more her bid for independence along with a new life. As a woman no one expected her to flourish. She would.

When they reached the end of the road to Mayfair, Timmie the young black stable boy strode out to greet them. He grinned at her. One top tooth was missing. He lost it in a race when a competitor nudged him along with his horse into a ditch.

"Hello." She dismounted before Michael could come to help her. Feeling his hands on her waist was sure to cause unruly sensations she didn't want to deal with before she spoke with him.

"Brush Duster and Gypsy. Duster is here for the night. I'll be out to see to the horses when I'm done with Mr. Flannigan."

She watched him bristle. Will he posture and get all out of joint? His displeasure with her intention would never change her plans.

He stepped up beside her, keeping pace as they walked through the huge front door. "Done with me?" he asked while his hand gripped her elbow turning her, forcing her to look at him. To no avail she tried to wrench her arm from his hold.

Michael no longer smiled. His face assumed an austere mask of what might be indifference. She understood what this man felt was far from indifference.

Clare beckoned Old Suzzy. The woman was another one of the black slaves. She was tiny, barely reaching five feet tall. Her dark skin was wrinkled with age. She had the warmest big brown eyes Clare had ever seen. Several times the woman cleaned Sophie's wounds when their uncle hit her. Old Suzzy knew more about her life here than any other living soul.

"Miss Clare." She grinned showing a few missing teeth. Wrinkles crinkled around her eyes. "Mighty glad to see you. You here to stay?"

"Will you bring a pot of tea to the office, please?"

Old Suzzy nodded before she took off down the long hallway to the kitchen. Clare took a moment to straighten her skirt. She walked into the office. She remembered William Brinkmeyer sitting behind the huge oak desk. Her uncle would smile at her. Even then at thirteen she understood there was nothing good behind that smile. Uncle Brinkmeyer was an evil selfish man who cared nothing about anyone except himself.

Clare remembered a lot of things she'd rather not recall. She hitched in a deep breath of air realizing she'd given Michael time to walk around her then assume an in charge position behind the huge desk.

He did not.

Instead, he leaned negligently on the doorframe legs as well as his arms crossed. This time he seemed to school his features, a lazy somewhat insolent smile plastered on his face. Clare didn't know what to make of this.

She sucked air.

This man would not give an inch. Who sat behind the desk would not matter to him. Certain that he didn't think she could manage the men who worked for her, she meant to convince him otherwise.

Old Suzzy brought in the tea. After she looked from her to Michael she scurried from the room. Michael pushed away from the wall then sauntered to the decanter of brandy on the sideboard. He poured himself a glass then saluted her. So much was being said without words.

"What is this business you're going to enlighten me with?" he asked before he downed the snifter in one gulp. Michael set the glass down.

Deciding she needed to sit before her knees buckled, she poured her tea. Behind the desk she rested both hands on its smooth top. The wood barrier gave her confidence. She sat; sipped her tea thinking about what she needed to say first. Silence thundered in the room. It seemed she could hear everything yet nothing.

Before she started she tugged in some courage in the form of oxygen. "Life around here will not be the same now that I've returned."

"I gathered as much. How pray tell do you mean to change life?" He poured more brandy. He didn't choose to sit.

Clare thought to start with the less controversial of topics. "To begin with we will no longer grow tobacco." Intuitively, she watched his face. He was calm, showing no emotion at all.

"The land would not take too much more of that crop. Tobacco sucks the life out of the dirt. Most planters rotate crops or allow the land to lay fallow. Your decision seems reasonable to me."

"We won't be doing either." She placed a lemon slice in her tea then poured milk before adding a sugar cube. "I've other plans for the land."

It seemed she caught his attention. "What do you intend?" Actually, he appeared intrigued.

"I'm going to free the slaves. Don't believe in slavery. Link gave me permission. Not that I need it." When she was nervous she talked too fast. That was what she did right now. He would know.

"Good." After that statement which thoroughly surprised her, he leaned both hands on the desk she knew he usually sat behind during conversations of this nature. "What is going to happen to them? They will starve. My God, woman they are like children. Even though I approve wholeheartedly, you can't just pronounce them free."

She pulled herself up straight thinking he had no right at all to question her. "Link and I discussed this particular problem not that it has anything to do with you. I've set a course of action that will be followed to the letter."

"What brilliant strategy did the two of you come up with?" His bland tone didn't surprise her. He was waiting for her to mess up before he jumped in with his opinions thereby assuming control.

He would learn soon enough she was in charge here. "We will rent land to each family. They can plant crops as well as sell them. Your job will be to collect the rent on the properties after they have begun to make a living."

"So far you make sense."

The acknowledgement was sweet of him. She didn't think he meant to be sweet. "We will build new homes for those who want to stay."

"What about the ones who don't? What will happen to them?" He pushed away from the desk, pinching the bridge of his nose.

"I'm going to encourage them all to stay then I'll hire a person to teach them to read and write. They will need those skills to survive as well as prosper." On the defensive now, she needed to turn the exchange around. Taking charge here was imperative if she meant to run the plantation.

"Good luck with that. How do you expect to keep this place running without funds from the crops? Where is the coin going to come from to build new homes for all the people you've freed."

"Those are all good questions. However, I want you to know if you continue to manage the properties, your job description will change. You will be doing most of the teaching." She held up her hands, "Not the reading and writing."

"Figured as much." He sat down with another glass of brandy in hand, his long muscled legs stretched out in front of him appearing totally relaxed. "I'm waiting."

"For what?" she asked surprised. Keeping her gaze from roaming the length of him was nearly impossible. Clare touched her lips recalling his kiss, the warmth, how he traced her lip with his tongue before plunging deep inside. She recalled his taste, his sent. That was a month ago, a mistake. One she wouldn't make again.

His grin was slow, lazy, his arrogance undeniable. "My job description. Perhaps I'm to attend to the physical needs of the new owner since we are sharing a bedroom."

"You!" Heat bathed her face. "How dare you imply something like that!"

"Me, yes, who else? A moment ago you were thinking about the kiss we shared the other evening. You know the evening we watched the sun go down in the west. We shared a bottle of wine as well. Oh, did it happen nearly a month ago? You have a fine memory, Clare. Shall we see if the kiss will still taste as sublime as the first time?"

"I have no physical needs you will attend to." Her breath stuck in her throat. In that one moment he took over the discussion. He made her recall in vivid detail that moment.

"You should understand, I won't share my bed with you unless you are naked." His gaze traveled the length of her before insolently settling on her heaving bosom. "You want me now. We can visit the master chamber then see if we are as compatible in bed as I believe we are. We haven't had a chance for anything more than a few kisses."

Clare understood the conversation turned to a topic she didn't understand too well. He was outrageous in his words. He was all male and powerful. She would do well to remember that fact when dealing with him.

To get back on track was her immediate goal. "You will collect the rent monies, make sure they have seed to plant as well as the tools the men will need. They will most likely have to be instructed on what will be best for the land. I've heard wheat or corn are good crops for the soil that has been tasked to the limit. The families may also plant vegetable gardens for their use if they would like to do so."

"You heard right. I'm sure we will think of other issues that might arise then deal with them together. Now, what are you going to do with the studs you brought in? What are your plans for the stable that has been reconstructed these last months since your brother-in-law has been in the states. He didn't leave before he thought it was ready."

She breathed a silent sigh of relief when he stopped pursuing this bedroom situation. Nonetheless, he maintained that arrogant air that only men would understand what was needed. He was wrong.

"Mayfair Hall will no longer be a tobacco plantation. It will be a stud farm. A sign has been commissioned that will read, Mayfair Racing and Stud Farm. Duster has bloodlines going back to Fearnought. I've two pregnant mares both with lines that go back to Medley who was bred in England by Lord Grosvenor. Link has been busy, as he has lined up two mares that Duster will cover. We should make a great show of this. The men bringing the mares are each paying two hundred pounds, which is the going rate in England. At the moment I'm not certain how much that is in American money."

"So," Michael tapped his long bronzed fingers together before he joined them beneath his chin is a powerful steeple. "You've got everything figured out. Or, should I say Link has brought about this wonderful scenario for you. A woman cannot command. If she attempts such a feat, men won't obey."

Enthusiastically, she nodded relieved he seemed to be taking this change in stride while she tried to forget the condescension in his tone along with his words about a woman's ability to lead men. Clearly, Michael Flannigan didn't believe women competent to run a stable such as this one. "Link has been an immense help. However, the success will be up to me."

"Except the sharing of my bed." He leaned closer to her. "Link has nothing to do with that. I'm sure he would not be pleased. As you said, he is across the ocean."

"I've that covered also." She felt prim and proper. After all, she was a spinster. She was on the shelf. While they discussed this new situation for Mayfair, she realized she would simply allow him to have the master chamber. The bedroom as it appeared now reminded her too much of Uncle William.

"You do?" He sounded surprised yet at the same time a bit intrigued.

Curtly, she nodded. "I will take the adjoining room. You may stay in the large room. I've no problem with that."

His curses shocked her to the tips of her slippered feet. "Mr. Flannigan!" Her heart heaved against her chest.

His scowl returned. He appeared dangerous and dark. His green eyes closer to the darkness of leaves on an oak rather that the soft green of moss. "Do you care so little about your reputation?"

Blindsided, maybe more confused, Clare didn't understand what to make of his words. "What does our sleeping arrangements have to do with my reputation? If we are sharing or not sharing a bed, who would know? Who would even care about what we do in the privacy of Mayfair Hall?" She didn't want to feel quite so baffled. Didn't wish for him to believe she didn't understand what he meant.

She didn't.

"Are you stupid or naïve or both?" He rose from the chair. His pacing took him in circles around the dark blue Aubusson carpet. He paused at the window looking over the land, his hands clasped behind his back.

Clare made a mental note to change the draperies. The fabric was too dark. The room needed a brighter look. He turned, a scowl creasing his forehead. His hands were fisted.

She wanted to understand what was traveling through his man's brain. Nothing he'd been telling her made sense. At first he teased about taking her to his bed naked. The next thing she knew he was telling her if she slept in the adjoining bedroom, her reputation would never recover. "I take exception to that. What is it that you want, Mr. Flannigan? What exactly are you trying to describe?"

His feet took him to a point directly in front of her. With a finger beneath her chin, he slowly lifted. His gaze bore into hers. Her breath caught in the back of her throat. "I should show you. God knows it's probably the only way you'll understand. You're too damn innocent."

Clare pushed away from him as well as the desk. "You ass..." Her words trailed off when his large hands gripped her shoulders. It didn't seem he was going to let her go.

He pulled her close. The scent of brandy caressed her as his breath whispered across her face. One month ago he tasted of the sweet wine they drank, the white Bordeaux from the Stewart vineyard in France. She ran her tongue across her bottom lip, leaving a path of moisture. She did want another kiss, perhaps another one after that. Nonetheless, she didn't want him to know that.

With all her might, she pushed away from Michael understanding if they were going to maintain a working relationship, they could not dally. Sharing kisses would not be conducive to business. It would prove to be distracting. Clare wasn't at all certain if dallying meant just kissing or if the word entailed more. Nonetheless, she didn't want to take the chance she would melt in the heat of his arms again.

One time was enough. A month ago she melted. This afternoon was not going to see a replay of that frivolous evening. Her push seemed to bring them closer. His mouth hovered inches above hers. "You want me to kiss you, admit to the fact." His voice was husky, a different sound from the norm.

She was shaking her head. Lifting one hand from her, he ran one hand through the length of her hair. He stared hard at her. A muscle along his jaw ticked warningly.

"No, no I don't."

"Tell me to keep my hands off you but don't lie to me. Kiss me, Clare. Kiss me like you did before. I want to taste your sweetness, feel your sultry heat. After that maybe we can talk in a more adult way about our sleeping arrangements."

"There is nothing to talk about." Her hands on his chest pushed. He didn't move.

"Oh, but I do believe there is a great deal of discussion to be had." His lips found hers. Unable to help herself, she met his tongue with her own, delved inside the warmth of him. Clare wanted to cry with the desperate need he induced. She needed to put this man out of her thoughts. He was too big a distraction to her plans. If she gave him the chance, he would ruin everything. In order to prove herself, she would have to be strong.

When he lifted his head to look at her, to move a few strands of damp hair from her face she found her voice, "Stop, Michael, please...don't do this to me."

~ * ~

Well, hell, he didn't want to stop. There wasn't one doubt in his mind she liked what he did to her. No, he wanted to keep kissing her until she agreed to marry him, until he couldn't breathe. Yesterday, after speaking with Link, he believed he had the three months until she turned twenty-one to convince her to his way of thinking. After that it would be more difficult for him to maintain the land he wanted, the land he should own.

Now she thought to take on her sister's shoes by sleeping in the adjoining room. If he had his way, she would never become the next harlot of Virginia. The difficult part of all this was that he did want her naked in his bed. He wanted to give her a woman's pleasure. Needed to hear her howl at the moon when she climaxed her silken white body beneath his. His emotions were in such turmoil; he didn't know what to think.

He wanted to be a gentleman where Clare was concerned.

Hell, he wasn't a gentleman. Never had been.

Link made it abundantly clear she was not to be present when Duster covered a mare. She was a virgin. Clare shouldn't see something so carnal in nature. Short of tying her somewhere, he didn't understand how he could prevent her from doing whatever the devil took her mind to do. From all she spoke of just now, she would make sure she played an integral part of this business, all of it.

When Link explained this dream of hers to become independent, well, he promised to give her that illusion as long as possible. Michael understood if she ran out of funds, he was to write to her brother-in-law immediately for more money. Clare's brother-in-law was going to use his substantial groats to keep her dream alive. Now, Link counted on him to be a silent partner is this ill-fated adventure of Clare's.

The difficult part of all this was that he as well as Link hoped she succeeded. Neither had an iota of hope it would, at least not without a man's interference. The other men would never take orders from her. Blast it all, she needed him to have a superior role in this venture of hers.

He kissed the lass.

After she asked, he stopped.

Even while lust surged straight to his groin so potent he had few rational thoughts, he set her aside. Actually, he was surprised he didn't toss her on that big desk then with her legs wrapped around his flanks teach her about a woman's pleasure. His imagination ran rampant. If he was going to succeed and see his dreams materialize, he needed to curtail his carnal thoughts.

Michael didn't want to stop and think about all these plans of hers. When he did, he realized Link supplied her with all she needed to make a success. Duster would bring top dollar as a stud. Two mares were lined up to test Duster's prowess. If he continued to advertise, there would be more within the week. He could race Duster as well as Gypsy. Duster was fast. Link told him the stallion did best at the quarter mile. Gypsy was in for the long haul. The stallion possessed a heart that never quit. The horse was quickly gaining an impeccable reputation in the racing world. While he wanted to ride Gypsy, the problem was that he was just too damn big for a jockey. Link also made certain he understood that under no circumstances was Clare to race. She would try to do so. He would have to be a step or more ahead of her to succeed.

He agreed.

She would try.

He grinned, a huge grin. Another possible tussle with Clare might be fun. "When do you want to begin telling the slaves they are free?"

She stepped away from him, wishing for more distance he felt sure. He strode to the big desk then sat down. For a few seconds while he tried to school his emotions, he shuffled the papers he'd been working on before he rode into town.

"Timmie and Old Suzzy should be told first. They will help us with the rest when the time comes. Link thought we should start building the new homes before we do anything else. The freed men can help."

He agreed. "Over the last five years Mayfair has acquired no new slaves. Some have died. At this moment we have only twenty-five families. Twenty-five new homes will need to be built. What are you going to use for capital?"

Air shifted in then out of her lungs, her breasts moving provocatively with each tiny breath. "Link wished to give me money for that. I told him no. I plan to use my dowry. The money is deposited in the bank in town. It is more than enough to cover the initial expenses then some. By the time I need more, we should have stud fees. Perhaps we can win a few races." She paused thinking about the funds there. "I'm not at all certain that Link considers that money my dowry though."

Michael leaned back, his hands resting on the desk while he played with the pen twirling the stem between his fingers. "Don't suppose it matters. Link made it clear to me, whatever money you needed would be supplied. The question now is what type of homes do you wish to build."

"Yes, well, they cannot be too fancy. They need to have a floor as well as two bedrooms and a kitchen, of course, a living area."

"Much fancier than anything they live in now. Have you seen the hovels they call home? I suppose I should have made improvements. However, the funds were not there nor the permission. I've spent the last five years bringing the plantation up to standard. We've just begun to make a profit."

Michael watched her move around the room. The soft swish of her skirts gave him ideas he shouldn't have. She was graceful. Her hips rounded while her breasts were small. He wondered what color the tips were. He guessed a soft enticing pink.

"I understand. Before my sister and brother-in-law left, Link made arrangements for the construction of the homes. The building should begin tomorrow. I do expect you to oversee this."

"What will you do with the overseer? The man who makes sure the slaves do their jobs?" The man was evil. Once he discovered the man's true nature, he meant to fire him. Had not done so yet. The arrival of the Stewarts put a stop to much of what he planned. "You need to get rid of the man. I was making plans. Since you are taking control of the reins so to speak, I suppose you will wish to see him."

"No, I don't wish to see Raynard or speak to him. My interest is with the racing along with the stud farm. You will tell the man not to come back. Since there will be no more slaves, we will have no use for his services. I wish I could ask you to write some type of letter that would acknowledge his credentials. I can't."

"No, I would gag on the words. If you commanded it, that would be my first act of disobedience. In most things I can be loyal. In that I cannot." He watched her for a reaction to his words. Commanding men for her would not be possible. She was such a tiny, delicate slip of a woman. No man would take orders from her.

"Don't expect obedience necessarily. I do, however hope you will continue to give me an honest opinion. I know horses. I don't know anything about the workings of a plantation."

"Very well, advice I've plenty of. Shall we start with the freeing of Old Suzzy then Timmie so we can see how that will go?" He was eager to begin this new chapter for Mayfair Hall. In time all would come together as planned including the seduction of Miss Clare Carter-Brown.

"Yes, that would be a good idea. After that will you show me around the plantation, especially the slave's homes."

"I will call for Old Suzzy." He stood then rang the bell that would bring the slave to the office, the soon to be servant. Michael understood the old woman would not be pleased. This was the only life she knew. She would believe she'd done something wrong. His wording would have to be impeccable. "She will be here in just a moment." He stood behind the desk. Clare appeared resigned to the fact that at the moment he held the power. "Would you like me to tell her or would you appreciate the privilege?"

"Perhaps you should. It's been seven years since I've been at Mayfair Hall. Old Suzzy has taken orders from you while I was gone. If I tell her she is now a free woman, she will not believe her ears." Her voice was so calm and quiet the sound quite discomfited him.

To Michael, Clare seemed too damn serene when there should be a modicum of anxiety building. What she was about to do would have all the slaves on tenterhooks until they figured out what was now happening to them. "If that's what you would like."

He tapped the pen he'd been toying with on top of the desk. Wished to whistle while he watched Clare's face turn pale with what he assumed would be anxiety. Well, hell, her skin was white to begin with. Now her skin appeared to be a death mask.

Old Suzzy walked into the room. When she looked between them, her face paled it that was at all possible. She clasped her hands in front of her. "Massa," she whispered. "Did I do something wrong?"

Michael sent Clare a look she might not appreciate. While he expected this Clare did not. "Perhaps you would like to sit."

She dropped another shade closer to white. Old Suzzy sat, her fingers gripping the pour chair so tight it turned her knuckles even whiter than her face. "Massa?"

"Rest easy, Old Suzzy. You've done nothing wrong. We want to give you a bit of good news," Clare said softly.

Well, it seemed she couldn't keep her nose out of this situation. Clare touched the old woman on the shoulder if that tiny gesture could reassure her. The lady stiffened with the contact.

Might as well get this over with. "We, Clare and I," he pointed to her. She stiffened slightly tilting her chin into the air. He cleared his throat. "Neither one of us likes slavery. Another person should not own people. We plan on changing the plantation from farming to racing. In this case, we will have no need of slaves to keep the place running."

Old Suzzy promptly put her hand to her forehead. Her old eyes going vague and hazy, she slid from the chair to pool on the floor.

"Oh my!" Clare blurted before she rushed to her. She felt the woman's forehead. "She fainted? Is that a good or bad sign? Tears are running down her cheeks."

"A bad sign." Shaking his head at his stupidity, Michael strode to the kitchen to retrieve a basin of water along with a soft cloth. By the time he returned, Old Suzzy was sitting in a more comfortable chair moaning emitting gut wrenching sobs. Clare shot him a glance that pretty much told him what he thought. He'd gone about telling her about her freedom all wrong. She must have assumed he meant to sell her to another plantation.

Well hell! He jabbed his hands through his thick dark red hair. Hair so dark it was nearly chestnut in color.

He crouched down in front of her, taking her elderly leathered hands in his. "We aren't going to sell you. Clare and I want to give you your freedom. We will pay you for working here, for serving us just as you've been doing for years and yes, years. You deserve more for your loyalty." Yes, she did merit more from them. He would contrive some way to give her something she would cherish as much as her freedom.

Blank, foggy, deep brown eyes stared at him. Obviously, she didn't believe the words. Either that or she didn't truly understand what his words meant. He would have to elaborate more.

"I don't want to work for anyone else." It seemed she was finally able to speak. "Want to stay here."

"You aren't going anywhere, Suzzy, unless you want to. This is your home for as long as you wish it to be so."

"I don't understand. I'm a free woman?" Surrounded by his hands her bony fingers were shaking. She was thin and frail. If she had to leave, she would die.

"Does that please you? Your duties will be the same. The only difference is that you will now be paid to perform them," Clare said coming around to stand in front of her, her smile huge. "You can have a new home with the other people who choose to stay or you can remain in your room on the third floor. Where you want to live is your choice."

It still appeared she didn't comprehend all they told her. "You're not going to kick me out? I have choices?"

"No and yes," Clare said softly tears spiking her lashes. "You're important to me. I remember when you used to help Sophie when Uncle William hit her."

Old Suzzy grinned back. "I want to keep my room. What will I do with the money you pay me? Never been paid before."

"No, don't suppose you have." Michael grinned, relieved now that she seemed to grasp her new situation. "You can do with it whatever you wish. If you like, the first time you're paid I'll drive you into town. You might like a new dress or a bonnet."

She was nodding her head as if she thought over her new situation and was well pleased. "My children and my grandchildren will be freed too?" Her smile grew huge then suddenly she frowned. "What if they want to leave? You can't give them that choice."

"Free men and women can go where they please. I couldn't stop them. You would have another choice to make," Clare said thoughtfully. "I hope they choose to remain with us."

"May I go tell them?" she asked seemingly eager to spread the news. She stood, still a bit shaky around the knees, quickly sitting down.

"No," Michael picked up her hands again. "That is something I must do. This will come as a huge shock to some. Just as you didn't believe the good fortune, there will be others. Can I trust you to keep the secret for a few days?"

She nodded.

"Good. I promise you won't have to wait long. Now, you're done for the evening. Clare and I are going to take a stroll to the stables. Want to talk to Timmie next. Perhaps I will contrive a better way to give him the message." Yes, he hoped he could figure this out.

A few seconds later, Old Suzzy vanished up the steps to her room. Clare looked at him. He grinned ignoring the fact he bumbled the first telling of the news that would certainly shock the surrounding planters.

He held up his hands, laughing, "I know I did an atrocious job. Doubt if you could have done better. This freeing business is not going to be easy to explain. However, I'm more than eager to begin."

"No, I don't suppose the telling will be at all easy."

He strode from behind the desk, holding his hand out to her, "Should we go see Timmie. If you think you can do better, please be my guest."

"Perhaps you've learned from your mistake." She laughed softly tilting her chin to look into his eyes. "I'm certain I would bungle the job worse."

"That is what I thought."

Good lord, her hand felt so small, her fingers wound between his larger ones. The feeling was right. They needed to discuss her return to Leslie Hall before he did something he might come to regret. He didn't think he could stay away from her when she was one door away from him.

It was late afternoon. Heat still buffeted the soft grass around Mayfair Hall. Timmie would be tending the horses. They stepped inside. Clare found the pail holding apple slices and carrots. Without paying heed to him, she approached Duster first. She rubbed his nose then whispered something to him. With greed, he took the food offerings before he nudged her. If he didn't know better, the horse grinned. She stopped at Gypsy next. He wondered what she told him. Ah, but he had to find Timmie. He wondered what he would say to the lad that wouldn't frighten him to eternity.

Timmie was mucking out Jingle Bell's stall. He deliberated on who could have given the little mare that atrocious name. It must have been one of Link's many children since the mares came with the Stewarts. One evening, a glass of brandy in his hand, a glass of wine in Sophie's, she told him all about Link's children. How he adopted and loved all of them. He had a heart of gold. The children were ones who had no home. Link provided love as well as shelter. The other mare that came with Clare was Maid Marion. It was a much better name.

"You about finished, Timmie?" Michael rested one arm on the stall. He went over in his mind what he did wrong with Old Suzzy in his explanation. There had to be a better way. He should have explained her life wasn't going to change. Well, of course, it would change.

Timmie nodded. "Just about ready to head for home. My stomach is rumbling offly hard. What do you need?"

Michael paused thinking and thinking, trying to form words that wouldn't terrify the lad. Well, the lad was nearing seventeen. He supposed Timmie was very nearly a man now.

"First, I don't want you to panic when I start speaking. You will always have a place at Mayfair. This will always be your home if you wish it to be. Clare will always need you to tend to her magnificent horses."

"Panic?" His eyes widened with apprehension. "Don't know what you are getting at, Sir."

"Promise me you won't lie down and start wailing or I won't give you the good news. Don't want to see you pounding your fists on the floor."

Timmie nodded slowly, his breath seeming to be held tightly in his chest.

Michael thought that to be a very good sign. "Would you like to be a free man, Timmie? Clare and I can do that for you. If you want to stay and work with the mares as well as the studs, I will pay you decent wages. If you want to race Duster and Gypsy, you can do so." When the man didn't dissolve into hysteria, Michael was pleased with himself.

Though the young man's eyes seemed to be crossing while his smile grew fat. Perhaps he was getting the hang of the telling. For tomorrow he would work on his delivery. It would be the last time. He would have to make certain all understood their choices.

When Timmie sat on a stool, tears streaming from his eyes, Michael wasn't at all certain he did it right this time either. Mayhap he patted himself on the back a bit too soon.

"Why are you crying, Timmie? I would think you would be happy, perhaps dancing a jig or two. Do you want to remain a slave?" He thought maybe his words were too harsh. Michael couldn't imagine anyone not...well hell, the youngun' had to be happy.

"I've never been happier." He sniffed before wiping the tears from his cheeks with the back of his sleeve.

"Good, good then," Michael patted Timmie on the shoulder, relief swamping him although now he didn't know what else to say. "Perhaps you could tender this happiness with something other than tears."

"Can I tell my ma and pa?" Timmie did grin. He smiled so wide his white teeth flashed the missing tooth quite evident.

"No, Timmie not yet. We plan on freeing all the slaves. However, first we have to build everyone a new home. Tomorrow, Timmie, we will have a meeting with everyone who lives on Mayfair lands. We will find out then how many people are staying so we will understand how many houses we will have to create for all our new tenants. No one will go into the fields. I'll be there before dawn to make sure of that. We will celebrate."

"I'll see to it that we have lots of rum punch," Timmie said. "If that's okay with you."

Ah, so they were able to get the rum punch. He'd have to think about someone confiscating the rum from the house. The thought of anyone sneaking inside to steal it stole his breath. Raynard would never allow the slaves rum. Yes, he'd have to think about that some more. Now that they were free they could have all the rum they could afford to buy.

"I'll see that my cook supplies the rum punch. We won't drink too much though. Everyone will get a cup, no more."

The scream he heard next ripped him apart. It was Clare. She was screaming again and again. What the devil was happening? She was supposed to be close by listening and evaluating his performance. His breath caught while he tried to understand. Nothing made sense. Timmie and Michael rushed from the stables toward the loud yelling.

She sounded as if she were dying. His heart lurched. He was terrified. The shrieks didn't stop. He ran and ran, Timmie behind him, the lad's boots pounding against the hard dirt. When did she leave the stables?

What he saw made his blood curdle. His stomach rolled in endless waves of agony. A young woman, one of the black slaves, was strung up, her hands above her head. Her clothing was torn, welts from Raynard's whip lacerated her tiny body. Clare was on her knees, her arms crossed in front of her face. She must have tried to stop him from beating the girl to death. Raynard sent the whip against Clare, hitting her while she tried desperately to grab the leather from his hands. He saw that Raynard hit her back twice, the fabric of her gown torn by the stinging weapon. He must have hit her again in the front after she turned. She clutched her shirt to hold the material together.

"Stop! Stop it now!" Michael roared as he raced faster toward the man. He should have fired the man months ago. What the devil was going on here? Timmie ran behind him.

When he reached Raynard, he hauled back his fist hitting him square on the jaw. The man crumpled, his large body sprawled on the ground. He hoped he broke his jaw. Michael turned to Timmie. "Run, fetch Mammy Jo, tell her what happened here. She'll know what to do. Find someone who can carry the girl back to her home. I'll have Old Suzzy go to her with some healing cream as soon as possible." She couldn't be more than fourteen or fifteen. Why was Raynard punishing her? The overseer strung her up by her hands then laid into her with his whip.

Michael turned kneeling in front of Clare. He pushed sodden hair away from her face. She looked up, her eyes filled with pain as well as tears that spiked her lashes. "Cut her down, please." Her voice trembled. She got the words out before she moaned softly.

His hands fumbling with the ropes, he released her. The girl fell to the ground, weak from the loss of blood. Michael slipped off the jacket he wore then covered her exposed body with it. "I'll find out what happened here. Can you tell me?" he asked wishing he knew her name.

"I refused him," was all she said as she huddled, her arms crossed in front of her while she clung to the jacket.

Yes, he heard the rumors that Raynard eased himself with the slaves. For some reason, he hadn't believed the gossip. He was stupid. Of course, the man would believe they were his to do with as he pleased. They were property after all. In time she would be all right. The wounds would heal.

Well, hell...

Michael hauled Raynard to his feet, his fist ready to slug this man again who deserved the punishment and more.

The man blinked at him several time. He looked confused. Appeared to not understand his fury. "What are you so fired angry about? She's just a little black whore. They are all the same. Meant to be used by whites."

Gritting his teeth together in his rage, he tried to calm himself, said the words as slowly as possible. "Get off Mayfair land now. Pack your things and leave immediately. Send someone here who can tell me where you will be staying in the village. I will see that you are paid through the month. If you know what is good for you, don't ever let me see you again." Michael didn't ever remember being so angry he shook.

Clare held out her hand to him. He pulled her to her feet. She moaned softly. "You will explain yourself after I've seen to the lacerations. He could have killed you. Why didn't you call for me or run back to get help? You knew I was close by."

"Mr. Flannigan, I'm here." It was Mammy Jo. She stopped running when she saw the girl huddled on the ground, clutching his jacket. "I brought Big Tom. He's going to carry her home. Don't you worry about Janey here. I'll tend to her. She'll be fine. Do you need help with your little lady?" She fussed over the girl even when Janey was in Big Tom's arms.

"No, I'll take her back to the house then tend to her myself." After that he would lecture her on her folly.

~ * ~

Biff Gideon and Busby Turnpin sat in the Deer Head Ale house sipping on the latest draught of ale created by the owner. Biff thought the brew was delicious. He ordered another pint. The owner experimented with different brews monthly. Some creations were good, some not so tasty. This was one of his best. Two large pretzels sat on platter along with what looked to be delicious crab cakes. There were bowls of hot melted cheese to dip the pretzels. Biff thought he'd died then gone to heaven everything tasted so delicious. Heaven wouldn't take him. He knew that. Still, he could dream.

"Heard Link Stewart and his harlot bride left her sister in Virginia," Busby pointed out. "You remember the girl, Sophie? She used to take lovers to that cottage on their land. Brinkmeyer, her uncle never knew how to stop her. She wore harlot gowns, painted her face so she looked the hussy."

"Yeah, I remember. She painted her face just like the women who work at Miss Bessy's place."

"Saw Clare just this afternoon. Her face wasn't painted. She wasn't wearing a dress that showed off her womanly charms," Busby pointed out while he chewed on a crab cake. "Don't think the younger sister is anything like Sophie."

"You don't think she's like her sister?" Biff asked as drool pooled behind his lips. He didn't have to think very hard about Clare being naked and beneath him, all that soft white flesh in his hands. His groin throbbed. He tossed back his ale then pulled off a chunk of the pretzel before dipping the end in the melted cheese while he tried to calm his unruly body.

"You mean a whore?" Busby tossed back his head then hooted. "Nah, she's a pretty little thing. While Brinkmeyer was alive he kept her all gussied up in little girl clothes. She wasn't anything like her sister then though she could be now."

"Clare Carter-Brown was a little girl at the time. Did you see her in town the other day? She's a grown woman now. What I saw was a little flirt asking for a man to have his way with her. Why that manager of hers picked her up by the waist before helping her mount that stallion she was riding. He had this light of possessiveness shining his eyes. Men don't think that way about a woman unless he's taken her." Biff was thinking that he'd like to see what she was willing to give to him that she was giving Flannigan. That little house where Sophie took her lovers was still standing.

She would be so soft and white. Her pretty white tits would be big enough to fill his hands. Pure lust surged to his man parts. He groaned with the pleasure of it all.

"You thinking you'd like to be the stallion she was sitting on top of?" Busby chortled.

"Wouldn't you?" Once more Biff thought about her creamy breasts tipped in soft pink. Yeah, he'd keep her for himself. It didn't even matter to him if she was well used. Flannigan probably had her already.

"Think we should ride on out there to see for ourselves if she's willing and warm? We should flip a coin to see who gets her first. What do you say?"

Other Books by Christine Young
Available at Rogue Phoenix Press

Don't Hustle Letty
Good Girls Book One

She's a good girl...

As tempted as Scarlett was, she had too many secrets to let someone enter her world—secrets that would send any reasonable man to the farthest ends of the earth. Bobby was far from reasonable and despite her desperate attempts to hold him at bay, he would not let her past destroy their future. With her escort service, Scarlett used men and their insatiable lust for women to capitalize on the means to survive and prosper. She vowed to never wed, to never put herself in the control of a man.

...nonetheless he has other ideas.

Lord Robert Munroe, with his newly acquired title of marquis goes to Scarlett's for training on how to comport himself. The marquis, better known as Bobby, knows how to pick a pocket as well as get into a bloke's home to steal them blind. What he doesn't know is how to be a gentleman. When he sets his sights on the prim Miss Scarlet, Letty, to his way of thinking, he decides she is the woman he wants to call his wife. He tempts all that she is with sweet words and tender coaxing until she is unable to refuse all he hopes to give her.

Connal's Eternal Love
Sweet McKenna Book One

A few days shy of All Hallows' Eve Connal McKenna, Laird of Clan Chattan stands on the parapets of his castle. Bonfires line the hillsides while his clan prepares for the upcoming festivities. Drawn by the whispering of the wind, Connal McKenna feels a strange restlessness in his soul. Setting out to discover the wickedness that is calling to him, he discovers his mate. With gentle words and sensuous kisses, the auburn-eyed highlander conquers his mate, the beautiful, defiant Wynnie Adair who he comes upon during an evening ride. She must ultimately put her trust in the only man who can save her from the ruthless plans of her father and succumb to his gentle coaxing.

In Brady's Arms
Sweet McKenna Book Two

Forced to run from the only home she knows, beautiful, headstrong Lillian Townsends seeks shelter in the wild highlands where the McKenna clan live. Trying to avoid a betrothal contract signed by her stepfather to an aging lord, she is desperate to find a means to sidestep the inevitable, including a marriage to the oldest son of the laird. Lilly is enamored of the young lord who pursues her with unrelenting determination flashing his devilishly handsome charms. She is hard pressed to resist.

Besotted from the first moment Brady McKenna sees Lilly, he is determined to find a means to coax her into his arms and bed. With only the promise of carnal pleasure as his mistress, Brady relentlessly pursues the woman who has unwittingly forged a place in his heart. She is like no other woman, proud, defiant and enchanting. Despite his father's advice to stay away from her, he cannot. He boldly seeks her out and makes her his own.

Nobody but Walker
Sweet McKenna Book Three

The Highland Lass...

She was brought up, adored and loved by a doting mother and father ardently protected by her brothers. She was everything sweet and innocent until she was faced with betrayal and an unexpected and out of wedlock pregnancy. When she gave her love to a man who couldn't return her passion and commitment, she was left devastated and furious. Faced with the loss of her child if she didn't comply to his demands, Crissie McKenna followed him to Belfast then on to his country home to discover he was already married.

...The Irishman

Stunned to find out his one and only encounter with the woman he wanted to love forever created a child, Walker Endicott, Earl of Briarwood, claimed his child as his only heir. Walker threatened all her previously held values even while he thrilled her senses. From the moment he first saw her to the second she ran after him begging him to make love to her, his captivating masculinity held her fascinated. In his arms she would know tempestuous passion, bitter despair, and a soaring joy that would humble them both before the power of love.

Roby's Moonlit Night
Sweet McKenna Book Four

Once she'd been a pampered child with high expectations for her future blessed with love. Then she became an innocent pawn in a terrible game of greed and power. Now, with a noose around her neck, Pippa was to hang before she had the chance to unveil the men who drove her from her home, before she had the chance to live.

Roby McKenna was a man blessed with endless charm and wit. While he searched for his eternal love across the Atlantic in a new land, he would have to come home to find her. His silver blue eyes could sparkle with amusement or harden to steel gray with displeasure. He had all the women a man could want or need. As he grew older, mistresses were not enough. A quirk of fate brought him to the gallows, a spark of destiny made him claim the condemned Pippa as his bride.

My Sweet Broc
Bad Boys Book One

He's a bad bad boy...

Broc Wallace is a fun-loving rake who never thought any beautiful woman could melt his heart. He lives life in the present enjoying the camaraderie of his friends and the pleasures of his mistress. When Bliss races into his life, he is ill prepared to deal with her secrets or give up the tenor of his life. When the truth is revealed, he finds himself unable to forgive and forget the betrayal.

...but she's sweet for him

Bliss MacTavish knows she's playing with fire when she refuses to tell this bad boy her name. He tempts her with sweet whispers of seduction knowing her innocent nature will be unable to refuse all he yearns to give her. Deciding to follow her heart, she finds the repercussions more than she bargains for when she gives herself to this bad boy.

Crazy for Cam
Bad Boys Book Two

He's a bad bad boy...

Lord Cam MacEwen, Viscount of Rosehill, tries his best to be proper and court the lady of his dreams in the acceptable way. The feat proves impossible when the lady in question uses every means at her disposal to tempt him. He fights his jealousy for another man as well as the need to make her his own, finally giving in to her irresistible passion.

...but she's crazy for him.

Chelsea MacTavish wants the bad boy she fell in love with and kissed just before her eighteenth birthday. With feminine wiles and irresistible allure, the sensuous lady plans to best Cam at his game of hearts and make him forget his need to court her properly.

Falling for Flynt
Bad Boys Book Three

He's a bad, bad boy...

Fascinated by Hope's loss of memory yet haunted by her sultry beauty, Flynt is irresistibly drawn to the stoic miss—and into her troubles with the sultan who wants her for himself. When he discovers she is the sister of his best friend, his pride keeps him from pursuing her and making her his.

...but she's falling for him.

Raised in a harem but now penniless, alone and without her memory, Hope must discover a way to remember all that she has lost. She finds a way to continue with her life as a servant in Flynt's home. The first sight of Flynt steals Hope's breath as well as her heart. Can she overcome her fears and give herself to the man she fell in love with.

Dancing With Donal
Bad Boys Book Four

He's a bad bad boy...

Once a bad boy always a bad boy, Donal Chamberlin's carefree ways come crashing down around him when he meets the ravishingly beautiful Daryl MacTavish, the innocent little sister of one of his best friends. He is determined to win her heart as he sets his sights on marriage and an heir. His past gets in the way of his quest when a woman he once loved threatens Daryl's life.

...but she's dancing with him.

Daryl has seen the control her sister's husbands hold over them. She yearns for a life where she makes decisions for herself. No man will have power over her. But no man kisses her the way Donal does. No man can make her forget all her goals leaving her helpless to give up her dreams. Yet Donal is determined to dance through all the barriers she thrust in front of him, pursuing her until she says yes.

Loving Leslie
Bad Boys Book Five

He's a bad bad boy...

Leslie Stewart, Duke of Southcliff is stoic, set in his ways, a spy who is used to having his life well ordered. He expects life to continue on in this perfectly conventional fashion. He assumes his bad boy status while keeping mamas and debutantes at arm's length. An heir is needed but Leslie has every intention of finding a woman who doesn't covet his wealth and tittle. He is irresistibly drawn to the headstrong young lady who becomes more beautiful as she develops into a woman.

...but she is loving him.

When Leslie kisses Lacie MacTavish, she knows even at the tender age of fifteen this is the man of her dreams. Forced to wait until she comes of age, Lacie withdraws into herself. Now she is eighteen and Leslie has returned from a mission for the British Government ready to claim her as his bride. She refuses him and he must find a way to seduce her and in the process create a burning passion within her, which she cannot deny.

Pleasing Arie
Bad Boys Book Six

He's a bad bad boy...

Arie Demir has never been denied anything in his life. He takes what he wants. What he undeniably yearns for is the beautiful redheaded spitfire he sees in a restaurant in Glasgow. At every turn, she confuses him by disputing his power over her. Alison refuses to accept the fact he owns her. While Arie tries desperately with patience and tenderness to drive her wild with new sensations, his scorching kisses ignite the fires of her very soul to make her understand he is all she will ever want.

...but is she pleasing him?

Alison Fletcher never expected to find herself kidnapped and sold to a whorehouse then bought by a Turkish sultan to become his slave. She vows to never surrender to the arrogant man who believes he owns her. She is stunned by the magnificently handsome man who awaits her compliance. Unexpectedly, she finds Arie the lesser of all the evils. The hidden depths of his mesmerizing dark brown eyes hold her into their power; his muscular embrace makes her weak with desire. She is his to do with as he wishes.

Graham's Wicked Kiss
Bad Boys Book Seven

He's a bad bad boy...

Graham Chamberlin is stunned to find three young boys dangling from the trees lining the drive to Runningmead Manner. On further inspection, he is astonished at their obsession to protect a young woman who has been brutalized by her pimp. The woman he discovers hiding in a third-floor attic room is gravely injured. He takes the silver haired stowaway under his wing. Clearly, Graham's new guest is a lady with many secrets. He is determined to unlock all the mysteries surrounding her.

...But she can't resist his wicked kiss.

The years since Ria left the convent where she was raised have been a nightmare. Her secrets are dangerous—as is the powerful man determined to find her. Handsome Graham Chamberlin is clearly a gentleman with secrets of his own, but staying with him could mean the difference between life and death for Ria. With each passing day, her handsome host turns Ria's convalescence into an increasingly sensual escape. Now her greatest challenge may be imagining anything less than a future in his arms.

Feeling Etienne's Love
Bad Boys Book Eight

He's a bad bad boy...

Etienne Dubois is the son of a wealthy vineyard owner who craves the excitement of putting his life on the line. Working with the French government and as a confidant of King Charles X give him reasons for living. An encounter with a beautiful young woman in a plush bordello in Paris has him rethinking his roguish ways. Etienne never expects to become a father especially from one encounter with an innocent prostitute who whispers his name and has him rethinking his well-ordered life.

...But she can't help feeling his love.

Elisa Moreau, the only daughter of Angelique Moreau, the owner of an exclusive bordello in Bordeaux, France, has loved Etienne Dubois since she was six. Unfortunately, until an unexpected encounter at a brothel in Paris puts the two of them in the same room, Etienne doesn't even know she exists. Confused but wanting Etienne and this chance meeting to never end, Elisa gives herself to the man who has held her heart in hands for what seems like her entire life.

All I Want Is Link
Bad Boys Book Nine

He's a bad bad boy...

Merry Stewart is wildly unpredictable. Left alone to run wild over the Bordeaux and Scottish countryside she becomes impetuous and daringly bold. Over the years, she's found she can bedevil her softhearted brothers into allowing her exploits to go unnoticed. As a young woman she has learned she can do as she pleases when she pleases. Now, Merry has set her amorous sights on the Duke of Weston—a man she has never met but has every intention of marrying. No other suitor will satisfy her—especially not the exceptionally striking, horse breeder, Devlin Mathews.

...she's the woman of his desires.

Posing as commoner Devlin Mathews to escape a potentially fatal confrontation, Devlin is enthralled and infuriated by the audacious, duke-hunting dark haired vixen. Bedeviled at every opportunity, he finds dealing with the tiny she-devil exasperating as well as intriguing. Without revealing his true identify, the infamous rogue pledges to thwart Merry's plans to wed the man of her dream-never imagining the bewitching strategist would turn out to be the only woman he would ever dream of marrying.

Devlin's Angel
Bad Boys Book Ten

He's a bad bad boy...

Merry Stewart is wildly unpredictable. Left alone to run wild over the Bordeaux and Scottish countryside she becomes impetuous and daringly bold. Over the years, she's found she can bedevil her softhearted brothers into allowing her exploits to go unnoticed. As a young woman she has learned she can do as she pleases when she pleases. Now, Merry has set her amorous sights on the Duke of Weston—a man she has never met but has every intention of marrying. No other suitor will satisfy her—especially not the exceptionally striking, horse breeder, Devlin Mathews.

...she's the woman of his desires.

Posing as commoner Devlin Mathews to escape a potentially fatal confrontation, Devlin is enthralled and infuriated by the audacious, duke-hunting dark haired vixen. Bedeviled at every opportunity, he finds dealing with the tiny she-devil exasperating as well as intriguing. Without revealing his true identify, the infamous rogue pledges to thwart Merry's plans to wed the man of her dream-never imagining the bewitching strategist would turn out to be the only woman he would ever dream of marrying.

Foolish for Piper

The pickpocket...

Piper has spent her life surviving the streets of St. Giles Parish in London, a den of iniquity and crime. Masquerading as a boy she escapes the whorehouses the young girls are sent to as they come of age. The day she encounters Brett MacLachlan begins the same as every other one. When she picks his pocket, she has no idea her life is going to change irreversibly.

...and the mark

Handsome aristocrat Brett MacLachlan has come to London for his amusement only to find his world turned upside down by a thief and her dog. From the moment he spots her, Brett knows there is something intrinsically wrong. In his arms, Piper discovers passion and joy. Yet secrets of her past haunt her, and a scar will tell the true tale as well as her identity.

Taylor's Destiny

She traveled to another time and place to change destiny...

Enjoying a day of sailing, Taylor Maxwell never expected after a suffering a concussion she would wake up in another century. A resilient independent woman in the twenty-first century, the blond beauty is ill prepared for life in the 1800s. Her first sight of the naval captain who rescues her makes her heart stop, giving her hope for her future.

His life is transformed by a woman who appears from nowhere...

Born to a life of ease, Reid Stewart defies the dictates of those born to aristocracy and chooses a life of adventure in the navy and as a spy for the crown. When he discovers a nearly naked woman on the bow of small sailing ship, his heart warms. His love for Taylor and his need to protect her from a man who pursues her might cost him his life as well as hers.

Caitlin's Duke

She played a fiddle in an Irish pub...

Caitlin O'Shea Is the most beautiful woman Roc Leighton has ever seen. With her blue violet eyes and long black hair she captivates him. In turn he mesmerizes Caitlin. Caught in the power of his gaze as he watches her, she is wise enough to know he desires her but will never give his heart to her. Caitlin has vowed to never be any man's mistress.

And fell in love with an English Lord...

Roc knows the first time he watches her play the fiddle and dance around the pub, she will be his next mistress. Despite her protest, he will find a way to convince her that her place is with him. While Caitlin's determination to keep her vows, fate takes a cruel turn and she is forced to seek refuge with Roc.

Catching Meara
Book One in the McKenna Clan Series

Meara Thorton was a feisty, world-class computer hacker—cornered by the FBI and shockingly given the chance to be their newly acquired technical analyst. Brilliant and intuitive, yet aching with the loss of everyone she has cared about, her restless heart led her to discover a love she fought and a world she didn't know could possibly exist.

Sweet Sexy Sadie
Book Two in the McKenna Clan Series

From the first time Sadie's eyes met those of Brody McKenna in the hot Sierra Madre Mountains, theirs was a potent attraction—not gentle, slow, and easy, but hot, hard, and all-consuming. The daughter of a dysfunctional family, Sadie had dreams no man could wrench from her with hot sex and an all-consuming passion. She'd challenge this alpha male with all the strength she possessed. But her red hair, fiery temperament, and indomitable spirit obsessed Brody...and he knew he had to find a way to show her he was more than he appeared and convince her to make a life with him.

Sweet Misbehavin'
Book Three in the McKenna Clan Series

Cast adrift after fleeing the home of Jokul, the ice demon, Atantsi, a firestarter, grew to womanhood as she moved through time to keep the demon from finding her. Though stubborn and courageous, she was ill prepared to use powers she had not been taught. Her first sight of the intoxicating Carr McKenna left her breathless, and her second encounter gave her hope for a future she never thought she had.

A playboy, a second son and a shifter, a man who thought his life would be carefree, Carr McKenna was shocked to discover the woman he'd paid as an escort is a firestarter who is running for her life. He is the leader of all the McKennas around the world and that he has multiple powers. His passion for Margo and the need to defend her might cost him his life as well as hers.

Sweet Talkin' Sugar
Book Four in the McKenna Clan Series

Lyonesse McKenna, was dreaming, or was she? From the instant Lyn saw Deacon McClain across a black jack table in a crowed Las Vegas casino the unmistakable attraction sent Lyn's senses flying into overdrive. Her family of shapeshifters believed in soul mates. She'd always been skeptical yet she couldn't help but question the way her heart sped when he looked at her.

When Deacon appeared in Las Vegas he knew his first job was to save Lyn from a Sea Demon, but the next order of business was to convince her he would someday mean more to her than she'd ever expected. But her stubborn nature and unbendable spirit consumed Deacon...and he had to chase away all the demons real and imagined in order to win her heart.

Sweet Surrender
Book Five in the McKenna Clan Series

Ripped from her family at the top of Infinity Cliff, Kimi McKenna finds herself thrust somewhere into the future. Dark elements threaten to destroy the earth unless Kimi can work together with the white witch to stop the destruction. Confused by her mate's role in the conspiracy, she refuses to acknowledge the connection. But amidst raging fire and attacks on the people she is coming to hold dear, she allows Maska O'keefe into her heart.

Maska O'keefe has loved the beautiful shapeshifter for years. Unable to save her life years ago, he vows to watch over her as he is given a second chance to convince her that even though he is a witch and not a shifter, they are indeed soul mates. Kimi's divided loyalties between her family and the cause she is now a part of will determine their relationship. Only the part she plays as the messiah can bring this to a conclusion in the final battle.

Dakota's Bride
The first book in the Lakota/Pinkerton Series

When Emma St. John received her brother's letter imploring her to escape her stepfather's vengeful scheme and to trust Dakota Barringer with her life, she was willing to chance it. But the handsome, brooding riverboat owner Emma found in Natchez a danger of another kind. For Emma soon found herself surrendering to an unrelenting desire.

Raised by the Sioux when his parents were killed, Dakota had been betrayed once before by a white woman. He wasn't about to trust another, especially one claiming that her stepfather, a powerful U.S. senator, had framed her as a murderess. But he couldn't let Emma's intoxicating effect on him. Now Dakota would risk his very life to protect the innocent beauty who had seduced him with her tender love.

My Angel
The second book in the Lakota/Pinkerton Series

A BEAUTY IN BUCKSKINS
When her father decided to send her to a finishing school back East, Angela Chamberlain refused to be confined to stuffy drawing rooms. Instead, the daring spitfire who could shoot like a man and ride like the wind longed for a life of adventure and romance—and she knew exactly who could give it to her. Devil Blackmoor was a hired gun with a dangerous reputation. But Angela was willing to go to the ends of the earth to capture the handsome devil's heart.

A DEVIL IN DISGUISE
He'd come to America looking for excitement, but Devil Blackmoor got more than he bargained for when he encountered a beautiful rebel who answered his kisses with a wild innocence that touched his very soul. Yet standing between them were more obstacles than either ever dreamed. For Devil had strapped on a gun for the wrong man. And that made Angela his enemy. Now he'll have to choose between his duty and the woman he loves more than life.

The Locket
The third book in the Lakota/Pinkerton Series

The year is 1894. Seeking revenge for crimes against his family, Misha Petrovich follows a path that leads straight to Ariel Cameron's boarding house in Mist Harbor, Oregon. A family heirloom in Ariel's possession leads Misha to believe she is guilty. The locket has been handed down to the oldest girl in the Petrovich family for generations. Ariel is innocent of wrong doing, but her father is not. Misha is torn by his feelings for Ariel and his need for restitution against her father. Knowing that the relationship between them is fragile, Misha does everything in his power to protect Ariel's father. His efforts are to no avail when her father is shot. Ariel comes to realize Misha's steadfast courage and determination to protect her and her father despite what has happened to his family. Ariel's love and devotion heals Misha's heart.

The Talisman
The fourth book in the Lakota/Pinkerton Series

Running from a marriage that lasted one night, Dr. Moriah McKeown discovers the land she has settled on is coveted by determined and lawless men. Yet the proud young woman who once vowed never to abandon her home has second thoughts when her adopted children are threatened. Her only recourse is to enlist the aid of a dark, dangerous gun for hire.

Haunted by the past and a betrayal he will never forgive, Ian Civanovich uses his fast gun and his reckless courage to forget the faithlessness of a woman in his past. He will trust no female—nor will he rest until the threat hovering over Moriah McKeown is put to rest.

Forever His
The fifth book in the Lakota/Pinkerton Series

Struggling to come to terms with the part she played in Jacob St.

John's death, Etta Barringer resigns from Pinkerton Agency and seeks peace and solace in a Rocky Mountain Cabin.

Jacob has vowed to discover the reason Etta has betrayed him, sold him out to his enemy and left him for dead.

Isolated in their cabin, they discover their love for each other and learn to trust. But the trust is shattered when Jacob learns she is married to his sworn enemy; the man who left him in the desert to die.

Allura's Secret
Twelve Dancing Princesses Book One

Allura McClellan is horrified by her father's decision to take out an ad in the Times awarding her to the man strong enough and smart enough to win her hand and uncover her secrets. She's an intelligent young woman who takes great delight in the freedom allotted to her by her father. She's well aware that marriage would effectively curtail the adventures she's shared with her sisters and cousins.

Hunter Gray is nothing like the other men who've arrived to vie for Allura's hand in marriage and everything that goes along with it. However, he is the first to refuse to concede defeat and pursue her despite her attempts to disguise her true appearance. It's her temperament that is of more concern to him than her looks. Hunter has worked all his life with the hope of someday owning his own land. Now that it looks like there's a very real possibility that everything he's ever wanted is within reach nothing is going to deter him – including Miss Allura's disagreeable disposition.

Amorica's Wager
Twelve Dancing Princesses Book Two

Amorica Hepburn was sent to London to find a husband. Finding a man was the last item on her agenda. With her two cousins, Amorica wagers she can dissuade her suitor before the others. Despite her efforts she discovers a chemistry that cannot be denied. Suddenly she is the arrogant man's wife, pledged to a marriage neither desire. But swept off to his ancestral home above the Dover cliffs and into his strong embrace, Amorica is soon possessed by a raging passion for the husband she had vowed to despise...

Damian Andrews couldn't afford to trust the emerald-eyed spitfire who happened upon his secret. Amorica's hatred of all men of his kind only inflames the war that rages between them. Still, he can not control the intense desire his stubborn bride inspires, or make her surrender to his will until he has conquered the headstrong beauty on the battlefield of love...

Ravyn's Marriage of Inconvenience
Twelve Dancing Princesses Book Three

A REGAL BEAUTY
When the duchess decides to wed her to a wastrel and a fop, Ravyn Grahm takes matters into her own hands and declares her engagement to another man. Instead of fessing up and telling her great aunt what she has done, she goes through with the pretense. Ariec Lakeland is the bastard son of an earl and has a dangerous reputation. But Ravyn is willing to do most anything to keep the duchess from discovering the lie.

A DEVIL-MAY-CARE SMUGGLER
He'd bought land in America, looking to put down roots and end his life of adventure, but Ariec Lakeland got more than he bargained for when he encountered a beautiful heiress who made a promise she didn't want to keep. But the promise could not be undone and standing between them were more obstacles than either ever dreamed. Ariec had made plans to spend the rest of his life in America and that was at odds with Ravyn's plan of living in England and running her father's estate. Now, he'll have to choose between his dreams and the woman he loves more than life.

Christel's Sunrise
Twelve Dancing Princesses Book Four

He Made Her An Offer...

Life has thrown Christel McClellan some experiences that could have devastated a less determined woman. Beautiful, self-assured and fiercely independent, she is trying to forget the loss of her stillborn child. But is the child alive?

She Couldn't Deny...

Life is carefree for Ryder MacLaren who loves to see what is on the other side of the sunrise. Laird of Clan MacLaren, he is wealthy, handsome and happily unencumbered...until stunning Christel McClellan enters his life. When he hears her story, he believes the child she thought dead has been sold to a wealthy buyer.

Storm's Passion
Twelve Dancing Princesses Book Five

SHE MADE A PROPOSAL...

Life strikes Storm Graham a shattering blow when she learns her father has bartered her to a man she detests. Storm is beautiful, self–assured and fiercely independent, and refuses to be a pawn in her father's schemes, yet she can find no way out of this bargain made in hell. Going on the offensive she asks the wealthiest man on the eastern coast of England to marry her, never believing she might fall in love.

HE TRIED TO REFUSE...

For Hadden Johnston life has provided everything he ever wanted, including a sanctuary for homeless children. He is wealthy, handsome and happily unencumbered...until stunning Storm Graham marches into his life and proposes a marriage of convenience. Yet this type of marriage to a woman who inflames his senses is far from acceptable. If he's going to be tied down, he will move heaven and earth to have this woman warming his bed.

Gotta Have Fayth
Twelve Dancing Princesses Book Six

A regal beauty with raven hair and piercing blue eyes, Fayth Graham is unwilling to parade herself in front of the wealthy Lords of England during the season. Seeking a means to dissuade any man wishing to wed her, she seeks a way to ruin herself for marriage. When she unexpectedly meets a man with sparkling gray eyes and an infectious grin, she decides this is the man who will keep her from agreeing to obey.

He returned from six months at sea, looking for a few nights of pleasure with a willing lass, but Jarret Kinsley got more than he bargained for when he met a beautiful debutant who responded to his kisses with a wild innocence that touched his heart. Yet the obstacles looming between them might rip them apart. Both had vowed never to marry, so when consequences of their dalliances got in the way, Jarret would have to choose between the life he's always desired and the woman he loves more than life.

Ella's Pleasure
Twelve Dancing Princesses Book Seven

A WHISPER OF PLEASURE
Ella Hepburn was an auburn haired debutant from the harsh Scottish coastline—a wild innocent to be seduced and tamed. A spirited beauty, she captivated Drake Montgomerie's jaded heart—while succumbing to the smoldering desire she felt for her unyielding suitor.

A WHISPER OF DANGER
In Drake Montgomerie's glittering world of money and privilege, young Ella discovered passion and desire could overcome everything she'd been taught to resist—entangling Drake, the heir apparent, in a lethal coil of aristocratic family intrigue. But grave peril would only nurse the sparks of a love that knew no limits and a magnificent ecstasy that would not be denied.

Eveleen's Seduction
Twelve Dancing Princesses Book Eight

A WHISPER OF SEDUCTION

A brutal attack on Eveleen Hepburn's cherished island off the Scottish coastline leaves her shattered and bewildered. Learning a man she once trusted can kill as easily as he can breathe even though the deed saves her life, creates questions that need answers. An innocent beauty, she enchants Logan Maxwell's cynical heart—giving in to the raging passion she feels for her mysterious suitor.

A WHISPER OF INTRIGUE

In Logan's Maxwell's world of espionage and privilege, young Eveleen discovers truths about herself she never expected, and a need for passion and love can overcome all her fears if she learns to accept certain truths. She finds herself entangled in a lethal battle for land that was once owned by French nobility, taken from them during the revolution and sold to Maxwell. But grave peril would unleash the flames of love that simmers, creating a magical union that cannot be refuted.

Tavia's Deception
Twelve Dancing Princesses Book Nine

WHISPERS OF DECEPTION

When her father decides to send her to London for her season, Tavia Hepburn resolves to see the world instead. The raven haired beauty decides to disguise herself as a lad and find employment on a ship bound for Barcelona as a cabin boy. But she never bargains on finding passion and love to a red haired sea captain who rescues her from certain death.

WHISPERS OF MURDER

For James Macmurra, the world is black and white until he meets a young debutante, who turns his world upside down. He's unable to deny Tavia's intoxicating effect on him. In a match tense with obstacles, unwillingness to divulge secrets, and unforeseen peril, irresistible desire and passion grows into undeniable love. James would risk his life to shelter and protect the innocent debutante who seduces him with her sweet love.

Larena's Fascination
Twelve Dancing Princesses Book Ten

WHISPERS OF FASCINATION
Fiery, free spirited Larena Graham never wanted to marry a duke. She is thrilled to be in love with the fourth son of an aristocrat, Gavin Broon. But when it seems Gavin ignores her, she set her sights on politics and bettering human life. Unsuspecting intrigue and a plot against her, she continues her dangerous plans despite Gavin's wishes.

WHISPERS OF TRUST
Gavin has every intention of properly courting the beautiful Larena until he must leave the city in order to put his affairs in order. Returning to London, he finds the woman he means to make his own is embroiled in political protests that could lead to a prison ship. Larena must learn to trust the handsome Scotsman whose most pressing mission is to protect her and keep her from harm.

Tira's Education
Twelve Dancing Princesses Book Eleven

WHISPERS OF EDUCATION
Learning how to build ships is Tira Hepburn's only dream until she meets Jamie Lundin and her world is turned upside down. With her raven black hair and vivid green eyes, she tempts Jamie and pushes him to defy his vows. She never bargains on finding an irrevocable love and a passion to a man who cannot fulfill her dreams despite his burning desire for her.

WHISPERS OF A BARGAIN

Arrogant and self-assured Jamie is brought up short when Tira captures his heart. All his carefully made plans are put to the test when he decides to teach her the art of ship building if she will spend a week with him alone on his ship. He is unable to deny Tira's intoxicating effect on him. When Tira leaves him behind unwilling to live with him without the benefit of marriage, he races after her. Jamie will risk everything to shelter and protect the innocent debutante who seduces him with her sweet love.

Aidan's Love
Twelve Dancing Princesses Book Twelve

Whispers of Love

Aidan McLellan has loved since she first set eyes on him as a young girl. Spontaneous, wild and eager to grow up, Aidan haunts his waking thoughts day and night, insinuating herself into his life. With her fiery red hair and sparkling sapphire eyes, she seizes Blade's heart even while he tries to resist the innocent child until she becomes a woman.

Whispers of Courage

Blade has waited what seems a lifetime to claim the woman who captures his heart as a little girl. Claiming his inheritance before his younger brother takes what is rightfully his, Blade must convince Aidan of his sincerity after years of avoidance and wed her before his father dies so he can return home, securing his rightful place. Everything is put to the test when his life as well as Aidan's is threatened by the man who once called him brother.

Twelve Days to Love

When Archer Steele shows up at Calanthe Durand's failing plantation with an alligator over his shoulder, Cali thinks she's never seen a more handsome man. During the war she had to defend herself and her servants from both union and confederate soldiers. Independent and self-sufficient, she vows to never marry.

But Archer Steele has different ideas. The first time Archer sees Cali in town, he feels an instant attraction. He decides he will do everything and anything to convince the beautiful Miss Durand he is worthy of her love. During the weeks leading up to Christmas, he gives her twelve gifts in hopes she will fall in love with him. Yet they are faced with challenges they must overcome before Cali can commit to a marriage.

Door to Heaven

Jessica Lawrence is the stepdaughter of a woman born in the twentieth century transported back in time to the year 1868. An acclaimed suffragette, she raises Jessica to believe in the equality of women. Jess Law believes everything she was taught, and when the time is right she becomes a private investigator. Courageous and impetuous, Jess finds danger in her quest to save all women from white slavery. Her passionate mission results in a wedding to Roc Newman, a man she knows can steal her heart...

Roc can't trust the sapphire-eyed spitfire who invades his home in search of secret papers and knocks him flat with her karate moves. Jessica's refusal to obey his wishes serves to inflame the war between them. Still, he cannot control the intense desire his reluctant bride inspires, or make her surrender her independence, until he has conquered the headstrong beauty on the battlefield of love...

Rebel Heart

HER REBEL SPIRIT DEFIED HIS OUTSIDERS SOUL...She was velvet and silk, eyes the color of a summer storm and amber hair. Victoria DeMontville, because of a promise and a codicil to her father's will, was forced to marry one man to protect her from another. She hated Cameron Savage with a fierce passion. But to hold on to her genetic research and find a cure for the deadly Signe virus, she must pretend to love the enemy at her door, come with weapons of fire to melt her icy heart...

HIS OUTSIDERS TOUCH IGNITED RAGING PASSIONS... He wore a mask, disguised as the Phantom, a true legend come to life. Even as war and debate over new genetic research engulfed them all, he would find his greatest adversary in the beauty who'd branded him an outsider and barbarian, the woman he was born to possess, his soul mate.

Safari Moon

Solo St. John, a wildlife photographer, is preparing for a trip to Alaska. Suddenly, Solo finds women of all sorts invading his privacy, his home and his office, all cooing nonsense words and blatantly throwing themselves at him. Solo doesn't know why, and he has no idea how to rid himself of the persistent women. He finally decides to beg a favor of his best buddy Nyssa Harrington.

In love with Solo for the past ten years and knowing he doesn't return her feelings Nyssa doesn't want to talk to Solo. She knows if she accepts his phone call, she will not be able to resist the temptation to hope again.

Straight to Heaven

Running from demons, Alexandra McMurdie stumbles into Forbidden Ground where up is down and elements of nature are contested. Though a strong independent woman in the twenty-first century' she is unprepared for life in the 1800s. Her first site of the formidable James Lawrence makes her heart skip a beat, giving her cause to reconsider her desperate need to find a way home.

Born with a silver spoon, James' life was torn apart during the War Between the States. Moving west he vows to put the life he once knew in the past. When he discovers a half-frozen woman near Gold Hill, his heart begins to thaw. His love for Alexandra and his need to keep her from a man who has pursued her through time might cost him his life as well as hers.

A Valentine's Anthology

The Lending Library-a fantasy by Christie L. Kraemer
Faeries try to fit into the human world when the forest where they make their home is destroyed by a mysterious enemy.

Chasing Rainbows-a contemporary romance by Genene Valleau
An eccentric aunt, an inventive uncle, a mother who wears poodle skirts, and a brother who wears pearls provide a hilarious backdrop for the courtship of a young woman who yearns for a "normal" family.

The Gift-an historical romance by Christine Young
A man and a woman on opposite sides of the Civil War get a second chance at love after one final battle returns soldiers to their war-torn homes to rebuild their lives.

A St. Patrick's Day Tale
Christine Young, C. L. Kraemer, Genene Valleau

Tumble through time...
...to Ireland in 1817, when tensions are high between Protestants and Catholics and fae people guide the fate of villagers. A lovely Catholic lass stumbles upon the weakly ritual fisticuffing between Irish lads. She falls into the lap of a handsome young Protestant. Family ties, grudges, and two conniving faeries threaten their budding love. But the faeries outsmart themselves when they hijack a time machine that has mysteriously appeared in their forest and are whisked to...
...Eugene, Oregon in the 20th century, amid a property feud between the local faeries and night elves. The conniving faeries from Olde Ireland try to stir up more mischief. However, a warrior gnome convinces the magic folk to control their own destiny, and forces the intruding

faeries to take refuge in the time machine again, spinning their way toward...

...A modern day castle in western Oregon. An eccentric inventor is determined to reclaim his wayward time machine and save his beloved wife from her latest misadventure. If only they can travel safely past the black hole...

a May Day Anthology

Christine Young, C. L. Kraemer, Rosemary Indra, Genene Valleau

Highland Miracle — Christine Young

HURTLED THROUGH TIME, Sean Michael Sterling, landed in the midst of a May Day celebration he didn't understand, assuming the role of Laird Sterling.

ILLIGITAMATE CHILD OF NOBILITY, Reagan Douglas searches for a way out of her half brother's house.

Defying the Odds — C.L. Kraemer

The night elves on the hill aren't happy without their magic. They concoct a plan to punish those who were involved in the act that rendered them almost human. Meanwhile, Uther, the rogue night elf, has returned to woo the Librarian to be his eternal mate.

Love in Bloom — Rosemary Indra

When childhood friends reunite it takes two fairies and a matchmaking daughter to help them admit their true love for each other.

No More Poodle Skirts — Genie Gabriel

After drifting for years in the innocent age of the 1950s, a woman struggles to join today's world by finding a career and a new love, with some help from her zany family.

Once Upon a Christmas Moon
Christine Young, C. L. Kraemer, Genene Valleau

TWELVE DAYS TO LOVE

When Archer Steele shows up at Calanthe Durand's failing plantation with an alligator over his shoulder, Cali thinks she's never seen a more handsome man. During the war she had to defend herself and her servants from both union and confederate soldiers. Independent and self-sufficient, she vows to never marry. But Archer Steele has different ideas. The first time Archer sees Cali in town, he feels an instant attraction. He decides he will do everything and anything to convince the beautiful Miss Durand he is worthy of her love. During the weeks leading up to Christmas, he gives her twelve gifts in hopes she will fall in love with him.

BOOTS AND BLADES

An ancient evil from the old country has arrived in the high desert of Oregon. Gnome children are vanishing then re-appearing, showing various stages of traumatization. Tiamoon, warrior gnome, will put her skills to use alongside Killian, a handsome warrior, also in need of a cause.

CHRISTMAS PAWSIBILITIES

With their world destroyed and their space ship malfunctioning, the dogizens of Planet Canid have little choice but to crash land on Earth. They face tortuous experiments at the hands of the Geeks in Green...or they can trust an eccentric inventor and his zany family to deliver the Canine Queen's puppies and help them celebrate new lives.

VISIT OUR WEBSITE
FOR THE FULL INVENTORY
OF QUALITY BOOKS:
http://www.roguephoenixpress.com

Rogue Phoenix Press

Representing Excellence in Publishing

*Quality trade paperbacks and downloads
in multiple formats,
in genres ranging from historical to contemporary romance,
mystery and science fiction.
Visit the website then bookmark it.*

www.ingramcontent.com/pod-product-compliance
Lightning Source LLC
Chambersburg PA
CBHW07064718O626
46817CB00006B/2275